RAY O'MEARA

the Aberrationists

THE PARLIAMENT HOUSE

Edited by Bianca Visagie, Rebecca Milhoan, & Aimee Bounds

The Parliament House

www.parliamenthousepress.com

To Mom and Gram,
who taught me what heroes are

ONE

Fire and Phantom

WILLIAM KENDRICK AWOKE to the soothing sound of a female voice drifting into his darkened bedroom. He grinned dreamily, listening to the comforting chorus of 'You Are My Sunshine' as it wafted into his room. He had not slept well in weeks, but as he opened his eyes and sat up, he was pleased to notice that he finally felt rested and relaxed. Planting his feet on the cool hardwood floor, he stood and shuffled over to his window, where he opened the shades and was surprised to find that the sun had yet to show itself. From his second-story bedroom, he saw no cars on the street, but that was no shock—Pinewood Avenue was always quiet. Shrugging, he turned around and headed out into the hallway.

The old floorboards creaked beneath his feet as he made his way to the landing. Supposing it foolish to walk down the warped old stairs without the aid of a light, Will flipped the switch to his right. He flinched as the bulbs of the foyer's modest bronze chandelier flickered and sparked, refusing to provide the illumination that he desired.

Unnerved, Will used the song emanating from the kitchen

as a security blanket. He began to hum along, following the sound of the melodic voice, but stopped suddenly on the sixth step when he saw a figure lurking just outside kitchen doorway. The lanky shape stood motionless, seemingly waiting for Will to approach. When he gathered the nerve to descend the remainder of the staircase, he saw that the figure was covered from head to toe in a quiltlike patchwork of various fabrics. It was like a horrendous, life-sized ragdoll, complete with threads worming out of its face where its right eye should have been. "Who are you?" Will tried to ask, but the words wouldn't come. It was as if his tongue had gone numb.

Nonetheless, an answer came. The figure rasped an unintelligible response, barely above a whisper, and pointed a long finger toward the door to the kitchen. Obeying the creature's tacit request, Will finished his descent, all the while keeping two wide eyes locked on the mysterious intruder. *"Please don't take my sunshine away…"* Only as he drew closer to the kitchen did Will notice that he was still humming the song that was somehow permeating the entire house. The quilted figure stepped back into the shadows until it had completely disappeared, and Will entered the kitchen, where he found his mother working diligently at the stove.

"The other night, dear, as I lay—oh!" Will's mother blushed as she turned and realized that her son was standing behind her. "You scared me, Will."

"Sorry, mom," Will said, distracted.

"Breakfast will be ready in just a minute. Do you have time before school?"

Out of habit, Will looked to his watch, but discovered that he had forgotten to put it on. Glancing instead at the darkness outside the kitchen window, he responded, "I have a feeling I've got time."

His mother nodded and turned back to the frying pan. Will could see bacon hopping in the pan, but the familiar aroma was strangely absent. In fact, it was this absence that first made him note the sterility of the kitchen. The pale gray-tiled floor complemented the slate countertops and the cold steel appliances. Everything was immaculately clean—not a cold, blue coffee mug out of place as they hung uniformly beneath the cabinets, not a smudge on the colorless walls. Even his mother was perfectly coiffed for this time of day—or night, as the case may have been. The smoke from the stovetop wrapped around her like a mist, dimming what would have been the most vibrant colors in the room: her sky-blue housedress and her golden blonde hair.

Something was wrong. The silence of the kitchen was deafening now that his mother had stopped singing. The bacon grease didn't sizzle and spatter, the refrigerator didn't whir, and the coffee maker didn't gargle. All but his mother and her smoky aura maintained an uncomfortable stillness and silence. Will fidgeted in the corner. "Mom? Did you notice that we have bulbs out in the foyer?"

"Do we?" she asked as she tilted the pan, sliding its contents onto a clean white plate. Without saying another word about the bulbs, she resumed humming the tune from earlier, and handed Will a plate brimming with scrambled eggs, juicy bacon, and two perfectly-toasted slices of bread. "Why don't you go join the others in the dining room? I'll be right there."

Will did what he was told, his anxiety somewhat abated by the prospect of enjoying his mother's fantastic cooking. Upon entering the dining room, he took a seat at the rectangular table, next to his father and opposite his sister. They both smiled at him but said nothing as they scooped forkfuls of eggs into their mouths. Within moments, his mother had joined them, and the table was complete. "So," asked Will's father, "are you going to do it today?"

Having no idea what "it" was or even to whom the question had been directed, Will did not initially answer. However, upon his father repeating the question, he responded, "Me? Do what?"

"You know," said his father, "Tell them."

"Um, sure," Will answered, still unaware of what his father was talking about. He eyed his plate hungrily and worked to get the perfect ratio of bacon to egg on his fork. Placing it into his mouth, he expected to taste the salty, savory meat and the fluffy egg, but instead was unpleasantly surprised to find himself with a mouthful of what felt like flour. He coughed the substance out instantly and was again shocked when he saw the color of the cloud of dust that he spewed. Puffs of gray ash escaped from his mouth as he spat out a dark, viscous liquid.

"Is there something wrong?" asked his mother. Trying desperately to wipe the sulfuric taste off his lips, Will looked over at her and went wide-eyed with horror. Where his mother had been enjoying her breakfast just moments earlier, now sat a charred corpse. Her blonde hair was nearly nonexistent, and the few strands that clung to the burnt scalp were frayed and blackened. Her sundress hung in tatters over her scorched flesh, blistered and bloody from head to toe.

Nauseated at the sight of the creature that used to be his mother, he looked around the table and saw his sister and father in similar conditions. The smell of burning flesh reached his nostrils as he knocked over his chair and stepped away from the table. His sister's deformed face, mandible exposed, rasped, "Run…"

Not needing to be told twice, Will ran to the front door as quickly as his legs could carry him. His hand on the knob, he paused for an instant to look back, and although nothing appeared to be following him, he opted to play it safe and get out of the house. When he stepped outside, though, he immediately knew that he had made a mistake. This was not the front lawn he knew, with its stone path stretching to the sidewalk through rows of colorful zinnias. Instead, he stood alone on an expansive, empty field, save for one building off in the distance, barely visible in the pre-dawn darkness. He felt unsafe here, as though something could come at him from any direction, so he headed toward the lone building, constantly looking back, but seeing nothing, not even his house.

Arriving at the simple stone building, he read the name etched into the arched entryway: *Trammell*. He also noticed that the building had only flimsy wooden doors, and would offer little safety, but he entered anyway. He walked as quietly as he could down the singular marble hallway, lined on each side by cement slabs engraved with indecipherable words. The path was dark, but a faint stream of light from the door that he left ajar allowed him to see what looked like a body slumped against the wall on his right. Approaching it, he crouched down to see again the charred corpse of his mother, this time her eyes shut, unmoving, and looking thoroughly dead. With a shudder, he stood back up and continued along the path, passing his sister's body on the left, trying not to get too close. Finally, as he knew he would, he reached the third body, this one sprawled across the center of the floor. He attempted to step gingerly over his father but received a jolt when the corpse grabbed his ankle.

"Tell them!" It moaned before he was able to violently pull away.

He ran the rest of the way to the end of the hall, where he found nothing but a stone statue, half-covered in moss and vines. The piece portrayed a stoic man with terrible eyes and a puffed-up face, almost like that of a toad. Will looked around the base of the statue for a plaque, or some other source of explanation, but found nothing. Having reached a dead-end, he decided that the only thing to do was to turn back.

But this plan evaporated as soon as he turned around. In the distance, in the light of the archway, stood a figure cloaked in darkness. Will pressed his back against the statue, gripping the suffocating vines anxiously as the wooden door slammed shut and the interior was plunged into darkness. Will opened his mouth to scream, but nothing came out. He was sweating now, his whole body trembling as he continued to try to cry for help. His attempts stopped when he saw a flicker of light. The figure lit a lantern and was now walking toward Will at a slow, steady pace.

Step, step, click. Step, step, click.

He heard the same rhythmic pattern over and over as the figure drew closer, and soon enough, he was able to see why. The individual, clothed in a long black coat and a wide-brimmed hat, carried a stick that seemed like more of a prop than a cane. He saw the dark figure approach his mother's corpse, jab at it with the stick, and, after considering it briefly, move onto his sister.

It was when the figure reached his sister that Will's hair truly began to stand on end, for now he could make out the individual's face—or rather, his mask. The flickering light was reflected in the cold glass eyes of an expressionless ceramic mask with a long, curved beak. While it poked the corpse of the young girl, the figure's head tilted back and forth, like a bird considering a worm.

Whereas earlier he could not make a sound, now Will could hear nothing but the sound of his own breathing and the *step, step, click* of the masked figure coming closer. He felt sweat running into his eyes and over his lips as the phantom now leaned into his father's corpse, the sharp, downturned beak only inches from the charred remains. Will jumped as his father's body twitched and the phantom reared himself back up. With a lightning-fast movement, the phantom brought his stick down on Will's father's head with a sickening *thwack.* It then poked at the remains, and, seemingly satisfied that the body was truly deceased, moved on.

Will knew that he was next. With the three bodies

accounted for, the figure *step, step, clicked* over to Will until the two were standing face to face. Will attempted to remain silent, but every drop of sweat seemed to hit the floor with a thunderous splash. He stared into the large, blank eyes of the phantom, and the phantom stared back, cocking its head first to the left, then to the right. And then it was over. The dark figure turned away and began the long walk back down the marble hallway. Will waited until the phantom was past his father's body before peeling his soaked back off the statue behind him and heaving a sigh of relief.

It was this sigh that finally caught the phantom's attention. Will wore a look of panic as the creature spun back around, let loose a blood-curdling screech, and hurled the flaming lantern like a grenade at Will's face.

The dream ended in a fiery explosion, and Will shot up in his bed, dripping perspiration. "This can't keep happening," he said to himself as he looked around his room, seeing that he had once again woken before his alarm. Since the alarm would have gone off in ten minutes anyway, and since there was no way that he was going back to sleep after the dream that he just had, Will decided to try to calm down in the shower.

The only problem that the shower relieved was the sweat, however. He shut his eyes while the warm water ran down his face, and he replayed what he could remember of the dream in his head. The odd thing was, he could remember everything. For nearly eighteen years, Will had not had one dream that he could recall in the morning—not until this past week, when he awoke every day covered in sweat and trembling from head to foot. Something was up, and Will, not normally an alarmist, decided that it was probably time to ask for some help.

WHEN WILL ENTERED THE KITCHEN, he saw his mother, Emily, sitting at the table with a cup of tea and the morning paper. Had she looked up from the paper, she would have seen that her son was visibly shaken. Instead, Mrs. Kendrick wished him good morning, asked if he'd like a Pop-Tart, and continued to fill in her crossword puzzle.

"No, that's okay," Will answered. "Not hungry."

"Humpf," Emily muttered, placing her pencil on the table and making eye contact with her son. "That's new. What's wrong? Is it about a girl? Should it wait until your father gets home?" Will's father, Dr. Robert Kendrick, had left for the hospital nearly an hour earlier.

"Nah. I guess it doesn't really matter who I talk to. It's just..." he paused, making circles on the tabletop with his fingertip. "It's just that I've been having nightmares. God, I sound like such a baby."

His mother smirked. "Everyone has nightmares, hon." She held her cup in front of her face with both hands, her elbows on the table. "What are they about?"

"That's the thing," Will said. "I have no idea. It's like I'm in someone else's screwed-up life."

"How so?"

"Well, for starters, you and Dad are in the dream...only it's not you and Dad."

"Okay, you've lost me," Emily laughed. "Maybe you *should* speak to your father about this."

"No, it's..." Will struggled for the words to explain what he meant. "I treated the woman in my dream like she was my mother, but it wasn't you. It was some woman I'd never seen before. She was blonde."

Emily blew a strand of her own mousey-brown hair from her face and shrugged. "Dreams can be strange, Will."

"I know," he said, "but this dream has happened a lot lately. Some things are different every time, but some stuff is the same. For example, do we know anyone with the last name 'Trammell'?"

Emily shifted in her chair and gulped more tea than she had intended. She coughed a couple of times, set the teacup down, and said, "Trammell? Doesn't sound familiar." She stood to bring her cup to the sink and waited there for a moment, staring out the window to the backyard. "It's getting late, Will. You should get going. Aren't you supposed to pick up Andy?"

"Yeah, I'll go," said Will, grabbing a small pile of books from the table. Judging by her tone and her decision to end the conversation, Will assumed that his mother was not concerned about his dreams, and so he shouldn't be either. Still, one more thing was bothering him, and as he headed out the front door, he called back, "Hey mom! When I was young, did you ever sing 'You Are My Sunshine' to me?"

"What a strange question," she answered, smiling warmly. "But no, I don't recall doing that. I didn't even know you knew it."

"I don't," he said, troubled, and left for school.

EMILY WAVED to Will as he pulled out of the driveway and bolted the front door as soon as he was on his way. She pressed her back to the door, and with trembling hands, dialed her husband. "Robert, you need to come home."

TWO

The Trammells

THE WAY that things were going, Will half expected 'You Are My Sunshine' to play on the radio while he drove the short few blocks to the Lunsfords'. Still, the fact that it didn't certainly did not make Will feel any more comfortable about his dreams. He couldn't shake the fundamental questions that arose from them: who were those 'parents'? Who was Trammell? Why 'You Are My Sunshine'? What about this business of a sister? He'd never had a sister…that he knew of. Perhaps he did, though. Will was, after all, adopted, but he had never heard anything about a sister.

Not quite knowing how he had gotten there, Will now sat in the Lunsfords' driveway, waiting for his best friend Andy, who soon came stumbling out of the house, arms filled with books and loose papers, mouth filled with bagel. After a brief struggle with the door handle, Andy plopped himself into the Prius' passenger seat and buckled up. Andy would never let Will take his foot off the pedal until everyone was buckled up. It wasn't that Will was a bad driver—on the contrary, there were no blemishes on his albeit short driving record. No, that was just how Andy Lunsford operated. He was not Will's conscience so much as his own personal safety officer. Having barely taken a risk in his life, Andy lived vicariously through Will's impulsiveness. He admired it, though he had never quite felt the urge to experience it firsthand. At the same time, Will knew that Andy, whom he had met in grade school, had a good head on his shoulders despite his nagging behavior, and had often found that having such an anchor was a helpful thing.

"Is this seatbelt broken?" asked Andy.

"What? No."

Andy shrugged. "Okay. It just didn't click the first time. At least not audibly, you know?"

Will rolled his eyes. "Did you bring that book I asked you about?"

"What book?"

"That book of dream interpretations that you have. I texted you on the way over here."

His friend gave him a stern look of disapproval. "You shouldn't be texting while you drive. You're gonna get pulled over. Or kill someone. Remember that *Twilight Zone* episode?"

"No. And texting didn't exist back then."

Andy bit off another piece of bagel, and with his mouth full, uttered, "Granted. But the guy hit a kid. Then he pretended not to, so his car started acting all crazy…basically haunting him. Creepy stuff. If you watched that episode, you'd never text while driving again."

"You know I hate all that supernatural crap," said Will, waving Andy off.

"Yet you wanted me to bring a book of dream interpretations? That's a bit too metaphysical for you, isn't it?" Andy thought for a minute. "You trying to impress a girl?"

"Yes, Andy," Will deadpanned. "I'm trying to impress a girl by showing her your book of dream interpretations."

"Who?"

Will hit Andy playfully in the back of the head. "It's those dreams again, man. They keep coming back. Four days in a row now."

"I figured. You look like hell."

"Thanks." Will knew that Andy was right. He could feel his eyes getting puffier by the minute.

"So the dreams…the ones about the fire?"

"Yeah. There's always some sort of fire or explosion at the end. But things are getting weird. Really specific details are starting to repeat."

"Like what?"

"Like names. Does the name 'Trammell' mean anything to you?"

"Um…well, I think there are a couple of baseball players named Trammell. Could it be referring to either of them?"

"I really doubt it. Then there's this guy with a creepy mask, and a statue, and a song that I don't know. But in my dream, I do! I know it!"

"Weird, Will," Andy admitted. "That stuff could all definitely mean something. I'll check the book when I get home. Or we can check online later. There're tons of sites for that kind of stuff. But dude, I seriously think you're being haunted or something."

Will sighed. "There's no such thing as ghosts." Having arrived just in time for the first bell, the two friends joined the hordes of students filing into the school. "So how about we head to the library after school?"

"Uh-huh."

"I figure they should have plenty of dream interpretation books, so we won't necessarily need yours. And I'd rather do this here at school. I think my mother's starting to think I'm crazy."

"Okay," Andy replied absentmindedly.

"I'm sorry," said Will. "Am I boring you?"

"Huh? What? No!" Andy replied, snapping out of it. "Never! I was just enjoying the view." He motioned very obviously toward Samantha Foster, who stood chatting with her girlfriends across the hall. Her too-blond hair, too-tan skin, and too-white teeth led Will to believe that high school was simply a formality for her, as she was clearly destined for greater things that she would almost certainly not have to work for. "Sam's something, huh?" Andy mused.

"She is something," Will agreed. "But once again, I'll remind you that she doesn't know that either of us exists."

"Well I don't think that's true," said Andy, sounding slightly affronted. "*I*, in fact, got a smile from her just the other day when all that crap spilled out of my locker. And you, my friend, are on the baseball team."

"But I suck."

Andy wrinkled his nose as if to say, "Yeah, kind of," but was thoughtful enough to keep the words from escaping his lips. "So anyway," he said, opting to change the subject, "library later. I'll be there."

Will waved a casual hello to the school librarian, Mrs. Privit, as he entered the otherwise empty room after school. He briefly considered enlisting her help in looking through the stacks for books on dream interpretation, but Mrs. Privit was known to turn each search into a learning experience, so he decided that he would just wait for Andy to arrive instead. In the meantime, Will would stick to a reference method that he was much more comfortable with. He sat at one of the vacant computer stations and desperately tried to hold back a yawn. *Okay*, he thought to himself. *Let's start simple.* He typed in the name 'Trammell.' Over one million results were found, but a headline on the third page caught Will's attention. It was from a Philadelphia-area newspaper, and the headline read: *Officer and Family Perish in Blaze.*

"Trammell and fire," he muttered. "Interesting." Will

clicked on the article title, the monitor went blank for a moment, and then, rather than a newspaper article, one image appeared: that of an old Victorian-style house with flames coming through the broken windows. Will searched the screen for the back button but saw none. The toolbars were gone, and the lone image took up the entirety of the monitor. He turned to ask Mrs. Privit for assistance, but she was no longer at the circulation desk. Returning his gaze to the monitor, Will could almost swear that he saw the flames begin to move, slowly licking the sides of the house. Will looked more closely, and sure enough, the flames were undulating. It was as though he were watching slowed-down news footage of the blaze.

"This is crazy," said Will, leaning back in his chair. He took a moment to rub his tired eyes, and when he opened them again, not only was the strange image still on the monitor, but it was showing on every other monitor in the room. "Um, Mrs. Privit!" he yelled, standing up and frantically looking around the empty library. "I think I need some help here!"

Will jumped as an icy hand grasped his shoulder. He slowly turned around and was taken aback to see the shape of Mrs. Privit inher brown pantsuit, her horn-rimmed glasses dangling from her neck, her tightly pulled-back gray hair. Everything was intact except for her face. Where her typically sour expression should have been was a blank slate without a trace of eyes, nostrils, or lips. Will remained frozen as the mouthless creature rasped, "I'm here to help."

"Yo! Earth to Will!" yelled Andy, slamming his books down on the table about two inches from Will's ear. Will woke up and looked bleary-eyed at Andy, the impression of his watch etched into his right cheek.

"What?"

"I said I'm here to help. Jeez, you look worse than this morning," Andy said with genuine concern.

Will ignored his friend for the moment and looked around

the room like a cat following a housefly. The computer monitors were all blank, and Mrs. Privit was once more at her post behind the circulation desk. He stared at her for a few moments until their eyes met, she gave an obligatory half-smile, and returned to the solitaire game on her computer.

"Will, you want to just go home? We can do this another time," Andy suggested.

"No," Will responded, snapping out of his haze, "I know what we need to do. Hop on one of those computers. We need to look up 'Trammell' and 'fire.' Maybe 'Philadelphia' also."

Andy nodded. "I can do that. You take a minute to wake up."

Will winced and rubbed his head. It had been a long day, and he didn't see it getting any better. Opening his bloodshot eyes, he saw Sam Foster looking at him with an expression bordering on concern but edging closer to indifference. "You've got a watch on your face," she said, motioning with her finger to where the impression had been made upon his cheek.

Will gave a defeated nod. "Awesome," he replied, rubbing his right cheek futilely as Sam sauntered away.

"Hey buddy," Andy called. He looked over his shoulder from where he was seated at the computer station. "You need to come see this."

Will wearily pulled a chair up next to Andy. "What is it?"

"I don't know," said Andy, whose face had drained of any color, "but it's something. Check it out."

The article that Andy had retrieved was from the archives of the *Philadelphia Inquirer*. It had been written nearly fourteen years earlier, and the headline read '*Officer and Family Perish in Blaze*,' just like it had in his dream. "A fire in Pennsylvania fourteen years ago? What could that possibly have to do with me?"

"Just read it," Andy said.

Will read quietly enough to avoid being shushed by Mrs. Privit but loudly enough for his friend to hear. "'One of Philadelphia's finest was killed on Monday in an early-morning explosion at his home in Thornbury Township. In all, four people died, including Officer Daniel Trammell, his wife Linda, daughter Kimberley, 12, and son William, 4.'" He stopped. "Andy, their son's name was William."

"Yeah, Will," he responded. "And he'd be our age now, wouldn't he?" Andy added.

"Will...this *is* pretty weird, isn't it?"

"I don't think you realize how weird it is," said Will, his hands shaking as he held the printed article. He held the page up for Andy to see and pointed to the pictures of Officer Trammell and his wife. "In the dream that I had last night, these two people were my parents."

THREE

Up in Flames

MUCH OF THE ride home took place in silence. By the time they pulled into the Lunsfords' driveway, Will was so lost in thought that he didn't notice Andy get out of the car, and was startled when his friend came around and tapped on the driver's side window. Will lowered the window enough for Andy to lean in with his thick fingers. "Will, you're adopted."

Will, disappointed by what he thought was going to be a worthwhile statement, met his friend's announcement with a distinct lack of enthusiasm. "Yes, I know. Thank you."

"I think you know what I mean, Will. The Trammells' son was named William. Same age. What if...what if there was some kind of mistake? What if the kid didn't die? What if the kid is you?"

Will twisted his lips into a doubtful expression. For some reason, he didn't want to let on that he had been thinking the same thing since leaving school. "Seems a bit of a stretch, doesn't it?" he replied, trying to convince himself as much as Andy. "That would've been a pretty big mistake...and you'd think that someone would have realized sometime in the last fourteen years."

"Yeah, I guess." Andy released the window and straightened up. "You should ask your parents about it, though. I'm sure they'll be straight with you if they know anything."

"I'm sure," said Will as he backed out of the driveway. His mind immediately leapt back to the conversation that he had had with his mother earlier in the day and the odd way that she had reacted when the name 'Trammell' was mentioned. Stopped at a traffic light a few blocks from Andy's house, Will removed the newspaper article from his pocket and scanned it until his eyes landed on a name. *That's it*, he thought. When he heard the honk of the car behind him, he threw the paper down on the passenger seat and continued home, driving faster than before.

WILL ARRIVED home to find that he was alone. A note in his mother's handwriting on the refrigerator explained that she and his father had run out to a few stores and would be home in time for dinner. Will threw the note away and paused, looking around the kitchen, which seemed different now. In fact, the whole house suddenly seemed colder, almost foreign. He stepped quietly through the house, walking as though he were afraid of waking some unseen creature, stopping to examine each shadow for signs of movement. Finally, convinced that he was truly alone and that no faceless monsters were going to appear anytime soon, he entered his room, locked the door, and set the newspaper article down on the plaid comforter.

He sat on the bed to take a closer look at the article. *The explosion occurred at roughly 4 a.m. its vibrations could be felt several houses over, say residents, many of whom were still shaken from the event. Houses on either side of the Trammell residence were also damaged, but the fireball decimated 257 Grant Street, leaving little but cinder by the time the flames were extinguished.*

No official conclusion has been reached about the cause of the disaster, but the possibility of arson has not been ruled out. While residents claim that the Trammells were ideal neighbors, it is no secret that Officer Daniel Trammell's line of work made him the target of a number of vendettas over the years. Most notable, perhaps, was Trammell's involvement in the recent arrest of alleged weapons dealer Chilnos Villovich.

When asked about the possibility of Villovich's involvement, Trammell's longtime partner, Officer Edward Garza, declined to comment. However, Trammell's precinct has vowed that all possibilities will be examined.

The story went on to get neighbors' reactions about the sound and size of the fireball, the damage to their property, and how long it took to extinguish the blaze. Will only really cared about the Trammells, though, and was again distracted by their photographs, which appeared at this point on the page. They were an attractive couple—him muscularly built with short-cropped black hair, and her a petite, pretty, blue-eyed blonde. Will looked at their photographs for a long moment, feeling a hazy kind of bond that he was half convinced was the result of an overactive imagination. Looking at the clock, he realized that not only would his parents be home soon, but it was almost six. He didn't know much about the newspaper business, but he feared that if he waited too long, there would be no one there to answer his questions. He couldn't take another night of unsettling visions. Pulling his phone out of his pocket, he dialed the number that was on the bottom of the printout, below the *Philadelphia Inquirer* logo.

The phone rang at least eight times, and Will was worrying that he'd have to give up when a frazzled young woman answered: *"Inquirer..."*

"Um, yes, hi. I'm calling for one of your writers. Jim Mitchell. I'm not sure if he still works there, but I—"

"Mitchell, you said? Jim? Not sure. I'm new here. Lemme check. Hold please."

While the recording played a listing of all the advertising options for the *Inquirer*, Will came to realize that he had absolutely no idea why he had called. Jim Mitchell, the reporter who had covered this story fourteen years ago, was about to get on the phone, and Will was going to say what, exactly? "Do you know who my real parents are? Do you know why I have nightmares?" Will's palms began to sweat as he waited and they practically began to drip when he saw his parents' Navigator pull into the driveway. "Damn," he muttered. "This was stupid." He was about to hang up when the recording abruptly stopped and the receptionist got back on the line, this time with a much different tone.

"Hon, you said you were looking for Jim Mitchell?"

"Yes. Please."

"I'm very sorry to tell you that Jim passed away earlier this year."

Will was silent. He wasn't quite sure how to react. "I... sorry for your loss," he said, wincing. Stupid. Stupid stupid stupid.

"Um, thanks. Me too," she responded. "I mean, I'm sorry for *your* loss. Did you know Jim?"

"I...no..." said Will, hearing his mother coming up the stairs. "Just checking to see if he was dead. Thank you! Bye!" He hung up and remained seated on the edge of his bed as feelings of disappointment and mortification battled for supremacy. He didn't have time for either, though, as within moments the familiar sound of his mother's footsteps could be heard approaching his door. There was soon a soft knock. "Will, are you in there?"

"Yeah," he said, hurrying to hide the article under a stack of papers near his laptop. "Just a minute," he added. He rushed to the door and opened it to see his mother holding a plastic shopping bag.

"I'm not, um, interrupting anything, am I?" Emily asked.

"What? No," said Will, blushing slightly. "I was just making some calls. What's up?"

"Well," she said, entering his bedroom, "I realized today that it will be less than a month until your graduation! So while your father and I were out, I forced him to go to the mall with me. I picked up a few shirts for you, and this tie." She removed a handsome navy blue and tan tie from the bag, laying it carefully on the bed. As she did so, Will noticed that she seemed to be avoiding eye contact, whether intentionally or not, and that she was speaking more quickly than usual. He deduced that she was still a bit shaken from the morning. "What do you think? I liked it, and your father liked it, and I know that you're not a fan of wearing ties to begin with…I mean you probably only own, what, two? So I figured that you probably wouldn't take it upon yourself to get one. *Or* it would be the day before graduation, and you'd say, 'Mom, I need a tie,' and then we'd be out of luck, wouldn't we?" She caught her breath and glanced at him with a quick smile before promptly reaching back into the bag, removing a crisp white shirt and laying it first next to the tie before placing the tie on top of it. "So? Do you like it? Or would you rather another one?"

"It's…it's great, mom. Thanks."

"Okay then," said Emily, as she turned to leave the room. "Try on those shirts tonight, just so that I know they're alright. Also, we brought Chinese in. Come on down when you're ready."

By the time Emily had finished her last sentence, she was out of Will's bedroom and well on her way to the stairs. Despite the effort that his mother had taken to avoid the discomfort that she clearly felt during the morning's conversation, the past few minutes had only strengthened Will's desire to find the truth about the Trammells—and about what his mother was so anxious to hide from him.

WHILE HEADING DOWN TO DINNER, Will decided to try another approach with his parents—one that he hoped might be less disconcerting. When he entered the kitchen, he saw that his parents had already begun eating, but his father put down his fork and wiped his mouth, trying to hide a guilty grin behind his napkin. "I'm sorry, Will," said Robert Kendrick. "I tried to wait, but I'm famished. Work was crazy today, and, as I'm sure you heard, I was lucky enough to be dragged to the mall afterward."

"Only the promise of Yummy Panda Kitchen persuaded him," Emily chuckled.

This made his father laugh as well, though that was no great accomplishment. Everyone who had ever come into contact with Dr. Robert Kendrick agreed that his appreciation of a good joke, or even a not-so-good joke, was one of his more endearing qualities. Dr. Kendrick was universally known as a somewhat quiet, rather jovial family man, but he was serious when he had to be, and at the hospital, he was. He never joked about his patients, and colleagues and patients alike considered him a straight-shooter. It was this reputation that Will would rely on to get him through the approaching conversation.

"So how was school?" Robert asked.

"It was fine. Nothing really special."

"That doesn't sound fine to me," his father responded. "These last few weeks should be the best of your high school career! Enjoy them!"

"Yeah, you're right," Will conceded. "I'm just really tired lately."

"Probably the stress of your baseball schedule. But that should be ending soon, right?"

"Soon enough. I have practice in the morning, so I'd better get some sleep tonight," said Will, taking a forkful of General Tso's.

"You'll do great. You're getting better and better."

"Thanks. Hey, do you know who my birth parents are?" For the second time in an hour, Will displayed his lack of tact, and this time there was no hanging up. He looked down at his plate of food, hoping that maybe the past few moments would rewind themselves.

Robert cleared his throat and once more wiped his mouth. "Excuse me?"

"Yeah, I know that wasn't the best segue, but I've just been wondering about it."

Robert glanced quickly at Emily, who took it upon herself to take an interminable sip of wine at that moment. "Well do you mind if I ask why the sudden interest?"

Will shrugged. "I don't know. A variety of things. I mean, I'll be graduating from high school soon, so I guess it just made me think about things." He took a quick sip of iced tea. "Plus I keep having these dreams."

Robert put his fork down and smiled. "Ah, the dreams. Your mother was telling me about that issue while we were at the mall. I wouldn't worry about them. I firmly believe that they're stress-related. Once you pass your finals and finish up the baseball season, I guarantee they'll go away."

"I agree with your father," Emily chimed in.

"I'd buy that if the dreams weren't so vivid," Will said. "Did Mom tell you about the name? Trammell? Do you know anyone by that name?"

"Do I know anyone by that name? No. I've never met anyone named Trammell. I'm sure I've heard it before. It's not incredibly uncommon, after all. In fact, I'll bet you saw it before, and it just reappeared in your dream for some reason. Probably the editor of one of your school textbooks...a name that you see every day but don't really pay attention to. That tends to happen with dreams."

Will nodded to placate his father but pressed on. "So my birth parents are not named Trammell?"

Perhaps realizing that he had wiped his mouth every time Will had asked him something, Dr. Kendrick now adopted a new tell, removing his wire-rimmed glasses and cleaning them with a cloth from his pocket. "I'll tell you what," he said. "Give me a week or so. I'll gather all of the information that I can about your birth parents, and all three of us will go over it together." He paused to replace his glasses. "You're right, Will. You're going to be heading to college next year. You're an adult. There's no reason that you shouldn't know your own family history. Will you give me a few days?"

Will nodded, smiling faintly. If he could trust anyone, he could trust his father.

LATER THAT NIGHT, he lay in bed thinking that for the first time in several days, he would get a good night's sleep. Had he not spoken to his father about his concerns at dinner, he would have stayed up all night trying to figure out his connection to the Trammells and the reason for his nightmares. Instead, he could rest easy knowing that his father would do the legwork, recalling that he had never let him down before.

Will had gone to bed relatively early in an attempt to get at least eight hours of rest before he had to get up for practice. While the night was beautiful and breezy, there was still a decent amount of noisy traffic on Pinewood Avenue, so he rose to shut the window. That was when he heard his parents, who had also left their window open, talking in his father's study below.

"Why did you have to call him?" Will heard his mother ask. She sounded as though she was near tears.

"I just had to, Emily," said Dr. Kendrick in a tone that was firm, yet kind. "We're not equipped to deal with this situation, but he is. He'll know how to handle what's going on with Will."

"I'll bet," said Emily, not without a tinge of bitterness.

"We knew that this day was coming, Emily."

"It's just…insane. He's still our little boy."

Robert's tone softened to the point that Will has to strain to hear. "He's old enough to do what he has to do," he said. "Brandt will be here tomorrow."

FOUR

Brandt

———————

HAVING NOT GOTTEN the peaceful night's sleep that he had been hoping for, a bleary Will Kendrick dragged himself out of bed and left for baseball practice without encountering either of his parents—a circumstance for which, considering the previous evening's conversation, he was quite grateful. After parking at the field, he took a moment to send Andy a quick text: *Meet me at the field ASAP. Very important.* While others may have ignored such a text at 7 a.m., Will knew that Andy wouldn't be able to resist, having not heard anything further from Will since their discovery in the library.

Will got out of the car and realized with some discomfort that he could not remember the ride there. He remained lost in thought for the first half of practice, repeatedly falling out of sync with his teammates during drills as he spent more concentration on replaying his parents' discussion in his head. It was not until around 8:30 that he snapped out of it, alerted suddenly to the presence of Andy Lunsford, whose rotund form could be seen lumbering toward the bleachers, where it joined another much more pleasant form.

Batting practice had just begun when Andy reached the bleachers and found himself one of only two spectators, the other being Sam Foster, her golden hair iridescent in the morning sun. "Hey," he said cheerily, taking a seat on the second row, careful not to get uncomfortably close to Sam, who sat higher up on the fourth row of bleachers. "What are you doing here?"

"My brother's on the team," she replied. "And since my parents were too busy to drive him, I was lucky enough to get that gig." She pointed to a tall, muscular young man stepping up to the plate. "There he is. Kenny."

"Oh yeah," said Andy. "A year younger than us, right?"

"Yup," she answered. Then, with a quizzical look, she asked, "Why are *you* here?"

"Me? I'm just a fan. Just love baseball," he lied through his teeth as he looked back over his shoulder at Sam. "I saw people on the field and thought there was a game going on. Guess not. Just practice. Can't win 'em all, huh?" Sam forced a smile. "Don't worry, though," Andy continued, "if any balls come flying this way, I'll catch 'em. I could be out there myself. I just choose not to be."

"Good to know," said Sam, who resumed what she supposed was her sisterly duty of watching Kenny's turn at bat. Luckily, she didn't have to watch for long before he cracked one into the outfield. She clapped halfheartedly, while Andy clapped wholeheartedly.

"He's great!" said Andy, turning around again.

"Thanks," Sam responded.

"I heard that he was a good football player, but I didn't know—Jesus Christ!" Andy screeched as a ball clanged onto the bench within two feet of where he sat. He turned quickly toward the mound and shot a glare at Kenny, who offered an apologetic wave. "Just a precaution," he said as much to

30

himself as to Sam while he moved up a level on the bleachers. "I would've had that, had I been looking."

"My hero," Sam said flatly.

With one more hit, a line drive that shot past the pitcher, Kenny Foster was finished, and Will Kendrick stepped up to the plate. "That's your friend, right?" Sam asked as Will took his first strike.

"Yeah. That's Will. He's pretty good." Will swung at the second pitch and took his second strike. "Well, usually better."

"I've gotta tell ya, he's been off all morning. The coach has been on his case, but he just seems to be dragging."

Andy wore a look of concern. "I think he's got a lot on his mind lately."

WILL DID HAVE a lot on his mind as he geared up for the third pitch. What was his father referring to when he said that he was old enough? Who was Brandt? And what about the dreams? He glanced for a moment over to the three figures on the bleachers. Wait. Three figures? Will took a step back and rubbed his eyes with his sleeve. Sam and Andy were there, but there was indeed a third individual now seated on the bottom row, directly between his two classmates. Dressed in a pale gray suit, he was already out of place at a high school baseball team's practice, but more disturbingly, he had no face. Just as in the library, this individual had no discernible features from the neck up. *Almost like when they pixilate the face of an eyewitness on the news*, Will thought.

Unfortunately, as he thought this, his third and final strike flew by. "Come on, Will!" shouted his coach. "Where's your head at today?"

"Not here," Will said, throwing his bat and helmet onto the dusty ground. "I'm done."

Will knew that his coach and teammates were still speaking

31

to him as he walked off the field, but he refused to acknowledge, refused to take his eyes off the faceless figure as he stomped over to the bleachers, determined to finally get some answers. However, as he came within twenty feet of the stands, the figure turned its expressionless head toward him for a moment and faded from sight.

"No!" Will yelled, infuriated and slamming his fist onto the end of Andy's bench. "What the hell?"

"What, Will?" Andy asked, growing more and more concerned. "What's going on?"

"That's what I'd like to know," said Will. He paused for a minute, registered the look of confusion on Sam's face, and said to Andy, "Let's get out of here. I need to talk to you."

"WILL, SLOW DOWN!" Andy huffed as he raced to catch up. Will was walking as quickly as he could to his car, hoping that others from his team would take the hint and leave him alone. "What is going on? Is this still about the Trammell thing?"

"Yeah. It is," Will answered. "Something's going on with me, and it's not my imagination. My parents are in on it—and someone named Brandt."

"Brandt? Is this someone else I should be looking up?"

"No," said Will. "Apparently my father already took the liberty of looking up Mr. Brandt. Whoever he is, he'll be paying me a visit soon."

"How soon?"

Will took a breath and shrugged. "I don't know. But soon. Let me stay at your place tonight?"

"Sure, yeah. Whatever you want."

"But Andy, no one can know that I'm there."

"No one…as in, not even my parents?"

"Not either of our parents," said Will. "I don't feel entirely comfortable at home right now, and honestly, I'll be interested to see how my parents react if I'm not around in the morning."

"Will, I don't know about this. Why don't you just sit down and ask your parents directly about the Trammells? Maybe this Brandt guy knows. Maybe that's why they're bringing him in." Andy sighed. "You know I don't like all this sneaky stuff. It makes me nervous."

"Everything makes you nervous." Will paused, looking his worried friend in the eyes. "Listen. You know that I don't buy into all that superstitious, paranormal mumbo jumbo, right?"

"Right."

"Andy, these coincidences have me scared. I saw the name 'Trammell' in my dreams, and I have a strong feeling that I'm connected to them."

"Okay, but…"

"And if the other parts of my dream are at all real, then I could be in an incredibly weird situation and some serious trouble," said Will. "Let me crash at your place tonight. I can meet you in the backyard after dark. I'll text you."

Andy pursed his lips and nodded slowly. Will could tell that Andy didn't approve of the idea, but Andy could tell that Will's fear now extended well beyond his nightmares.

DURING HIS SHORT RIDE HOME, Will planned his next steps. His parents would probably be out, as they usually were at this time on a Saturday, and he'd have plenty of time to pack some things without attracting any attention. Then it was simply a matter of laying low and acting natural until darkness fell, at which point he'd find his way to the Lunsfords. Perhaps after a day or so of not having him around, his parents would decide to let him in on what was going on. If not, it would be up to him to find out on his own. It seemed like a simple enough plan – one that was immediately jeopardized when he pulled into his driveway and noticed that, not only were his parents home, but there was also an unfamiliar brown hatchback parked on the street in front of their house.

"Brandt," Will muttered to himself, already feeling an inexplicable hatred for this mysterious individual. He sat for a moment, his stomach turning with anxiety, before he took a breath and headed toward the house.

Once inside, he could smell fresh-brewed coffee and hear a muffled conversation emanating from behind the closed door of his father's study. Will entered the study without knocking, and found, to no surprise, three people who were clearly disturbed by his sudden intrusion. His mother, who was standing with her back to Will, looking out the window to the backyard, reacted the least, simply turning for a moment to give Will a slight, sad smile. His father stood immediately from his leather armchair, followed soon after by the man who sat opposite him in a matching chair—a man whom Will did not recognize.

"Will," Robert said, again removing his glasses and nervously wiping them clean. "What happened with baseball practice? Did it end early?"

"I think I quit the team," Will responded matter-of-factly, throwing his mitt onto an end table, his gaze fixated on the stranger standing behind his father. The man cut an imposing figure, as he stood several inches taller than Robert Kendrick and looked as though a smile might be painful to produce. Will couldn't determine his age, particularly because his skin was dark and hardened as though from years of outdoor work. Most of his face was covered by a black beard that showed hints of his age through several gray streaks that had begun to infiltrate it. His black, expressionless eyes met Will's and did not blink. Nothing in this man's grim appearance lessened Will's feeling of dread. In fact, if anything, the feeling was heightened.

"Quit the team?" Robert asked. "But—" He abandoned this train of thought when, replacing his glasses, he noticed the apparent staring contest between his son and his guest. "Never mind. We'll talk about it later." He stepped aside to allow for a handshake between the two. "Will, this is Mr. Brandt. He's an old acquaintance of mine."

Brandt stepped forward and took Will's hand in a crushing grip. "Hello, Will," he said in a gruff voice. "It's a pleasure."

Will refused to return the forced kindness, instead opting to get right to the point. "Are you a doctor as well?"

"No," Brandt answered. "In fact, I was a patient of your father's once."

"When?"

"A lifetime ago."

"Why are you here?"

"Will!" said his father with a look of dismay. "Is there a reason why you're making Mr. Brandt feel so unwelcome?"

Emily gave a barely audible chortle that Will was able to pick up on, and so—he could tell—was Brandt. "It's alright, Robert," said Brandt. "I have a feeling that Will already knows that this is about him. Don't you, Will?"

Will nodded slightly. "I knew that you were coming."

"How did you know?" asked Brandt. "Because of your dreams?"

"No," Will answered, shooting his parents an icy glare. "Because of an open window." Emily, standing at the window in question, sighed and turned away, clearly unable to face her son. "And what do you know about my dreams, Mr. Brandt?"

"Only what your parents have told me. I hear that they are rather vivid and rather disturbing." He paused to read Will's facial expression. Determining that Will agreed with his assessment, he continued. "I may be able to help you, Will. But I need to hear from you what these dreams are about."

"Why should that matter? You're not a shrink, right?"

"Far from it. But I think you might be surprised by my insight."

Will chuckled bitterly. "Yeah, okay. Sure. Ready? My parents—these parents that you see right here," he said, motioning toward Robert and Emily, "are not my parents in my dream." He removed a piece of paper from his pocket and unfolded it, holding it up so that Brandt could clearly see the smiling faces of Daniel and Karen Trammell. "These people are. And I see their name in the dream as well: Trammell. That's how I knew to look this up. That's how I knew they also had a son named William."

"I see," said Brandt pensively. "Is there more?"

"There's always more," Will responded. "It's like freaking Oz, but instead of a scarecrow, a tinman and a lion, I get some sort of living ragdoll, a creep with a bird mask, and a statue. And it always ends with fire. Always." Will stopped to take a breath. "So what does it mean, Mr. Brandt? Am I going crazy? Am I some sort of psychic now?" He shook the newspaper article in Brandt's face once more. "A useless psychic who can only see things that've already happened?"

Brandt stood stoic in the face of Will's frustration, fazed neither by his sarcasm nor his rising voice. Ignoring Will's questions, Brandt asked, "Who else knows about these dreams?"

Andy's name was on the tip of Will's tongue, but he held back. "No one. Only the people in this room."

Brandt nodded, but Will couldn't tell whether the man believed him or not. "I believe," said Brandt, "that I know what the dreams mean, but I can't tell you now."

"Ha!" Will plopped himself into the chair that his father had recently occupied. "Unreal."

"Damn you, Brandt," said Emily, with particularly spiteful emphasis on the man's name. "Enough of the games! You don't understand the position you've put us in!"

"No, Mrs. Kendrick," Brandt answered, this time with

some passion in his voice. "You're the one who doesn't understand." He turned to face Will once more. "Will, I'll be back tomorrow, at which point I'm going to ask you to trust me. You'll need to come with me for a while. I plan to bring you back safe and sound, but that's really all that I can tell you at this point."

Will screwed his face into an expression of indignation. "No way!" he replied, looking to his parents for backup. Since her exchange with Brandt, Emily had been sitting and sobbing in the corner, Robert comforting her. Their eyes met Will's, but both offered only looks of reluctant resignation.

Will couldn't believe what was happening. "And what if I don't go with you?" he yelled, this man Brandt suddenly becoming the personification of everything strange that had happened to him recently, and thus, in Will's mind, an entirely appropriate recipient of his rage.

"If you don't come with me, you'll put your parents' lives in danger…not to mention your own."

"Is that a threat?"

"I deal in facts, William. I will be here tomorrow morning. If you don't come with me, the fact is that your family will be in very real danger."

"And I don't deserve to be given a reason? I don't deserve to be told where you're taking me or what I'm supposed to be doing?"

"You absolutely deserve it," Brandt conceded. "But you're not going to get it." He looked around the room with his onyx eyes. "Not from me and not from your parents."

"Will, this needs to be done," said Robert.

"Listen to your father," said Brandt.

"Adopted father," Will retorted.

"Listen to your father," Brandt repeated. "I'll see you in the morning." With that, the grim figure excused himself from the room. The Kendricks sat in silence, save for Emily's sighs, until they heard Brandt's beaten-up hatchback drive off. Finally, Robert took his arm off Emily's shoulder, stood, and attempted to break the silence.

"Will, I don't like this anymore than —"

"You know what, Dr. Kendrick?" Will interjected, being very careful not to accidentally say "Dad." "You can go to hell."

He left the study, fully expecting to be followed to his bedroom, but Robert held his wife back. Will heard him say, "We all need to collect our thoughts, Emily. We'll talk to him tonight."

WILL SPENT the rest of the day in his bedroom. Every solution to his problem seemed to be easily dismissed by Brandt's tone earlier. He could have just called the police, but his parents were obviously in on whatever Brandt was planning, and Will would have looked like a lunatic basing every accusation on bad dreams and hallucinations. He toyed multiple times with the idea of either calling or texting Andy, but worried about placing his friend in danger. Brandt may have been full of it, but if anything, he did not seem the type to make things up. After a few hours of deliberating, Will finalized his decision to leave Andy—and anyone else that he knew—out of his current situation.

He sat on the edge of his bed for quite a while, wondering when his parents would come to talk to him, and considering whether he even wanted them to. He heard someone he assumed was Emily pacing in front of his closed door several times, but no one entered. Will was initially surprised by the lack of response from his parents, but eventually feelings of anger and betrayal took over. He rose from his bed, intent on taking control of his own destiny. If this Brandt character wanted him so badly, he'd have to find him first.

Taking a duffel bag from his closet, he quickly but quietly began packing some of his favorite items of clothing, including T-shirts, jeans, sneakers, a baseball cap, and a watch that his parents had given him for his sixteenth birthday. He stood in place for a moment, looking around the room for anything else that might prove useful on the road, but the rest—video games, books, and such—seemed suddenly expendable. Having packed everything that he might need for a few nights on the road, he slid the bag under his bed and walked nervously around the room, stopping now and then to look out the window, waiting for dusk.

WHEN THE SUN began to set, still not sure of where exactly he was going, Will pulled the bag out from beneath the bed and went to the open window. After raising the window to allow enough room for himself to squeeze through, he took one last look around his room, this time deciding to take a framed picture of himself and his parents taken before his junior prom last year. He looked at the picture of the three of them smiling and began to have second thoughts. What if he really was in trouble? What if Brandt was right, and by not going with him, he was putting the couple that he had always known as his parents in danger?

Will took a deep breath and placed the picture into the duffel bag. He'd go hide out for a few days. He'd see whether they looked for him or not. He'd contact them and play hard-ball—see whether they were willing to tell the whole truth about what was going on. It wasn't like he'd never see his parents again. He nodded as if to affirm his own actions and made his way through the window, onto the roof of their garage. He slowly lowered himself down onto a trashcan on the side of the house before jumping onto the grass. Looking back only briefly out of fear of getting caught by his doubtless vigilant parents, he began running. He ran a block or so to the corner, where he made a quick right and headed for a wooded area that ran behind their development. He wouldn't stay there, as it would be too obvious, but there was a shortcut to the neighboring town that would buy him some time to figure out where he'd be able to safely spend the night.

Will was just making his way out of the woods when darkness fell completely. It was now that he was standing on the beautiful grounds of the Greendale Library that he truly comprehended his distinct lack of a plan. No one had followed him as far as he could tell, and one cursory glance at the library parking lot told him he was alone. He took this opportunity to drop his bag onto a bench in order to rest his shoulder. He stretched and looked around, seeing a McDonald's sign glowing in the distance. The idea of a Big Mac made his mouth water, and he admitted to himself that he would have to stop to eat somewhere, as he had not had the forethought to pack food. Will decided to head to McDonald's as his next destination, and leaned over to find his duffel bag's strap. He fumbled in the darkness for only a few seconds before he felt a strong hand grab his arm and a needle prick his neck.

FIVE

Searching

ANDY LUNSFORD HAD BEEN so busy killing zombies that he had nearly forgotten to go outside and look for Will. After all, Will had promised to text before he left home, and as no text had ever come through, Andy easily found himself immersed in his video games. Still, at around nine, Andy shut off the Xbox and dutifully went out onto his family's back porch. There he sat for the next half hour until the beams of his parents' headlights shone into the backyard, signaling their return from the bar. After squinting one more time into the darkness and rasping a hushed, "Will? You there?" to no response, he called it a night and went inside.

Just before turning in for the night, Andy felt a slight but growing concern for his friend and sent a simple text to see whether plans had changed. He laid his phone on the nightstand near his head and turned on the television to keep him awake until he received a response. It didn't work. Within five minutes, Andy was fast asleep, but it didn't matter anyway, as an answer never came from Will.

· · ·

ANDY NOTICED this when he woke up in the morning, and he grew more and more troubled. True, it was easy to rattle Andy, but it was not nearly as easy to rattle Will. When Andy had last seen his friend, Will seemed perturbed like never before. Andy knew that it was out of the ordinary for Will not to respond to a text, and even stranger considering he had not shown up as planned the night before. For a moment, Andy simply figured that he'd see whether his friend showed up for school, but recalling that it was Sunday, he quickly scratched that notion. "Well," said Andy, who had a greater penchant than most for addressing himself directly, "I guess I'll just head over there."

Within an hour, Andy was showered, dressed, and riding his bike to the Kendricks' home. Andy hardly had a chance to knock before Emily answered. In what would have been a bizarre snapshot, the tearful Mrs. Kendrick looked down at the plump figure whose face seemed comically compressed by a heavy, oversized helmet.

"Oh," she said, trying her best not to sound disappointed. She stood for a moment looking at her son's friend, almost as though she wanted to say something but didn't know if she should. After a few seconds, though, she was replaced by her husband, who had rushed to the door behind her and gently shuffled her aside when he saw who the visitor was.

"Hello, Andy," said Dr. Kendrick.

"Hi, Dr. K," Andy responded. "Is Will around?" he asked.

"He's not, actually," Dr. Kendrick replied. "In fact, he probably won't be around for at least a few days." Dr. Kendrick looked around to ensure that Emily was out of earshot and motioned gently for Andy to take a step back. When he did, the doctor followed him onto the front porch and closed the door quietly behind him. "I'm sure you've noticed," Robert said, "that Will hasn't been feeling so well lately."

"Well, I know that he hasn't been sleeping well."

"Exactly. We had a family discussion last night, and Will's

gone to spend a few nights at his grandparents' place in Raleigh. You know, not too far, but just far enough to provide a change of scenery for him."

"So he's missing school?" Andy asked, knowing that Dr. Kendrick was a stickler for making Will attend every day.

"Y-yes," Dr. Kendrick answered, hesitating only slightly. "He's been under a lot of stress lately. But with any luck, he'll be back by next week, and everything will be back to normal," he said with a smile.

"Is Mrs. K alright? She didn't look too good."

"She's fine," said Dr. Kendrick with a nod. "Just a bit of a rough morning. But I'll tell her that you were concerned."

"Okay, then," said Andy, getting back on his bike. "See ya soon." With that, he left Robert Kendrick standing alone on his porch. The conversation could have continued, Andy thought, but why bother? Something had clearly happened to Will, and Dr. Kendrick was not about to say what. "That's fine," Andy said to himself. "If they don't want to tell me, I'll just find out myself. 'Grandparents' house' my ass."

UPON RETURNING HOME, Andy immediately hopped online. He read through the entire article about the Trammells twice but could not figure out where to go from there. He was sure Will believed the Trammells to be his birth parents, and Andy wanted to believe as well, but the report of William Trammell's death was staring him right in the face. What Andy needed was information beyond what was provided in this article. Skimming it a few more times, one name kept catching Andy's eye: Officer Edward Garza. "That's our man," muttered Andy, quickly opening a new window to search for a way to contact the Philadelphia police force. As Philadelphia was a big place that Andy knew little about, it took quite a few tries to reach anyone who had ever heard of Edward Garza.

43

Finally, after nearly an hour's worth of wrong numbers, he spoke to a Detective Ramos, who informed him that Garza had retired two years previous and who understandably refused to give any personal contact information.

Crestfallen, Andy sat with his elbows on the desk, squishing his face in his hands. *There must be a way*, he thought. A few seconds later, a small chime drew his attention to the bottom of the screen, where he had minimized his Facebook page earlier. Normally, the notification that Sam Foster had requested him as a friend would have made his day, but instead, he was drawn to an advertisement on the side of the page: *See who's searching for you*, it read.

"Yes!" he said, louder than he had intended. "The wonders of technology. Thank you, Sam." He leaned in to give a peck to the image of Sam, who had somehow become the symbol of his success, and typed "Edward Garza" into the search box. There were several matches, but none from Philadelphia, and none old enough to have been a police officer fourteen years prior.

Andy then tried "Eddie Garza" and found more success. Again, he received several matches for the name alone, but this time, there was one from Philadelphia who matched the probable age of his quarry. "This has to be you," he said. "Thank God for old people on Facebook." With that, he crafted a lengthy email relating Will's situation and including his own contact information. Having sent the message, he sat back contentedly. Now all he would have to do was wait for a response. In the meantime, he'd check out Sam's photo album.

SIX

The Aberration

WILL WOKE UP SLOWLY, his head gently bobbing and his bleary eyes bombarded by the light of the newly risen sun. It was only when he attempted to rub his tired eyes that he realized his hands had been restrained. As his vision focused, he saw his hands were tied tightly together in front of him, and a quick attempt to move his feet confirmed that his ankles had been bound as well. He raised his head to look around. It had been several years since his last camping trip, but he immediately recognized his prison as the interior of a dated RV, empty save for a briefcase, a few olive-colored canvas bags, and himself. Most of the shades were drawn, blocking his view of the road, but the sun shone through the front windshield, making it difficult for him to discern the shape of the individual in the driver's seat. Will had a gut feeling, however, that he didn't need to see the man's face to know who he was.

"Brandt," he rasped, noting how dry his mouth was.

Sure enough, Brandt, much of his face shaded by a weathered wide-brimmed hat, glanced back at Will and nodded. His captor turned his attention back to the road, but addressed Will while looking into the rearview mirror every now and then. "That was very stupid, Will," he said. Will, not knowing what he meant, responded only with a glare. "Running away like that doesn't say much about your character." Brandt paused to watch Will struggle with the thick rope that bound his wrists. "Still, catching you out by that library kept me from having to deal with your mother again."

Will stopped struggling long enough to say, "She's not my mother," and then went back to work, twisting his hands in all manner of unnatural ways.

"We'll get to that," said Brandt. "First, a few things you should know. The number one thing you should know right now is that you're not escaping from those knots. I don't care how many action movies you've seen. I've searched you. You've got nothing on you that will help you to get out of those ropes."

Will stopped struggling as Brandt completed his last statement. As much as he hated Brandt right now, his words seemed to be in earnest. "What about my phone?"

"I'm afraid I had to destroy that."

"*Destroy?* Who do you think you are?" Will screamed.

"You can always get a new phone," said Brandt, calmly, "if that's what's important to you."

"And when is that going to happen? Right before you bury me in a ditch somewhere?"

Brandt was obviously unamused. "Well, that brings me to my next point." Brandt pulled onto the shoulder of the highway and turned to face his seething captive. "Since we met yesterday, I've told you nothing but the truth. I'm going to tell the truth again now, so listen carefully." The tall man stood up, stooping a bit, and walked toward Will until he was within a few feet. He squatted and rested his forearms on his knees before continuing. "You're about to be asked to do something very dangerous, but something that I think you'll ultimately find worthwhile. If all goes well, this…task…won't take long at all. When all is said and done, once you've done what you need to do, I intend to bring you right back to South Carolina. There, you can continue to live your life as you have been all this time. You have my word on that."

Will's breathing came a bit more regularly at this point, but Brandt could still see the fear and uncertainty in his eyes. "So you're not going to…you know…"

"Kill you?" Brandt suggested. "No. In fact, I'm here to see to it that you live through this. Now, if you're going to be kicking and screaming the entire time, you're only going to make my job more difficult, you see? And then if harm *does* come to you, it won't have been my fault." Brandt stood, rubbing his knees as if they ached. "But if you follow my instructions to the letter, you'll not only live to tell the tale, but I'll turn you into something of a hero. Now how does that sound?"

Will didn't feel as though he had much of a choice, but he could sense that Brandt needed him at least as much as he needed Brandt, so he decided to press his luck. Clenching his jaw, he replied, "That doesn't work for me. You know about my real parents. I know you do. If I'm going to come along with you, I want to know about them."

Brandt cracked a crooked smile for the first time—one that Will felt he could do without seeing again. "Sounds like a deal. As a matter of fact, I was going to tell you anyway."

Will wasn't thrilled with this response, as Brandt had effectively removed any sense of victory, so he tried for one more concession. "So do I have to stay tied up?"

"Not if you can behave yourself."

"I'll be fine," Will promised. "I won't try anything."

"Good," Brandt said, grabbing one his green bags and drawing a beautiful but intimidating ivory-hilted knife from it. He crouched again and laid the blade against Will's bottom lip. Will could taste the metal as Brandt's eyes, surrounded by dark circles, hovered only inches away from his. "Just remember, William: if you try anything, you'll never find out about your real parents. Deal?" He moved the knife away, allowing Will to give a solemn nod. "Alright then. Come on. We've got a lot to cover."

WILL SOON SITUATED himself much more comfortably at the small dinette in the back of the RV as Brandt squeezed himself onto the bench opposite him. "Who *are* you?" Will asked, opting to forego pleasantries.

"I'm not one for philosophical questions. You'll have to be more concrete."

"Fine," said Will. "How do you really know my father, um, Robert Kendrick?"

"I already told you yesterday. I was, in fact, a patient of your father's once. He's a good man. Trustworthy."

Will snorted. "If you say so.

WHAT ABOUT YOUR FAMILY? Are you just this creepy man-of-mystery loner? Do you have a wife? Kids? I'm guessing not."

"No family," Brandt answered quickly. "Not a good idea in my line of work."

"Which is?"

Brandt looked ahead without the slightest acknowledgment.

"DO you at least have a first name, or do I just keep calling you Brandt?"

"I think we've got more important things to discuss than my life story."

"Fine, *Brandt*. You're serious about letting me go back home after I do you this favor?" Will asked.

"I am."

"So where are we going?"

"Boston."

Will nodded. "I've never been there. So what am I supposed to do in Boston?"

"Now that," said Brandt, "is a loaded question. We'll get to that shortly. First, there are some items that I need to fill you in on. And you're not going to believe most of what I say."

"It's been a strange few days. Try me."

"We'll start at the beginning. As you've already guessed, you were born William Trammell."

Will nodded. This was no surprise, really, but it was still a strange feeling to finally know the truth. "Okay, but if I am the William Trammell who lived in Philadelphia, I'm supposed to be dead."

"You are indeed. In reality, the nature of the explosive that was planted in your family's house didn't allow for the proper identification of any bodies. Nearly everything was incinerated."

"So the rest of my family could still be alive?"

Brandt looked Will in the eyes, shaking his head. "No, the rest are gone."

"But you just said—"

"Believe me. They're gone. Do not hold out hope of seeing them again."

Will lowered his head, upset that he would never again see these people that he didn't remember having seen in the first place. "So they were murdered, right? By that Russian guy?"

"Villovich? No. But it was certainly made to look that way. They were, in fact, murdered, but by someone else entirely."

"Who?"

"We'll get to that."

Will was getting frustrated now. "Well then why? And how did I get away?"

"They were killed because of you."

"Me?"

"More specifically, your blood. Your blood is your story." Brandt paused, as if not quite knowing how to continue. "The murder of your family had nothing to do with your father and everything to do with you. You have enemies that you're not even aware of. You've had them since birth. Hell, even before that."

"But why?"

Brandt thought for a moment. "Tell me, William—do you believe in the paranormal?"

"Like witches and ghosts? No. At least I didn't until my dreams started making sense."

"You'd be wise to start," said Brandt. He sighed and laid his hands on the table in front of him. "Before I go on," he said, "I need to inform you that I've always considered myself a practical man. A realist. I never had any use for ghost stories or other flights of fancy. In order for me to believe in something, I've got to see it—and I've seen more than you can imagine. So, William, do you trust that I'll tell you the truth?"

Will nodded and said, "I do," anxious to hear what Brandt had to say.

"Very well. In order for you to understand your part in things, I'll need to go back to the beginning."

"Of what?" Will asked.

"Of everything," Brandt replied. "For as long as people have existed, they've been surrounded by forces that even their most ambitious scientific advancements could not explain. Much of this *can* be explained, though, by the presence of demons."

"Demons? Like red guys with horns and tails?"

"Not necessarily. You see, demons are not simply the devils that you learn about in Sunday school. They are forces, often unseen, that are not of the human world. They may be good, they may be evil, or they may be anywhere in between—like people. Regardless of the demon's moral character, one thing is for sure: they are extremely powerful."

Brandt struck Will as the kind of person who would roll his eyes through a haunted house movie, so his belief in the supernatural was surprising. By the same token, though, Brandt's staunchness and conviction lent a credibility to all of the ridiculous things his captor was saying. Will decided to lean into what he was being told, at least for the time being. "So what about other monsters, like vampires and zombies and werewolves?"

Brandt stroked his thick black beard as he weighed how to answer the query. "They exist," he said finally, "though perhaps in ways you wouldn't expect. But they are not your concern."

"So what *is* my concern?"

"I'm getting there," Brandt said. "Since the beginning of time, demons have interacted with humans. This often involved taking human form and, um, lying with people."

"You mean lying to?"

"No. I mean lying with. They had sex, Will. You're seventeen. Shouldn't your mind go right there?"

"That's nasty."

"Be that as it may, it happened. The result of these unions eventually became referred to as 'the demonic strain,' and later simply 'the Aberration.' In short, demon blood mixed with human blood to create a sort of hybrid. Children of these unions would often find themselves with special abilities that their purely human peers did not have. For instance, some could alter their appearances, hence the basis for your typical werewolf legend."

"Cool," said Will, now totally enrapt.

Brandt gave him a disapproving look and continued. "The immediate offspring would typically be more powerful or would need to exert less energy when tapping into their demonic traits. In most scenarios, even those with the Aberration were ignorant to the fact that they possessed it. They would marry pure humans and the strain would become more diluted with each passing generation. Still, there were plenty of individuals who were perfectly aware of their…condition and could exercise their traits at will."

"So how come everyone doesn't know about these people?"

Brandt smirked. "They do. They just don't realize it. You have to understand that the paranormal frightened people even more in the old days than it does today. I mean, how do you explain individuals who can part seas, walk on water, and raise the dead? In short, they become the stuff of legends, of supposed fiction, folklore, and even religious doctrine."

"No way," Will said in a hushed tone, realizing the enormity of what he was being told.

"But you can research that more on your own time," said Brandt with a dismissive wave of his hand. "Back to our story. Most of these demons—mainly the most harmful—were banished long ago, but the Aberration still exists today."

Suddenly something clicked for Will. He was putting the pieces together…at least he thought he was. "I have it, don't I? That's why I've been getting those dreams?"

Brandt nodded. "You do."

"So is that my power? I have weird dreams? That sucks."

"To be honest with you, William," said Brandt, "I didn't expect that. For the past fourteen years, I was under the impression that you only had one special ability—one that has nothing to do with dreams."

"And what ability is that?"

"The ability to avenge your family's death. You're a killer, Will."

SEVEN

Blood Feud

WILL SAT QUIETLY as Brandt stood to get himself a bottle of water from the mini fridge at the far corner of the camper. "Water?"

Will nodded. "Yes, please," he said softly, without inflection, lost in a sea of thoughts. "And while you're at it, could you explain what you mean by 'killer'?"

Brandt removed his hat and sat back down, passing a bottle to Will. "I can try," he responded. "This whole situation in which you currently find yourself started with two men: Roderick Gleave and Desmond Duquesne. They both lived in England during the nineteenth century, and both were extremely powerful. Your great-great grandfather, Roderick Gleave, was a sorcerer on par with some of the most powerful. Duquesne, on the other hand, was a diabolist. Do you know the difference?"

Will simply shook his head. He was lost already.

"Didn't think so. A sorcerer is the polite name for someone who uses their inborn demonic powers."

"What's the impolite name?" Will asked.

"Well, they really hate being called magicians. It's kind of like calling an escort a whore." Will smiled slightly at this. Brandt didn't. "Of course, others would simply call them freaks. No offense."

"None taken…I guess. So what was the other guy?"

"A diabolist is someone who seeks power through other means, typically by finding ways to communicate with the demon world. Duquesne, for instance, had no innate magical talent but was adept at summoning demons, to whom he gladly sold his soul. Thus, he gained power to rival that of Gleave."

"Okay. Just so that I'm clear," said Will, "Sorcerers are like natural athletes, while diabolists are kind of like regular guys who get all 'roided up?"

"Not an entirely inappropriate metaphor," Brandt replied. "In fact, there's more to that metaphor than you know. You see, people who use what we'll refer to as 'magic' are very much like athletes, in that their abilities have physical limits. An Olympic runner may be able to keep an impressive pace for a matter of minutes, but can he do it for a matter of days? Not likely. No matter how he conditions himself, his body will eventually wear out. The vast majority of sorcerers are the same. Their abilities are often incredible, but they are not without limits."

"What about the diabolists?" asked Will. "Do they have the same limits?"

Brandt shifted in his seat a bit, betraying some uncertainty. "Depends," he answered. "That gets into more complicated matters that I'm not an authority on. I can only speak to what I know."

"So are you an Aberrationist?"

"A what?"

"Aberrationist. I just thought of that. People don't say that? I'm going to make it a thing."

"People do not say that, and you are not going to make it a

54

thing. It's awful," Brandt snapped. "And no, I do not have demonic blood. And glad of it. It's nothing but trouble."

"I see," said Will, sensing that he had hit a nerve with his traveling companion. "So…you were telling me the story of my great-great grandfather?"

"Yes," said Brandt, his gruff voice a bit more composed. "Gleave and Duquesne were two immensely powerful individuals, and they happened to be relatively friendly with each other as well. I say 'relatively' because, as everyone knows, the friendship between two people like them can only ever be tenuous at best." He took a brief sip of his water and continued. "Anyway, very few people know exactly what happened, but eventually there was a falling out between the two, leading to a bitter feud that continued for the rest of your ancestor's life. Gleave made many attempts on Duquesne's life, but it was in vain, since Duquesne's most recent deal with a demon had granted him apparent immortality."

"Immortality? So no matter what, he couldn't be killed?"

"Well, almost," said Brandt. "With this kind of business, there's almost always a loophole, and before too long, Roderick Gleave found it. He discovered a prophecy—a very reliable one —that stated that his male heir would have the means to finally kill his rival, Desmond Duquesne. There was one problem, however…"

"He didn't have a son, did he?"

Brandt shook his head. "And not for lack of trying. The Gleave bloodline lived on, but it never produced a male heir, until guess who…"

Will gulped as Brandt poked him in the chest with a large, forceful finger. "You win the prize."

"And that prize is?" Will asked, fearing that he already knew the answer.

"The opportunity to finally put an end to Desmond Duquesne. In other words, the opportunity to kill the man who ordered the death of little William Trammell fourteen years ago."

ONCE WILL HEARD that Duquesne was responsible for the death of his birth parents, his questions ceased. It wasn't that he didn't have any—in fact the problem may have been that he now had too many. He remembered a hydra that he had seen in a movie once. Each time the hero cut off a head, two grew in its place. Suddenly, his personal history resembled this creature. For each question that Brandt had answered, several more popped up. Brandt, sensing that the conference had reached a satisfactory ending place, returned to the wheel of the RV, allowing Will time to digest the plethora of information that had just been thrown his way.

It was fifteen minutes or so before Will joined Brandt in the front of the vehicle, strapping himself into the passenger seat and staring blankly forward through the windshield. After a few more minutes, Brandt broke the silence: "So. Have you ever killed anyone?"

Will immediately shook himself out of his haze and shot Brandt an incredulous look. "What? No! What's wrong with you?"

Brandt kept his eyes on the road and shrugged. "Didn't think you had, but figured I'd ask," he said. "I really just wanted to see your reaction."

"Oh? And how'd that go for you?"

"To be honest, I'm a bit more concerned than I had been previously."

"Why is that?"

"William," Brandt responded, "twenty minutes ago, I told you who ordered the death of your family. I also told you that it is your responsibility to kill that man. Yet, when I even mention the idea of doing so, you respond with shock and disgust. Where's the righteous anger? Where's the desire for justice?"

Will shook his head. "It's a lot to take in, I guess. I don't know. It still just doesn't seem real to me."

"It's real," Brandt said, finally turning to look him in the eyes. "Like I've said before, I deal in facts. Unfortunately, I feel that we have an uphill battle ahead of us."

"Why? Because of the way I just reacted?"

"No, not just because of that. As a matter of fact, I've had a sinking feeling since I first met you yesterday."

"What the hell? What did I do wrong yesterday?" Will demanded.

"You quit," Brandt answered.

"Quit what?"

"You quit the baseball team. At least, that's what you told your father. And frankly, I can't stand quitters. Never could."

"I'm just not that good at baseball. I thought I might have been, but—"

"I don't need your life story," Brandt interrupted.

"Whatever. You're the one relating my current situation to baseball," Will argued. "It's not the same at all."

"It *is* the same. If you can't do something as simple as hitting a ball with a stick or taking a few laps around some bases, how the hell do you intend to do something that obviously turns your stomach? How do you expect to be able to kill a man?"

"It's an adjustment, Brandt. Excuse me if I'm not the heartless killing machine that you apparently are." Brandt shot an intense glare in his direction, but Will continued, "Despite what this Duquesne guy's apparently done to me, you can't expect me to go after him guns blazing. I've never held a gun in my life, unless you count Super Soakers."

"Well, that's going to change, starting now. Consider your training underway."

"So you're changing hats from kidnapper to mentor now?"

"You can call me whatever you want," said Brandt. "That really doesn't matter. As of today, though, I'll be giving you every lesson you'll need to go up against the man who had your family killed. So take note. Your first lesson: quitting is not an option."

"Thanks, Yoda," Will responded, rolling his eyes. "Very inspiring. I need to go back to something that you said before that amazing life lesson, though."

Brandt, not amused by Will's flippancy, nonetheless opted to indulge him. "What's that?"

"You've actually said a few times that Duquesne is responsible for my family's death, or that he had my family killed."

"Right. What's your point, William?"

"You never came out and said that he actually killed the Trammells. Did he?" Will asked.

"Did he physically plant the bomb that killed your family? No. Of course not. He has people for that."

EIGHT

The Illusionist

EMIL HAVELOCK STARED into the black waters of the Indian Ocean, hoping for his latest wave of nausea to pass. He wiped the moisture from his face with his bare forearm, but within seconds, he was saturated again with a mixture of perspiration and mist from the waves lapping angrily against the side of the weathered fishing boat. He closed his eyes and listened to his companions speaking, more for distraction from the sound of churning water than anything else. After all, he couldn't understand a damn word they said. This strategy failed, however, and he dry heaved. When he opened his eyes and found himself inches from the surface of the water, he quickly pulled himself up and sat stiffly on his bench, now facing his fellow travelers.

He was furious at his own nausea. He hated showing weakness normally, so he absolutely despised himself for the display that he was putting on in front of the two clowns he traveled with. Emil Havelock—the infamous mercenary, the best at what he did—was being made to look like a weak-willed coward in front of a glorified librarian and a hired hand. This would not stand.

He glared as his colleague, a stocky man with round, tortoiseshell glasses, struggled to translate their agenda to their guide. The guide was a dark-skinned Tanzanian prone to making wild hand gestures, as he did now. Havelock hadn't taken the time to perfect the pronunciation of the man's name, nor did he care to. Instead, he had taken to referring to him as Cheshire, as he was barely visible at times like this, when the moon had ducked behind the clouds, save for his brilliant white teeth. He watched the exchange between Brisbane and Cheshire for a few more moments before, with one dramatic, dismissive gesture, Cheshire returned to his place at the helm of the small craft. Brisbane, clearly exasperated, removed a handkerchief from his pocket, wiped the mist from his thick lenses, and then the sweat from his brow. He strode gracelessly over to Havelock and plopped down onto the wooden bench next to him.

"Well?" said an annoyed Havelock. "Are you getting through to him?"

"My Swahili is rusty," Brisbane answered in his surprisingly guttural voice. "I believe I'm getting through, though. He just isn't eager to go where we need him to go."

"He's a prick."

"He's afraid."

"Afraid of what? Me?"

Brisbane laughed. "No, actually, despite your repeated threats. It's dangerous enough to travel these waters at night, but you should know that Pemba Island is considered by many to be one of the most haunted places in the world. The native people in and around Pemba take this very seriously. Our guide says that the particular shore to which we are heading is a hotbed of witchcraft and paranormal activity."

Havelock smirked. "Well, that only confirms that we're on the right track." He removed a wrinkled piece of paper from the pocket of his black shorts and held a set of numbers up to Brisbane. "We *are* going to these coordinates, right?"

Brisbane had memorized them earlier and waved the paper away. "Yes, yes. I checked multiple times. He's not happy about it, but he's taking us there."

"That's all that matters," Havelock responded. "Of course, if he doesn't get us there in the next ten minutes," he said, raising his voice to get their pilot's attention and removing a pistol from his vest, "our friend Cheshire is going to have more to fear than just ghosts."

WHETHER AIDED by Havelock's subtle encouragement or not, the small craft reached the cove within ten minutes, and the mercenary leapt eagerly into the waist-high water. He took a moment to survey the area, noting the sense of isolation created by the high cliffs on either side of the shoreline and the dark, dense forest just past the pale sand of the beach. The setting would have been idyllic in the daylight; in the dark of night it was foreboding. "You coming?" he asked as he looked back to his colleague, who was again engaged in conversation with their guide.

"As soon as I convince our friend here to stick around," Brisbane answered. "He seems to be getting cold feet."

Sure enough, Cheshire appeared to be adamantly refusing to stay adrift while Brisbane and Havelock completed their task. He shook his head, and with wild eyes, pointed to the forest. From what Havelock could decipher, he was repeating one phrase over and over again with a tremulous voice. "What is he saying?" Havelock demanded.

"He's saying that this area beyond the beach," Brisbane responded, pointing to the gently undulating foliage, "is the witch's land. That no one goes there…at least no one who plans to come back."

Havelock gritted his teeth and again revealed his gun as he waded back toward the boat. "You tell him that we plan to come back, and if he's not here—"

Brisbane silently motioned for his partner to calm down and reached into his pocket, producing a thick wad of currency. He handed it to Cheshire and spoke briefly in Swahili. Cheshire nodded. Before Havelock could ask, Brisbane explained, "He'll wait here for the other half. You see, I have my own methods of persuasion." He rolled up his pants and flopped into the water alongside Havelock.

As they waded toward the beach, Havelock raised his brow and muttered, "We're not really going to pay him that much for this, are we?"

"Of course, Emil. Mr. Duquesne has authorized me to use these funds in any way that I see fit. That's how important this assignment is." Havelock grumbled, but Brisbane added, "However, once we're safely back to the mainland, if our guide were to mysteriously disappear, I suppose we could pocket the money, no? Our friend Duquesne would be none the wiser."

Havelock flashed a crooked grin and slapped a wet hand against Brisbane's back. "I didn't think you had it in you, Professor, but keep thinking like that, and we'll make this a productive trip."

THE TWO TRAVELED down a narrow dirt path leading through the thick brush for nearly a quarter-mile before either said a word. The only sounds that could be heard were the crunching of Brisbane's footsteps and the small thwacking noises that he made when he periodically swatted at the countless flies and other insects that formed a cloud around them. Havelock walked ahead, his footsteps silent, more calculated. He wore a determined look as he cut a swath through the jungle, the only exception being when he would throw a frustrated look in Brisbane's direction and hold a finger to his lips.

After being shushed three times, Brisbane, oblivious to all but the pests surrounding him, rasped, "I can't believe that I forgot bug repellant."

"I can't believe that you decide to talk when I tell you to shut up."

"Well I'm sorry," said the older man, slapping a fly from his shin. "I just didn't realize how much walking would be involved."

"We haven't even gone that far," Havelock hissed. "You're no Indiana Jones, are you?"

"I'm twice the archeologist he was."

"Good, Georgie. I'm glad that you're confident in your abilities as compared with a fictional character."

Brisbane grunted and slapped his leg again. "Check our location, will you? If we entered the forest at the correct location, we should be getting close."

"No need," said Havelock. "Listen."

This time, Brisbane stayed quiet, and he was soon able to make out the faint, rhythmic beating of drums. "Sounds like a ceremony," he whispered.

"Yeah. Or maybe it's 'ghosts,'" Havelock said, using air quotes.

"After all that you've seen, you don't believe in ghosts?"

"I never said that. I just don't believe in the ghosts of Pemba. You?"

Brisbane shrugged uncomfortably. "I don't know. I've traveled around the world. I've seen some strange things. I suppose that ghosts wouldn't be out of the question. Especially here. The place seems..." He paused as they entered a circular clearing surrounded by shoulder-height fronds that performed an eerie dance in sync with the warm breeze. He finished his thought: "...sinister."

Havelock didn't say a word, but silently readied his pistol. He had had this feeling before. The feeling of being hunted… and he didn't like it. The beating of the drums had gotten louder by this time, a steady *thump, thump, thump* that reminded him of *King Kong*'s Skull Island. Something was coming, alright, he thought, but it wasn't a damn monkey. The beats grew in both volume and intensity as Havelock and Brisbane neared the center of the circle, so much so that the latter clasped his hands over his ears like a child and ran for the path on the opposite end of the clearing. "Come on!" Havelock could just about hear him over the ritualistic thumping. Brisbane had nearly reached the barely-there path. "Let's get out of—Jesus!"

Havelock watched intensely as a pale figure emerged from Brisbane's intended path, sending the man crashing to the ground in shock. "Emil!" he shouted, scurrying backwards on his forearms, never taking his bespectacled eyes off the figure. "Shoot it!"

"It won't work, George," Havelock answered.

"Just do it!" The shape advanced. It was human in appearance, but ethereal, almost translucent, at first. Within seconds, it took solid form, and, though it remained a sickly pale gray, appeared as a young woman dressed in rags. The two men remained still, Havelock standing with his gun poised, Brisbane propped up on his elbows, caked in dirt and breathing heavily. They watched as several more figures appeared, all very much akin to the first. Two shapes appeared, followed by three more, and then another two, all making their way through the tall grass surrounding the clearing. The figures, chanting softly to the beat of the drums, slowly closed in on the two intruders, until Havelock fired a single shot at the one in the center, the one that had appeared first. As he expected, the bullet breezed through the figure's incorporeal chest. Brisbane's eyes widened. "They are ghosts!"

"Not quite," said Havelock. The bullet may not have

injured the shape, but at the very least, it stopped them from advancing. In fact, the chanting and the drums had stopped as well. "What now?" Havelock muttered, dragging George to his feet. The form of the young woman opened her mouth as if to answer his question, but her jaw soon unhinged and dropped nearly to her chest. Her teeth elongated into crooked daggers reminiscent of a monstrous deep-sea fish, and her arms followed suit, stretching until her pallid hands touched the ground. Within moments, the ghostly young girl had mutated into a hunched, skeletal beast. The creature let out a guttural roar, and with that, its seven companions began their transformations. Brisbane watched in horror as they found themselves surrounded by these ashen grotesqueries that once again crept toward them, this time with an unnatural gait, walking on all fours with their elbows turned out in front of them. He heard them gnashing their teeth and turned to Havelock.

"What do we do?" he asked in a panic. "This is why you're here. What do we do?"

Havelock briefly appeared to be ignoring his partner as he gazed intensely from creature to creature. When he did finally speak, he simply said, "We run."

"Good! Which way?"

"That way."

Brisbane looked to see that the direction in which Havelock was pointing was straight across the clearing and would require them to somehow weave through several of the beasts. "But that's where they all are!"

"Exactly," Havelock responded. "So that's where we need to go. Come on." He holstered one of his guns and grabbed Brisbane's arm. At first, he seemed to be lugging dead weight, but after a few steps, Brisbane picked up the pace out of the sheer terror of being left behind. Brisbane closed his eyes while Havelock ran headlong into the gaping jaws of one of the creatures. The professor braced himself, expecting to be torn apart at any moment, but then his face felt the sharp blades of tall grass and he realized that, somehow, they had made it through the horde of creatures. He didn't turn back. Instead, he diligently followed Havelock, who had by now released his arm, down a steep slope to what appeared to be the outskirts of a small fishing village. Brisbane looked around at the line of ramshackle houses that stood along the singular dirt road; only a few were barely illuminated by flickering lanterns.

"You think she's in one of these?" he whispered.

"No," said Havelock. His attention was not focused on the village, but on another slope similar to the one that they had just hastily traversed. "Look. There's another path here."

Brisbane, just now realizing that he had dropped his flashlight during their last encounter, took a few cautious steps toward the spot, and squinting, answered, "This doesn't look like much. It's not well traveled."

"It's a trick," Havelock responded as he crouched down and began to remove branches from the entrance of the path. "These branches came from those trees back there," he said, pointing to a grouping of trees in the distance that Brisbane could hardly make out. "Someone placed them here to cover the path. It's too amateur for Simms. Must've been the natives trying to protect her."

"But why?"

"I think I know," he said, "but we'll find out for sure in a minute. Come on."

BRISBANE FOLLOWED his partner down the treacherous path, stumbling multiple times but refusing to let on. Havelock, of course, had no problem managing it, and Brisbane did not want to seem any less capable, though he most definitely was. A few minutes and several scrapes later, he caught up to Havelock in a clearing that housed a solitary cabin, which appeared to be in much better shape than any of the other local dwellings. "This must be her," Havelock said. Brisbane nodded and approached the door. He raised his fist, but Havelock caught his wrist. "Seriously?" he rasped. "You're going to knock?" He shook his head in disappointment. "Element of surprise, George." Using the butt of his gun, Havelock gave the flimsy doorknob a swift crack, sending it falling with barely a clink to the dirt below. He rammed the door with his shoulder, probably harder than he had to, Brisbane thought, and entered the cabin with his gun at the ready.

Brisbane didn't know what to expect when he entered the cabin, but he was surprised nonetheless. The cabin felt homey, as though it were in the Adirondacks rather than a remote African island. A teapot was set to boil on a small cast iron stove, a modest fire burned in the fireplace, and the walls were decorated with local art, mostly consisting of woven, tapestry-like pieces. In the far right corner of this single room sat a middle-aged woman who could not have seemed more out of place on the island of Pemba. Her skin had a pinkish complexion, not from being in the hot African sun, but from rosacea, Brisbane could tell. Rather than wearing the traditional garb of the island, she wore an old Disneyland T-shirt and a pair of jeans. When the two approached her, the woman looked up from a puzzle that she was completing and took off her bifocals, letting them settle on her chest, hanging from a string around her neck. She smiled faintly, leaned both hands on the table in front of her, and said, "I was wondering when someone would come for me."

"Nice trick with the monsters, Miranda," Havelock responded.

"I try."

"Pretty clever operation you've got here. Let me see if I've got this straight," said Havelock as he browsed her small ice chest. "First you convince these savages that their island is haunted, and then you offer them protection from the ghosts and goblins…hence why they'd be so eager to keep you their little secret for all these years. They think that if anything happens to you, the bogeymen will get them." He found a bottle of water and helped himself, nearly finishing the entire thing in one series of chugs.

"Very good, Emil!" she said in a patronizing tone. "Did you figure that out all by yourself, or did you need your friend here to help you?"

"Ms. Simms, my name is George Brisbane." He removed his hat and stepped forward to shake her hand, but she remained unmoved.

"I know who you are, Dr. Brisbane, and I know why you're here."

"So you know that we're here for the Heart?"

"I do."

Havelock, who had finished his water, returned to the conversation. "And are you going to play nice and hand it over, or do we have to make things messy?"

Miranda sighed. "I'm getting too old for this, Emil. As far as I'm concerned, I did my best. I played my part."

"Good decision," said Havelock. "Now where is it?"

She hesitated for a moment, looked at Havelock's cocked weapon, and begrudgingly motioned toward a door behind her that was partially obscured by one of the handmade tapestries. After receiving a nod from his colleague, George Brisbane gently removed the tapestry and stepped through the door. In the meantime, Emil kept his sights focused on Miranda, holding the gun in one hand and wiping his brow with another. "Christ, Miranda, isn't it a bit hot for a fire and tea?"

She shrugged. "Doesn't bother me."

After a few seconds, Brisbane, also sweating profusely, came back from the other room. "Emil, you'd better come look at this." Emil glared at Miranda as if to say, "What have you done now?" and hurried to meet George in the other room. The teapot began to hiss, but Miranda stayed where she was.

Havelock swore loudly as he stepped into the back room. The room appeared to be the size of a storehouse and was stocked with what he estimated to be hundreds of thousands of blood-red stones, each about the size of a tennis ball, and all matching the description of what they had been charged to find. "How can I possibly know which one it is?" Brisbane asked.

Emil didn't answer but went back through the doorway to find Miranda standing in the same spot, the teapot now at full whistle. "Aren't you going to get that, Miranda?" he asked harshly. "No, of course you're not." He moved quickly toward where she was standing and reached a clutching hand out to her shoulder. His hand passed right through the shape just as his bullet had passed through the ghostly figure's body earlier. "Goddamn it."

Brisbane came out to meet him, panic written all over his face. "Emil, the stones...they're not real."

"Of course not." Havelock gritted his teeth. "She took the real one. You stay here in case she doubles back. I'm going to find this bitch." Brisbane nodded and watched his partner race back out into the darkness.

Once Havelock was out of sight, Brisbane removed the teapot from the stove and turned his attention back to the phantom Miranda, who remained standing behind her unfinished puzzle of an old-fashioned carousel. As the teapot's howl settled down, he said, "I feel like a fool speaking to a mirage, but I must know how you are doing this."

"You must have read up on me," the image said, replacing her glasses and returning her attention to the puzzle. "You must have been well aware of my capabilities before you came here."

"Well, yes," George replied, "but I had no idea of the extent. I knew that you could conjure illusions, but I had no idea that you could give such life to them. It really is quite extraordinary."

"I couldn't always do this, but, as they say, practice makes perfect."

"In order to do this, you people—"

"Us people?" the image repeated.

"You know..." Brisbane searched for the proper words. "People who have abilities like yours...they're finite. I know that you have your limits."

Phantom Miranda nodded matter-of-factly. "Yes. This kind of interactive illusion takes energy. It's very tiring and takes a great deal of concentration...concentration that I'm going to have to break now that your friend is coming to find me."

"He's not my friend," said Brisbane in a petulant tone. "Regardless, if you give him what we came for, no harm will come to you."

The image smiled. "We both know that that's not true. But thanks for trying, Professor. No, now that you've found me, found the Heart, a whole world of harm is coming to everyone. In a way, I'm glad that I won't be around to see it."

With that, the image faded, and Brisbane was left alone in the cabin with the mirage's words echoing in his mind.

HAVELOCK RAN AS QUICKLY as he could through the wooded area behind the cabin, the scent of sea salt growing with every step he took. This trail had been traveled recently by someone else, and he was willing to bet that the only one on the island brave enough to venture out amongst the "ghosts" was Miranda Simms. She could have headed into the village, but he would have noticed this before, and besides, she was probably more concerned about getting off the island. It was logical that she would make a break for the shoreline, where she more than likely had a vessel of some sort lying in wait. He was impressed that she had been able to navigate herself so quickly through the dense foliage, but then, she had been hiding out here for years. She would have been a fool not to have prepared for this moment. Havelock frantically pushed branches out of the way, but there were always more, their razor-like leaves slicing at his face, hands, and arms. He could tell that he was getting close when he started hitting patches of mist that were creeping in from the ocean, and sure enough, after vaulting over a fallen tree, he found that his feet had landed in gray, moonlit sand. He had reached another large cove surrounded by forest on three sides and sea on one. The quiet of the cove gave the impression of isolation, but footprints in the sand said differently. He raced to catch up with their owner, his legs burning from the exertion. He could handle the run, but Miranda had experienced significantly more difficulty. He found her near the start of a long, skeletal fishing pier to which were tied a handful of beaten-up rowboats.

Still several yards away from his prey, he leveled his gun at her chest. "No more tricks, Miranda."

To his surprise, she nodded in sullen agreement. "You know I can't keep this up forever, Emil. I have my limits."

"Your kind usually does," he responded. Miranda offered a grimace, but no reply. Sensing her weakness, Havelock held out his open hand. "Give me the Heart, Miranda," he said.

Still, she only stared at him, meeting his cold blue eyes without a hint of fear. When she broke her silence, she said, "He won't win, you know. Someone will stop him."

Havelock allowed himself a chuckle that echoed eerily through the surrounding caves. "Someone like who? John Brandt? Frances Whitworth?" he retorted. "Not likely. See, the thing about me is, I always manage to be on the winning team —and that's not because of blind luck."

"No," she said, "it's because you're a scumbag."

Havelock's bemusement was beginning to fade. "Don't push me, Miranda."

Miranda waved him off. "Oh please," she said. "I've dealt with far worse than you. I've helped take down people who would make you turn tail and run like a frightened bunny." At this, she sighed, gripping the blood-red stone as tightly as she could, her knuckles turning a deathly white. "And my only regret is that after all of my grand adventures, I'm to be killed in the middle of nowhere by nothing more than a stooge."

Havelock did his best to swallow his anger, but even in the moonlight, she could see his visage darken. "And what makes you so sure that you're going to die tonight?"

Miranda smiled. "Because unless I'm dead, you're not leaving Pemba with this stone."

He shrugged and took aim. "Oh."

GEORGE BRISBANE WAS MARVELING AT the sheer number of illusory stones that Miranda had created when one by one, they began to fade from existence. Within a few moments, the stones were gone, and the empty storage space began to shrink. Brisbane backed out of the room quickly, afraid that it would collapse upon him, but it eventually did stop shrinking, and he realized that he had been standing in a space no larger than a walk-in closet. He shook his head in amazement and settled into Miranda's torn, stained brown sofa, waiting for the return of his partner. After several long minutes of hearing nothing but the sounds of insects through the hole where the front door used to be, he heard quiet footsteps, and Emil Havelock appeared at the doorway shortly thereafter. He looked winded and a bit worse for wear, but Brisbane did not care about any of this. He only cared about the stone that Havelock held firmly in his right hand.

"The Heart of Murena." Brisbane's eyes widened as Havelock handed the gem to him. "Incredible," he mused. "From David and Goliath to Elizabeth Bathory, do you realize how many historical and mythological figures have been linked to this stone?"

"I don't really care."

"You should," said Brisbane, offended on behalf of the stone. "We are holding one of the most coveted items in archeological history. Do you know why this is called the Heart of Murena? Even though historians had been searching for it since biblical times, it was found during the eighteenth century inside a lamprey."

"A what?"

"A lamprey. A parasitic creature found in lakes throughout the world, with the exception, ironically enough, of Africa."

"Wow," Havelock said with feigned interest. "This is thrilling, but I still don't really care. Let's find Cheshire and get the hell out of here."

Brisbane started walking to the door but hesitated briefly. "And what about Ms. Simms?"

"Let's just say that these islanders should be thanking me. I solved their ghost problem."

NINE

Conspiracy Theory

ANDY LUNSFORD HAD NEVER FAILED a quiz in his life until the third day after his best friend disappeared. The circumstances of his disappearance reeked of something unsavory, but Andy could not put his finger on what that was. The puzzle occupied his thoughts to the extent that the once straight-A student was now having quizzes handed back with the dreaded "See Me" written in bloody red ink on the top of the page. But he didn't care. Something bigger than a chemical equation quiz was afoot, and Andy found himself up against a wall. He knew that his friend was not actually William Kendrick but William Trammell, but he had no way to prove it. He knew that Robert and Emily Kendrick were knee-deep in this conspiracy, but he couldn't prove that either. As an outsider, his hands were tied; however, this irrefutable fact could not stop him from obsessing over Will's situation.

He sat with the "'See Me" quiz on his desk, in plain sight of his fellow students, who were all conspicuously peering at each other's grades, his eyes fixated on the clock, which was now only seconds from three. He tapped his foot anxiously, waiting to start his journey past Will's house to see whether there was any sign of his friend.

When the bell finally rang, Andy crammed the quiz into his already overstuffed backpack, slung the bag over his shoulder, and ran from the room, evading the gaze of his chemistry teacher, Mr. Sullivan, who no doubt meant the "See Me" as an *immediate* request. He had only made it past a handful of lockers when he ran into Sam Foster, nearly knocking her off her feet. "I'm so sorry," said Andy, blushing.

"It's alright," said Sam, sensing Andy's embarrassment. "You okay?" she asked. "You seem kind of anxious."

"Yeah, I'm fine," he answered tersely. "I just…I have to get out of here quickly today."

"Oh. Okay," said Sam, not used to getting what she assumed was a brush-off. "Is your friend alright? He hasn't been around, has he? I mean, I haven't seen him since that day at the field when he was acting weird…"

Andy shrugged. "I don't know. I think he's been kidnapped. Or killed. Maybe both. It's a long story."

Sam let out a chuckle, but abruptly stopped herself when she noticed the earnest look on Andy's face. "You're being serious right now, aren't you?"

"Yup."

"You can't really think that he was kidnapped…or worse. Who would do that?"

"It's hard to say. Seems to me like there's some secret cabal that may have come after him."

Sam stared blankly at Andy. "What's a cabal?"

Before he could explain further, they were interrupted by Mr. Sullivan, who placed his hand on Andy's shoulder. "Mr. Lunsford, I believe I asked you to see me regarding your quiz. I'm concerned about how your grade has dipped."

Andy sighed. "I…Mr. Sullivan, I really don't have time—"

"Mr. Sullivan," said Sam, "I know you really want to talk to

Andy, but I was hoping you'd have time to talk to me too. I know I haven't been doing so well."

"That's fine, Miss Foster," the teacher responded, surprised at her sudden interest in academic improvement.

"Great! I'm going to go first. Okay? Thanks." She ushered a befuddled Mr. Sullivan back into the classroom while she mouthed "Go" to Andy and made a shooing motion with her hand. Andy smiled as he hurried into the stairwell, glad to have a co-conspirator of his own.

TEN

Into the Woods

WILL WOKE up in a foul mood, the crick in his neck from leaning his head against the passenger-side window taking forever to subside. He rotated his head, trying desperately to crack his neck. When that failed, he simply slammed the back of his head against the headrest and moaned, "This sucks." Brandt continued to concentrate on the road, paying no attention to Will's complaint. "Where are we?" Will asked, noting the steep gray rock walls that were looming on either side of the highway.

"Pennsylvania."

"Oh." Will looked at the clock. It was now almost five, and as if on cue, his stomach gave an empty, echoing rumble. "I'm starving," he said.

"You're not starving," Brandt responded. "But if you're hungry, open the glove compartment. There should be something in there."

Will was pretty sure that there were no burgers in the glove compartment, but he begrudgingly decided to make do with one of the granola bars he found there. "So how long before we get to Boston?"

"I never said that we were going straight there," said Brandt. "We'll be sticking to these parts for just a little while longer. Welcome to the Poconos...your new classroom."

"The Poconos? The only reason that people come here is to ski." Will paused, waiting for a reaction that never came. "And, you know, it's May."

"Exactly. It should be nice and quiet at this time of year. Perfect for what we've got to do."

Will raised an eyebrow at Brandt. "You mean training me to kill an otherwise immortal diabolist based on the fact that I have magic blood? Yeah. Sounds like fun for the whole family. Brandt remained stoic. "Jesus, Brandt. You'd think *I* abducted *you*. Ever laughed before?"

"How about instead of telling jokes, you make some decent use of your time and do some research?" Brandt retorted, motioning to the briefcase that Will just now noticed.

Will rolled his eyes. "Research. Sure." He grabbed the case next to his seat and opened it to find roughly a dozen file folders, each one labeled with a date range, the first being '1862-1899' and the last '2000-Present.' Will opened the former, and found himself facing a portrait labeled 'Sir Desmond Duquesne, 1869.' This painting portrayed a thin, older gentleman in a black suit sitting in a velvet chair and holding an ebony cane with a silver handle. The man had a slight, mischievous grin.

Setting the 1869 print to the side, Will opened the most recently dated folder, and, as he thought he might, found a color photograph labeled 'Sir Desmond Duquesne, 2012.' Placing this photograph alongside the older image, he looked back and forth between the two, and it did not take him long to realize that either they were not the same person, or the artist from the 1860s was simply inept. "They don't look the same,"

Will said aloud. "I thought you said that this was the same person? I mean, they look as though they could be related, but these are two different people. Couldn't this more recent one be a descendant?"

"Gee, I never thought of that, William. I'd better turn around and bring you home. My mistake," Brandt said dryly. "Keep reading."

"Fine," said Will, "but I don't need an attitude from the guy who stuck a needle in my neck. I'm going to the back." Brandt ignored the comment, and Will took the briefcase and its contents to the table in the back of the RV. He spread the folders out, lining them up in ascending order, but noticed that one was missing. "1980-1999 is missing!" he shouted to Brandt.

"I know."

"Why?"

Brandt shrugged. "Just don't have it. Not sure where it went."

Bullshit, Will thought. *That's when my family was killed, and he doesn't have that folder?* Will glared at Brandt, who appeared much more interested in finding their exit than worrying about the missing folder. "Whatever," Will muttered, and he opened the '1862-1899' file again. This was the thinnest of the files, mainly containing handwritten letters in fanciful penmanship that Will could barely decipher, though to be honest, he really did not try all that hard. More of a visual person, he searched for additional pictures and found only one in that file. It was another portrait, this time of a much larger man. Like Duquesne in the previous portrait, this man was dressed in Victorian garb, but the similarities ended there. Tall and barrel-chested, he cut an imposing figure. Most disconcerting, though, was his face. While Duquesne had the look of someone who had just remembered a punchline, this man looked like someone who had never smiled before in his life. His large, toad-like mouth was bent into a stiff frown, set under a pair of dark, foreboding eyes. Will noted that the man's complexion seemed ashen—it had a gray tone. While Duquesne was apparently a murderer, Will could not help but think that this man, in life, may have been no less wicked. As he looked into the dead eyes of the Victorian gentleman, a wave of familiarity washed over him. With a shudder, he dropped the portrait, which promptly slid from the table and landed face down on the floor of the RV. On the back of the portrait was written 'Sir Roderick Gleave.' It was dated 1871.

Will did not immediately pick up the print. Instead, he sat lost in thought, recalling the dream he'd had several days ago. The moss-covered statue had undoubtedly been a likeness of Roderick Gleave, his ancestor. But how was any of this possible? Now, sitting in this RV, being driven into the mountains by a lunatic, Will felt the full force of the past twenty-four hours' madness. He was confused, anxious, and he missed his family. Overwhelmed by a sudden urge, he shouted to Brandt, "Pull over! Now!"

Startled, Brandt veered off to the side of the road, tires screeching. Will fumbled with the door handle for a second, then promptly bolted from the RV, ran down a steep embankment, and vomited.

WILL WAS KNEELING on the bank of a small creek. With his eyes tightly closed, he tried to let the soft sound of running water lull him back to a sense of calm, but recent events had taken their toll, and he struggled to control his breathing. He hadn't even heard Brandt's door slam, so his eyes shot open when the older man clutched his shoulder in a firm grip. "Here," Brandt said gruffly, handing Will a bottle of water. Shrugging off Brandt's hand, Will sat on the grass, his knees bent in front of him. "You sick?" asked Brandt. "Or is this something else?"

Will shut his eyes again and sighed. "Something else."

Brandt simply grunted in response and turned back toward their vehicle. "You'll be fine in a few minutes."

"Thanks for the concern," Will murmured, not caring whether Brandt heard him. He listened as Brandt removed some items from the RV but did not turn to see what they were. He had seen enough of Brandt and his RV for one day. It felt much better to look at the clear water of the creek running at his feet. In a moment, Brandt was standing beside him again, this time toting two large canvas bags and a lit cigarette. "You want one?" he asked, flicking a bit of ash into the creek.

"No."

"Suit yourself." Brandt surveyed the area. They had left the highway while Will was looking through the files, and were now on a quiet side road nestled between two large expanses of forest. "This seems as good a place as any. Stay here for a few minutes. I'll be back." With this, Brandt splashed through the shallow stream and made his way into the wooded area. It was then that Will noticed the hunting rifle slung over his shoulder. Before he could say anything, Brandt turned back and added, "And William—when I say stay here, I mean it. Trust me when I say that you're much better off with me than with anyone else who might be out there looking for you."

ALMOST IMMEDIATELY UPON seeing Brandt disappear into the woods, Will instinctively reached for his cell phone and cursed himself for forgetting that Brandt had disposed of it. He looked at his watch, noted that it was nearing six o'clock, and laid back on the grass, resigned to the fact that even if he were to run off now, he would not get very far before darkness fell, especially considering that he had no idea where he was.

Will gazed at the clouds for as long as he could until the bright May sun appeared suddenly from behind one. He closed his eyes and thought, *Maybe there is enough time for me to get away. It is mid-May, which means I've got an hour or so of sunshine...* His mind wandered at the thought of that word... *You are my sunshine...* The song that he had heard in his dream, the one that he had never heard before, was again running through his mind. *It means something*, he thought. *If that statue represents Gleave, then what does the song represent? And what happened to that file? What is Brandt hiding?*

"William!" Will opened his eyes to see Brandt's silhouette looming above him, and his face went pale with unease as though the older man had been able to read his thoughts. If Brandt sensed what Will had been thinking, he kept a poker face and simply muttered, "Come with me" as he began walking back to the forest.

Will got to his feet and followed Brandt down a lightly-worn path for a quarter mile until they came to a clearing where the canvas bags lay. Brandt leaned his rifle against a tree as he asked, "So, I guess you've never been hunting?" Will shook his head in response. "Well, this is as good a place as any to start learning how to shoot."

Will looked at the canvas bags that had been thrown down amongst the leaves and twigs. One was open, revealing a cache of weaponry. A feeling of nausea began to rise from the pit of his stomach once more but he was able to suppress. "Why do I need to know how to shoot?"

Brandt shook his head. "Have you been paying attention to anything? You need to kill Desmond Duquesne."

"I don't feel overly comfortable with this."

"I don't care." Will glared at Brandt, searching for any hint of his true intentions, but got nothing. "He had your family killed," Brandt continued. "And deep down, as ridiculous as this all sounds, you know that I'm telling the truth."

Any slight desire for revenge that Brandt had kindled within Will earlier that day immediately died when the reality of these weapons stared him in the face. He believed that Duquesne had had his family killed, but something about the urgency and outlandishness of this situation did not ring true. There was something unsettling in Brandt's insistence upon another man's death, but at the same time, what choice did he have? Brandt was the man with the RV. He was the man with the files. He was the man with the guns.

"I don't have a choice, do I?" Will asked.

"No. You do not," Brandt replied, crouching to rummage through a bag of handguns. "Here," he said, removing one particularly nasty-looking piece. "I need to see what you're made of." Brandt held the gun out to Will, who carefully took it by the handle, surprised at its heft. "Hold it firmly, now," he said, grabbing Will's hand and contorting it to match the shape of the gun. "Good. Now, you see that tree just over there?" Brandt pointed to the largest tree in the vicinity. "All I want you to do is take a shot at it. Easy as that."

Brandt stooped to retrieve his pack of cigarettes from a nearby stump, and when he turned around, Will's handgun was aimed directly at his chest. "And all I want you to do," said Will, "is give me your keys."

ELEVEN

Eddie Garza

EDDIE GARZA WAS ABOUT to leave the bar when he received a text message from his daughter: *Had a great time. Back home safe. Pics online.* It was bad enough that the Phillies had lost again, but now he had this to look forward to. When he got home, he would be obliged to view pictures of the fun family vacation his thirteen-year-old daughter had taken with her mother and new stepfather. They had gone to Rome—the place that he had begged his wife for years to accept as their vacation site, but no, she had always insisted on someplace tropical. So, upon receiving the text, he reclaimed his stool and ordered another beer.

"Thought you were leaving," said the young bartender. "Not that I mind," he added, picking up the tip that Eddie had left for his latest drink.

"Think I need one more," Garza said. "Hey, how old are you, Joe?"

"Twenty-six."

"Jesus. Only a few years younger than my ex-wife's new guy. Sick, huh?"

Joe grimaced as if to say, "If you say so," and Eddie caught the awkward vibe.

"Sorry, Joe. Didn't mean to involve you."

"It's alright. That's why I'm here." Joe scooped up a basket of complimentary popcorn and laid it in front of Eddie. "He the reason why you need another drink?"

Eddie shrugged. "Eh. Not him necessarily. Just the situation. They just went on their first 'family' vacation with my daughter. I need to check out the pictures on Facebook when I get home, apparently."

"Just do it here. Drink in hand. It'll go a lot better," he laughed.

Eddie waved his phone around with exasperation. "I know nothing about this thing. I don't know how the hell to get online with this."

"Give it to me." Joe took the phone, and after a few taps, said, "Got it. You're on. Just type in your info."

"You type it in. I hate that phone" said Eddie. "The email's EGarza12@mymail.com. Password is 'Ashley.'"

"Daughter's name?"

"Yup."

"You should know better than anyone, by the way," Joe said as he typed, "that you shouldn't give out your log-in information. I may just steal your identity one day."

"And you should know better than anyone," said Eddie, making a shooting motion with his fingers, "that I'd track ya down in two minutes flat." The two chuckled until Eddie added, "Anyway, I really only use that damn site to keep in touch with Ash. I barely have any other so-called 'friends.'"

"Well, you have a message," said Joe. "Want me to open it?"

"Who's it from?"

"Let's see…it's from an Andy Lunsford?"

"Lunsford? I have no idea who the hell that is. Sure. Open it. Probably trying to sell me something."

Eddie watched Joe open the message. The bartender's eyes went wide. "Well, this is interesting."

"What?"

"Didn't you tell me your partner was a guy named Dan? The guy who died years ago?"

The alcohol in Eddie's blood seemed to evaporate at the mention of this name, and he straightened up on his stool. "Yes. Why?"

"You need to see this," said Joe, handing the phone back to Eddie.

Eddie started reading aloud. "Detective Garza, you don't know who I am, but I know that you were involved in the investigation of…" As his voice trailed off, he looked around the bar nervously and continued reading to himself.

Joe looked on intently for a few moments, until Eddie had finished reading, and asked, "Is everything alright?"

A strange look had come across Garza's face, the look of someone who is uncertain whether he should laugh or cry. "Shit," was his only response before he left his untouched beer at the bar.

EDDIE MOVED DOWN the street as quickly as his feet would carry him. It did not take long for him to reach his apartment, as it was located above a realtor's office only a few doors down from the bar. He barely touched a step as he flew up to his third-floor loft and let the door slam loudly behind him. Immediately, he turned his computer on, intending to book the next possible flight out of Philly, and as the outdated device hummed its familiar start-up noise, he unlocked the top drawer of the desk and removed a thick, leather-bound journal.

Eddie cleared the surface of his desk by throwing random bills, Post-it notes, and photos onto the floor so that there would be enough room for the contents of the journal to spill out. When they did, they included dozens of newspaper clippings regarding the explosion that had killed the Trammell family fourteen years prior. Paying no attention to these stories with which he was all too familiar, he picked up each one and shook it. After shaking out four different newspaper articles, he grabbed the fifth, and out fluttered a small piece of white paper about the size of a business card. All that was written on it was a phone number and a name. "It's been fourteen years, Agent Whitworth," he said to himself as he dialed the number. "Let's hope you're not retired too."

TWELVE

Memorytown

WILL FELT good as he pointed the gun at Brandt's chest. For the first time since he had read about the death of the Trammells, he felt as though he had some semblance of control, some say in how this situation would unravel. Unfortunately, this sense of satisfaction was short-lived, as Brandt's reaction was not what he expected. Rather than showing any sort of anxiety about being shot, Brandt's face twisted into a cruel smile. This only served to annoy Will, who repeated, "Give me the damn keys. I'm getting out of here."

"Are you?" Brandt asked with his condescending smirk.

Will did not respond immediately, but gingerly toyed with the trigger, wondering what would happen if he actually did shoot Brandt. Wondering if he could. "I swear," Will said, "I'll shoot you."

"Then do it," said Brandt, taking a step closer.

"Stop," said Will as he tried to still his tremulous outstretched arm. Then, with a quickness that Will did not think him capable of, Brandt took Will's wrist in his vice-like grip and moved closer, pressing the muzzle of the gun against his own chest.

"Do it," Brandt repeated. "You won't. Because deep down you know that I'm telling you the truth, and you know that you need me."

Will glared at Brandt and pressed the weapon harder still against Brandt's chest. "You're right, Brandt. I won't do it. Because I'm not a killer," Will responded.

Brandt's dark eyes peered down at the weapon in Will's hand. "I guess I've seen what you're made of," he said, and in one swift motion, Brandt twisted Will's arm behind his back, forcing him to drop the weapon onto the forest floor. He shoved Will forward while keeping his arm locked behind his back and slammed his face against the trunk of a large oak tree. "Do you think I would have handed you that gun and *not* expected you to point it at me? It was all about teaching you another very important lesson: don't test me. The next time you try something like that, you're in for a world of pain. Do you understand?"

Through his teeth, Will was able to mutter "Yes," and Brandt threw him away from the tree, forcing him to the ground.

"You need to grow up and realize that not everything revolves around you."

Will spat a small amount of blood from his busted lip and started laughing. "That's where you're wrong, Brandt. See, what *you* need to know is that I'm not the idiot kid you take me for. You can say over and over again that I need you, but the needle in the neck, the lessons, the briefcase full of clippings and photos—all of that adds up to the fact that *you* need *me*. So you can threaten me all you want, tough guy, but at the end of the day, I'm your only hope, aren't I?"

Brandt's scowl betrayed an intense anger that Will had not

previously seen in him. Still, Will was satisfied that he had made his own point in spite of his captor's alleged 'lesson.'

"I want to make a deal with you," Will added. "If we're going to continue on this mission—or whatever you're calling it—we need to be partners."

Brandt's reaction to this proposal was simply to take a seat on a large, low stump. Grasping his knees with his hands, he leaned forward and asked, "And what exactly would this entail?"

"I'll do what you tell me to do, within reason, but I need a few things in return for my cooperation."

"Like what?"

"A guarantee that I go back to my family as soon as this is over."

Brandt nodded. "That was always the plan, should you live through this."

"Awesome," Will said facetiously. "Two more conditions—to be fulfilled immediately."

Brandt raised an eyebrow. "Oh?"

"I want the truth. Up until now, you've been giving me only what you think I need to know. That's not for you to decide. I want to know what your deal is and exactly what you're expecting me to do. No more 'mystery man' gimmick. This isn't all about some fourteen-year-old murders, and if it is, I want to know why you care so much."

"And your third condition?"

"I want a decent meal—not a stale granola bar from your RV. We're going for burgers. Your treat."

"Let's get the last two over with," Brandt responded. "Grab one of these bags. I know a place nearby that should be safe to talk."

. . .

AFTER A SILENT FIVE-MINUTE drive that felt more like an hour, the two pulled up to an antiquated wooden sign that said 'Memorytown' in faded, old-time lettering. Will looked around and soon determined that Memorytown's best days, appropriately enough, seemed to be behind it. All that remained of what was once a vibrant tourist destination was a cluster of dilapidated cabins, a murky lake with a handful of rusty paddleboats resting on the bank, and a large red building with black shutters and a chalkboard advertising when local bands would be playing gigs. Having parked the RV, it was into this building that Brandt silently led the way.

Upon entering, Will was surprised to see signs of life. The building turned out to be a fully functional tavern, complete with about two dozen customers who were dining on food that immediately made his mouth water. The Tavern itself was decorated in the style of a hunting lodge or a winter retreat house. An impressive stone fireplace sat dormant below the mounted head of the largest moose Will had ever seen. Against another wall was a brown bear, standing on its hind legs and overseeing the diners with a hungry maw gaping beneath its cold marble eyes. The moose and bear were not alone; the Tavern's grisly collection also included a one-eyed gray wolf, a mountain lion, and a number of local species of birds. Some birds, such as the hawk, were perched on faux-branches far above the tables, while others, like a horned owl, were displayed in an attack posture, swooping from the rafters, talons bared, looking to prey upon the oblivious patrons at the large, horse-shoe bar below.

"Come here often?" Will asked Brandt, trying to ease the tension.

Brandt didn't bother responding with more than an eye roll. He subsequently motioned to the bartender as if to say, "We're taking this table." The bartender, a heavyset older man in a plaid shirt and a full gray beard, nodded, and Brandt and Will took a seat at a table directly beneath a large chandelier constructed from deer antlers.

In a matter of seconds, a thirty-something waitress arrived at the table wearing a wide, genuine smile. "Well, how are you two boys today?" she began. "Out for some father-son bonding?"

Brandt snorted. "I am *not* his father."

The waitress was obviously taken aback by his abrupt tone and looked about ready to apologize before Will chimed in, "We get that a lot."

The waitress's cheerful countenance returned. "Just two pals, then. I gotcha."

"Well, to be honest," said Will. "I don't even know this guy! He kidnapped me, so I told him that the least he could do was take me for a burger."

Brandt lowered his menu and stared at Will's incredulous expression. There was a moment of pregnant silence before the waitress and Will both burst out laughing. Brandt attempted to follow suit, but laughing, especially on cue, was not his forte.

"Well okay then!" the waitress chuckled. "I hope he's at least paying!"

"Oh, he'll pay!" Will responded with a quick glance toward Brandt. "What're you drinking, pal?"

"Coffee. Black," Brandt said, addressing the waitress while shooting daggers at Will.

"I'll have a Coke," Will said. "And a water."

"You got it, boys. Be right back."

With that, the waitress was off, and once she was beyond earshot, Brandt leaned in and muttered, "You think you're pretty funny, don't you? A real charmer, huh?"

"Oh please," Will retorted. "You should consider yourself lucky that the guy whose lip you just busted up isn't running around this place telling everyone who will listen about what a certifiable sociopath you are."

Brandt pretended to ignore this threat, but when he looked back down at his menu, Will knew that he had made his point. "Do me a favor," said Brandt, "Order me the ribeye. Medium rare. I've got to run and make a phone call."

"Now?"

Brandt looked at his watch. "Yes. Now. And remember, don't try anything stupid. I'll be standing right outside that window," he said, pointing to a payphone near where they had parked the RV. "When I get back, I'll explain things a bit further."

"Fine," Will answered.

"And try the onion rings. They're delicious."

Will watched as Brandt left the Tavern, and as soon as the door was shut behind him, he waved their waitress over. "So, what'll it—"

Before she could get her question out, he blurted, "Burger. Medium. Ribeye. Medium rare. Please give me your cell phone for a minute. I'm sorry, but it's an emergency and mine died."

"But I—"

"Please! It has to be quick! I just have one quick text to send! I'll pay you for it!"

The waitress moved to take her cell from her pocket, but Will could see that Brandt was watching intently through the window. "Never mind," Will said. "Gimme this for a minute!" He grabbed her pen instead and wrote a quick message on a napkin. "Will you send this message to this number for me as soon as you can? It's something very important that I forgot to tell a friend."

The waitress looked at the message for a moment and said, "That's it?"

"That's it. And listen, it kind of has to do with a surprise for that guy who's coming back in here now, so don't let on, okay? Please?" He looked nervously out the window to see that Brandt had hung up the payphone and was on his way back in.

"Um, okay. I'll do it during my smoke break," said the waitress.

"Thank you!" he said, just as Brandt again took his seat. "Oh! And an order of onion rings!"

The waitress smiled warily over her shoulder as she walked away. "Everything alright?" Brandt asked.

"Super," said Will, who could tell that he was probably more than a bit flushed. "So. Explain away. Who are you, and why do you have such a need to avenge *my* family's death?"

The older man sighed and began, "My name is John Brandt."

"Can I call you John?"

"You may not."

"Does anyone call you John?"

"They do not." Will nodded, and Brandt continued. "I have a military background. Served in the Gulf War. I lived to see the completion of my tour, but I wanted more excitement, so instead of coming back, I traveled the world looking for adventure—you know, stupid kid stuff. The trouble was, I had no funds, and really, I had very few skills, so I took up with a group of...how can I put this...unsavory characters. They were problem solvers—sometimes bounty hunters, sometimes merce- naries...depended on the day and whom you asked."

"So you were a hired gun."

"For a while, yes. Death didn't bother me. During my brief stint in the Gulf, I had seen some truly horrible things. I was, I thought, essentially immune." During this last sentence, Will couldn't help but notice Brandt flinch ever so slightly, but he made no mention of it and allowed the man to continue. "For years, I traveled the world, honing my 'craft,' if you could call it that. When I wasn't on assignment, I'd take excursions to some of the most remote places on earth to hunt animals most can only dream of seeing in zoos."

"Like what?"

"Let's just say, if it's got a pulse, I've probably stopped it at some point." He waved his hand around the room, as if he had personally killed and mounted every beast in the place, but Will got the point. "Eventually I made my way to India. I wasn't there on assignment—I was getting tired of that lifestyle. I had just always wanted to see the place. However, while I was there, I met someone who was on a different type of assignment, and she introduced me to, well, your people."

"My people? You mean the Aberrationists?"

"Stop that. But yes.

This woman's name was Whitworth, and she worked for the government. She was there to stop some magical bigwig from making trouble and she recruited me to help. Of course, I didn't believe her at first, just like you probably don't believe a lot of what I've told you, but then I saw it with my own eyes. I saw those freaks do things that no normal person could do. They were dangerous, and Whitworth was persuasive. Before I knew it, we were practically partners, and we were able to take down this mystic bastard. It felt nice doing good for once. So, when that mission was over, I signed on with the group that Whitworth worked for. I was intrigued by this new world that had been opened to me…and who wouldn't be? This was the stuff of movies and comic books, and now it was happening in real life.

"Anyway, I had a good run with this group, this 'Collective'…and by 'good,' I mean 'long.' However, sometimes an event happens that makes you realize things are not as they appear. You know how that is," said Brandt, pointing a gnarled finger at Will. "A number of years ago, the glamour wore off, and I realized that this gig wasn't all fun and games. It wasn't like the movies, despite what I had originally thought. In short, I came to realize that these 'gifts,' as many would call them, are nothing of the sort. Whether a sorcerer, a diabolist, whatever, the use of these powers is unnatural and can only lead to trouble."

"What happened that made you feel this way?" Will asked.

Brandt nodded at the waitress as she placed their food on the table and waited for her to step out of earshot before answering. "It was a mission. It went wrong. Innocent people died. I don't want to talk about that. What you need to know is that, after that mission, I vowed to do what I could to put a stop to this magic bullshit once and for all."

"And killing Desmond Duquesne is a step in the right direction?" Will suggested.

Brandt nodded. "Duquesne is the worst of the worst, as far as I'm concerned, and he's planning something that will make him even more powerful than he already is. If he pulls it off, more people will die."

"But the catch," said Will, "is that you need to use magic to kill him. You need to use me."

"I do."

"So what happens? I kill Duquesne and then you kill me? After all, in your perfect world, there would be no demonic strain. The way I see it, that means I've got to go. How do I know you're not lying about letting me go back to my family when this is over?"

"I'm the first to admit that most people shouldn't be trusted," Brandt answered. "However, now that I've met you, I'm not too worried. Your gift seems to be nothing more than clairvoyant dreams. I'm not worried about you as a huge threat to humanity. You've been prophesied to kill Duquesne, and I feel that it's my duty to ensure that it happens."

"How do you know the prophecy is accurate?"

"Because," said Brandt, looking down at his bloody steak that had been sitting untouched in front of him for several minutes. "It has to be."

THIRTEEN

Whitworth and Donovan

ANDY SAT in the small Main Street Coffee Shop looking anxiously at his watch. It was now past six o'clock, the time when Detective Garza had said that they would meet up. *He's probably just lost*, Andy thought to himself. *He's probably never been in this area before.* He tried to reassure himself that he had taken the right course of action by contacting Garza, but he couldn't help but feel a sense of dread while he waited for this stranger to show up. Andy was not a risk-taker and meeting up with this strange man from the Trammells' past was definitely outside of his comfort zone. About to give up on his wait, he stood to throw his coffee cup away and noticed a dark-haired, middle-aged man coming through the door.

"Detective Garza!" Andy shouted, waving him over to his table, full of notes for his upcoming history exam.

Garza gave a cursory wave in response, embarrassed that his name had been shouted across the nearly empty coffee shop, and approached Andy with an open, outstretched hand. "Please, call me Eddie. My days on the force are behind me. You're Andy, I guess?"

"Yup." Andy immediately felt more at ease once he had shaken Garza's hand. He looked a bit worn around the edges, but overall, Andy got the feeling from the amiable tone and firm handshake that this was someone who he could trust. "Thanks for coming all this way."

"Listen, Andy. I appreciate that you got in touch with me, and I took the next flight out as soon as I saw your message. I have to warn you, though, if this is some sort of prank, I'm not going to appreciate you wasting my time. What you wrote about the Trammells isn't something to joke about."

Although Andy recognized that this threat was more earnest than harsh, his pulse quickened as he stammered, "I-I would never do that. Will's my best friend. I'm just worried."

The detective took a long critical look into Andy's eyes, as he had done with so many suspects during his time on the force, and determined that whether or not the boy was crazy, he was at least sincere. "Okay, Andy. I'll trust you, but I have to admit that this whole situation has me a pretty confused."

Andy chuckled nervously. "You and me both."

"Well," said Garza, taking a seat at Andy's table. "Let's start at the top. You seem to think that your friend Will, who has gone missing, is really William Trammell?"

"I think so," said Andy, "and since you were Trammell's partner when he was killed, I figured I'd get in touch with you about it."

Garza nodded. "They never found all the bodies, you know. So it is possible that William Trammell and your friend are one and the same." He paused to think for a moment. "Still, how would he have gotten all the way down here?"

"Don't know," said Andy. "That would be why I contacted you, since, you know, you're a detective."

"Well, then," said Garza, "let me grab a cup of coffee and start detecting. Can you lead me in the right direction?"

Andy nodded enthusiastically. "This is so cool," he said.

"It's like one of those buddy cop movies where the grizzled veteran and the funny new guy need to work together to solve a high-profile murder mystery!"

Eddie grimaced. "But you're not a cop."

"No."

"And this isn't really high-profile."

"Don't kill my dream, Eddie."

Eddie shook his head and paid for his coffee while Andy packed up his materials. As they headed out the door, Eddie said, "So I'm assuming the first stop I should make is William's house. Do think that his parents will speak to me?"

"They're being a bit shady about this, honestly. They definitely won't talk to you unless I'm there. Even then, who knows? But it's worth a shot since you came all this way, right?"

"Suppose it is. And Andy, have you told anyone else about this?"

"No. You?"

"Just one. She's going to meet us at the Kendricks'. Hopefully she'll be able to help persuade them to talk."

EDDIE AND ANDY arrived at the Kendricks' doorstep only a few minutes later, and Andy immediately noticed that Dr. Kendrick's car was not in the driveway. "This could be a good thing," he said. "Maybe Mrs. K will crack a little more easily." Following a slight hesitation, he rang the bell. When Mrs. Kendrick came to the door, Andy thought she looked more haggard than he had ever seen her, and felt sympathy mixed with the confirmation that something was amiss.

"Andy," she said, forcing a smile. "What are you doing here? Who is this?"

Eddie didn't let Andy answer, but removed his baseball cap and said, "Eddie Garza, Mrs. Kendrick."

"Oh," she responded, not knowing how to react. "Nice to meet you, Mr. Garza."

"I know that this is awkward, but do you mind if we come in, ma'am?" Andy heard the *Law & Order*-style detective voice coming out of Eddie as he asked this.

"Well, I suppose," she said, opening the door more widely, "but could you please tell me what this is about?"

"I can try," Garza answered. The three of them stepped into the living room, where Eddie and Andy took seats on the sofa and Emily sat herself in her husband's armchair. "Mrs. Kendrick, Andy here got in touch with me because he thinks I might have a connection to your son." At this, the remaining color began to drain from Emily's face. "You see, I'm from up north, and I used to be on the police force with a man named Daniel Trammell. Is that name familiar to you, ma'am?"

"N-no," she answered.

"I see. Well," Eddie attempted to continue, but was interrupted by another ring of the doorbell. An exasperated Emily excused herself and returned in a moment, looking more ashen than before, with two more visitors—a man of about forty in a plain black suit and a significantly older woman in a colorful paisley blouse whose stout, plump build stood in stark contrast to her taller partner's sharp features. As they entered, the younger of the two nodded cheerlessly and stood against the wall, but his partner beamed a delighted smile and walked eagerly forward to heartily shake hands with Eddie. "Detective Garza!" she said, clasping the man's hand far longer than necessary. "It has been so long! I hope you've been well! Thank you for the call!"

Garza, taken off guard by the old woman's enthusiasm, simply answered, "I've been fine, ma'am. It's nice to see you looking so well." He offered an explanation to Emily: "These folks work for the FBI. On the day of the explosion that killed the Trammells, Ms. Whitworth here approached me with her card. I've kept it all this time, and when I heard from Andy, I gave her a call."

Emily nodded, but did not seem enthralled by his story. "And your partner is Mr. Donovan, I believe?" Eddie continued.

Whitworth and Donovan nodded in unison, and as Donovan remained upright the living room entryway, Whitworth plopped herself on the sofa betweenEddie and Andy. "I should have asked, Mrs. Kendrick," she said with a distressed look. "May I sit?"

"I don't see why not," she said with as much politeness as she could muster. "But if you don't mind, I'd really like to hear from Detective Garza as to why you are all suddenly in my house."

"Of course, of course," said Whitworth, clasping her hands on her knees. "Detective, I assume that you were in the midst of an explanation. Please continue."

Garza gave a quick glance to Donovan, who had begun to pace slowly around the room, and continued his story. "Detective Trammell was killed about fourteen years ago now. He and his family were incinerated in a bombing. It seems, though, that your son, according to Andy, may have been experiencing the resurgence of some repressed memories...memories that led both him and Andy to think that he might actually be Daniel Trammell's son, William."

"Mr. Garza, you came all this way to find out whether my son is really the son of your deceased partner? A man who has been dead for fourteen years?" Emily asked.

"I did," Garza said softly. "Mrs. Kendrick, I consider what happened to the Trammell family to be the biggest failure of my career. Of my life. I've lived without closure for these past fourteen years, and it would be such a tremendous relief if I found that the boy was alive. He was like my own son in a way. So you see, this is very important to me."

Emily sat silently for a few seconds before Donovan chimed in, "It's important to us as well, Mrs. Kendrick. We were investigating the murders and always suspected that the boy might be alive somewhere, since a body was never found. You could say that we've made it our mission to find him."

"Oh, stop being so darned cryptic, Mr. Donovan," said Whitworth with a grin. "Mrs. Kendrick, I'm going to be honest with you."

"Please do," she responded.

"I love this sofa," she said, giving herself a slight bounce on the cushion.

"Um...thank you?" Emily said.

"No, thank you," she smiled. "Delightful. Could sit here all day." Then she stopped bouncing and replaced her grin with a serious, but compassionate expression. "Now, about your son. Mrs. Kendrick, I'm going to go out on a limb and guess that William is not here."

She nodded in agreement. "That's true. And regarding this whole Trammell issue, I really can't answer any of your questions. I simply don't know the answers, and I'd be more comfortable speaking to you with my husband around."

"Of course, Mrs. Kendrick. Of course. I understand completely. Can you at least tell me, though, where your son is right now?"

"He's with a relative who lives out of state. Now please. I don't feel comfortable with this. I need to ask you all to leave. Perhaps you can come back when my husband is here, but I would ask you to at least call first. This is very overwhelming."

Having reached a stalemate, they all sat wordlessly and uncomfortably until Andy's phone suddenly played a brief snippet of *The Twilight Zone* theme. "Sorry," he said, his face reddening. "Just a text."

"From Will, by any chance?" Eddie asked.

"No," Andy replied. "Some number I don't know." He looked at the text, which read: *Memorytown. Boston soon.* Realizing at once who the message must have been from, he shut his phone off and shoved it back into his pocket in a suspiciously speedy manner. Luckily, no one seemed to be paying much attention to him anymore, as they had picked up their conversation where it had left off.

"Mrs. Kendrick," said Donovan, "before we leave, Agent Whitworth and I are going to ask if we can search your son's room. Do you have any objection to this?"

"Would it matter if I did?" asked Emily, who seemed shell-shocked.

"No," Donovan replied. "I asked as a courtesy."

"I do hate to intrude upon your family's privacy like this," said Whitworth. "But could you show us the way? We'll be as unobtrusive as possible. I promise. You can even stay in the room and observe, if you'd like."

Emily sighed. "Fine. Andy, Mr. Garza, I'm sure you'll understand if I say goodnight now. This has been a bit much for me." She looked at Andy when making this last statement as if to say, "How could you?"

Andy, regretting having led the party of strangers to the Kendrick house, nodded sullenly and headed for the door, followed by Eddie Garza. "Please, Mrs. Kendrick," Garza added on the way out, "if you change your mind and want to talk, do get in touch. Here's my number." He took a pen and the crumpled receipt from his coffee out of his pocket and jotted down the digits. She shook his hand, he passed through the front door, and she was left with the two government agents.

.   .   .

GARZA CURSED as he stepped off the Kendricks' front porch. "Emily's obviously hiding something, but if she's that tight-lipped on her own, I'm sure when her husband's around the two of them will be even less likely to give up information. All this way for nothing."

"Not necessarily," said Andy. "About that text I got in there...I think that while you were coming south, Will was heading up north. Check it out."

Andy showed the text to Garza. "It's small," he said, "But it's something. I'm obviously not going to get anywhere with the Kendricks, so I may as well find William himself."

"But all we know is that Will is going to Boston. Finding one guy named William in the city of Boston will still be like finding a needle in a haystack."

"That's why I'll have to rely on Agents Whitworth and Donovan to find out something that we didn't. They seem to want to help," he said. "And if I lose contact with them, I've always got my secret weapon."

"Which is?"

"You."

EMILY PAUSED with her hand on the door leading to William's bedroom. "Are you sure that this is necessary?"

Whitworth rested a reassuring hand gently on her shoulder. "I won't be intrusive," she reiterated, "and this will only take a moment or two."

Something in her tone led Emily to believe her, so she turned the knob, granting the two strangers access to her son's room. Whitworth entered first, followed by Emily and then Donovan. While Emily had expected that the agents would begin ransacking the place, Donovan stood absolutely still, and Whitworth moved about the room with her arms behind her back as if taking in an art exhibit. She nodded as she noted certain items such as the bats leaning against the corner of the room and observed, "Your son is athletic? Plays baseball?"

"He does."

"Is he good?"

"I think so," said Emily. "He doesn't."

Whitworth frowned. "That's a shame." She picked up one of the bats, swung gingerly at the air, shook her head, and leaned it back in its corner. She next picked up a pen that was lying on Will's mess of a desk, and again shook her head.

"Are you looking for something specific?" Emily asked.

"Who knows?" Whitworth responded in a hazy, withdrawn tone. "Ah! A mitt!" she said, noticing the glove that Will hand been carrying on the last occasion that Emily had seen him. "Well-worn!" She now held the glove in her hand, and, with her eyes closed, her smile devolved into a slight frown. Careful to avoid Emily noticing this, she quickly fixed her expression and addressed her host with her usual joviality. "Mrs. Kendrick, that—as they say—is a wrap."

"That's all you needed? Just to look around?"

"That's it, ma'am," said Donovan. "Sorry for disrupting your evening like this. We'll be going now."

"O...kay," Emily responded with a look of confusion. She led them down the stairs and onto the front porch, where she received yet another phone number, this time from Whitworth.

"I know that it's hard to believe that two complete strangers could care about the well-being of your child, so I do not expect you to do so just yet. However, if you and your husband, after discussing things, decide that we seem trustworthy, please feel free to give a call. No pressure, Mrs. Kendrick."

She didn't know what to say to this, so she said nothing as Whitworth and Donovan waved a quick goodbye and headed for their black sedan. Part of her wanted to run after them as they drove off, but discretion got the better of her, and she decided to see what her husband thought of this latest development. She sat on the top step of her porch as the sun set, unsure whether she had done the right thing for her son, and whispered, "I hope you're okay, Will."

"THE COP THINKS that we're feds?" Donovan asked as they drove down Pinewood Avenue.

Whitworth shrugged. "I can't remember telling him that, but if that's what he believes, all the better."

"So was that all a waste of time? Please tell me it wasn't."

"Nothing is wasted if you know how to use it properly, Mr. Donovan," Whitworth answered.

"What did you find out?"

"The boy was carrying that baseball mitt when he came home the other day. When he arrived home from practice, there was an unfamiliar visitor waiting for him, conferencing with Dr. and Mrs. Kendrick. I'm willing to bet that the boy's with that visitor now. I'm willing to bet that he's with our old friend Brandt."

"Damn," Donovan growled. "This is going to be a real pain in the ass, isn't it?"

"Oh, I don't know. We do have one more lead."

"What's that?"

"The strange boy—Andy. He received a text he did not want others seeing. He hid it almost immediately, but it wasn't lengthy. It was a message from someone currently in Pennsylvania and heading to Boston."

"You're thinking William Kendrick sent the message? That Brandt's taking him to Boston?" Donovan asked.

Whitworth nodded. "It makes sense, doesn't it? What are the chances that Mr. Lunsford received that text from anyone *but* our boy? It's simple logic. Duquesne is in Boston; Brandt wants Duquesne dead; Brandt takes the boy to Boston."

"That bastard's going to get the kid killed."

"I don't know," said Whitworth, gazing out the window at the salmon-colored sunset. "I think that he might actually be the boy's best chance at remaining alive. After all, I'd rather know that he's with Brandt than in the custody of Desmond Duquesne."

FOURTEEN

New Covington

AGENT JAMES LAWRENCE held his flashlight firmly in one hand and rested the other on his holstered gun as he walked slowly and softly through the halls of New Covington. He had only been on the security payroll for about a week, but that already felt like one week too long. During the day, New Covington sat on a sprawling and bustling estate, always alive with activity. When night fell, however, the Duquesne Compound, as many called it, took on a different personality entirely.

Despite the feeling that he was traversing through a haunted mansion, Lawrence had not been truly unsettled until he saw Duquesne's collection illuminated by moonbeams. Throughout the labyrinthine hallways of New Covington, there were, displayed as though in a museum, hundreds of masks from around the world. Some were African tribal masks, carved from indigenous woods and large enough to cover the majority of a person's body. Others were masks from various Asian cultures, many depicting demons—what Lawrence knew to be referred to as *oni*. There were the old Grecian masks of comedy and tragedy, as well as Venetian masks with grotesquely elongated noses. *Regardless of the mask,* Lawrence thought, *not one of them looks welcoming in the moonlight.*

When he reached the double doors at the end of the long hallway, he was relieved to leave the watchful masks behind, but a new kind of anxiety overtook him. This was the night that he had been looking forward to all week. Emil Havelock had been sent abroad. If Lawrence wanted to avoid anyone above all others, it was him. This was the time to take a closer look at Duquesne's operation, which meant, hopefully, that his time at New Covington was coming to a close. He'd get what he needed tonight and make sure it was enough. Then he'd disappear.

Agent Lawrence turned the brass handle on the door at the end of the hall and opened it slowly and quietly. The ballroom was illuminated by the moon and stars shining through the domed glass ceiling. The room certainly did look beautiful, the light twinkling through the grand chandelier, making intricate kaleidoscope designs on the immaculate marble floor.

As he walked the perimeter, Lawrence ever so gently tapped on the mirrors and panels lining the walls of the ballroom. Finally, after several attempts, he rapped on one panel whose reverberations sounded only slightly different than its identical brothers. This was the way in, he thought, or at least one of the ways in. He pulled on the sconce above his head, but nothing happened. He felt for a hidden switch along the sides of the panel, but still nothing. Desperate, he got down on his hands and knees and tried searching the bottom of the panel. With his face pressed against the cool marble, he felt a slight draft coming through a slim crack between the floor and the wall. This was definitely it. He stood again, frustrated at his lack of progress. He gave the panel a once-over with the aid of the flashlight, but still had no luck.

Time was running short. Although Havelock was away, there were plenty of other residents at New Covington who were perfectly capable of finding him, not the least of which being Duquesne himself or his faithful butler, Ridgley. Lawrence smirked. *Who has a butler these days anyway?* With that thought, he was about to begrudgingly call it a night when a slight movement in the mirror next to him caught his eye.

Lawrence leaned over, expecting to see his own reflection in the mirror, but he was shocked to instead be met with the one black, emotionless eye of the Patchwork Man. Mustering every ounce of his composure to keep from jumping out of his shoes, Lawrence watched as the figure stepped fully into the frame of the mirror, pointed to its left with a dramatic flourish, and with a snap of its fingers, dissolved, leaving Lawrence once again looking at his own reflection. As calmly as he could, he looked behind him into the empty, placid ballroom, which did, in fact, remain empty and placid. There was no one there with him. He turned his flashlight back to the mirror and aimed its beam at the area that the Patchwork Man had pointed out, finding a small switch on the gilded frame of the full-length mirror. "Gotcha!" he whispered. "Thanks, you creepy bastard." Agent Lawrence flipped the switch and the panel to his left jutted out the slightest bit. He grabbed the edge, pulled the door open, stepped into the coolness of the hidden chamber, and silently closed the door behind him.

Had it not been for his flashlight, Lawrence would have been immersed in total darkness as he walked several yards along an unlit stone passageway. There must have been a light switch somewhere, he thought, but he had missed it and wasn't eager to backtrack now. After all, there was every chance that the light switch in a hidden corridor was rigged to an alarm or similar sensor. He stopped for a moment to remove his gun from its holster. He had barely taken another ten paces when he felt the floor beneath him gradually sloping downward. He followed this curving slope until he saw the spot where it leveled out, and proceeded to scan the abysmal cavern with his flashlight.

What Agent Lawrence saw amazed him. The cavern was easily the size of the ballroom that he had left moments before. In fact, the space appeared as a grim reflection of the ballroom, complete with similar stone pillars along the periphery. He got close to one of these pillars, feeling its craggy surface and realizing that several shapes were carved into it, one on top of another. He ran the flashlight's beam up the pillar and counted six unique characters, none of which he recognized. *They look ancient*, he thought. *Seems more like a job for Whitworth.* Pausing for a moment to confirm the deafening silence of the cave, he holstered his gun and removed his phone from another pocket. It took a few attempts, but he was finally able to get some decent shots of the six markings on the column in front of him. He shone his light around the cavern and counted twelve pillars, each with six distinct runic symbols. Seventy-two characters in total—far too many for him to photograph tonight, but hopefully Whitworth would be able to work well enough with the six pictures that he got. Not surprisingly, Agent Lawrence's phone did not have service in Duquesne's subterranean lair, so he exchanged the device for his weapon again and continued his exploration of the cavern. The space reminded him of a temple, albeit a very sparse one. The plethora of characters etched into the stone gave the room a primeval quality, and the scant amount of furniture consisted of a handful of tables covered with an array of antique books, what looked like a sacrificial stone altar in the center of the vast space, and a very out-of-place armchair not far from it. At best, the room looked like a work in progress, but Lawrence's imagination quickly ran through the possibilities of what Desmond Duquesne planned to do in here. The thoughts made the hair on the back of his neck stand up.

Agent Lawrence walked over to one stack of books, his

footsteps echoing more than he would have liked on the cold stone floor. He shone his light on one book which was already open, but again saw more symbols that he could not decipher. "They picked the wrong guy for this job," he said to himself. Whitworth knew more than twenty-six languages...most of them dead ones. Lawrence knew English and about enough French to pass a high school midterm. He knew this much, though—these books were written in neither English nor French, nor any language he could readily identify. He took one last picture—this time of the open book—and lifted the gun again. He headed back to the sloping entranceway as quietly as he could but stopped short when he spied what appeared to be a wrought iron door on the far right wall.

The door opened with a tinny creak and Lawrence marveled at the fact that Duquesne hadn't secured his secret chamber more thoroughly. Once through the door, he found himself in another tunnel, this one sloping upwards and giving Lawrence a feeling of claustrophobia. This could have been attributed to the increasing warmth he felt as he walked, as opposed to the refreshing coolness he had felt in the previous chamber. He figured correctly that this passageway was leading him onto the grounds of the estate rather than back into New Covington. In a few more yards, he had reached another door —this one wooden—which opened outward, making quite a racket as it knocked over several shovels that had been leaning against it. Agent Lawrence fumbled with the tools but was unable to prevent them from crashing to the ground. The clanging of the shovels subsided, and Lawrence found himself peering cautiously through the grimy window of the tool shed located on the south lawn of the compound. Seeing no signs of life outside, he took a moment to gingerly place the tools in what seemed to be their proper places and stepped out of the shed, closing the squeaky door as slowly and quietly as possible. He looked at his watch. He was now three minutes overdue to take over for the guard at the front gate. He holstered his weapon once more and took a moment to send his photos to Agent Whitworth. After confirming that they had been sent, he began his walk across the compound to the gate on the east lawn.

The moonlight on the lawn made it easy for Agent Lawrence to make his way toward the front of the house, but he had only walked a few yards before he thought he heard someone else walking behind him. He paused briefly, confirmed that he heard footsteps on the dewy grass, and turned quickly, shining his light on a figure that quickly threw his right hand up to block the glare. "Who's there?" Lawrence demanded.

"Oh dear," said a calm voice with a faint British accent. "I'm so sorry for startling you."

"Mr. Duquesne?" Lawrence asked, hoping that he was wrong but knowing that he wasn't. Sure enough, once the older man's eyes adjusted to the light, he lowered his hand, revealing a patient smile and perfectly coiffed hair. It had gone prematurely white, so that it did not hint at his true age, nor did his face, which had reportedly undergone a number of slight surgeries through the years. He still appeared to be in his early sixties. He was clad in black silk pajamas and a thin black robe and carried nothing but one of his ever-present walking sticks —this one an ebony cane topped with a silver raven's head.

"Guilty," said Duquesne. "Just out for a bit of a stroll. I tend to get a bit listless at night, and I often get the impression that my wife doesn't mind if I take my time coming to bed," he chuckled. Agent Lawrence grinned nervously. "And how about you, sir? How goes your evening?"

"Oh, it's fine," Lawrence replied. "I just thought I heard something near that shed over there," he said, motioning to the small square structure with his flashlight beam. "So I figured I'd check it out before I headed back for gate duty."

"Heard something, did you?" Duquesne said, as though he didn't quite believe him. "And did you find anything?"

"No, sir." Lawrence smiled. "All clear."

"Ah. I see. Well, thank you for your diligence, mister…I'm sorry, but your name is escaping me. What is it again?"

"Jackson, sir. Harold Jackson."

"Harold Jackson," Duquesne repeated slowly, grinning. "Walk with me, Mr. Jackson," the older gentleman said, waving his walking stick in a gesture of invitation. Lawrence complied, walking in step with Duquesne in the opposite direction of where he was supposed to have been going.

"It's a lovely night, isn't it?" Duquesne mused. "It reminds me of that song, 'On a Clear Night You Can See Forever.' Are you familiar with the musical of the same name?"

"Um, no sir," Lawrence answered.

Duquesne appeared to be in a trance while gazing up at the moon, but soon shook it off. "My apologies," he said. "My mind tends to wander sometimes. A side effect of getting on in years, I suppose." They continued to walk in silence for several paces before the moment that Agent Lawrence had been dreading arrived. "So, my friend, are you going to tell me the real reason that you were in that tool shed?"

Lawrence tried not to appear rattled, but he tensed up. "Like I said, Mr. Duquesne, I heard—"

Duquesne stopped walking, and Lawrence followed suit. "Come now. Let's not be so formal. I'll tell you what. You may call me Desmond, if I can call you James."

Lawrence had been trained for moments like this, and without blinking, responded, "But my name is Harold, sir."

The old man chuckled. "I can tolerate many things, but I can't abide liars. Now, Special Agent James Lawrence, what exactly did you find in the chamber below us?" Lawrence did not answer, but nonchalantly moved his flashlight from his right hand to his left. In response, Sir Duquesne waved his cane disapprovingly. "Oh dear," he said. "If you are preparing to remove your weapon from its holster, please rethink that. After all, the people who sent you must have informed you that shooting me is rather pointless." Lawrence had indeed been briefed on the futility of trying to kill Duquesne, but he wasn't sure what else to do. The confidence that Duquesne was exuding all but confirmed that Lawrence wasn't about to get one over on his opponent. He remained stoic, trying to think of something, as Duquesne continued. "Let me ask you this, James. I imagine that you took a few photographs while down there. Did you already send them along to your superiors? Whitworth, no doubt?"

"I did," Lawrence admitted.

Duquesne's grin disappeared momentarily but returned with a shrug of his shoulders. "Well, I guess that ship has sailed, then. Nothing to be done about it."

"They'll figure out what you're up to, Duquesne," Lawrence said. "And they'll stop you."

"I do suppose they'll try."

"That is," Lawrence continued, hardly believing that these words were escaping his mouth, "unless you have someone on the inside. I can help you."

Duquesne raised an eyebrow at this unexpected offer and shook his head in a disappointed manner. "Agent Lawrence, do you not think it odd that I knew exactly who you were? Consider this: if I already have someone on the inside, why would I need to hire you? Redundancy is bad for business."

Lawrence was now visibly shaken, sweating in the late spring heat. "But...but I..."

"Oh, stop blubbering, James. Here. Take this. You look a sweaty mess." Duquesne removed a clean red handkerchief from a pocket in his robe and handed it to Agent Lawrence, who wiped his face obediently. "Do you have a family, James? Children? Wife?"

"N-no, sir. My line of work doesn't really allow it."

Duquesne nodded. "Prudent. I'm glad to hear it. I would have felt just terrible otherwise."

Lawrence, sensing danger, reached for his gun, deciding that even if he couldn't kill Duquesne, he could injure him enough to get away. He was wrong, though, as Duquesne was too quick and gave the agent's right hand a vicious crack with the ebony cane, forcing him to drop the gun onto the grass. Lawrence barely had time to react before Duquesne, in one fluid motion, drew a long blade from the cane's hollow sheath and took a vicious swipe. Agent Lawrence saw a glimmer of silver in his peripheral vision just before the blade sliced through his throat.

Duquesne watched stoically as the agent's body thudded to the ground and began to twitch. "Oh James," he said to the agent as he picked up the red handkerchief and wiped the blade clean, "Don't do that." Upon reassembling his walking stick, he bludgeoned James Lawrence's head several additional times, the raven's beak going to work with sickening *thwacks*, until the corpse stopped its spasms and his victim's face was barely recognizable.

Duquesne raised his cane again to see the dark matter now staining his silver raven and winced at the realization that he may have just ruined one of his favorite canes. He dropped it to the ground and removed his phone from the same pocket that had previously held the now blood-soaked handkerchief. He said as he dialed, "It's not that I mind being shot, James. It's just that my daughter gave me these pajamas, and I'm quite fond of them."

The phone rang only twice before a tired voice answered, "Yes, sir."

"Ridgley!" Duquesne's face brightened, as though he hadn't expected anyone to answer, when in truth, Mr. Ridgley had never let a call go in all his years of service. "Are you awake, my friend?"

"Of course, sir," Ridgley lied.

"Good man. Listen, I hate to be a bother, but I've made a terrible scene down here on the east lawn."

"How unfortunate, sir," Ridgley offered. "Would you like me to take care of it?"

"Yes, that would be most helpful. I'm afraid that the sight of it would give the grounds crew an awful fright if it were still there in the morning."

"Very good, sir. I shall get on it immediately." Ridgley paused. "Sir, may I ask what the nature of the mess is?"

"Oh, I ran into that Agent Lawrence. We had a little chat, and I'm afraid that I had to—oh no!"

"Sir? Sir, what is it?" asked Ridgley with urgency.

"Oh, Mr. Ridgley, I feel just terrible. Earlier, I asked Agent Lawrence if he was familiar with the musical 'On a Clear Night You Can See Forever' and unfortunately I just now realized that the musical in question is really called 'On a Clear *Day* You Can See Forever!' Oh, no wonder the poor man was puzzled." He sighed, crestfallen. "Ridgley, do you ever wish that you could go back in time to right a wrong?"

"Of course, sir."

"If only I could do so." Duquesne looked down at the corpse. "I'm very sorry, James. How careless of me. But the mind does wander..."

"Sir, while I have you on the phone, I received word about an hour ago that we have an approximate location of Mr. Brandt and the Trammell boy. I thought that I'd tell you in the morning, but since you're obviously up now..."

"Oh, well that's exciting news," Duquesne responded, snapping to attention. "Are they close?"

"Pennsylvania, sir. The Pocono Mountain area."

Duquesne stood in thought for a moment before saying, "I suppose we should do something about this."

"Agreed, sir, but Mr. Havelock is not due back from Africa until tomorrow afternoon."

"Let's not waste time, Mr. Ridgley. Throw a team together to dispose of those two troublemakers."

"Very good, sir. Will there be anything else you'll need tonight?"

"Oh, no thank you, Mr. Ridgley. I'm…wait. Is your wife there with you?"

"She is, sir."

"Excellent," he said, smiling once more. "Could you ask her where she has hidden the…what are they…Nutter Butters? And make her promise not to tell my wife that I asked."

FIFTEEN

The Assassins

AFTER DINNER and a brief discussion with the bartender, it was discovered that the ramshackle cabins scattered throughout Memorytown had been shut down years ago, so it was fortunate that Will and Brandt had the RV at their disposal. Fully sated from dinner, they drove the vehicle to an empty lot adjacent to the woods. These woods would be the location of Will's training the following day, and Brandt, in exchange for his earlier candor, was insisting that they get an early start. Still, Will did not feel all that tired, and as Brandt prepared himself for a short night's sleep, he asked permission to step outside for some air.

Brandt did not look thrilled with the idea but felt that Will's compliance in asking was at least a step in the right direction. "Don't go far," he replied.

WILL WALKED across the parking lot of the Tavern and sat on the bank of the lake, realizing for the first time just how filthy he felt. His jeans crackled as he bent his knees, the dirt from his early scuffle in the forest caked onto the denim. The burger had hit the spot earlier, but now he was sick to his stomach. Tomorrow, Brandt would try to teach him to shoot a gun again. He would try to train him to kill a man—a man he did not know. Suddenly, a terrible thought came to him. What if Brandt was running a scam? What if this kindly old man whom he had seen in the photographs was not really the villain? What if he was being asked to do Brandt's dirty work, only so that someone else could take the fall? Too many things about this scenario remained uncertain. Tomorrow, he would see what Brandt had to say about this. For tonight, though, he would try to calm himself by listening to the hoots of the owls and the barely audible splashes of fish coming to the surface to feed.

WILL WAS AWAKENED at daybreak by the sound of Brandt's rifle butt hitting the floor next to his cot. "Look alive, kid," said Brandt. "There's water and a cereal bar on the table. Eat it now or later. I don't care. But be outside in five minutes regardless."

"Can't you just shoot me instead?" Will groaned, burying his face in the pillow.

"There's every chance of that happening depending on how annoying you are today, but you're not getting out of your training that easily."

"Damn," Will muttered, straining to sit upright. "Today's going to suck."

When he dragged himself outside, he saw that Brandt was already leading the way into the forest with his trusty bag of weapons. "It's going to be a beautiful day," Brandt said. "With any luck, you'll get the hang of things quickly and we can shoot something for dinner."

"Yay," Will responded with a distinct lack of enthusiasm.

Brandt dropped the sack when he had reached a quiet

clearing and looked back at Will with disdain. "Why aren't you wearing shoes?"

"Because it's early and I hate you," Will said, yawning.

"Neither one of those are reasons for not wearing shoes."

Will shrugged, approached the bag, and removed a hunting rifle. "So what do I shoot?" he asked nonchalantly.

"Christ. Nothing with that," he answered. "Let's start with something a bit smaller." He gingerly took the rifle from Will's hands and replaced it with a nine millimeter handgun. "This isn't the most commonly used weapon out in these parts, but it'll do the trick much better in the city. You won't get too far walking around Boston with a rifle unless you're reenacting the Revolutionary War."

"Guess that makes sense," said Will. As he got used to the feel of the gun in his hand, he added, "Speaking of which, I'm wondering just how exactly I'm supposed to kill this man and get away with it."

Brandt took the gun, loaded a clip into it, and returned it, saying, "You just let me worry about that."

Will gave an incredulous look and said, "Yeah, well here's the thing. If I get caught, all that stuff about going back to be with my family will pretty much be a moot point, no?"

"Don't think that I haven't thought this through, William. You have to kill the man, yes. No one ever said that you need to take responsibility. All roads will lead back to me, and I'm ready to take the fall for the death of Duquesne."

"You're kidding."

"You should know by now that I don't kid."

Will almost said, "Thank you," but felt that the sentiment would be an understatement. This brief exchange had sparked the feeling that this guy was for real. For the next few hours, Brandt and Will spoke about little else but how to hold the weapon, how to load it, how to fire it, and how to conceal it while maintaining easy access. "I feel like a badass secret agent," said Will.

"Uh huh. Very badass," Brandt responded. "But all you've shot so far are trees. Let's try something new." He reached into his bag and pulled out a carton of eggs. For the next several minutes, he paced the perimeter of the clearing, sometimes stepping into the woods beyond, resting eggs gently between branches, on logs, in the hollows of trees, and in the crevices of broken stumps. When all twelve eggs had found homes, Brandt simply said, "Go."

Will understood what he had to do, and, with the exception of one reload, took twelve consecutive shots—one at each egg. When the forest had finished ringing from the gunshots, Brandt walked over, patted William on the back, and said, "Missed every damn one. By a mile. Now, consider going for accuracy instead of speed, eagle eye. Start again. Only aim at that one egg in the tree hollow over there," he said, pointing. "We are not moving on to another egg until Humpty Dumpty there has been shot to pieces."

Will concentrated, aiming the barrel of the gun carefully at the egg, not so much as an attempt to gratify Brandt, but rather to prove to himself that he could do it. "I can do this," he said. He pulled the trigger and lowered the gun, fully expecting yolk to be running freely from the hollow. However, the egg remained untouched. In fact, the tree itself remained untouched.

"Try again," said Brandt. Will tried again, concentrating more on his aim and his steady grip on the gun every time. And every time, he missed. "Goddamn," Brandt sighed. "This is going to take longer than I thought."

BY THE END of their session, Will had successfully shattered five of the twelve eggs that Brandt had initially set up, and had successfully wasted hundreds of Brandt's bullets. If anything, the day's exercise had helped Will to concentrate on something other than his abduction and his longing for home, but as the sun began to set and they packed the supplies back into the canvas bag, Will remembered to ask one of the questions he'd thought of last night while sitting by the lake. "Brandt, I know that you said Duquesne had my family killed, but what's the urgency now? What is this guy about to do that's so bad?"

Brandt hefted the bag onto his broad shoulders and started back toward the RV. "I don't know many details of the ritual. I do know, though, that the man is obsessed with immortality and will do anything to get it."

"But he's already immortal, right?"

"He's lived a long time, but all his initial ritual did was slow down the inevitable. He can't be killed—except by you, of course—but given a few more decades, Duquesne may very well pass away. He knows this, and he's gathering what he needs to extend his lifetime…indefinitely."

"And this new ritual may kill people?"

"It *will* kill people. It *may* unleash hell on earth."

"Oh."

WHILE WILL and Brandt made their way back to the RV, their previous parking space outside the Memorytown Tavern was occupied by a jet black BMW convertible that had just come screeching into the lot. A tall man dressed in a black overcoat slinked out of the passenger seat, while a shorter, more muscular man leapt from the seat behind him and began sniffing the air. "I smell power," he hissed.

The final member of this trio, a young woman with blazing red hair and a long leather jacket, stepped out from behind the wheel and, looking around, said, "I smell boredom." She neared the bank of the lake and poked at the remains of a small bird that had been picked clean by scavengers. "This place is dead." She stared intently at the clean, hollow bones, and with awkward, jerking movements, the skeleton reassembled itself. The undead creature hopped onto the girl's outstretched finger as she gave her compatriots a crooked smile. "Time to liven things up."

SIXTEEN

"Guess What I Can Do"

HAVING DECIDEDLY FAILED to reach the level of hunting for his own food, Will convinced Brandt to take one more evening meal at the Tavern once they had washed away as much evidence of a day in the woods as they could. "We'll go back out again tomorrow," Brandt said between oversized forkfuls of salmon.

"That's fine," Will responded. "By the way, how do you know that by the time I learn to shoot, I won't shoot you? Aren't you at all worried about that?"

"Should I be?"

The look in Brandt's dark eyes quickly convinced Will that this was the last concern on Brandt's mind. Wishing he could take back his question, he averted his own eyes and looked into the darkness beyond the Tavern's parking lot. "There's a guy out there," said Will, moving back and forth to avoid the reflection from the neon Bud Lite sign above the bar.

"Where?" Brandt asked, not really caring.

"In the trees just beyond the parking lot. Weird."

"What's so strange about it?"

"Well, I didn't know it was a guy at first. I thought it was an animal. Seems like he has red eyes."

Brandt cupped his hand over his brow and pressed his face to the window. "Probably a hunter. Looks like he's got infrared glasses. Impressive."

"Yeah. Cool," said Will, and he fell back to eating his ribs. Brandt, on the other hand, slowed his eating, which had only minutes ago been ravenous. He peered through the window once more, this time apparently deep in thought. "What is it?"

"Nothing," Brandt said. "But I'm finished here. We should head back soon."

"Give me the money and I'll pay," Will offered. "I'll meet you back there. I want dessert."

"You're pushing it," Brandt muttered.

"I know. The perks of being a captive." Will smiled. "Seriously, though, when I get back, I want to look at those files again. The ones about Duquesne."

This seemed to appease Brandt, and Will truly did want to dig into those files to try to connect some dots for himself. With that settled, Brandt handed Will a wad of cash, once more threatened him not to wander off anywhere, and left for the RV. Once Will was convinced that Brandt had made it back to their vehicle, he counted out enough for the bill and a tip, pocketed the rest, and, before leaving the restaurant, craned his neck to look around the perimeter of the bar. He tried to see whether the waitress who he had asked to contact Andy was there, but when she did not appear after a few moments, he gave up his search and headed outside.

The moon reflected off the lake, revealing a gaggle of geese that drifted placidly across the surface. Will made his way for the second time in as many nights to the edge of the water, where he found what looked like a gumball machine filled with pet food. He deposited a quarter and received a handful of pellets, which he promptly began scattering among the geese.

When the geese realized that he had run out, they glided leisurely beneath a wooden bridge that led from the Memory-town Tavern's defunct patio dining area to a barely noticeable trail into the woods across the lake.

The bridge was lined with a series of faintly flickering lanterns, which was the only reason Will was able to make out the figure standing on it. The man wore all black, looking like an antiquated undertaker in his long coat and gloves. Will stood transfixed as he took in the sight of this dark, lanky figure. He was awed by his height—the man must have stood nearly seven feet tall, dwarfing the rusted guardrail that ran the length of the bridge. Will could not make out any facial features, but he could see that the man held something in his hands.

After what felt like an eternity of staring, the man slowly raised his occupied hand and fit a Seussian top hat onto his skull, which only served to make him appear that much more an unnatural and ghastly apparition. The man adjusted the brim of his hat and tipped his head slightly toward Will, who, realizing that this man had been staring at him for just as long as he had been, instinctively got to his feet. He now noticed a distinct mist rising from the still water of the lake. Thinking that he had heard a noise behind him, he jerked his head to look, but saw nothing out of the ordinary in the parking lot. Turning back to the bridge, he saw that it was now empty. The geese had made their way to the back of the Tavern, and the ghostly Goliath had vanished. Will felt a knot in the pit of his stomach. Something was wrong, and he needed Brandt.

Despite his attempt to tread softly, every step that Will took on his way across the parking lot seemed amplified. Still he walked on, looking back toward the lake often, but only saw the empty bridge as it grew fainter in the distance. When he neared the end of the first lot and began to descend the small grassy hill into the further lot where the RV was located, he noticed that his feet were barely visible in the growing mist and so paid close attention to where they were landing. In his attempts not to trip, he almost smashed his face into the side of the RV, which seemed to appear out of nowhere.

"Hey," said Will as he entered the vehicle, making sure to lock the door behind him. Brandt looked up from a fishing magazine that he had taken from the bar earlier. "Is it possible that we could have been followed here?"

Brandt stood up and tossed the magazine aside. "I don't know how anyone would have known we'd be here, but anything is possible." As he said this, he flicked off the one light that he had been reading by and crouched over to peer through the drawn blinds.

He frowned as Will said, "Someone was watching me by the lake—a strange-looking guy. Very tall. Dressed all in black."

"Theatrical? Tall hat?" asked Brandt, still looking out into the gathering fog.

"Yeah. How did you—"

"Damn." The older man moved quickly to his canvas bag and began emptying its contents. "Isn't that clever?" he mused.

"You want to clue me in?"

"The guy that you saw in the woods while we were eating... he wasn't a hunter. And those weren't infrared goggles. Those were his eyes. He's known as Stalker. He's a mercenary, just like your friend in the top hat."

"So they work for Duquesne?"

"As far as I knew, they were locked up tight. I guess they're out, and I guess Desmond Duquesne is outsourcing again." He loaded a clip into the nine millimeter Will had been practicing with earlier and handed it to him. "Hold on to this."

"Okay," Will said nervously. "So what's so clever?"

Brandt holstered a handgun of his own and grabbed a taser from a small black case that Will had previously assumed held ammunition. "Well, you may have noticed that the tall fellow has a 'skill' of his own."

"The fog? You said the weather was supposed to be clear tonight. As soon as I saw him, the fog started."

Brandt nodded. "Kingsley Ratchford. Calls himself Steampunk. The man's a human fog machine, which makes him ideally paired with Stalker. Steampunk brings in the fog, so we can't see, but Stalker can. His senses are off the charts. If we go outside, he'll see and hear our every move."

"Then we don't go outside," Will retorted. "Let's get out of here."

"That might be the best course of action," said Brandt, shoving Will out of the way to get to the front of the vehicle. As soon as he reached the driver's seat, though, Will heard Brandt mutter, "Shit." He too rushed to the front, and, looking over Brandt's shoulder, saw through the windshield the tall man, Steampunk, holding what looked like a torch, its flame burning a hole in the mist and reflecting off of the round industrial goggles that he wore below the brim of his top hat.

Will pointed past Brandt. "Is he holding—"

Steampunk's arm moved with a mechanical jerk, letting loose a flaming bottle, which landed with a crash on the roof of the RV. "They're smoking us out," said Brandt with no small hint of concern. "Follow me as closely as you can, and don't look back. Have your gun ready."

Brandt unlocked the door and swung it open, only to have Will grab his shirt and pull him back. "Wait!" Will shouted. "I need those files!"

Brandt considered this for a moment before looking into the rearview mirror to see dark smoke billowing from the roof. The RV was rapidly heating up. The ceiling wouldn't hold out much longer. "No time," he said. "We'll have to do without."

Will glowered, and, ignoring Brandt's response, fumbled to gather the open files that he had left out on the table. "I said 'no,'" Brandt growled, grabbing Will forcefully by the arm and leading him out into the night. A bullet lodged itself into the door as they ran toward the wooded area where they had trained earlier. Desperate to see that the documents stayed intact, Will's hopes were dashed when he looked back to witness the flaming roof of the RV cave in.

With no chance of seeing any of the documents or photographs again, Will was resigned to following Brandt, who had released his arm and was running at full speed into the forest ahead. He struggled to see Brandt through the dense fog, especially since he was so hesitant to keep his eyes open—he had almost lost one when a branch came out of nowhere and scraped the side of his face and through the flesh of his ear. He did not feel the steady trickle of blood, though, as Steampunk's miasma had dampened his face, his hair, everything. He kept pace with Brandt until, flinching at the sudden appearance of a particularly foreboding holly bush, and frightened at the prospect of blinding himself with a thorn, he shut his eyes for the briefest of moments and veered off track. Now officially lost in the haze, he searched desperately for any sign of Brandt but saw nothing. At the same time, he did not see the dreaded red eyes of Stalker, which he took as a good sign. Maybe Brandt had distracted him? Either way, he did not want to take any chances, so considering what Brandt might do in a similar situation, he threw himself onto the damp ground.

Will looked around and realized that the mist rose naturally, and he was able to see a bit further from this low vantage point. He briefly considered taking a risk and calling for Brandt, but he soon decided that that was probably the dumbest course of action, and so did not expect Brandt to call for him either. He was truly on his own, but he knew that he could not last long by staying in one place. Though short of breath, Will tightened his grip on the gun in his hand and began dragging himself through the dirt on his elbows, heading in what he hoped was the direction of the clearing where he had trained. This, he imagined, would be where he'd find Brandt.

He shuffled through what was gradually turning to mud for several yards, stopping often to listen for rustling that was not his. During one of these stops, he spotted a tall blurry figure that he took for Steampunk in the distance, but was relieved that, having less visual acuity than Stalker, his would-be assailant faded off into the fog before too long. Several minutes later, Will came upon a much more welcome sight. Hiding behind the trunk of a large oak tree, he saw a grouping of white shards half-buried in sedge. He tenuously reached his hand toward them and felt a warm, sticky substance on the ground. Egg yolk. He had successfully reached the clearing, but where was Brandt?

As Will waited for a sign of Brandt, he sat up against the tree trunk and held the gun with both hands, resting them on his bended knees. He noticed now that his hands were shaking and felt, for the first time, the sting of the gash running along the side of his face. *This is crazy*, he thought. *I should just run. I want to go home.* He considered how long it would take to get to the road they had come in on and wished he had paid more attention from the start. He cursed under his breath, and heard, as if in response, a raspy unfamiliar voice saying, "Where's the kid, Brandt?"

Will's eyes shot wide open, and he peered around the trunk against which he rested. Now he saw the red glow of Stalker's eyes, like two rubies hovering in the void. Their burning gaze was not pointed in Will's direction but was fixated on a point near a bog of dead trees just beyond the clearing. Cautiously and quietly, Will stood, craning his neck forward, and found that he could barely make out the shape of Brandt standing opposite the mercenary, his hands raised and presumably disarmed. Will sighed. If what Brandt had been telling him all along was true, then these men were here for him, to stop him from killing Desmond Duquesne. Despite his reservations about Brandt and the way that the situation had been handled, he couldn't let someone else die for him. With that thought in mind, he stepped out into the clearing, no longer caring about how loud his footsteps were. "I'm here," he said in a quavering voice, his gun aimed at the stranger.

As he got closer, he heard Brandt growl, "You idiot." Will stared as one of Stalker's bulging red eyes pivoted like that of a chameleon. With one eye remaining on Brandt, the man broke out into an inhuman laugh. "Is this really him?" he asked Brandt. "I assumed you'd been training him! I guess you didn't get to the part where he doesn't announce his presence to someone who wants to kill him!" His laugh reminded Will of a hyena that he had seen once on the Discovery Channel—it was just as raucous and just as chilling. Still, it didn't last long as the man grabbed an obviously injured Brandt and held him as a human shield between himself and Will. One arm was wrapped tightly around Brandt's throat, while the other held a handgun much like Will's against Brandt's temple.

"Shoot him," Brandt muttered through blood-stained teeth.

Stalker's laugh once more pierced the thick air, and Will grew concerned that the laugh was sure to bring Steampunk this way before long. "Yes!" Stalker agreed, both eyes now fixed on Will. "Shoot me!" Will wanted to, but he knew that there was no way that he would be skillful—or lucky—enough to put a bullet between those reptilian eyes. "You know I'll just find you if you run," Stalker continued. "So what's the harm? Afraid you'll hit your buddy here?"

"Just do it!" Brandt gasped as Stalker's forearm tightened around his throat.

Will stepped forward once and took aim at Stalker's face. *I need to do this*, he thought. *Otherwise, they'll just keep coming after me.* Stalker's laugh turned into a chuckle and then faded out altogether. "I don't have all day, boy. Either you shoot or I do. What will—"

"Now!" Brandt demanded. Will pulled the trigger and felt

the recoil in his tensed muscles. The shot was deafening, so he was not able to hear Brandt yowl when the bullet entered his shoulder. He did, however, see Brandt take advantage of Stalker's surprise to twist his arm in a sickening motion. Will didn't hear the break, but he saw it. Stalker nursed his hand momentarily as Brandt fell to the ground. Holding his mangled limb to his chest, Stalker aimed his gun at the back of Brandt's head and said, "Turn around, you son of a bitch. I want you to see this."

Noting a small window of opportunity, Will ran at full speed into Stalker, whose right eye pivoted just in time to see a body flying toward him. Stalker was muscular, and Will felt as though he had run headlong into a brick wall, but he heard a crack that he took for one of Stalker's ribs, and as he fell to the ground, heard another, larger crack and a subsequent splash. Crawling to a ledge that looked over the bog, Will saw that Stalker had fallen several feet and had been impaled on a dead, crooked tree. Stalker's body gently slid down the crimson branch that rose from the murky water like a gnarled, skeletal arm. Before long, the mire had claimed him, and all that remained were two glowing red orbs that gradually faded into darkness.

Brandt dragged himself over to look down at the scene, saying, "I guess we know why you suck at baseball. Your true calling was on the football field."

Will sat up and couldn't help but grin. "You just sort of made a joke."

"Figured this was as good a time as any." Brandt gave a faint grin that quickly gave way to a painful wince. He held the shoulder that Will had shot, trying to stem the flow of blood with his dirt-covered hand.

"What can I do?" Will asked, sensing the urgency that Brandt's bloody clothes implied.

"That bastard," he said, motioning toward the now placid

bog, "got me in the leg." He turned to show Will a hole in his left thigh that was barely distinguishable though the dark, sticky substance caked onto his flesh. "I need pressure on that, and obviously on my shoulder. I can keep the pressure on the shoulder while you take care of the leg."

"Right," said Will, not really knowing what to do. He sat in thought for a moment before Brandt interrupted, "Today would be nice…"

"Sorry!" Will removed his shirt, which he hesitated to use since it was filthy to begin with, and wrapped it around Brandt's leg, using his knowledge of action movies as his only basis for doing so. "Good?" he asked when finished.

Brandt seemed less than impressed, but simply said, "Good enough." He held out his left arm for Will. "Tear off my sleeve. I'll use that for the shoulder."

Will nodded and went to do so, but then heard the rustle of leaves from near the clearing. "Shit," said Brandt. "I forgot about the other one. Give me my bag," he ordered, pointing to the satchel he had taken from the RV. Will handed the bag over, and as Brandt pulled out the taser, he whispered, "Get back where you were before. I'll take care of this." Will did not hesitate to run to the large oak tree behind which he had been previously hiding, and crouched there, awaiting the arrival of the tall man. Brandt, in the meantime, did his best to work through the pain of his gunshot wounds and played possum, spreading himself out on his stomach with his good arm holding the taser.

It was not long before Steampunk emerged from the woods, flintlock pistol at the ready. His eyes, as opposed to Stalker's, were dead. He scanned the area with his thick, black goggles, taking no note of Brandt at first, but, deciding that the coast was clear, ultimately heading over to the prone body. Steampunk sloshed into one of the shallow creeks that led down to the watery tomb that his colleague now lay in and crouched to check Brandt's pulse.

Will worried for a moment that Steampunk would actually not find a pulse…that Brandt had bled out. This fear vanished, though, when in a quick movement, Brandt shot the taser's barbs into the mercenary's chest. Will watched as Steampunk silently convulsed, losing his stovepipe hat and falling to his knees. At this point, Brandt stood as quickly as his injured body would allow and took a vicious swing at his assailant with a large, fallen branch. The force of the blow sent Steampunk reeling backwards into a thorny bush, where he lay motionless.

Upon seeing Steampunk collapse, Will moved from behind the tree and approached Brandt, who was looking substantially paler than before. Walking cautiously toward the fallen mercenary, he asked, "Is he dead?"

Brandt gave a wet cough and groaned. "Can't tell from here. Either way, he's down for the count. Forget about him. We've got to get out of here."

Will nodded in agreement. "But how?"

Breathing heavily, Brandt gave this some thought, then responded, "I need a phone. Are you injured?"

"Nothing serious."

"Good. Run to the Tavern. Get a phone. Bring it to me. I'll get us out of here."

"You want to give me the number?" Will asked. "I can use the payphone."

"No," Brandt answered sternly. "I'm afraid they may have somehow traced the call that I made from the payphone earlier. Get me a cell that I can dispose of afterwards."

"Alright," said Will. "I'll be right back."

With that, he was off, bolting back through the woods as though he had grown up there. Instinct kicked in, and suddenly he seemed to know every turn and remember the location of every log, creek, and low-hanging branch. He deftly maneuvered himself back to the flaming wreckage of the RV within a matter of seconds, stopping only once to consider the damage done to the smoking vehicle, and determining that anything inside was now well beyond saving. Will accepted this unfortunate truth and picked up the pace again as he raced toward the flickering neon of the Tavern's beer advertisements.

As he ascended the creaky wooden steps that led to the bar's entrance, Will noticed that the fog that Steampunk had produced seemed to be thinning out. At the same time, the bar seemed much quieter, much more deserted than it had been earlier that night, or even the night before. Sensing trouble, he opened the door slowly, just barely jingling the leather strap laden with bells that hung on the opposite side. Despite the ambush that he had half expected, there seemed to be only one customer seated at a small, square table near the bar. The woman had unnaturally red hair and piercing green eyes. She was young, maybe in her early twenties, and seemed entirely out of place in a backwoods bar, her long leather jacket hanging past her seat and nearly to the floor. She nursed a martini in one hand and pointed in a circular motion to Will's bare chest. "Sorry, muffin," she said. "No shirt, no service." Will followed her eyes over to a spot on the floor where the bearded barman lay—a lifeless heap of plaid and denim.

Other bodies were scattered around the restaurant, some slumped over tables, but most, including the waitress who had been so helpful the day before, were splayed out on the hardwood floor. Will had never seen so much death in one place. Whoever this girl was, he was more frightened of her than he was of Stalker and Steampunk combined.

"Who are you?" asked Will, now realizing that he had forgotten his gun on the ground where he had tackled Stalker.

"Name's Candace," she said as she stood, took the last sip of her martini, and dropped the glass to the floor.

"You're here to kill me too?" Will was stalling, though to what end, he had no idea.

"Let's just say you're not out of the woods yet...so to speak," the girl replied. She gracefully stepped from her seat to her table to a barstool to the bar, where she stood and smirked. "Hey. Guess what I can do." Candace removed her gaze from Will and looked right past him. Confused, he turned and peered at the large moose head that resided above the stone fireplace. The head and its mount began to quake, shaking bits of stone and plaster to the floor below. As Will looked on in amazement, the moose blinked its glass eyes, twisted its neck, and let out a thunderous, angry bellow.

SEVENTEEN

Dead Things

BRANDT TOOK the pressure off his shoulder wound long enough to rummage through the satchel. Nearly empty now that the taser lay useless in the babbling creek, it was not difficult for him to find a set of zip tie cuffs. It was, however, difficult to prop Steampunk's limp body up against a tree and bring his hands behind it to be restrained. Still, after several painful attempts, he managed. He then promptly sat back down, concerned that his leg wound would become infected. *It will be alright though*, he thought. In a few minutes, Will would be back with a phone, and he would call his contact again. They'd be out of here in no time. *That is*, he thought, *unless Stalker and Steampunk were not the only two sent after us.* He reassured himself that Will would be fine, noting that the boy was still armed. He breathed a small sigh of relief and leaned back against a tree opposite Steampunk. It was only then, with Steampunk's control over the weather fading, that Brandt noticed Will's handgun sitting uselessly on the ground.

· · ·

"SO WHAT'LL IT BE?" Candace asked. "I don't care for guns. They're so, you know...humdrum. There are, however, plenty of options in this place when it comes to how I could kill you." With an outstretched hand she beckoned for the bartender to rise, which his lifeless body did, though not without some trouble. The corpse staggered to its feet, moving with awkward, jerking motions behind the bar, its face contorted, jaw hanging low, neck twisted in an unnatural manner. With a sneer of disappointment, she waved her hand and let the body slump to the floor once again. "Too fresh," she said. "Harder to control." Her eyes darted over to the one-eyed gray wolf near the door, and it too came to life with a jolt, tearing its paws from the wooden pegs on which they stood and shaking in a disturbing manner, almost like a marionette that was being played with for the first time. When it achieved some semblance of balance, it paced over to the doorway through which Will had just arrived. Candace wore a satisfied smile. "Much better."

"How are you doing this?" asked Will, backing away from the animal and toward the bar on which Candace was perched.

"You mean you can't?" she laughed. "Just takes a little concentration."

"Good to know," he responded, and in one quick swipe, took Candace's leg out from under her, sending her crashing onto the bar's surface. The reanimated wolf went limp, but Will opted not to press his luck by heading toward that door. Instead, he ran through the swinging wooden door to the kitchen, figuring there must be a back exit through which he could escape.

In the meantime, Candace had recovered. She rubbed the small of her back and glowered at the kitchen door, still swinging slightly. "Little bastard." Pointing to the wolf, she gestured for it to rise again. Not satisfied with anything less than seeing Will torn to shreds now, she glared intensely at the stuffed brown bear that stood against the wall to her right, made a similar motion and brought it to life. It stretched its massive arms and strode forward once with each hind leg before falling to all fours and letting out a blood-chilling roar.

Will's eyes went wide as he heard the roar, and though he was hidden away in the kitchen, he knew exactly what it meant. He pushed against the metal bar of the door labeled 'Fire Exit,' but the door did not give. The thought of being torn apart by a zombified bear lent some urgency to his actions, and he shoved his body repeatedly against the door, but to no avail. Looking around the kitchen, he saw no windows, but plenty of knives. *I might need to fight my way out of here*, he thought, his stomach sinking at the prospect. Grabbing the largest knife he could find, he ran back to the swinging door, opened it, saw the wolf lunge at him, and swung it shut again. The wolf's body landed with a thud against the door.

Will hurriedly blocked that entryway as best he could by dragging a small stainless steel table across the floor. It wasn't heavy, but it might buy him some time. He looked to the other side of the kitchen. There was another, identical door that led to the other side of the horseshoe bar. Not wanting to be surprised again, he ran to peer through its small square window. He saw nothing for a moment but the red-haired girl flashing him a menacing smile from atop the bar. Distracted by her taunting, he fell backwards when the sight of the bear's maw suddenly appeared in the window. The bear took a furious swing at the door, which swung open, revealing the creature in its entirety, and then swung back, hitting it on the snout. These animals could move, but they didn't have the brains they were born with.

The wolf angrily scratched at the other door, but Will was more concerned with the substantially larger creature standing behind door number two. He sat on the floor, pressing his back against it, realizing too late what a bad idea that was. With another furious swing, the bear broke through the center of the panel, its claw barely missing Will's already-damaged ear. A dull pain radiated through Will's upper body. He felt as though someone had dropped a cinder block on his back, and his head throbbed.

The room stopped spinning in time for Will to formulate one last-ditch idea for escape. He spied an air vent above one of the prep stations against the back wall of the kitchen. The furniture looked like it would make for an easy climb, so he ran over and leapt onto the lowest surface, knocking over cutting boards, utensils, and baking pans. With all the noise, he barely heard the bear barrel through the door, smashing what was left to splinters. It immediately spotted Will and roared with antici-pation as it neared him. Frantically, he placed the knife in his mouth, as he had seen heroes do in movies, and upon cutting both corners of his mouth, decided that this was a bad idea. Instead, he stuck the knife into one of the fiberglass ceiling tiles and continued his ascent, knocking ceramic dishes to the floor and climbing the shelves which housed them. The bear was gaining on him, and with a strong swipe, tore the flesh of Will's calf. He winced in pain, but carried on with his escape plan, fumbling with the latches that held the vent's screen in place.

Having only successfully undone one latch, he submitted to the searing pain in his leg. Afraid of receiving another wound, he grabbed the knife back from the ceiling as if he were pulling a sword from a stone. He looked down at the gaping jaws of the bear that was trying, fruitlessly, to climb the slippery metallic prep station. He stabbed at the bear whenever it came near enough, but noticed that whenever he made contact, it felt like stabbing a piñata. He was clearly dealing with the husk of a living being. This was made even more evident by the fact that the creature showed no sign of feeling any pain, regardless of how well-aimed Will's strikes were. *This is it*, thought Will, tugging at the vent with one hand and stabbing at the dumb creature with the other. *I'm dead.*

CANDACE SQUEALED with delight when her bear broke through the kitchen door and was almost giddy when she heard the smashing of dishes, pots, and pans. She was not as thrilled, though, when she looked to the other side of the bar to see her wolf having trouble just making it through the swinging door. It was growling ferociously and scratching with all its might, but it just could not grasp the concept of this impenetrable barrier. She sighed, alit from the bar, and, tossing her hair, made her way over to the frantic creature. "Do I need to do everything?" she muttered. With a wave of her hand she motioned for the wolf to stand down, which it did. She opened the door wide, saw Will attempting to stave off the bear with a carving knife, and went back to grinning. "Go help your friend out, sweetie. Finish him."

Having gotten the okay, the gray wolf leapt into the fray, much to Will's dismay. A sinking feeling quickly turned into a painful one when the eager wolf jumped recklessly onto the prep station, sending Will plummeting to the rubber mats on the floor below, which did little to cushion the landing as they were covered with bits and pieces of ceramic plates. He moaned in pain as both creatures bore down on him. They were close enough that he expected to feel their breath, until he recalled that neither was breathing. Still, he could hear the grumbling of the bear and the snarling of the wolf as he closed his eyes, resigned to his fate. After that, he heard nothing.

Surprised that the room was suddenly silent, Will cautiously opened his eyes to find the two creatures still standing over him,

frozen in position. Not wanting to look a gift horse—or bear—
in the mouth, he slid out from under them as quickly and as
quietly as he could. It was the right move, as only seconds later,
the wolf slumped into a pile of dishes and the bear's full, dead-
weight came crashing down onto the floor. There they stayed,
as lifeless as they had been when he and Brandt had first
entered the Tavern the night before.

Leaning on an overturned metal table, he dragged himself
to his feet, the pain from his leg shooting through his entire
body. When the initial shock of the pain wore off, he limped
slowly through the remains of the kitchen door to find his
would-be murderer sitting at the bar next to a thin, bespectacled, dark-skinned man whom he had never seen before. "Are
you here to kill me too?" Will asked wearily.

The man swiveled on his barstool and gave a warm smile.
"No, Will," he said as he stood and pushed chairs aside to get
to him. "I'm here to help." He placed one of Will's arms over
his shoulder and accompanied him to a seat of his own at the
bar. The man gingerly took Will's wounded leg into his hand,
shook his head, and scooted behind the bar. He fished around
for a minute or two and came back around with two bottles of
alcohol, one clear and one amber-colored. He poured the
amber drink into a shot glass and motioned for Will to drink it.
Without hesitation, Will tossed back the drink, winced and
swallowed back the reflux that was rising in his throat. Not
satisfied, the man-made him drink one more time before grabbing Will's leg again and pouring the clear alcohol over it. Will
screamed, feeling the burn of the alcohol much more acutely
than the wounds he had received in the heat of the earlier
melee. He dug his fingernails into the leather of the bar stool,
and when the pain had subsided enough, poured a third drink
for himself.

"Who are you?" Will asked, his voice cracking as he
winced.

"My name is Simon. I know Brandt."

"Lucky you."

Simon gave a knowing grin. "He's rough around the edges, but he's trying to do the right thing."

Not having the strength to argue, Will nodded in resigned agreement and looked past Simon to Candace, who sat at the bar in some sort of daze. "What happened to her? What happened to the animals?"

"I told her to stop," Simon said matter-of-factly.

"Oh," Will responded.

"It's my thing," said Simon, elaborating. "I can get people to do what I tell them to."

Will put down his shot glass, suddenly interested. "That's awesome."

Simon chuckled quietly. "Awesome. Horrific. It's a matter of perspective." He sealed the bottle of clear alcohol back up and placed it in its proper slot behind the bar.

"If you don't like doing it, then why do you?" Will pressed.

"I only do it when I have to. When it's a matter of life and death," said Simon. "Which this was, and continues to be, actually. So we've got to do something about that. If you'll excuse me…"

With that, Simon turned back to Candace and, looking into her emerald eyes, asked, "Who are you to contact when your job here is finished?"

She did not answer right away, but stared angrily back at Simon, her crimson lips twisting ever so slightly. "Why isn't she answering?" asked Will.

"She's resisting," Simon responded. "Strong-willed people can do that. I think our answer is on its way, though."

Sure enough, as soon as Simon repeated his question, Candace uttered, "Emil Havelock."

He nodded. "I figured as much. Candace, please use your cell phone to call Mr. Havelock and tell him that your mission is accomplished, that you have successfully killed both William Trammell and John Brandt."

She glared at Simon again, but begrudgingly removed her phone from her jacket pocket and dialed. "She knows that you're making her do this, doesn't she? She knows that you're pulling her strings."

Simon nodded slowly. "She may. I've never been on the receiving end of it myself, so I could not accurately tell you what it feels like." Will noted the reluctance in Simon's voice whenever he spoke of his ability, so he chose to forgo the rest of his questions for now.

"Mr. Havelock," Candace said, without any hint of coercion, "You can tell the old man that they're dead. Yes, sir. Excellent. I'll come for my money in the morning."

Simon ensured that the call was ended before he continued with the remainder of his instructions. "Now go. I need you to leave this place and not look back. Go home, wherever that may be. Whatever you do, do not go to Boston to collect your fee. In fact, forget that the money was ever offered to you."

Candace's green eyes stayed locked with Simon's for longer than Will was comfortable with. She momentarily seemed to be pushing back, but soon rose from her stool and left the Tavern. Simon followed to ensure that she had gotten into her car and driven off. Once this was settled, he returned to Will.

"Should we just let her go like that? What if she hurts someone else or comes back for me?" Will asked.

"We don't have time to weigh all of the options, Will. She's out of our hair now, and that's what matters."

"If you say so... Who is Emil Havelock?"

"Desmond Duquesne's personal fixer. He handles most of his dirty work.

DON'T WORRY about him now. Where is Brandt?"

"He's in the woods. He's hurt."

"Let's get you in the car first; then I'll head out to find Brandt," Simon suggested. "I think this would be an appropriate time to end your days as woodsmen. It's time we went to Boston."

EIGHTEEN

A Nasty Piece of Business

MOST BOSTONIANS WOULD HAVE FELT HONORED to receive an invitation to New Covington, but Eleanor Hornbeck was far from elated. As she drove her 1996 Volvo through the wrought iron front gate and onto the sprawling grounds, she noted the pomposity of the estate, which seemed to her as phony and as overrated as its residents. The Duquesnes were akin to royalty in Boston—known to be one of the wealthiest and most generous families in the world. But she saw right through that. Absent were the butterflies that many experienced when pulling up to the impressive columns that lined the front entrance; in their place were what felt like a dozen burning ulcers that only worsened after she handed her car off to Desmond Duquesne's right-hand man, Ridgley.

Eleanor made no attempts to hide her disgust when she spotted Ridgley's toad of a wife lumbering in her direction. *Here we go*, she thought, and popped another two Rolaids into her mouth.

"What, are ya sick?" Mrs. Ridgley asked in place of a greeting. She stopped short, hesitant to come closer lest the answer be an affirmative.

"Just an ulcer," Hornbeck replied, curving her lips just enough to present a feigned smile.

"Oh," said Mrs. Ridgley, waving her up the steps. "I've got a few of them myself. Otherwise I'd come all the way down these stairs for ya. But I've gotta save my strength."

Not sure whether Mrs. Ridgley truly had an ulcer—or in fact, knew what an ulcer was—Eleanor followed her up the wide concrete steps that led to the front door of New Covington. "Yes, well mine feels especially bad," said Eleanor, "since I'm just getting over a nasty cold as well. I've been feeling like if it's not my stomach, it's my throat, and if it's not my throat, it's my nose."

"And so on," said the unsympathetic Mrs. Ridgley, who led her into the main hall rather unceremoniously, letting the door nearly close in Hornbeck's face. "I've got the allergies," Ridgley continued, "so I know sinus pain. It's constant." She paused as she motioned for Hornbeck to follow her up the steps, and perhaps sensing that the guest was preparing to speak again, added, "Plus I just broke my toe this morning. Hence, why I can't guide ya all the way up to Mr. Duquesne's office, though ya know I'd love to."

All that the disgusted Eleanor Hornbeck could see when she looked back at Mrs. Ridgley's exaggerated smile at the bottom of the stairs was a conspicuous snaggletooth and a pair of eyebrows that were just close enough to touch when her face wore the right expression.

"I wouldn't want you to put yourself out, dear," Eleanor responded before she continued climbing the flight of stairs. "Don't want you to end up in traction."

Glad to be rid of her reluctant companion, Eleanor strode down the long hallway toward Desmond Duquesne's office, her therapeutic sneakers squeaking on the polished marble floor.

Approaching the opened door, she peeked her head in, and finding no one, made herself at home in one of the plush maroon chairs stationed off to the side near a wall covered entirely with leather-bound books. *What a waste,* she thought, eyeing the volumes lining the walls. If *she* had this kind of money, she would never fritter it away on books. *If you want to read, go online,* she thought. No muss, no fuss. The leather chairs, however, she could get used to. *Still,* she thought, *I'd never be able to.* Khloe, Snooki, and Boo Boo—her cats—would surely tear leather furniture to shreds in no time.

Noticing a hair on her blouse, she picked it off, examined it and concluded that it belonged to Boo Boo before letting it spiral to the floor. While it was fluttering, she saw what she took for another dark cat hair, but when she tugged at it she realized it was a thread from her blouse that had now grown three times as long because of her fiddling with it. She held it fast at one end and tugged, but it still didn't break. Peering out into the hallway, she quickly brought the bottom of her blouse up to her lips, at the same time exposing a substantial, pasty stomach, and bit the thread. She quickly adjusted her clothing so that no one could tell the procedure had happened and let the thread join Boo Boo's hair on the oriental rug in Duquesne's office.

Anyone who spotted her in the room would have guessed from her shaking leg and the way she held her pocketbook on her lap that she was uncomfortable, and they would be correct, if only because of the peptic burning that had barely died down. Otherwise, her feelings swung more toward aggravation and impatience. She stared around the room, taking in the various masks that Duquesne had collected over the years hanging just below the ceiling around the perimeter of the room and concluding that the ugly things were nothing more than another gross misuse of funds. Sighing, she plopped her pocketbook onto the floor next to her and grabbed a book from the shelf. *The Pickwick Papers.* She flipped disinterestedly through the several hundred pages of text, stopping now and then to look at one of the black and white illustrations depicting pompous Victorian dandies standing around doing nothing. "Reminds me of my brother," she muttered.

Before she could restore the volume to its proper place on the shelf, the door to the office swung open, and as if caught mid-theft, she fumbled with the book until it landed spine-first on her toe. "Sh...shoot," she muttered, stooping to retrieve *Pickwick* as quickly as possible. "You startled me, Mr. Duquesne." She looked at the teenage brunette who had opened the door. "You're not Mr. Duquesne."

"No, I'm slightly less concerned about the state of Mr. Dickens than he would be," she answered with a warm smile. "I'm his daughter Daphne. Sorry for scaring you. I just wanted to look for my dad's copy of *Frankenstein*. I'm behind on an assignment and my teacher's a real hard-ass."

"Oh," said Eleanor. "Well, there's always that one jerk, right?"

Daphne smiled again. "My mom's my teacher. I'm home-schooled. That was the joke. I'm sorry. It was a bad one. Anyway, I'll leave you alone."

"No!" Eleanor blurted, a little too desperate to make up for her previous statement. "Your mother is a lovely woman, by all accounts. A beautiful, intelligent, kind woman. I was...I was just kidding too. Don't go! Let's chat. My name is Eleanor Hornbeck."

"Ah..." Daphne's smile gradually began to fade.

"I see that you've heard of me. Bad things, I'm sure," Eleanor prodded. When Daphne refused to take the bait, she continued, "I've wanted to meet you for so long, Miss Duquesne. I wonder if you might sit down with me some time for an interview. My readers would love to know what life is like for Desmond Duquesne's favorite child."

"That seems a little harsh on my brother, Miss Hornbeck. He's no saint, but—"

"Please, call me Eleanor," said Hornbeck.

"Eleanor," said Daphne, "I've got to be honest. I don't read your blog. I'm a book girl, as you can tell." She awkwardly reached her arm around Hornbeck and slid Mary Shelley off her shelf. "I'd feel uncomfortable giving an interview to a gossip blog."

"It's not a gossip blog," Eleanor retorted, getting defensive. "It is an arts and entertainment resource."

"Okay then. It was nice meeting you, Miss Hornbeck."

Daphne shut the door behind her before Eleanor could catch it. "Another member of this family who thinks she's too good for me," she fumed. "You just wait until you make an ass of yourself in public like your brother, you little bitch. Then you'll make the blog, whether you like it or not."

Eleanor had no sooner uttered this threat when Desmond Duquesne himself entered the room. Dressed impeccably as always in a slim-fitting suit and tie, he was all smiles as he closed the door behind him and approached her. "Miss Hornbeck!" he began. "What a pleasure it is to see you again. I cannot thank you enough for agreeing to meet with me today."

"Well," Eleanor said with as much joviality as she could muster, "when *the* Desmond Duquesne requests your presence it's not wise to say no." Not able to help herself, she added, "Although phones and computers are all the rage these days as far as communicating."

Duquesne chuckled and settled himself into the chair opposite hers. "Now, Miss Hornbeck, you know that I would have understood if you couldn't make it. I know how very busy you are."

"Not a problem, Mr. Duquesne. So what can I do for you?"

"First, it's Desmond," he replied, leaning forward and resting his forearms on his lap. "Now as you have probably gathered, I am not the most progressive as far as technology goes. I like to do things the old-fashioned way, because I am of the 'if it ain't broke' mentality. That said, I don't read many blogs, and I certainly don't make it a habit to read yours—no offense intended."

"None taken," said Hornbeck, now fully aware of the trajectory of this conversation.

"Do you have children, Miss Hornbeck?"

"No," she said. "My husband and I divorced years ago. He wanted them. I didn't."

"To each her own." Duquesne shrugged. "But my children are my life. I would do anything to protect them, so you can imagine the shock and dismay that I felt when I read the most recent item on your blog."

"The one about your son, Alexander?"

"Yes," he said with a hint of faded affability, "that one."

"Mr. Duquesne, before you ask, I will not be removing that item from my blog. There was no breach of journalistic integrity and everyone in the vicinity absolutely corroborated what a scene your son made at that nightclub."

"Well, I'm sorry Miss Hornbeck, but I guess I just don't see how that warrants a news item."

"It doesn't, Desmond," she answered. "I'm not in the business of news. I'm in the business of society and celebrity. People pay to watch the high and mighty, the rich and powerful, acting like asses—no offense intended. If your son chooses to get blackout drunk and hook up with every teen and twenty-something in Boston, that's his choice. But he's old enough to know that there is no guarantee of privacy anymore." She sat back and folded her arms, feeling as if her case had more than adequately been made.

Duquesne, on the other hand, leaned in and softened his tone. "Miss Hornbeck, my wife and I are embarrassed by our son's behavior as of late. There's no question about that.

However, bringing this negative attention to our family is not good for our relationships, and frankly, it's not good for business. I've lived long enough to know that you can't stop the presses, so to speak, but if you must write about my family, let me ask you one favor." He paused here to remove an envelope from his jacket pocket. Noticing the curiosity on Eleanor's face, he handed it to her, saying, "It's not money. It's an invitation. In a few weeks, I'll be hosting my annual masquerade ball. Antiquated, I know, but I'm an old-fashioned fellow and as you can see, I'm a sucker for a good mask. We aim to raise over $100,000 for charity this year. I hope you will consider attending. At the very least it should give you an interesting item to write about, but this time with a positive message."

Eleanor continued to smile politely as she slid the invitation into her pocketbook and stood to take her leave. "I'll consider the invitation, but no promises."

"Understood," said Desmond, also rising and escorting her to the door with a gentle hand on the small of her back. "Thank you again, Miss Hornbeck. I look forward to your RSVP."

ELEANOR'S SNEAKERS squeaked down the hallway as Duquesne looked on grimly. He did not need the kind of negative attention that Hornbeck's blog had been drawing to his family. Not now. Still, he could not place the blame squarely on her shoulders. Loathsome as she was, she was merely doing her job. No, his son was at least equally to blame, and it was Alexander's room that he entered soon after his conversation with Eleanor had ended.

Alexander Duquesne was in his early twenties, fresh out of college, and attempting to learn the least amount possible about the family real estate business to get by. He snuffed out his cigarette and walked away from the window when he saw his father enter. "Did you talk to the blog bitch?" he asked nonchalantly.

In response, Duquesne backhanded his son across the jaw with a vicious crack. "Watch your mouth," he said. "Yes, I spoke to Miss Hornbeck, but I wouldn't rely upon her to take it easy on you in the future. The woman is bitter and petty, and people like that will jump on the slightest opportunity to bring someone like you, and in turn, someone like me, down." Duquesne took the open pack of cigarettes from Alexander's nightstand, crushed them, threw them in the garbage, and walked away. Before leaving, he looked at his son with marked disappointment. "We'll see how eager you are to make head-lines. If anything like this happens again, I will disown you—publicly. Now make yourself presentable. We're leaving for the harbor soon."

Duquesne shut his son's door behind him and found Emil Havelock waiting in the hall. If he had heard the threat to Alexander, he was unfazed by it. "Welcome back, Emil. I trust all went well in Pemba?"

Havelock nodded, but seemed preoccupied. "Mr. Duquesne, we should talk behind closed doors." Duquesne ushered his head of security back into his office. Not bothering to sit, Havelock started speaking immediately. "Brandt and the boy are taken care of."

"Killed?" asked Duquesne. "Are you certain?"

Havelock nodded. "I received word late last night from one of your bounty hunters...the girl. She stated clearly that the two of them were dead and that she'd be on her way to collect her fee soon." Duquesne's head bobbed slowly as Havelock spoke. "Sir? What is it?"

"This was just a nasty piece of business," Duquesne sighed. "Having to kill the boy, I mean."

"True," Havelock acknowledged, "but having it done must be a huge relief."

Duquesne leaned back against his desk. "It is. So much so that I almost don't know how to react. For the past two centuries I've lived with this sword over my head, and now that it's finally and definitively gone, it almost feels…I don't know… like something's missing."

Havelock thought about how to respond, given that he did not follow Duquesne's thought process. Eventually, he offered, "Maybe what you need now is a vacation. Take a little time away now that you truly have nothing to worry about."

"No, no," said Duquesne. "I can't do that. Too much to do. In fact, now that the boy is gone, I can start planning my next stage in earnest."

"So what do you need me to do?"

"Nothing yet. You're back on your regular duties for now. I do still expect Whitworth and her group to try and stop me, but until that happens there is no sense in going on the offensive. After all, without the boy, whatever efforts they make will ultimately be futile."

Havelock nodded, and as he was about to leave the room, he turned back, saying, "Sir, just one favor to ask."

"Of course, Emil," Duquesne said kindly. "What is it?"

"I understand the urgency with which you wanted the boy dispatched, but next time, please have me do it. These independent contractors tend to be a bit…sloppy."

NINETEEN

A Wolf and a Bear Walk into a Bar

"Jesus," Donovan uttered, surveying the damage done to the kitchen of the Memorytown Tavern. He and Whitworth had arrived soon after the local police and fire officials, who had caught wind of what news sources would call the 'Memory-town Massacre' after following up on an anonymous phone call. When the Collective agents had entered the parking lot, they bypassed the Tavern in favor of the shell of an RV smoldering on the outskirts of a dense forest, threatening to ignite the nearby foliage. Luckily, there was no wind and the woods surrounding the area were curiously damp despite the dry weather the region had been having lately. Realizing that any assessment of the vehicle would have to wait until the fire was out and the remnants cool enough to work with, Whitworth gave her card to the officer in charge and requested that they be called when that time came. In the meantime, they would take a look at the scene inside the Tavern.

The restaurant was a sea of activity when the agents entered. Scattered throughout the bar and dining areas were lumpy black bags surrounded by probing medical examiners and caution tape. The agents immediately introduced themselves to an agitated young lieutenant who breathed a sigh of relief when they explained that their branch of the government dealt with difficult-to-explain phenomena. Wasting no time, the young man led the two agents past the bodies and through the smashed door of the kitchen.

Scanning the kitchen to find dozens of broken dishes, hundreds of utensils, pots, pans, and two large dead animals, Agent Whitworth answered her partner's "Jesus" with an understated "Indeed."

"Officer," said Whitworth, addressing the young man who had led them into the room, "I wonder: how do a wolf and a bear walk into a bar without so much as damaging the front door?"

What would have sounded to anyone else like the set-up of a bad joke was met with complete seriousness by the officer, who took a few careful steps closer to Agent Whitworth, leaned down to meet her shorter stature and murmured, "They've been here for years, ma'am" as though embarrassed.

"What's that supposed to mean?" asked Donovan, who had thwarted the man's best efforts at remaining unheard.

"It means what it means, sir," the officer stated. "I've been coming to this place since I was a kid. See that wolf?" he asked, pointing. "It has one eye. Just about every officer in here will tell you that there has been a one-eyed wolf in this place since the owner brought it back from the taxidermist over ten years ago."

"Interesting," said the nonplussed Whitworth. "And the bear?"

"The same," explained the officer. "Except that's been here even longer."

Donovan shot Whitworth an incredulous look, but she simply shrugged. "Stranger things have happened." She crouched down to examine the wolf first, and after rising with a dissatisfied expression, tiptoed through the ceramic pieces to the bear's outstretched paw and poked at it with a ballpoint pen from her pocket. One of her eyebrows rose as she poked, and she soon replaced the pen in her pocket and laid her hand on the brown fur of the bear's back.

"Um, ma'am…"

"It's alright," said Donovan, gently holding the young officer back.

"But she'll contaminate the crime scene," the officer protested.

"You've been watching too much television, kid. When one of your assailants is a stuffed bear, the rulebook kind of flies out the window."

Agent Whitworth had not been paying attention to the exchange, but remained transfixed until Donovan crouched down beside her and whispered, "So is our boy toast?" Whitworth gave a subtle shake of her head. Donovan's eyes went wide. He looked at the scene around them and was about to ask, "But how?" when Whitworth's phone began to vibrate. "The RV must be ready," said Donovan.

Whitworth checked the display on her phone and shook her head. "Hello, Peg," he said when he answered. "What's going on?"

"I'm sorry to bother you, Fran," said the raspy voice on the other end. "But you've got a package here at the office, and it's labeled 'urgent.'"

"Hmmm. Is it ticking?"

"Nah," said Peg. "And it's not booze, either. I shook it when it got here."

"Why would it be booze, Peg?" Whitworth asked.

"I don't know," she responded. "Why wouldn't it?"

"Fair enough. So you're thinking that I should get to the office as soon as possible, I take it?"

"All I'm saying is that the last time you got an urgent package, it nearly resulted in World War III. And I don't need World War III on my conscience this weekend, Fran."

"I'd never do that to you, my love," she answered. "We'll be on our way shortly. I've got to go now. Getting another call." With that, Whitworth hung up with Peg and answered the incoming call from the fire marshal. "Yes sir," she said. "Yes. Yes? Oh, that's interesting. Yes. We'll be right there. Keep him bound, please."

Lowering her phone, she said to Donovan, "The fire is out. Very little damage to the flora, which is nice to hear." She paused for a moment, trying to recall the conversation she had just had. "Oh!" she continued. "And they found our old friend Kingsley Ratchford shackled to a tree. Seems he is a bit worse for wear. I figure we'll take him home, save these boys some trouble.

"Officer," Whitworth continued, turning to their guide and handing him a card, "I thank you for your cooperation. It seems that our culprit may have just been found in the woods, but if you come up with anything else, please do let me know."

"Yes, ma'am," the officer answered, still confused by the events of the past several minutes.

"You're going to run out of cards," Donovan joked.

Whitworth chuckled, but stopped suddenly on her way out of the kitchen, saying, "Oh, and officer? We're going to need that bear."

TWENTY

A Plan of Action

"YOU TWO NEED A DOCTOR," Simon said, taking his eyes off the road briefly to glance anxiously from Will—who was in the passenger seat of the Elantra—to Brandt—who was passed out in the back seat, now stained with crimson blotches and streaks. Simon shook his head as he focused on the lonely stretch of highway in front of him. "So much blood," he muttered.

"I'm alright," said Will, despite wincing with every jolt of the car. "I think he's much worse than me."

"You may be right," Simon replied. "He's as tough as they come, but there's no sense in taking stupid chances. He just never learned that. When we get into Boston, we're going to have to give some real consideration to taking him to a hospital regardless of any objections he may have."

"How long have you known him for?" Will asked, sensing from Simon's demeanor that he might be more amenable to questioning than Brandt was.

"Oh, quite a number of years now."

"Are you friends?"

The tone with which Will had said 'friends' made Simon

grin. It implied that he did not see someone like Brandt as capable of having friends, which Simon found rather perceptive. "No, we're not friends. Not exactly."

"You worked with him too, didn't you?" Will pressed. "Did you work for the Collective? Or do you now?"

Simon gave a slight nod. "I did. I certainly do not anymore, but that is how Brandt and I first crossed paths. You know," he continued, "you're smarter than Brandt gave you credit for."

Not sure whether to be flattered or insulted, Will thanked Simon anyway. "You're the person that he called during dinner the other day, I guess," Will said. "He must have told you about me then."

"Only a bit," Simon answered. "He wouldn't stay on the phone, especially since he thought that you were conspiring with the waitress." Simon chuckled. "I bet you were, weren't you?"

Will felt much more comfortable with Simon than with Brandt, but he knew enough to remain tight-lipped. "Maybe. Either way, nothing came of it."

"Fair enough," said Simon with a knowing look. "So what has Brandt told you so far about this whole situation?"

"He told me that my real name is William Trammel, and that Desmond Duquesne had my family killed, because apparently I'm the only one in the world who can kill him."

"That's the gist of it," Simon said. "And he told you that he once worked for the Collective? I'm surprised you got that much out of him."

Will leaned forward to adjust the bandage Simon had wrapped around his leg. "It wasn't easy," he said. After a pause he added, "Can I ask you something?" When Simon nodded, he continued, "What you did back there…when you put the whammy on that girl, Candace…am I safe now?"

Simon pursed his lips and tapped his fingers on the steering wheel before answering, "You're safe *for* now." Not thrilled with this response, Will turned to gaze out the window, watching the glowing orange sun rise behind the line of evergreen trees that passed in a blur, indistinguishable from one another. "I'm sorry that I cannot give you a better answer, but Desmond Duquesne is a powerful man," Simon explained. "The one thing standing between him and true immortality is you. As you can imagine, someone who fears death like he does will stop at nothing to remove any and all obstacles from his path."

Will's gaze remained unmoved. "Do you fear death, Simon?" he asked.

"No," he answered in a voice no louder than a whisper. "If I did," he said with a forced, toothy smile, "I wouldn't be helping you."

NEARLY AN HOUR PASSED before another word was spoken. Brandt remained passed out, while Simon remained concerned that he would upset Will further. Truthfully, Simon was wishing that Will would fall asleep for the remainder of the car ride, but he was kept awake by both the throbbing pain in his calf and the constant stream of thoughts running through his head.

"Have you ever been to Boston before?" Simon asked as they reached the city limits.

"No," Will answered distantly.

"I think you'll like it," Simon said.

"You mean, once I finish killing whoever you tell me to kill?" Simon had no response, and so continued heading east into the city, deftly maneuvering through the rush hour traffic. "I know that Duquesne wants me dead," Will said. "And I guess I kind of understand why, if all that you say is true. What about the Collective? Should I be worried about them?"

"I don't see why you should be."

"Brandt seems to hate them. I guess Brandt just hates everyone but you, huh?"

"Even that's debatable," Simon responded. "As for the Collective, you'd be doing them a favor if you were to kill Duquesne. There's certainly no love lost there. The Collective has been aching to stop Duquesne for a long time now. They just lack the means."

"The means being me," Will suggested.

"Exactly."

"Are they government?" Will asked.

"They are—just not any branch that you've ever heard of."

"So why am I not working with them? Can't they provide me better protection? Wouldn't they be able to train me better? How come I've been recruited by the world's douchiest Dumbledore and not by the government?"

"Because Brandt got to you first, and frankly, their methods are often just as questionable as ours. In Brandt's words, the Collective is a group of—"

"Shady bastards," Brandt muttered from the backseat.

"Glad to see you're still with us," said Simon. "How're you feeling?"

"Like shit."

"Well, we're bringing you to a doctor," Simon stated.

"Like hell you are," said Brandt, struggling to pull himself upright. "We're getting this over with. Do you have any idea where Duquesne is going to be today?"

"I do," said Simon with a note of hesitance.

"Then we're going there. I just need to get freshened up."

Simon pulled over in front of a Hyatt, parked the car, and turned to face Brandt. "Freshened up? You're insane. You need to get *sewn* up. You've got multiple gunshot wounds."

"I've had worse," Brandt rasped. "Besides, the taxpayers will fix me up once I'm arrested for killing Duquesne." He looked out the window and squinted as the sun shone off the hotel's arched metal entranceway. "This place will do fine. Let's get checked in."

. . .

CHECKING in wasn't as easy as Brandt made it sound, since Simon was first required to stop at a clothing store across the street to purchase two cheap, black T-shirts and two coats long enough to hide both of his passengers' injuries. The shirtless Will slipped his T-shirt on right away, but for the injured Brandt the change to fresh clothing took a bit longer. Seeing Brandt struggle with his bloody shoulder injury triggered enough guilt for Will to offer to lend a hand. Brandt adamantly refused, though, and was able to remove his torn shirt amid a series of painful winces. With Brandt about to don the new T-shirt, Will could not help but notice that the man's back was blanketed with red, potholed flesh. At first, it looked as though Brandt had been dragged behind a truck, but Will had skimmed through enough of his father's medical books to recognize the wounds as burns. "Oh my God," said Will. "When did that happen? Are you alright?"

Unaware of what Will was referring to at first, Brandt caught the boy trying to peer around his back and worked through the shoulder pain to quickly cover-up. "It's nothing. Old injury. I'm fine."

"Don't worry about it," said Simon. "Let's go."

Will clenched his jaw as he stepped out onto the sidewalk, placing as little weight as possible on his right leg. He and Brandt limped in ahead of Simon amid curious stares from passersby. Simon tried his best to pass off their hobbled gaits, shrugging nonchalantly and saying, "Long ride." Once through the revolving glass door, Will watched intently as Simon spoke to the desk clerk, who, while insisting at first that there were no rooms, soon wore the same glazed look that Candace had only hours before. In no time at all, they were on the elevator heading to their room.

Once inside the small room with two double beds and three

bland paintings of red cubes, Brandt ducked immediately into the bathroom with a sewing kit that Simon had bought in the hotel gift shop to "fix himself up." Will, relieved to sit again, kept looking at his own leg to see whether blood was seeping out from beneath the bandage. Not yet. He peered around the room and addressed Simon. "You can make people do anything you want them to do. Why a crappy room with double beds? Why not a suite?"

Simon sighed. "It's bad enough that I had to do that to the poor girl. I wasn't about to make her lose her job over it." He sat next to Will and placed a paternal hand on his shoulder. "You're going to learn very soon that you are extraordinarily special. And I don't mean that in an 'everyone's special' way. I mean that you, William Kendrick, have incredible talents and abilities…abilities that very few other people in the world have. This does not make you better than them or more deserving than them. If nothing else, remember that every action has a consequence not just for you, but for everyone around you. Take these consequences into account before you revel in your gifts."

Will listened attentively as Simon spoke, and when he had finished, asked, "What happened?"

"What happened with what?" Simon responded.

"Something happened to you," said Will. "Every time that you talk about your abilities, you seem—I don't know—sad."

Simon removed his hand from Will's shoulder and sat with his head down and hands folded. "Like I said, you're smarter than Brandt gives you credit for. Yes, something happened. When I was your age, and I had just discovered that I could basically control anyone around me, I thought that it was the greatest thing in the world. Who wouldn't? I later found, though, that not only was I taking advantage of others, but others were taking advantage of me." He paused, considering whether to continue his train of thought. "Desmond Duquesne was one of those people. Like I said, he's a powerful man, and he has his own ways of making people do what he wants them to do. In a way, you and I are alike. Because of Desmond Duquesne, I lost my family as well."

"He had them killed?" Will asked, noting the tears beginning to well in Simon's eyes.

"No," said Simon, "but I know that I'll never see them again. I will never forgive him for what he did, and what he made me do. And because of this, because I was used, I refuse to use or manipulate others unless it is in the service of stopping Duquesne."

"But what about the hotel clerk?"

"I used my abilities on her as a last resort, and I did so for you and for Brandt. That was not for personal gain or pleasure."

"I see," said Will, and though questions remained, he opted to save them for another time. He turned on a local morning talk show and watched indifferently as he and Simon waited for Brandt to emerge from the bathroom.

It took nearly an hour, but Brandt eventually limped over to the television and unceremoniously turned it off. "We need a plan of action," he said to Simon. "Where will Duquesne be today?"

"At noon, he'll be at a ribbon-cutting for a new park that he funded down by the harbor. From what I know, he's scheduled to give a brief speech and then cut the ribbon. The problem is that the mayor will be there, as will several other high-ranking officials. This means, of course, that getting close to the stage with a weapon will not be possible. On the other hand, you don't want anyone to see that the shooter is William, so that works out." Brandt nodded as Simon continued. "There is an apartment building on Grant that would give him an excellent shot if we can get into the right unit."

"That's where you come in," Brandt said.

"Of course. I get us in, William takes the shot, I get him out of there, and you stay to take the fall. By now, Duquesne should believe both you and William to be deceased so his personal security should be a bit lighter than it would have been only yesterday."

"What about a weapon?" Brandt asked.

"I have a rifle in the car."

"Will, you haven't fired a rifle before," Brandt said. "We didn't get to that, but I'll line up the shot. All that you need to do is pull the trigger, understand?"

Will nodded but could think of nothing else to contribute otherwise. He felt a numbness coming over him, a sense that despite what had allegedly been done to the Trammells, and to Simon's family, he would not be able to pull the trigger when the time came.

TWENTY-ONE

The Box

AGENT DONOVAN IGNORED the turning heads as he sped through the streets of the Beacon Hill section of Boston. Agent Whitworth, on the other hand, gave friendly waves and pleasant smiles to the passersby who strolled the cobblestone sidewalks lined with beautiful brownstone shops and town-homes. She gave the impression of someone completely unaware of the large, bloodied bear sticking out of the trunk, bouncing on the old stones of Charles Street and held in place with only a sundry collection of bungee cables. This act continued until they reached the imposing gray structure now known as the Stonegate Hotel.

Once a prison, the building had been renovated into a five-star hotel in the most affluent area of Boston. They passed by the curved front façade and continued down the block, hanging a left and driving through a narrow alleyway behind the hotel. Beyond the alley was a large loading zone. Instead of heading for the loading bay doors, Donovan steered toward a boxy metal shipping crate against the far wall. With the press of a button on the steering wheel, the container swung open, revealing ample room for the car. They drove into the box, and as the door closed shut behind them, leaving them in darkness, Ratchford, cuffed in the backseat, grumbled, "Home again, home again."

"Jiggity jig," Whitworth added cheerily, and the car lurched slightly as the hum of hydraulic lifts began to echo through the chamber. Whitworth and Donovan did not typically enter their headquarters by means of the freight elevator but thought it more prudent than walking a dead bear and an angry captive through the busy lobby of a luxury hotel. This entrance tended to draw slightly less attention. After a slow descent, the lift settled in a standard parking garage filled mainly with black sedans like the one Donovan drove. The three walked silently through the garage, save for the echoes of their footsteps, until they reached a set of tall metal doors, next to which was a keypad. Whitworth turned to her partner at this point and said, "Would you handle this? I always forget these silly codes. They change so often."

Donovan nodded dutifully and pressed a few of the numbered buttons. Another panel opened, and Donovan submitted himself to the retinal scan. A flat square light above the doors turned from red to green, and the entryway opened with a quiet whirr. Once in the sterile, white room on the other side of the doors, Donovan swiped a keycard calling for yet another elevator to take them further below the Stonegate. "Mr. Donovan," said Whitworth, "would you kindly take this gentleman back to his cell? In the meantime, I'll head to my office. You can meet me there when you're finished."

"No problem," said Donovan, glaring at Steampunk. "I'll take good care of Mr. Ratchford here."

"I'm sure you will." Whitworth smiled and stepped out at her floor, leaving Donovan and Ratchford to continue their descent to the structure's bottommost level.

Whitworth, as a senior member of the Collective, had long ago been granted certain permissions to decorate her office in whatever way she chose. So, when she reached the end of a long, drab hallway and passed through the door labeled with her name, it looked as though she had entered the office of a museum curator. The walls, where not covered with original artwork, were lined with shelves, which were in turn filled with books, globes, abstract sculptures, and the occasional signed baseball enclosed in a glass case. Scattered among these items were anthropological curiosities: small skulls and skeletons belonging to creatures rarely seen in the wild, be they dead or alive. Whitworth felt that everything in the room reflected her history and personality—everything except for the unfamiliar music flowing from Peg's computer.

Whitworth turned to the left to see Peg, a gray-haired woman in her late seventies, bobbing her head with the beat as she typed away. "Hello, Peg," said Whitworth. "What is this music?"

"Alice Cooper," she responded, as though such a question hardly warranted a response. "You want me to put Sinatra on?"

"No, no, that's alright," Whitworth answered. "I could come to like this."

"Good," she said. "Now, Valentine wants a report on the William Trammell situation. Also, that package is on your desk."

"A late Christmas gift? Or an early one?" Whitworth asked rhetorically. She looked to see a plain brown box sealed with generous amounts of packing tape and marked simply with Whitworth's name and the word 'urgent.' "Peg," she said as she walked to her desk, "could you phone for someone to retrieve something from my car?"

She picked up the phone. "What is it?"

"Dead bear," Whitworth said.

She looked incredulously over her glasses. "Another item for your collection?"

"At some point," Whitworth said. "But first we need to examine it."

With that business out of the way, she took the package in hand and turned it to look for any hint of the sender. When she couldn't find one, she closed her eyes and concentrated, attempting to trace the path that the package took en route to her office, but she was unable to glean anything. With growing concern, she grabbed a silver letter opener from the top drawer of her desk and carefully sliced through the tape at the top of the package. She opened it, sending packing peanuts flying to the floor—much to Peg's dismay—and took a step back in shock. Resting in the center of the remaining peanuts was a woman's head, covered with long, black, straggly hair. The eyelids had been sewn shut, as had the mouth—at least, at one point it had. The decomposition process was well underway, and bits of the bluish flesh were missing to the point that the sewn-together lips were rendered moot by the exposure of decayed, crooked teeth lining the side of the face. One tooth fell out as Whitworth lifted the head from the box.

Peg stared at the head from across the room. "Looks like you were on Santa's naughty list this year."

Whitworth ignored Peg's quip, instead closing her eyes and concentrating. Peg, knowing that this process required silence, looked on without saying another word for several moments, until Whitworth's eyelids sprung open and she dropped the head unceremoniously onto her desk. "Peg, please page Mr. Donovan," she said with urgency as she ran to the door.

"Something wrong?"

"Yes. Tell him to meet me in the garage immediately and tell him to bring Hex."

"What about the boss? He wanted to meet with you for a report…"

"He'll have to wait," Whitworth said. "The game just changed. I need to go stop William Trammell from killing Desmond Duquesne."

TWENTY-TWO

Triggers

WILL'S LEG HURT. It was burning, and Will feared that he might have an infection despite the rudimentary care that Simon had provided in Memorytown. Perhaps the worst part about his injury though, was how much it reminded him that all he wanted to do was go home. His father would have been able to fix up an injury like this in no time, but now he did not know if he would ever see his father or mother again. He kept his head down during the short ride from the Hyatt to Boston Harbor, where Desmond Duquesne, among many others, was scheduled to be arriving shortly. Soon, he would be expected to kill this Duquesne person, a person whom he had never met. While he knew that Brandt and Simon expected him to share their hatred for the man, and while Duquesne *had* had his birth parents killed and recently sent a pack of lunatics after him, Will could not muster up the righteous indignation that would be necessary to shoot a man.

Will had killed a man yesterday, and although it did not strike him in the heat of the moment, the reality of the situation hit him when he had heard Simon mutter "so much blood." Will looked at the blood that had seeped through the bandage on his own leg. Then he thought back to the bloodied branch that had jutted from Stalker's chest as he sunk into the mire. He thought of the waitress, the bartender, and the rest who had been murdered so cavalierly by Candace. What would it look like when the bullet passed through Duquesne's head? Would this be the new image to haunt Will's dreams? So much blood...

Simon parked the car on a quiet street a few blocks from the water and led his two companions to a towering apartment complex that stood opposite the New England Aquarium and overlooked the harbor. Simon spoke for a moment to an impeccably-dressed doorman, asking him which unit would give the best view of the new park and its dedication ceremony. With the same glazed look that Will had seen before, the doorman answered, "Probably 6A, 7A, or 8A," and allowed the trio entrance to the building.

While Simon and Brandt consulted, Will intentionally stayed out of the discussion, having chosen to remove himself as much as possible from the murderous plot and the obvious enjoyment that was beginning to overcome Brandt as he felt Duquesne's hour of judgment approaching. Brandt was not exactly giddy; Will doubted that he ever had been. However, there was a glint in his eye as he cradled the rifle case with his good arm that showed how long he had waited for this moment.

The three stepped off the elevator and approached a door designated '6A' in polished brass characters. Simon knocked, and in a moment, the door was answered by a woman in her early thirties, dressed in the attire of a business professional. "Can I help you?" she asked, glancing nervously from one strange face to another.

"I'd like you to please let us in," said Simon. Will noted the placid, creepily-calm way in which Simon delivered his request and shuddered. He felt the influence, and if he had owned the condo, would most certainly have been compelled to let them in. The woman was similarly little match for Simon's power of persuasion, and without saying another word, she opened the door wide for them to enter and closed it once they had.

"We got lucky," said Brandt, checking out the sparse, modern apartment. "It looks like she lives alone."

"Tell me," Simon said to the woman, "do you live alone?"

"I do."

Simon smiled. "Excellent. Now, please go to your bedroom, close the door, and take a nap." The woman did so almost naturally but there was still something drone-like about her vacant expression as she walked into her bedroom.

Brandt, in the meantime, had opened a window and was checking out the view. "Are we okay?" Simon asked. Brandt looked down at the crowd beginning to gather near the beautifully landscaped parcel of land that would soon be dedicated the Desmond Duquesne, Sr. Memorial Park. There was a makeshift stage set up and a local cover band was completing their sound checks.

"This will do nicely," Brandt said, and he began to assemble Will's rifle.

EMIL HAVELOCK YAWNED. Today was going to be uneventful. In fact, with the kid out of the way, there was really no need for him to even attend the park's dedication, but one could never be too careful, and besides, work was work. If Duquesne felt like paying for security, why the hell would Havelock say no?

He leaned back against a bike rack and took out a cigarette as he watched Ridgley pull up with the family in a black Lexus. He gave an obligatory, uninterested wave and lit up. A crowd had started to gather, most of whom had had no prior knowledge of this event, but simply saw a stage, a band, and a bunch of fancy cars, so figured that something interesting must be happening. Most of the attendees were parents with young children, either out for a day at the new park or heading to surrounding attractions like the aquarium. He tried to suppress a scowl as loud, obnoxious children ran in circles around the bike rack, fighting the urge to trip them as they got close. "Brats," he muttered.

Bored, Havelock took out his phone to check for missed messages but, as he already knew, there were none. Before he could place the phone back in his pocket, it vibrated. When he checked out the text, his scowl deepened: "Kid still alive. Heading to Boston."

Duquesne and his family were now filing out of the car to a conservative round of applause, so it was too late for a change of plans without raising alarm. Still, if the kid *was* alive, he'd be here. Havelock could feel it. Eager not to leave anything up to chance, he quickly dialed one of the more recent numbers in his call log and in a moment, Candace picked up.

"You haven't come for your money," Havelock said, trying to remain calm.

"What money?" she asked. "Who is this?"

"It's Havelock," he growled. "Why haven't you come for your money? Is the kid dead or not?"

"What kid?"

Havelock hung up and threw his cigarette butt on the ground. "Shit," he said, frightening one of the unattended children back to her mother.

"WHAT DO you mean we've got to stop him from killing Duquesne?" Donovan asked as he arrived back in the garage holding a small pet carrier. Whitworth opened the barred door and removed a wiry black cat from the carrier. She petted her gently as she carried her, purring, over to the bear that had not yet been removed from the trunk of the sedan.

"It's time for you to work your magic, Hex," Whitworth said softly. She held the cat close to the bear's bloodied paw and urged her to take a sniff. She recoiled at first but realizing that she was dealing with an inanimate object, eventually took a few sniffs and then turned up her nose, seemingly bored. "Got it," said Whitworth. "Let's go."

The older agent hopped into the passenger seat of a different, clean sedan, while Donovan again took the wheel. "Again, why the sudden change? All that I've heard for years is that Duquesne's a danger, that he has to go, and that this kid is the only one who can make that happen. Isn't that what the prophecy says?"

"It is," said Whitworth, struggling to buckle up with Hex kneading her lap and Donovan screeching around the bend of the parking garage. Sensing that Donovan required a more developed answer, but still trying to process the new information herself, Whitworth simply added, "Let's just say that things just got much more complicated, and that, for the time being at least, it is imperative that we keep both William Trammell and Desmond Duquesne alive."

IT TOOK a few minutes for Brandt to set up the rifle and adjust the scope to his satisfaction, but once this was finished, he called Will over to the window and directed him to put his eye to the sniper scope. Will did so and immediately developed a queasy feeling as he saw the crosshairs focused on the face of the man currently standing at the podium. He had played video games that required the player to stealthily kill a target in a similar manner, but this was different. In a matter of seconds, he realized that he'd never play one of those games again.

"How does it look?" asked Brandt.

"Um, good," Will muttered. Will watched as the man at the podium motioned toward Desmond Duquesne, and he moved the scope ever so slightly to see a magnified view of his target. Duquesne stepped onto the stage with the vitality of a much younger man. He waved enthusiastically at a small group of people, beckoning for them to join him on the scaffold. Recalling the photo that Brandt had shown him a few days earlier, Will recognized the middle-aged, dark-haired woman as Joanna Duquesne. Behind her was a man in his early twenties, waving and posturing to the modest crowd as though he were an A-list celebrity. "Who is that?" Will asked aloud.

"Did you move the gun?" Brandt responded in a frustrated tone.

Ignoring his partner, Simon peered through the window next to Will's and answered, "Ah. That's Alexander Duquesne—Desmond and Joanna's son. From what I hear, he's a first-rate ass."

Will nodded, immediately agreeing with Simon's assessment. He wouldn't focus on Alexander for long, though, as he was soon gently moved aside by a young girl whom Will assumed was roughly his own age. "Is that Duquesne's daughter?" Will asked in amazement.

"Yes, sir," Simon responded. "Daphne Duquesne."

Daphne modestly, but confidently, smiled to the crowd that was politely applauding the appearance of the entire family. The ocean breeze at first caused Will's view of her face to be obscured, but when, in a soft fluid motion, she moved her silky brown hair aside, he saw that she was easily the most stunning girl he had ever seen. She whispered something to her mother, who gave her a knowing look and placed an arm lovingly around her shoulders. Will sat transfixed, watching her inviting pink lips give way to a luminous, genuine smile.

"Are you *sure* that's his daughter?" Will asked again, for the first time forgetting his reason for being perched with a gun in a stranger's window.

Simon, who had been watching Will intently as he gazed at Daphne, nodded. "Beautiful, isn't she?"

Realizing that he had given himself away, an embarrassed Will did not answer, but tried to neutralize his awestruck expression. He remained so distracted by this new development that he was startled when Brandt practically shoved him out of the way to readjust the scope. "Now don't move this again," he said when he had finished. "It's all set. When Duquesne is at the podium, take him out."

Will nodded but could now only think of how Daphne Duquesne's grace and composure would be destroyed with the tug of a trigger.

"I'M BREAKING my own rule here, you know," said Whitworth as Donovan parked the car as close as he could to the harbor. The elder agent slipped a collar around Hex's neck and flicked a switch on the small camera harnessed to it. "I hate to mix magic and technology, but I guess I'll need to make an exception this time."

"I don't see any other way," said Donovan. "If we're going to stop the Trammell kid from killing Duquesne, she might be our only hope. You sure a cat was the best choice, though? I mean, for sniffing someone out, shouldn't we be using a dog?"

"If we were sniffing out drugs, yes. But if you want to find an exceptional individual, you've got to use exceptional means." Whitworth gingerly placed Hex onto the hood of the car. "You know what to do, girl. Go. Find him." The cat stretched lazily, and as she did so, the black fur on her back parted in two spots. From these slits grew a pair of leathery wings, and the feline's eyes began to give off a violet glow. Hex took a few quiet steps across the hood of the car and then leapt, flapped her powerful wings and lifted off to the amazement of a group of children who had been running to the new park but now stopped to gape in silence at the impossible creature.

EMIL HAVELOCK, who did not have access to a flying cat, had to make do with his binoculars, but he managed. Knowing that Brandt would want a high vantage point, he scanned every window of two apartment buildings and a hotel before spotting the rifle set up on the ledge of unit 6A. He was off like a shot, too focused on his quarry to notice Hex as she glided overhead.

WILL COULD HEAR the smooth tenor of Desmond Duquesne's voice as he spoke into the microphone, opening his dedication to the park. He began by greeting and thanking several dignitaries, including various city councilmen, with whom he now shared the stage. He went on to thank his family and then repeated the word, "Family." He looked over the crowd of families assembled before him and smiled. "This revitalized park will become a place for your families to gather for generations to come, and you kids will be very lucky to say that you were here when it all began!"

"What are you waiting for?" asked Brandt. "Take your shot."

Will did not answer but continued listening. "I see many children here with their parents today. Do you know," he said, addressing the children in the audience, "that this great new park is dedicated to *my* father? He was a great man, and I know exactly what he would say if he were standing before you today. He would say that family is the most important thing in the world—more important than money, more important than fame. Always remember that, kids. I've been very successful in my life, but I would be nowhere if it were not for my father, or my wonderful wife and children who you see here on this stage today."

"What a crock of shit," said Simon, taking Will off guard with his intense anger.

"He seems to love his family," said Will.

"He *seems* to do a lot of things," Simon replied.

"If I shoot him," asked Will, removing his eye from the scope, "how am I any better than him? He destroyed my family, so I destroy his? Right in front of them? This is wrong."

Brandt stepped forward, pushing Simon aside. "I've waited too long for this. You need to kill this man, whether you want to or not," he growled. "Now get to it." He grabbed Will's head and forcefully turned it back toward the window. Will looked once more through the scope and returned his quavering finger to the rifle's trigger.

"I'M GETTING DIZZY," said Agent Donovan as he watched the images on the dashboard monitor. The glares of windows and the green blurs of trees whooshed by as Hex's collar-mounted camera chronicled her reconnaissance mission. Whitworth could relate, as she had already made the decision to look away, trusting Donovan's trained eye to pick up on anything of interest in the footage. She frowned as she watched Desmond Duquesne orate, almost glad that she could only make out a hushed, garbled version of what was being spoken on stage.

"Got them!" Donovan shouted as the image held steady on the open window of 6A.

"Excellent," said Whitworth, stepping nimbly out of the car. "Your knees are better than mine. Go on ahead. I'll catch up."

Donovan nodded and made a dash for the building that housed 6A.

. . .

WILL RESUMED LISTENING TO DUQUESNE, and though he had missed some of the speech while confronted by Simon and Brandt, he returned his attention in time to hear, "And so, with that idea in mind, I stand here today not only to dedicate this beautiful park to the memory of my father, but also to announce the development of a multimillion dollar youth center to be erected only five blocks from here, so that the children and young adults of this city may have a new, clean—and most importantly—*safe* facility in which to learn, play, and grow."

"Jesus," said Will as the applause erupted. "The guy is building a youth center."

"He's pandering to the crowd," said Simon.

"I don't care." Will stood and turned his back to the window. "I can't do this. This is too much for me."

"Goddamn it," Brandt fumed. "You can and you will."

"William," said Simon in a more measured tone, "you've come all this way. You need to do this." He paused to consider whether to continue, but eventually did. "You know that I can make you do it, William, if I absolutely have to."

"Don't get into my head, Simon," Will warned, tempted to turn the rifle on him but knowing that Brandt would disarm him in no time at all.

"If he's not going to do this willingly," Brandt argued, "then by all means tell him to. Think of your family, Simon."

Simon shot an icy glare in Brandt's direction before turning his attention back to Will. "William, I need you to—oh no..."

Will noticed that something had caught Simon's eye and crouched to look out the window. His eyes went wide. "Is...is that a flying cat?"

"Hex," Simon stated, looking to Brandt for instruction on what to do next.

At the mention of the creature's name, Brandt's face fell. He slumped back against the wall, looking utterly defeated, until he suddenly slammed his fist against the adjoining wall. While he failed to punch through the wall, he did let out a yowl from the exacerbation of his shoulder wound.

"What does this mean?" asked Will. "What does a flying cat mean?"

Before either Simon or Brandt could answer, another voice from the door of the apartment said, "I guess it means I'd better kill you quickly." All three sets of eyes now focused on Emil Havelock. The killer exuded a quiet menace as his gaze moved from one to another, but his silenced handgun remained steadily aimed at Brandt. "Is it just the three of you?"

The trio remained silent until Simon said, "Yes. It's just us."

Havelock shook his head. "You're a bad liar." He glanced quickly into the bedroom and "Now I'm gonna have to do her too. I hope you're happy." He moved cautiously to the door of the bedroom, pushed it open, and saw the young woman lying in bed, her back to him. Havelock stood against the door jamb for a moment, looking annoyed and trying to figure the best way to quickly dispose of the quartet.

"If you're going to kill us, you'd better do it," said a visibly exhausted Brandt.

"Shut up," Havelock retorted. "And you," he said, pointing to Simon, "not another word out of you especially. Now all of you get in here. C'mon. Into the bedroom." The three silently passed Havelock on their way into the bedroom, Will and Simon too intimidated to put up a fight, Brandt too worn down from the events of the past few days. When they were inside, Havelock took a bottle of vodka from a small liquor cart in the woman's living room, uncapped it, and began pouring it on the floor near the bedroom door. When the bottle was empty, he threw it onto the floor behind him and removed the lighter from his pocket. "Good night, kids," he said flatly, and let the small flame fall into the puddle of alcohol. The flames changed from purple to brilliant orange as they spread across the threshold of the room.

"So what now? You want to tell those flames to stop spreading?" Will asked Simon hysterically.

"Let's not panic," Simon answered. He moved to the bedroom window and opened it, but, looking out, found that a fire escape was nowhere in sight. The closest platform was the balcony extending from the kitchen at least ten feet away. Brandt, in the meantime, pulled the covers out from under the sleeping woman, sending her tumbling to the floor. Will, appalled at Brandt's disregard for another person, ran to the bedside to check on her, but found that she was still sleeping soundly under Simon's suggestion. When he got back to his feet, he saw that Havelock's silhouette had removed itself from the doorway, and there was now another man in its place, also holding a gun. As Brandt attempted to tamp down the flames, Will could barely hear Havelock say, "What the hell are you doing—" before a pair of gunshots silenced him. The new silhouette disappeared momentarily, but Agent Donovan soon entered the room with a running leap.

"Cover yourself and run," he urged, handing the woman's top sheet to Will. Donovan, paying no mind to either Simon or Brandt, removed the fitted sheet from the woman's bed, did his best to wrap her in it, and ran as fast as he could, following Will through the door and into the slightly less smoky living room. "Keep going," said Donovan. "Into the hall."

Will gladly did as he was told and ran into the hallway, knowing that he shouldn't use an elevator in a fire, but unsure of where the stairs were. He searched frantically for the metal doors until, turning a corner, he ran headlong into an older woman in a raincoat. "I'm sorry," said Will, "but there's a fire. Apartment 6A."

"Oh dear," said the plump woman without too much

concern. "That's not good. Let me go see to that. Will you watch my cat?"

Will now saw the black, winged cat gliding placidly down the hallway toward him. It didn't seem to want to stop, so Will instinctively held out his hands, allowing the creature to fly right into them. Once it did, the bat-like wings retracted, and to his amazement, Will stood holding a purring cat that had come to rest gently in his arms. "What is going on?" Will asked himself quietly.

As the stranger strolled toward the flaming apartment, she called back, "Strange days, William. Strange days!"

Chaos broke out within moments once the smoke that billowed from 6A hit the smoke detectors of the communal hallway. Residents of all ages pushed past a confused Will as he held the cat close to his chest, trying to keep it from being elbowed by the panicked apartment dwellers. When the sprinklers finally sprang into action, he stood beneath the fronds of a large fake elephant palm, futilely attempting to keep the old woman's cat dry, but it did not seem to mind the sudden shower as much as most felines he'd come across.

The residents of the sixth floor had all disappeared into the stairwell by the time Will spotted a worse-for-wear Simon walking toward him. He was followed by a limping Brandt and the scowling man who had shot Havelock. The entire group wore soaked, singed clothes, except for the woman, who brought up the rear and was perfectly dry thanks to a compact umbrella that she had taken from her coat pocket.

"What happened to Havelock?" Will asked. "And what about the woman in the apartment?"

"Mr. Havelock got away," Whitworth responded, "but the woman is safe. And now, so are you, William. Let's get you cleaned up."

· · ·

DESMOND DUQUESNE HAD NEARLY FINISHED his speech when he heard a series of gasps and noticed that he was losing the crowd. As the sound of a fire engine neared and event organizers hurried to clear the streets for emergency officials, the flames from apartment 6A reflected in the steely gaze of Duquesne's eyes.

TWENTY-THREE

The Collective

WILL SAT WEDGED between Simon and Brandt in the backseat of Donovan's car, the cat, Hex, curled up and purring on his lap. He didn't know quite what to make of the little woman sitting in the passenger seat, but the man driving seemed to be all business, which was reassuring in a way. Although the agent he now knew as Whitworth had assured him they wouldn't be harmed, she had been cryptic regarding where they were being taken. Still, Will sensed a legitimacy about these two, and since they had identified themselves as government agents, he felt in much better hands than he had been over the course of the last few days.

Despite the reservations that Brandt had expressed about his former partner, Agent Whitworth seemed entirely pleasant and forthright, if a bit odd. In fact, the tension in the car stemmed less from the reunion of Brandt and Whitworth and more from the dynamic between Brandt and Donovan. The latter raised an eyebrow as he peered at Brandt in the rearview mirror. "Never thought we'd see you again," he sneered. "You're like a gnat, you know that?"

Brandt, who had been silent until that point, turned his gaze to meet the reflection of Donovan's and answered, "You remind me of a few things yourself, kid. You know when you go into a gas station restroom, look in the crapper, and see——"

"Now, now, Mr. Brandt," said Whitworth, waving a disapproving finger. "Although I'm sure that we're all interested in knowing where your imagery was going to end up, perhaps that's a discussion best finished at another time. Things are far too tense right now. There's no sense in exacerbating the situation. Am I right, Mr. Donovan?"

The younger agent pursed his lips and nodded. Will could see him almost literally swallow his anger. Brandt turned back to his window, refusing to say more, and Whitworth, with a quick friendly wink to Will, turned her attention back to the streets as well. Will looked to his left to see what Simon's take on the brief exchange was, but he remained as he had been since they were ushered into the vehicle—silently staring at his own feet. Instinctively, Will began shaking his leg, but winced as a sudden pain reminded him of his hastily-treated wound that was probably all kinds of infected by now. He threw his head back and sighed, prompting Whitworth to pivot once more and ask, "Is everything alright, William?"

"Honestly? No," he responded, surprised at his own candor. "In the past few days, I've been drugged, kidnapped, shot at, and attacked by a zombie bear. Oh, and now I'm sitting here in a car with what's basically a bunch of strangers who apparently hate each other, being driven who knows where, and I'm holding a flying cat." At this, Hex looked up with an indignant expression.

"I can see how that might be troubling for you," said Whitworth.

"Can you?" Will retorted. "If so, can we at least talk about what's happening here? Some form of dialogue would be great."

Whitworth nodded. "We most certainly can. But not now. We're here." As she said this, the car once again entered the metal container behind the Stonegate Hotel, and with a loud slam, everything went dark. Unfazed, Whitworth's voice pierced the darkness. "Everything will be fine, and if you just give us a chance, I think that I can prove that. In fact, bear with me for today, and by tonight I'm going to have quite a surprise for you."

Will's recent circumstances had taught him to distrust surprises, but he did not argue. Instead, he simply listened to the hydraulics of the lift as it lowered them into the parking garage and thanked God when the lights came on that no one had killed each other in the meantime.

For the second time that day, Agent Whitworth passed through the two sets of whooshing metal doors and into the heart of the Collective's headquarters, this time followed by the small motley contingent. Will, the only one of the crew who had never set foot in the space before, took in the sights as he moved toward the center of the room, limping from the gradually increasing pain in his leg. The room, he was surprised to see, was vast but markedly empty. The Gothic architecture reminded him of Grand Central Terminal, which he had visited during a trip to New York with his father. He was amazed that such high ceilings were possible in a subterranean room and noted the intricate mosaic that hung above his head. The design on the ceiling depicted a large, luminous star—what looked like the North Star—set on a backdrop of midnight blue. Around the edges lurked black tiles, creating the appearance of a darkness being dispelled by the star...or encroaching upon it—Will couldn't decide which interpretation was correct. Simple, standard wooden desks were scattered around the room, creating an open office space with no divisions. Above them, surrounding the perimeter, hung dozens of clocks, ticking loudly in an arrhythmic pattern. The final detail that Will noticed, set above the clocks but below the mosaic ceiling, was a collection of the most grotesque gargoyles he had ever seen. They were unlike any creatures that had ever walked the earth, and he could almost hear their teeth gnashing and their claws scratching at the stone walls of the Collective head-quarters, aching to escape.

"So what do you think?" Whitworth's question echoed through the cavernous space.

"It's impressive," said Will. "It's just…I don't know…quiet. I expected to see hundreds of secret agents hurrying into top secret meetings and playing with high-tech gadgets."

Agent Donovan chortled. "Here's the thing they don't show you in movies, kid: when the government has a top secret agency devoted to paranormal activity, they don't exactly break the bank to fund it. Not many taxpayer dollars are at work down here, especially since several of the country's higher-ups don't see a need for us at all."

"So here we are," said the deep voice of a man who was emerging from a gated elevator on the far side of the room. "One happy little skeleton crew." The man who walked toward them now was tall, bald, and dressed in a tailor-made pinstripe suit. Upon reaching Will, he held out his hand and grasped Will's firmly. "You must be Mr. Kendrick…or Trammell. Which do you prefer?" he asked with a broad, blindingly white smile.

"I think I'll stick with Kendrick for now. I'm still letting the new name settle in."

The man nodded and continued, "I'm Nathanial Valentine. I'm the director of this little operation. And it is a pleasure to finally meet you."

Will smiled back, and after what seemed like an eternity, the handshaking finally abated. When it did, Valentine turned his attention to Will's companions and welcomed them with slightly less enthusiasm. "Simon, Brandt," he said, "it's good to have you back. Almost like nothing has changed, huh?"

Simon, trying not to look annoyed at the entire situation, accepted a handshake from Valentine and gave a halfhearted smile. Brandt, on the other hand, was not capable of showing as much restraint. He ignored the Director's outstretched arm and said, "I didn't expect things to have changed. Your daddy's still in the senate, so you're still in charge." Valentine slowly lowered his hand and slid it into his pocket. "In fact," Brandt continued, "I knew that nothing here had changed as soon as I saw that this incompetent douchebag was still on the payroll." With this, he pointed a crooked finger at Donovan.

An irate Donovan lunged toward Brandt, but Valentine held him back with an arm across his agent's chest. The Director smiled again and replied, "Like I said, nothing's really changed. Now, Mr. Brandt, you are looking a bit worse for wear, as is our young friend here. I'd like to conference about why we're all here, but not with you looking like this. Let's get you fixed up. Perhaps you could humor me and take a trip to the lab. I'm sure that Dr. Feng and Dr. Creswell can get you back in fighting condition in no time."

"An excellent idea, Nate," said Whitworth. "Come on, Will. There are some doctors here that can make that leg of yours as good as new." The group moved toward the elevator, with the exception of Simon and Valentine. Still, Valentine called after Whitworth: "Fran! You may want to prep them for Feng's, well, you know…" Will saw the Director making a circular motion with his finger as he pointed to his own face.

Whitworth looked distressed as she pulled shut the old-fashioned elevator's metal gate, and Brandt, sensing his former partner's discomfort, asked, "What happened to Feng's face?"

"An accident," Whitworth answered. "There was an incident a few weeks ago. It's healing, but he nearly died from blood loss. When you see him, you'll notice that there's something wrong, but try not to let on."

"I'm sure he's taking that well," Brandt said with what Will detected as a hint of sarcasm.

"He's taking it as well as you'd expect him to. He's not exactly a ball of sunshine to begin with, so you know, we just try not to talk about it."

With a slight lurch, the elevator came to halt, and Whitworth opened the gate. She, Donovan, Brandt, and Will stepped out into a sterile environment that looked more like what Will had initially expected. The short hallway that led to the lab was simply comprised of two white walls and one polished white floor. The only color came from a red blur beyond the frosted glass doors of the laboratory. This undefined mass took on a surprising form when the doors swung open and Will found a young girl in a red dress scurrying excitedly toward them.

"So what exactly happened to Feng?" Brandt pressed on, ignoring the girl.

"Not now," Donovan answered under his breath.

Brandt shot another glare at his rival, but perhaps because of the child's presence, thought better of pursuing the line of questioning.

"Hello, my love!" said Whitworth warmly as the girl wrapped her arms affectionately around the agent's legs. "I feel like I haven't seen you in ages!"

"It's only been two days!" she said.

"Like I said—ages!" the older woman replied with kind smile.

Will could not help but smile at this himself. The girl was adorable in her little red dress with her dirty blonde hair pulled back into a ponytail. She looked at Whitworth with her big blues eyes the way Will used to look with admiration at his adoptive grandmother.

While it was odd to see a child walking the halls of a secret government facility, Will eventually put two and two together as he saw a large, jolly-looking man in a slightly rumpled suit follow the girl from the lab with a porcelain doll in his hand. Surely this man was her father, and Will had stumbled upon a bring-your-daughter-to-work type of scenario.

"And how's our little girl doing, Mr. Jensen?" Whitworth asked.

"Just fine, ma'am," the jolly man responded. "Passed her tests with flying colors again. But," he said, now addressing the young girl, "*someone* forgot Lilabeth…"

The girl grabbed the doll from Jensen's clutches and hugged her tight to her chest. "Thank you, Jenny," she said. "I can't believe I forgot her!"

"It's alright," said Jensen softly. "You've been tired."

It was then that Will noticed just how very tired the girl actually looked. Her enthusiasm belied an exhaustion evident in the deep, dark bags under her eyes—bags that he had only ever seen on individuals much older than her. All at once, he felt sympathy toward her, but he did not quite know why. Whitworth saw him gazing at the young girl and immediately moved to introduce them. "William Kendrick," she said, "meet Miss Rose Pryor."

The girl looked up at him shyly from behind her doll and smiled. Will crouched down to meet her at eye level and said, "It's nice to meet you, Miss Rose Pryor. And who is this?" he asked, pointing to her doll.

"Lilabeth," she said. Rose handed the doll to Will as a way of introducing them, and Will took the toy gently, touched that she would be willing to share such an important object with someone whom she had just met. The doll was in excellent condition but looked to be an antique. It certainly wasn't a soft, Cabbage Patch-type doll that a child would cuddle with. No, this reminded Will of a doll one might find on an old woman's mantlepiece, its old-fashioned dress and tightly-curled black hair evidence of a toy made generations before Rose's time. Will had never cared much for dolls like this, as they reminded him of props from a haunted house flick, and Lilabeth was no different. Something about the item disturbed him. It was something about the eyes. They seemed too real. He found himself momentarily transfixed by them until Rose interrupted with, "She goes everywhere with me." Taking the hint, he handed the doll back and stood up.

"And is this your father?" he asked, motioning to Jensen.

"No," said Rose. "That's Mr. Jensen. He takes care of me. I call him 'Jenny.'" She started chuckling at this and explained to Will, "It's funny because it's a girl's name."

"That *is* funny," Will laughed. He turned to shake Jensen's hand and said, "I'm sorry. I didn't know. I just assumed…"

"It's alright, Mr. Kendrick," said Jensen. "Anyone could make that mistake. I do look after Rose like she's my own daughter, so I don't mind the implication."

"She's very special to all of us," said Whitworth, patting her on the head. "But I'm afraid that we've got to cut this visit short. William and Mr. Brandt have to see the doctors, just like you did. I'll come visit soon, okay, Rose? We'll have tea."

"That's Lilabeth's favorite," she said. "Sounds good." With a little wave, she and Jensen were off, and Whitworth led his group through the glass doors and into the Collective's labs.

The main room into which they stepped was no more welcoming than the hallway leading to it. Now, though, instead of being surrounded by white institutional walls, they were surrounded by file cabinets, metallic tables, and walls lined with fully-stocked shelves that houses bottles of every shape, size, and color. A young woman in a white lab coat approached them immediately, shaking her head as she neared William. "What is this?" she said, bending down to get a closer look at his injured leg. "It looks like you were mauled by a bear."

Will grimaced. "Yeah..." he said. "About that..."

The woman looked up in surprise, first at Will and then at Whitworth. "You're kidding."

Whitworth shook her head. "'Fraid not," she said. "This is Dr. Angela Creswell, by the way, and now you see why we pay her the big bucks."

She smiled faintly. Removing her glasses from the pocket of her lab coat, she rested them on her nose, gave Will's leg another once-over, and said, "You're going to need stitches. You're lucky that this doesn't look infected. When did it happen?"

"Last night," Brandt interjected. "Around the same time that I was shot. But don't you worry your pretty little self about that."

Dr. Creswell rolled her eyes and, for the first time, looked at Brandt. "Rest assured, Mr. Brandt, I won't. You're a tough guy, right? You'll live."

Donovan snickered, and before Brandt could think of a response, another man entered the room, saying, "Perhaps Mr. Brandt is not as resilient as we remember him to be." This second doctor, whom Will assumed was Dr. Feng, spoke in a soft, almost whispered tone, as though he were in a busy library rather than an isolated laboratory several stories below the surface.

"Could be, Feng," Brandt responded, "but then, from what I hear, you may not be exactly as I remember you either." Whitworth slapped her forehead and turned away, mortified that Brandt had already brought up the one topic of conversation that was supposed to have been off-limits. Feng, on the other hand, stood silent. He remained wrapped in shadows at the far end of the lab for a moment, but then seemed to glide effortlessly forward into the fluorescent light, exposing his face to the crowd.

Will tried to hide his shock at the sight of this poor man

whose face had obviously undergone major reconstructive surgery. Along the left side of his face ran a series of staples and a wound, shiny from a medicated cream that Feng had evidently just applied. From far away there was a chance that the doctor would have looked just as healthy as anyone else, but up close, one could tell that something was amiss. Despite the fact that a large portion of his face had been reattached, it laid like a puzzle piece that did not quite fit.

"I have seen better days," Feng conceded. "Now, does this hurt?" He laid his gloved hand on Brandt's injured shoulder and squeezed, causing Brandt to wince and yelp in pain. "I'll take that as a yes."

Donovan couldn't hide his delight as Brandt glowered at the doctor, but Whitworth cut his entertainment short. "Doctors, we leave these patients in your capable hands. Please do your best to help them out. Drayton, when you are finished fixing Mr. Brandt up, could you both please meet us in the conference room?" Dr. Feng nodded, led Brandt into a small examination room and silently shut the door. "Angela, since you have a better bedside manner, I figured you would be best to take care of young Mr. Kendrick. Take your time, but when you're finished, perhaps you could escort him to my office?"

"Will do," she responded.

"Excellent," said Whitworth. "Come on, Mr. Donovan. Let's go make sure that our old friend Simon is behaving himself and isn't making any interesting 'suggestions' to the Director."

With Whitworth and Donovan gone, Dr. Creswell turned her full attention to Will, directed him into a separate examination room, and said, "The pants have to come off, Mr. Kendrick." Will instinctively blushed at being told this by an attractive young doctor. His primary physician from home was his own father. Still, she remained unflappable and added, "We're all friends here."

Will gingerly removed his torn jeans, hesitating a few times as the denim, feeling more like sandpaper, brushed against his raw wound. Once in his boxers, he sat on the table and picked up on Dr. Creswell's last remark. "It doesn't seem like we're *all* friends here. What's the deal with Brandt and Agent Donovan?"

As Creswell began to swab his wound, she sighed and answered, "That goes back a long way. The simple answer is that they just don't get along. They come from two very different backgrounds and schools of thought, and when Brandt left the Collective years ago, Donovan was one of the main reasons. Not *the* main reason, but still, it didn't help." She paused as she arranged her instruments on the table and soon resumed, "The tragedy is that both Brandt and Donovan are very good at what they do. If they could find a way to get along, Brandt's bull-in-a-china-shop mentality and Donovan's more methodical approach could beautifully complement each other. They're just both too stubborn to let it happen."

Will nodded in understanding. "So there's nothing more to it?"

"Oh, there's plenty more to it," Creswell smiled, "but nothing that I'm going to get into now."

"Fair enough," said Will. "So what about Rose? What did she mean when she said Jensen takes care of her?"

"Rose," she answered, "is an interesting case. In many ways, you're similar. Her parents worked with us, but they were killed several years ago when she was obviously quite young. She lives here now, and Agent Jensen has been assigned as her guardian. He and Dr. Feng, for lack of a better word, protect her."

"From what?"

"From herself," Creswell responded. "You see, Rose is also like you in that she has what Dr. Feng coined the Aberration. She has power. By the way, what's yours?" she asked nonchalantly, as though she were asking his address or his favorite food.

"From what I can tell, I have clairvoyant dreams. That's how I was first able to put together that my birth parents were the Trammells."

"Interesting. So again you fall into the same category as Rose...kind of."

"What do you mean? She also has those dreams?"

"No, not quite. When I said that you fall into the same category, I meant that you both had latent abilities that expressed themselves without you willing them to happen. Many magic users discover their abilities in a similar way, and it can be startling, so I must say that you're handling it quite well. The rest of the individuals who have the Aberration work to actively bring their abilities forward. They are able to choose a 'talent,' if you will, and work towards honing it, like an athlete works toward mastery of a particular sport."

"Right," said Will. "Brandt mentioned that. So what is Rose's talent?"

"Hers I wouldn't describe as a talent," Creswell said, her tone sounding quite a bit grimmer. "More like a curse. Rose's power comes from her dreams as well. In fact, she may be the most powerful magic user I've ever come across, including Frances Whitworth. William, when Rose dreams something, it comes true."

Will allowed that to sink in for a moment before blurting, "What?"

"That's why she needs to essentially live in a sleep lab. She's too dangerous to the outside world. Every night, Rose is given a series of drugs and hooked up to a number of devices that monitor her sleep patterns. We can't allow her to dream. Often the pills work, and they essentially render her unconscious. They place her in a peaceful, dreamless sleep. However, nothing is certain, and so Mr. Jensen will watch the monitor and wake the girl if her brainwaves indicate that dreams are occurring."

"Wow," said Will. "What a terrible way to live. What happens if Jensen misses his cue? Are a little girl's dreams really that destructive?"

"Like any dreams," Creswell answered, "they are wildly unpredictable. If she dreams about Candy Land, then great, we have a room full of gumdrops and caramel. If her dreams head more toward the nightmare realm... Let's just say that a nightmare for Rose is a nightmare for all of us. If you don't believe me, take a look at Dr. Feng's face."

AFTER TENDING to his bullet wound, Dr. Feng followed Brandt into the conference room, where Valentine, Whitworth, Donovan, and Simon had already gathered. They were in the midst of a heated discussion regarding whether the captured Steampunk would be better off remanded to a federal prison, or whether he posed enough risk to be kept in one of the Collective's own holding cells on the lower level. This discussion was promptly stopped by Valentine once the door to the conference room had been locked by Feng. As the doctor approached his seat next to Brandt, Valentine called the meeting to order.

"Alright, now that everyone's here, I'd like to get started. We've got a lot to sort out, and we had best be on the same page," he said.

"We'll see," Brandt muttered.

In response, Valentine continued, "Let's get one thing straight. There are clearly people in this room who do not get along. However, I think that we're all in agreement that Desmond Duquesne is a threat that must be neutralized. If this is going to happen, we have no choice but to work together, especially in light of new information that was delivered to Agent Whitworth's office earlier today."

"What new information?" Simon asked.

"I'll gladly share that with the room, Mr. Simon," said Whitworth, "but let's get everyone caught up first, since an already complicated situation has become even more so over the past several hours." The individuals around the table almost unanimously nodded in agreement, with the exception of Drayton Feng, who remained stoic. "As we all know, nearly two hundred years ago, a disagreement erupted between Desmond Duquesne and Roderick Gleave. As the result of a complex ritual, Duquesne achieved invulnerability and an exponentially increased lifetime. However, it was later prophesied that Gleave's first male heir would be the key to finally putting an end to Duquesne."

"That male heir is William," said Brandt.

"Correct. So everything that we've thought all along remains true. William is the only individual capable of killing Desmond Duquesne. We also know from our surveillance, and from the deaths of Agent James Lawrence and former operative Miranda Simms, that Duquesne is planning a new ritual… one that appears to be far grander than his last."

"They got Miranda?" a dejected Simon asked.

Valentine nodded glumly.

Brandt gave what he felt was a requisite moment of silence for his former colleague and followed it with, "What new information could possibly come to light regarding a centuries-old prophecy?"

"You'd be surprised." Whitworth lifted a cardboard box from the floor next to her seat and placed it on the table. "Earlier this morning, this package came addressed to me. Inside the package was this head." Whitworth unceremoniously upturned the box and let the decomposed female head roll out onto the shiny wooden surface of the table to the sound of a collective, disgusted moan. "Sorry. Should have warned you. It's gross. Anyway, I worked my magic and found that this head belonged to a woman who once met with Roderick Gleave to address the very situation that we've been discussing. Friends and colleagues, you're looking at the woman who created the prophecy, the one who gave young William the ability to kill our mutual enemy Duquesne."

"Fascinating," said Simon. "So she had the ability to affect the future?"

"She did," said Whitworth. "I can't imagine the physical toll it must have taken on her to do so, but she was, in fact, a weaver of prophecy. Among the last of her kind, I would assume."

"I suppose we owe her some thanks, no?" Valentine suggested.

"No," said Whitworth. "Nothing so simple."

"It never is," Donovan groaned.

"Too true," Whitworth concurred. "Here's the rub. This entire time, we've been dealing with one prophecy, which is, of course, difficult enough. The problem is that there are *two* prophecies, and they are—well—conflicting."

"What do you mean?" asked Donovan.

Whitworth took a deep breath and began. "I read the head, and it told me quite a story. Once upon a time there were three sisters. Each had tremendous power. The first sister had omniscient knowledge of all that was happening in the present day. The second sister could see into the future. The third sister, though, the one whose head rests on our table, could *change* the future to a certain extent. Knowing this, Roderick Gleave approached the three sisters and demanded their assistance. He could not kill Duquesne, but the third sister gave him what he thought was the next-best thing: his heir would be able to kill Duquesne."

"Wait, wait, wait," said Valentine. "If the third sister was able to write prophecy and affect the future, why couldn't she have just made it so that Roderick *could* finish off his rival?"

"Prophecies are tricky things," said Whitworth, eyeing the wretched head. "They're not for the living. Roderick Gleave was already alive. His fate had been set into motion, so she could not change it. However, she could determine the path of his heir."

"So what's the problem?" Brandt asked.

"You see, these sisters were not all that they claimed to be. They foresaw the end days and they welcomed them. However, another prophecy existed, one that predated the sisters, one that stated that certain events could prevent this end time."

Simon sighed. "Okay. Let me get this straight. The sisters wanted the end of the world to happen, but there was a prophecy saying that it might be avoidable, and they didn't like this. Why didn't the third sister just change that prophecy?"

"Can't," said Whitworth. "Once a prophecy is made, it can only be changed by the one who created it. It's set in stone."

"So what can prevent the world from ending?" asked Valentine.

Whitworth cleared her throat nervously and said, "The Absence, according to prophecy, can apparently only be stopped through the united efforts of the houses of Gleave and Duquesne."

Brandt's eyes widened. "The Absence?"

No one responded, but no one needed to. The dismay around the table was palpable. Donovan leaned back in his chair and folded his arms, Simon stared at the rotting head's horrific eyes, and Brandt slammed his fist loudly against the surface of the table. Only Feng and Whitworth remained unmoved. Before long, Valentine leaned forward and said, "I get it! I get why she did it!"

"Indulge us," Feng hissed through barely-parted lips.

"The way the sisters saw it, they couldn't lose. Best case

scenario, Gleave's heir kills Duquesne. End of the world can't be stopped. Worst case scenario, the two families carry on their blood feud and never come together. End of the world won't be stopped. Right?"

Whitworth placed her finger on her nose. "Exactly. So here's where we are. William is capable of killing Duquesne. However, if he does, that merely continues the blood feud, as Nate calls it, and all but ensures that there will never be unity between the Gleaves and Duquesnes."

"And hence nothing will prevent the end. Well, that's just fantastic," said Brandt. "Any other bombshells you'd like to drop?"

"Just one. More of a tidbit than a bombshell, really. What you were aiming to do today? You know, having William shoot Duquesne? That would have just ticked him off. It's not the bullet that kills Duquesne, Brandt, it's William himself. He needs to touch him."

"Do you mean to say that I've been training him this whole time, and he could have offed Duquesne with a simple hand-shake?" asked an exasperated Brandt.

"Yup. That's exactly what I mean to say."

"So what do we do now?" Valentine asked. "I'm open to suggestions."

Donovan mused, "So we're looking for a way for Kendrick to kill Duquesne, but also looking for a way to get the two to work together at some point in the future..."

"Not gonna happen," said Brandt.

"Thanks, sunshine," Donovan responded. "Just thinking out loud. Who sent you the head, by the way?"

"Don't know," said Whitworth, visibly troubled by this. "I tried to find out, but I couldn't read the box. Someone is blocking me from knowing."

"Can we leverage this information to get Duquesne to see reason?" asked Valentine, returning to the subject at hand.

"From what we know of Duquesne, he's after power. He doesn't want the world to end any more than we do. We might at least be able to stop him from gunning for Will."

"He cannot be reasoned with," Simon averred. "He's a madman."

"But I'm willing to try," Whitworth offered. "I'm willing to bet that he's as unaware of this other prophecy as we are; otherwise he might not have been so gung-ho to sic Ratchford and the rest on Brandt and the boy earlier. Besides, we know that he's a narcissist. Saving the world would be quite a feather to put in his cap."

"I have another idea," said Simon. "His daughter." All eyes, even Feng's, were now on Simon as he continued, "When William saw Daphne, I could tell that he was smitten. We can use that. After all, what if the Gleave and Duquesne who save the world are not William and Desmond? What if they are William and Daphne?"

"If they were," said Brandt, "we could still kill Desmond."

"True," said Donovan, "but what happens when the girl finds out that William killed her father? You think she'll jump into his open arms?"

"We can use Simon for that," said Brandt. "He can make her love the boy."

Simon shifted uneasily in his seat as Brandt spoke about 'using' him and said, "I don't like the idea of messing with people's emotions like that."

"It's for the greater good," said Brandt.

"Perhaps there's a way in which William can kill Duquesne without Daphne knowing that it was him," said Whitworth. "Drayton, what do you think?"

Feng, who had appeared disinterested in most of what was going on, now snapped to attention and responded, "I'll analyze the boy's blood that I took from the bear's claw. His blood should do it. He may not even need to be in the vicinity.

Perhaps we can either inject Duquesne with the boy's blood or somehow make him ingest it? We'd just need to get someone close enough to make it happen."

"The surreptitious approach sounds like the best possibility so far," Whitworth concluded. "And I believe that Simon may be onto something when he sees the union of the two families happening between William and Daphne. Maybe we should arrange a meeting."

"Well, flirting with a waitress was the boy's only discernible skill thus far. Maybe this will work," said Brandt. "If we can get him to connect with the daughter and still kill Duquesne on the sly, everyone wins."

"We need to get the boy into New Covington. I'll handle that part," said Whitworth.

"We'd be throwing him into a hornet's nest," said Donovan. "What will prevent Duquesne from killing him immediately?"

"I will," said Whitworth. "I think it's time I set up a meeting with Desmond Duquesne. If you'll excuse me, I have a number of errands to run before that happens."

"What about the boy?" Simon asked.

"He'll be coming with me," Whitworth answered. "He's had a rough few days, and I'd like to give him a reprieve." Her phone interrupted her train of thought. "Oh, this day just gets more and more interesting," she said, looking at the number of the incoming call. "Looks like I'm going to be very busy," Whitworth muttered as she left the conference room. "Don't wait up."

TWENTY-FOUR

Frost and Wisp

"How're you doing with that?" Dr. Creswell asked as Will fumbled with the metal crutch she had provided.

"Are you sure this is necessary?"

"It can't hurt to use it for a few days."

"This might interfere with Brandt's plans for me to murder people, though," Will smirked.

"Is that a complaint?"

"Not really."

They reached the end of a hallway that seemed to go on forever with white door after white door on either side. But the final door on the left was different. It was an ornate wooden door with a cherry finish that seemed more apropos to a high-end restaurant than a government facility. "Well, here we are," Creswell said, placing her hand on the polished brass door-knob. "Frances Whitworth's office."

Heeding the doctor's unspoken invitation to enter, Will would have been engrossed by the interior of the office, had he not been distracted by an old woman at a desk in the far right corner. "Who the hell are you?" she asked with a sawed-off

217

shotgun aimed at his face. Despite hearing the question, Will remained speechless as he looked into the eyes of the gray-haired woman, who in turn stared intensely at him through her bifocals.

"Oh, for God's sake, Peg," said Creswell, entering behind Will. "This is William Kendrick."

"Oh," said Peg, lowering her weapon. "So you're what all the fuss is about?"

"Apparently," Will answered.

"Ms. Whitworth said that I should bring Will here to wait for her," Creswell said. "I need to get back down to the lab and keep track of some tests while Drayton's in a meeting."

"How's Dr. No-Face doing?" asked Peg.

Creswell shot her an incredulous look that barely hid a grin as she stepped out. "I'll give him your regards, Peg."

With the door shut, Will found himself alone with a possibly-senile, possibly-psychotic old woman with a shotgun. Somehow, he was more concerned about his own well-being than he had been with Brandt. "Okay, Mr. Magic," she said, turning back to her computer monitor. "Make yourself comfortable, but don't touch anything. This room is filled with things that will melt the flesh off your bones Indiana Jones-style if you rub them the wrong way."

Will chuckled as he looked at some of the odder baubles that lined Whitworth's bookshelves: shrunken heads, beautiful beaded necklaces, teeth the size of his fist, and several candles of varying shapes, sizes, and scents. "That was a joke, right? The melting flesh thing?"

"Maybe. You gutsy enough to find out?" Deciding that he was not, in fact, gutsy enough to find out, Will took a seat on a leather sofa opposite Peg and observed the rest of the room from a safe distance. Peg clicked away at the computer until eventually she asked, "What hand is higher, a straight or a flush?"

Will looked around the room to ensure that he was the only one to whom she could have been addressing her question, and upon confirmation responded, "Um...straight?"

Peg clicked and cursed under her breath. He couldn't hear which curse she used, but he could hear her mutter, "Gonna save the world, my ass. Can't even play poker."

ON HER WAY back to the lab, Angela Creswell was nearly run down by Frances Whitworth, who was dashing toward her office as quickly as her aching knees would take her. "I'm so sorry, my dear," she said. "So much to do."

She tried to continue on her way, but Creswell took her arm gently to slow her down. "Can I have just a minute of your time? I know you're busy."

Whitworth tried not to look put out as she responded with a quick nod. "Anything for you, dear. Go on."

"I'm worried about the boy."

"Medically?" she asked.

"No," the doctor responded. "His leg should be okay as long as he doesn't overdo it. I'm talking about his general well-being. Shouldn't we be preparing a place for him to stay?"

"Oh, I already have a place for him to stay," Whitworth said.

"Here? I mean, it's not ideal, but we could put him in one of the cells, just for now, just for his own safety."

"Let's not do that to the boy, Angela. He's been through enough. I'm going to take him someplace where he'll be safe. I'll make sure of it."

Creswell appeared unconvinced. "For the record, I don't like this. That boy was nearly killed. We should be keeping a close eye on him here. I'd hate to see anything happen to him."

"As would I, Angela, but we cannot continue to treat him like a captive. He's got to be able to trust us. Otherwise, we're no better than Brandt, and you saw how his 'gun to the head' approach worked out." She took Angela's hands in hers, looked her in the eyes, and concluded, "I swear on my life that we'll get this boy through."

HAVING UTTERLY FAILED to impress Peg, Will gnawed at his cuticles while he anxiously waited for Whitworth's return. Thankfully, he did not have long to wait, as only five minutes later the elder agent burst into the room with surprising energy and whisked Will out so quickly that he nearly forgot his crutch. Will struggled to keep up with the spry older woman as he followed her lead to the parking garage. "Why the hurry?" Will asked once he was in the car. "I don't have to kill someone now, do I?"

Whitworth laughed. "No, William. With any luck, that prospect will be off the table soon. However, I do need to have a serious discussion with you about the alternative."

Will nodded. He felt much more at ease speaking with Agent Whitworth about this situation than he had been with Brandt. "I'm listening."

"It can wait. I'm working on it." Will heaved a sigh. Brandt's plan had not exactly worked out brilliantly, and now he was expected to put faith in this woman who seemed earnest but may have had a few loose screws herself. As Will saw it, it was becoming an increasingly remote possibility that he was going to make it out of this alive.

Before long, Whitworth parked the car on a wealthy-looking street filled with small specialty shops and brownstones. "You look worried," she said. Will nodded, but no words came out. "I'm sorry that you're a part of this," she continued in a kind tone. "However, no matter how powerful someone is, there is always something beyond his control."

Will gave a half smile. He knew that she was trying to put

him at ease, but it was going to take a lot more than soothing words. He missed his parents and his friends; he wanted the comforts of home that he had stupidly left days earlier. "Hey," said Whitworth, placing her hand on Will's shoulder, "I know that you don't want life lessons right now, but I'm going to throw one more at you. You're frightened because you feel alone, but it's time to realize that you are not. In fact, troublesome times bring people together better than anything else. That said, are you ready for your surprise?"

"I guess so," said Will. "Where are we?"

Whitworth didn't answer but was unable to suppress a smile as she led Will up the stone steps of a nearby brownstone. The agent seemed giddy with anticipation. Once she rang the bell, she rocked back and forth on her heels until the door was opened by a woman whom Will did not recognize but who had a slight familiarity about her. She was smartly dressed in a black pantsuit, with a light colorful scarf draped over her shoulders. She had auburn hair just a bit longer than shoulder length, with a stark white stripe running down the right-hand side. The woman wore a pair of black-rimmed glasses, but she took these off once the door was fully opened. To Will's surprise, rather than folding them up and pocketing them, she let the glasses fall to the floor as she raised a hand to her face and covered her mouth.

Whitworth broke the awkward silence by saying, "William, it's my pleasure to introduce you to your only living blood relative—your aunt, Veronica Frost."

Neither nephew nor aunt seemed to know quite what to say at first, but Veronica broke the silence by saying, "My William…I…I can't believe it's you!" She wrapped her arms tightly around her long-lost nephew, and he hugged her back, if not with the same intensity. Wanting to hold onto him longer, she stepped back so as not to overwhelm him and said, "You don't remember me. I know. I remember you, though. Oh, my dear boy…you were only this tall when I saw you last." She lowered her hand to a point just above her knee.

Whitworth was positively beaming when she said, "Now is this a surprise, or what, William?"

William tried to speak, but no words came. This day had him officially shell-shocked. His reaction was not lost on Veronica, who, dabbing her eyes and regaining her composure, ushered the two visitors into her home. "I'm sorry," she said. "Come in, come in. I've been expecting you since Frances called earlier, but no amount of notice could have truly prepared me for this. Here, come into the living room. Get comfortable."

Will followed the woman into a living room far larger than the exterior of the house had suggested. For the first time in days, he felt solace in his surroundings. The windows were open and a cool evening breeze was beginning to billow the sheer curtains. He sat on a comfortable loveseat, and for the first time realized just how tired he was. Were he not essentially surrounded by strangers, he could have fallen asleep on the spot. Whitworth sat opposite him on a matching sofa, while Veronica stepped behind it and removed what looked like a cigar box from a bookshelf. Seating herself next to Will, she opened the box to reveal a sloppy stack of photographs, the topmost one portraying her younger self holding a newborn. "That's you," Veronica said, pointing to the child and placing the picture into Will's trembling hand. "I go through these pictures all the time, but when I heard that you were coming here…that you were actually alive…I made sure to set this one aside. After all, most of what you've gone through so far, from what Frances tells me, is quite difficult to believe. If I were you, I'd be suspicious of me as well. But it's true: I'm your mother's older sister. This picture was taken only four days after you were born. Your parents were so happy…" Here she began to tear up again, and instinctively, Will placed his arms around the woman and fought against his own tears. "And now I'm so happy, William."

After a moment, Will leaned back on the loveseat, slightly embarrassed at his sudden display of emotion. Veronica caught on and handed him a tissue from the box sitting next to her. "Here," she smiled. "Make yourself look all manly again."

He grinned at the comment but was soon mortified when a stunning young woman appeared in the living room entranceway. "Mrs. Frost?" she announced herself softly, hesitant to interrupt the family reunion.

Frost, doing her best to erase the traces of tears on her own face, waved the girl into the room. "Come on in, Gwen. Frances, I believe you've met Gwen?"

She stood to give the girl a friendly embrace. "Of course! How could I forget?"

Gwen smiled appreciatively and turned to face Will. "Gwen, this, at long last, is my nephew William. William, this young lady is Gwen Henley. She's a jack of all trades, but for simplicity's sake, we'll call her my personal assistant."

"It's a pleasure to meet you, Will," she said. "You have no idea how much your aunt has spoken about you...even before she got the good news that you were alive and well."

"Alive, yes, but hardly well," said Veronica with a look of concern. "My God, you look as though you've been through a war. Look at this!" she said to Gwen, who acknowledged his bloody clothes with a shudder. "Ms. Whitworth, I had no idea that you would return my nephew to me torn halfway to shreds!"

Whitworth gave an apologetic shrug. "It was between half torn to shreds and half burned to a crisp. I did what I could, dear."

Veronica smiled. "I know, old friend. Still, William, you are a wreck. Here's what I need you to do. First, Gwen will show you into the kitchen, where you can help yourself to a snack before dinner. You must be famished. In the meantime, it is my understanding that Ms. Whitworth needs to speak with me about some other matters. When we have finished our discussion, I'll come get you and show you where your room is and you can clean yourself up."

"I'll be staying here?" asked Will.

"Of course," said Veronica. "I'd have you stay nowhere else as long as you're in Boston. My home is your home, for as long as is necessary." Mrs. Frost could almost see the weight lifting off Will's shoulders when she extended this invitation. She placed her hands gently on Will's arms and said, "You've had a tough road, and I'm not promising that things will get any easier, but you've got more allies than you know—both friends and family—and you're safe. We'll see to that."

"Thank you," was all Will could think to say in response, but it appeared to suffice.

With an ominous "See you soon," Whitworth followed Veronica into her office and closed the door behind them.

"Guess it's just you and me," Will said nervously once left alone with Gwen.

"For the moment," she answered as she led him toward the kitchen. "Soon it will just be you. I've been asked to get you some clothes, so when we get to the kitchen, just write down your sizes for me, and any brands, designers, colors…whatever you prefer."

"Okay," said Will, mesmerized by the girl's legs, whose length was accentuated by the shortness of her skirt. Her golden-brown hair bounced with each graceful step and had an entrancing effect on him. When they reached the large, modern kitchen, he was instructed to take a seat at the granite island, which he did, and was then handed a pad and paper from a drawer next to the stove. He stared at the pad blankly and finally asked, "What's this for?"

"Your measurements," said Gwen with a bemused look.

"Boy, you must have really been through a lot after all, you can't even remember a conversation from thirty seconds ago."

"Oh. Yeah. Right. Sorry." If she had asked him to complete a calculus quiz, writing down numbers would not have been more difficult. His brain was so fried from the past few days that it took a full two or three minutes just to write down a few digits, but at long last, he reviewed his work and was satisfied.

"No specific colors or anything? You're giving me full control?" she asked as she tore the sheet from the pad.

"I give you permission to do whatever you want to me." He caught himself, and his face reddened. "Whatever you can to me. Whatever you can for me. You know what I mean... It's been a long day."

Gwen winked. "Gotcha. Help yourself to anything. Just don't fill up too much. Your aunt is an amazing cook. She'll make you a fantastic dinner." With that, Gwen left through the back door that led out onto a small terrace with an attached greenhouse. Will watched her leave through the back gate and promptly slammed his head down on the counter in combination of humiliation and exhaustion.

"I know what you're thinking," said a man's voice that Will did not recognize. His head shot up to see a distinguished gentleman with silver hair standing across the island from him, curiously and expertly lowering a red yo-yo in and out of his clutch. "And I can't blame you. She is a fine-looking gal. A bit old for you, though, isn't she?" His mouth widened into a mischievous grin once he had delivered his question. Will noticed immediately that the man was not a native of Boston, as his cadence was that of a slow-talking, silver-tongued Southerner.

"Maybe," Will responded. "But she's a bit young for you, no?"

The man laughed heartily. "You obviously don't know me too well." Will couldn't decide what to think of this man, but he got the feeling that like the yo-yo, he was being toyed with, though not necessarily in a mean-spirited way. "I know you, though," the man continued as he pocketed the yo-yo, opened the refrigerator, and began rummaging through Veronica's inventory. "At least, I know *about* you."

"Oh really?" said Will, playing along.

"Indeed, Mr. Kendrick" the older man said, tossing an apple to Will. He bit into a bright green apple himself, took a moment to chew, and stared at Will intensely until he swallowed. "For instance, despite your understandable admiration of the lovely Miss Henley, you just can't seem to keep your mind off of someone else...someone who you do not even know..." The man stopped for a minute and looked into Will's eyes as though trying to see into his soul. "Now don't tell me, don't tell me," he said. "I can guess this one. The person with whom you are besotted is...well oh my goodness...it's Daphne Duquesne! Now *that*, my friend, is interesting!" The man took another bite of his apple and raised his eyebrows. "Am I right?"

"You...how did you know that?" asked Will, thoroughly shocked.

"Lucky guess."

"Who are you? Are you Mr. Frost...my uncle?"

The man laughed again, though Will failed to see the joke. "No, no. I'm afraid that for many years now, Mr. Frost has been..." He made a throat-slitting motion and a croaking sound to not-so-subtly indicate that Frost had died. "I'm just a friend of your aunt's."

"A friend who hangs out in her kitchen?"

"If you must know, I was hiding in her bathroom." He motioned to a door that William had not previously noticed, out of which he must have stepped while Will's face had been buried in the granite countertop.

"Oh. Because that makes more sense. Hiding from what?"

"Whitworth. She still here?"

Will shrugged. "As far as I know. Why are you afraid of her? She seems like a nice lady."

"She's never cared much for me. I'm afraid that she sees me for what I am, which is, frankly, a terrible scoundrel." Will laughed. "No, no, it's true. I'm a selfish, lecherous old villain, and your friend Whitworth knows it. But hey, at least I'm honest about it, unlike so many others."

Will raised an eyebrow. "Does my aunt know how terrible you are?"

"Of course. But I've got more respect for that woman than I have ever had for anyone in the world. She's tough as nails... had to be once her husband and son died. When it comes down to it—and you'll learn this—she's the one you want on your side. I'd never want to stand opposite her. And so yes, I swipe an apple here or a bottle of wine there, but when the chips are down, she knows she can count on her old friend Wisp."

Will nodded in appreciation of the man's candor. "So you go back a long way? I didn't know that her husband and son were dead. She doesn't have any other family?"

"No, sir. You're it, so you can surely understand why she was so very excited to find out you had survived that terrible hit Desmond Duquesne placed on your family so many years ago. I haven't seen her this happy in years. Hopefully you're just what the doctor ordered."

"Doctor ordered for what? You make it sound like she's sick," said Will, concerned.

Ignoring this last question, the man glanced at his ornate gold watch and rolled his eyes. "Good lord, that Whitworth can prattle on, can't she? William, it's been a pleasure keeping you company here, but I do have an obligation at a local social club, so I will have to get going." He held out his hand, and William took it. "I expect great things from you, son. After all, anyone with your name is destined for greatness."

"Which name?" William asked facetiously as he shook hands. "Kendrick or Trammell?"

"Neither!" said the man as he acted taken aback. "I was referring to *our* name. William Kendrick, it was a pleasure to meet you. My name is William Wisp, and I'm sure that we'll be seeing a lot of each other. In fact, I'm going to make sure of it. Tell your aunt that I said good night." As suddenly as he had appeared in the kitchen, Mr. Wisp was off, and Will found himself alone for the first time all day. He hobbled over to the refrigerator and looked absentmindedly into it as if he were sleepwalking. His stomach rumbled at the sight of the vibrant fruits and vegetables, the paper-wrapped cuts of meat, and the pink boxes filled with mystery pastries from a local bakery. Still, any snack that required more energy than it had taken to bite into his apple was not appealing enough to be worth the effort. Lost in refrigerator hypnosis, he jumped when he felt a hand on his shoulder and squinted as he jerked his wounded leg.

"I'm sorry William," said Veronica. "I didn't mean to startle you, but Ms. Whitworth is gone, and if it's alright with you, I'd like to show you to your room." Will agreed and followed her back to the foyer of the townhouse. "I apologize that the room is upstairs," she said while she climbed the staircase located near the front door. "All of the bedrooms are up here. I could arrange to have the bed brought down to the living room if it would be easier on your leg."

William was touched by this offer of kindness and relieved to have found someone who seemed sane, reasonable, and compassionate. "I'd never ask you to do that," he said. "But thank you."

She led him into his bedroom, which was painted a light baby blue and housed furniture that seemed a bit young for the guest room in the house of a widow living on her own. "The room may appear slightly juvenile," Veronica admitted, "but it was my son's—your cousin's—room."

There was no denying the sadness in her voice when she said this. "What was his name?" Will asked.

"Matthew. Matt," she answered. "I'll tell you all about him, but let's get you cleaned up. Your bathroom is right through that door. You'll find all that you need in there. Gwen should be back anytime now with your new clothes. I'll place them just inside the bedroom door when they arrive. When you're all set, we'll see about dinner, alright?"

"Thank you, Aunt Veronica," he said, giving her a gentle hug, cognizant of the fact that he was still covered in blood and filth. After she had left, Will locked himself in the bright, immaculate bathroom. As he stood in the shower, he discovered a whole new set of injuries brought on by the day's excitement. In addition to the lingering pain of the cuts, scratches, and bruises left by his Memorytown adventure, the flash burns from Havelock's blaze practically sizzled as the water struck them. Still, he sighed in relief as the water ran down his body and left down the drain in a gray and red swirl.

Wrapping his towel around his waist, he cautiously stepped out of the bathroom and was surprised to see several shopping bags filled to capacity with clothes. He rummaged through and found several pair of jeans, easily a dozen T-shirts, a number of polos, boxers, socks, shorts, and three pair of shoes. He had expected a T-shirt and jeans. What Gwen had gotten him made the room look like Christmas morning.

VERONICA, in the meantime, had gone down to the kitchen to see what there was to throw together for Will. She decided he might enjoy it if she fired up the grill, which she rarely did, so she got the flames going out on the terrace and removed several steaks from the fridge. Not knowing his taste, she wanted to wait until he came back downstairs, but after waiting for thirty minutes beyond when she had heard the shower stop, she began to worry and hurried up the stairs to William's room. She knocked gently on the door. No answer. She knocked again, a bit louder this time, but still received no response. Finally, she cracked the door and said, "Will, is everything alright?" Upon hearing nothing in return, she peeked around the door and heaved a sigh of relief at what she saw. Asleep on his side, with both hands hidden beneath his pillow, William lay, fully clothed in one of the outfits that Gwen had purchased, sneakers and all.

Veronica smiled as she sat on the bed beside him and rested her hand on his arm. "Sleep, my love. You've earned it."

Will shuffled in his sleep and muttered, "Mr. Wisp says good night…"

TWENTY-FIVE

The Black Rose

FOLLOWING her brief meeting with Veronica Frost, Whitworth returned to her car and sat in silence. She removed her blazer and placed it on the passenger seat, and then, reaching into her blouse, exposed a chain upon which hung an antiquated but expertly polished gold ring with a flowing pattern of various-sized diamonds. It glimmered in the glare of the setting sun as she examined it briefly to ensure that the stones were all still in place. When finished, she held it up to her lips and whispered, "Please tell me I'm not going to get this boy killed." She kissed the ring gently, placed it back against her chest, and drove off to the second in her series of meetings.

This meeting would be slightly different in that she had no idea what to expect. She was surprised to have gotten the call on her way out of the meeting with the rest of the Collective, and was honestly not thrilled to be distracted in the midst of such an important operation. But the man who had requested the meeting had come all this way...perhaps there was some providence in it.

Whitworth walked into the Black Rose, a pub she usually

frequented alone as an escape from her subterranean work-place. This time, she scanned the bar for a companion and found him sitting in the shade of a back-corner table. "Detective," she said, "I have to be honest—I did not expect you to follow us all the way to Boston. I guess I was not the only one who saw the text sent to Mr. Lunsford."

"No ma'am," said Eddie Garza, nursing a pint. "It didn't really take all that much detective work to figure it out. Drink?"

Whitworth shook her head. "I really shouldn't. I'll be driving again soon, and I'm afraid that I'm a bit of a light-weight. I do enjoy these, though," she said, grabbing a handful of peanuts from the basket on the table. "So what can I do for you?"

"Well, Ms. Whitworth, I came all the way to Boston to try to find out if my best friend's son is alive. What I hope you can do is tell me that he is."

The agent cracked a nut, looked Garza in the eyes, and recognized his sincerity. "You truly care about the boy, don't you?"

"I cared about Dan Trammell, so I care about his son. I need to know what happened, because I can feel in my gut that the kid's not dead."

Whitworth nodded. "Your gut is correct. I can confirm that the young man is, in fact, alive."

Garza let out a short laugh, pounded the rest of his beer back, and slammed the glass down onto the wooden table. "Ha! I knew it! You've seen him?"

"I just left him. He's quite safe at his aunt's house."

Garza's hard features softened at this news. "He's got family here, huh? Well good. I'd like to meet her. Is this Linda's sister?"

"It is," said Whitworth, popping another peanut into her mouth.

"I'd seen her in pictures at Dan's place. I know that she and Linda were close. So where can I find them?"

"Detective Garza," Whitworth responded, "I feel that I can trust you, and I'm not often wrong about that kind of thing. Here's what I can tell you. William Kendrick is currently in a great deal of danger. Now, I'm working to get him out of this danger as soon as possible, but I'm afraid that things may get worse before they get better. I regret to tell you that I'm about to place him into a dicey situation."

"What are you talking about?" asked Garza, his cheerful demeanor vanishing rapidly.

"Over the next few days, I plan to take a number of calculated risks that will bring William into close contact with the man who ordered his family killed fourteen years ago." She looked furtively around the bar and whispered, "Desmond Duquesne."

"I won't let you do that," said Garza, clenching his fist. "Why would you even consider that?"

Whitworth remained calm and cracked another nut. "I have my reasons, and while this plan may not seem prudent on the surface, I believe that it may be the only thing standing between us and the end of the world. Besides," she added, "the gears of this plan are already turning."

"Don't give me this end of the world bullshit," Garza hissed, slapping Whitworth's bowl of nuts clear across the room. "You used me. I led you right to the kid, and now you're going to get him killed."

"You're right, Mr. Garza," Whitworth conceded. "We did use you. You were a means to locate William, and honestly, I never thought that you would. Since you did, though, and since you care so much about the boy's well-being, perhaps you'd be willing to help."

"Help? Are you serious? Why would I help you?"

"You wouldn't. Don't be silly. You'd be helping William."

Garza sat back and folded his arms, nodding for Whitworth to continue, and she did: "I'm willing to give you the address of Linda Trammell's sister, Veronica Frost. My only condition is that you do not make your presence known. Not yet. Not while our operation is ongoing."

"So what do you expect me to do, just sit and watch the house?"

"Exactly," said Whitworth. "I will pay you from my own pocket to guard that house and the people in it." She lowered her volume, leaned forward, and continued, "I'm having serious misgivings about the young man's security. It somehow leaked to Duquesne's bodyguard that he was in Boston, and as a result, the boy was almost burned alive earlier today. I need someone whom I can trust implicitly."

Garza's mood was softened by the old woman's display of integrity, but he was not entirely satisfied. "Can't I do something more than just sit on my ass and watch a house?"

"In the best of all worlds, Mr. Garza, I would have you escort the boy to Duquesne's compound, but with his resources, he'd be able to discover who you were in no time, and you'd fare no better than any of the other agents we've sent to spy on him. This is the next problem that I need to work on. You see, I'm not foolish enough to send William to New Covington by himself. People tend to disappear there, so I need to find someone to accompany him as an extra set of eyes and insurance that no harm will come to him. I need someone off the grid."

"I'm as off the grid as they get, ma'am." Whitworth turned quickly, upset that apparently some other patron had been lurking close enough to overhear her conversation. To her surprise, Andy Lunsford stood there, all smiles. "Don't worry, ma'am," he said. "I didn't hear everything. I was over there playing darts for most of the time, but if you want me to go with Will, I can do that."

Garza sat back again with a bemused expression. "Well, Ms. Whitworth, what do you think? Are you crazy enough to send Lunsford with him?"

Whitworth cracked a final nut and shrugged. "I just might be."

BACK UNDERGROUND, Brandt stared with disdain as Nate Valentine fumbled with his chopsticks. After nearly a dozen attempts, the Director came up empty-handed, save for a few grains of sticky rice that humored him by hanging on. "I'd ask if you were ever going to get the hang of that," said Brandt, "but it's been over a decade and you still haven't mastered your own job."

Valentine stabbed a piece of chicken with one of his chopsticks and gave Brandt a look that portrayed more disappointment than anger. "What exactly is that supposed to mean?" the Director asked.

Simon poked at his own food uncomfortably while Donovan jumped in, saying, "Don't even bother asking him, sir. He's just a bitter old bastard. Has he said anything positive or constructive since getting here today? I don't even know why you're putting up with this."

Valentine held up a hand to ask for silence and said, "No, it's fine. Let him say what he wants to say. I'm well aware of the problems you've had with me in the past, Mr. Brandt. Please indulge me and tell me what your current issue is."

"Let's see," Brandt began, with a triumphant glance at Donovan. "For starters, maybe you can explain how Stalker and Steampunk escaped your custody." Valentine remained silent. "I am assuming that the Brig still exists, and that, to your knowledge, they were still locked up?"

Valentine nodded. "We didn't immediately realize their escape. Nothing appeared on the security cameras, and no alarms were raised. Even if we had, we had no way of knowing they were under contract for Duquesne."

"Oh please," said Brandt. "You people have a way of knowing everything, if you feel like it."

"Look," said Donovan, "just because you two feel guilty about what happened to the Trammells, doesn't mean that—"

"Don't bring me into this," Simon interjected.

"And I don't feel guilty," Brandt responded. "I feel angry."

"And rightfully so," said Valentine, "but if we all work together, we can finally take Duquesne down."

Brandt snorted. "Doubtful."

"And why do you say that?"

"Because you don't have your own house in order! Murderers like Ratchford are escaping, and someone on the inside is very obviously letting it happen."

"We had a lapse in security," Valentine said.

"Bullshit. Someone in your organization is on Duquesne's payroll. How else would anyone have known to send the sideshow to Memorytown? How else would Emil Havelock have known that we were at the dedication ceremony this morning? Someone's on the take."

"If that's true, I'd say we're all suspects, no?" said Donovan, now aiming his glare at Simon. "After all, it wouldn't be the first time that you turned out to be the traitor, would it, Simon?"

"I'm not working with Duquesne," Simon said with quiet indignation.

"Not this time?" Donovan muttered.

"Enough," said Valentine. "If there is a leak, we'll find it and plug it."

"What if it's you?" Brandt asked, point-blank.

Valentine's normally steady temperature began to rise as he replied. "And what if it's Drayton? Or Angela? Or Peg? Perhaps little Rose is a spy for the other side. You'll find it much more productive to trust people than not, Mr. Brandt. I didn't get this far by being skeptical of everyone."

"No," Brandt said. "You got this far by kissing daddy's ass."

Donovan sprang out of his chair, but Valentine once more held him back. "Don't bother, Mr. Donovan. Brandt will feel that way about me until the day he dies. I actually feel sorry for him." He paused and looked around the table. This even silenced Brandt. "Come on, everyone. I treated you to dinner. The least you could do is eat it."

"So what do you plan to do with us?" Simon asked.

"Yeah. Are you locking us up in the Brig as well?" Brandt added.

"Should I be?" answered Valentine. "I'd like to think that we can all coexist long enough to deal with Duquesne. As they say in the movies, 'just don't leave town.'" Simon nodded in acceptance of this gesture of camaraderie and continued poking at his food. "Come on, Simon," said Valentine, "Eat something. You look thinner than ever. Need to put some meat on your bones."

Ignoring this, Simon asked, "Why did they kill Miranda? She was, as I understood, retired."

"She was as retired as any of us get," said Donovan, "but she made the fatal mistake of holding onto one of Duquesne's favorite toys."

"She thought it would be safe with her," Valentine added. "However, as her power diminished over the years, I guess her means of hiding it away did the same."

"What was it?" asked Brandt.

Valentine frowned. "The Heart of Murena—the relic that Duquesne used to lengthen his lifespan in the first place. Whitworth's afraid it's the key to what he's currently planning."

"Well, that's just great," said Brandt. "Where is she, anyway?"

"Taking the boy someplace safe for the night," Donovan

responded. "Then she had some errands to run. She wouldn't say where."

Simon chuckled knowingly. "She wouldn't say where because she knows there's a leak."

Brandt pointed his chopsticks at Valentine. "Or she wouldn't say where because she *is* the leak. Now wouldn't that be a kick in the ass?"

TWENTY-SIX

The Nowhere Men

SEVERAL HOURS after leaving Garza and Lunsford, Whitworth was feeling slightly better about the plan she had formulated for William, but there were still plenty of details about the past few days that left her perturbed. Something was not right, and the image of the rotting head that had been delivered to her office was the face that she gave to this feeling of discomfort. The fact that there was no return address on the package—and more importantly, that the package seemed to block any attempt she made to trace it—suggested a much different kind of magic than what Desmond Duquesne was capable of. Now, having arrived in the Pine Barrens of New Jersey in the dead of night, she prepared to approach those whom she was sure were responsible.

She parked the black sedan in a clearing near Mullica, turned on her flashlight, and began walking through the dense foliage. *I'm getting too old for this,* she thought when she nearly lost her balance over an exposed root. She continued on the slight trail for nearly half a mile, trying to keep the flashlight steady with one hand as she swatted at clouds of gnats with the other. At the end of the trail, she found an old cabin with a screened-in front porch that shielded a large, half-asleep man from the gnats, bats, and mosquitoes.

Whitworth approached the porch, and, after catching her breath from the walk and spitting out a bug or two, said, "Mrs. Leeds sent me."

The man on the porch cupped his hands over his eyes and said, "Ms. Whitworth? That you?" He laughed heartily. "You don't need the password, ma'am!"

"Can never be too careful, Harry. Protocol and all that…"

"Well, it's good to see you, ma'am! You step on back. You know the way. I'll go ahead and get things ready."

Harry disappeared inside the house, and Whitworth did as she was told, walking to the rear of the property and into another wooded area, this one darker and denser than the last. One difference, though, was that the swarms were no longer hovering around her head. In fact, there was not a living creature to be found and not a sound to be heard, save for the noise that her footsteps made on the dry dirt below. Despite being slightly more treacherous than the previous path, this one was shorter, and Whitworth soon found herself standing at the edge of the famed Blue Hole. A local legend in the Pine Barrens, residents—or Pineys—claimed many things about this unusually clear, vibrantly blue, almost perfectly circular pond. One legend said that it could never be found in the same place twice. Another suggested that it was bottomless—that it led straight through the earth. Other lore associated the hole with New Jersey's most infamous legend, the Jersey Devil, or claimed that it was infested with a particularly nasty and heretofore unclassified breed of shark. Whatever its origins, Whitworth knew the truth about its current function and could attest that it was stranger than fiction.

Only a few feet from where the trail ended, Whitworth saw

the familiar floating dock that she had used so many times before. Stepping aboard, she unraveled the line fastening it to the bank and slowly drifted to the center of the pond. Once in the middle, she felt a slight jolt as something latched onto the bottom of the dock, which was essentially a dozen boards nailed together rather shoddily. Water drained in a wide circle around the lift, and with a hydraulic whirr, the wooden vessel began to lower into the Blue Hole. She remained surrounded by water on all sides, bathed in an incandescent blue reflection, until she reached the bottom of the long Plexiglas tube. Once there, she opened the door, stepped through, and allowed the tube to fill back up with water, lifting the empty dock back to the surface. There, Harry stood ready to pull the dock back to the shore and sat waiting for the signal that would announce Whitworth's return from beneath the Blue Hole.

She walked down a hallway distinctly different from the one that she walked to get to her own office at Collective headquarters. This one was dimly lit, smelled of mildew, and was lined with cracked tile that barely saw any upkeep, considering that it was traversed so infrequently. The end of the hallway opened into what always reminded Whitworth of an aquarium. Rather than a standard four walls, the room was essentially a large bubble. The water from the Blue Hole flowed around the space, held back by no discernible barrier and illuminating the room like a giant fish tank. The rest of the space was black, and against the vibrant cerulean backdrop, Whitworth could make out the silhouettes of five individuals standing in a semi-circle around him. She stepped closer, and as she expected, the individuals' faces were blank slates, possessing no distinct features. These were people whose secrets were well-kept and whose identities were well-hidden. These were the Nowhere Men.

"Only five of you?"

A voice came from the man standing in the center: "It is

241

nearly three in the morning, Frances. Not everyone is willing to heed to your beck and call at all hours of the day and night."

A second voice added, "Even you must admit this is highly irregular."

"Says the man without a face," said Whitworth with a smirk. "It would seem that by this time, we'd all be used to the 'highly irregular,' no? But we all have our pet peeves. You don't like being called out to the middle of nowhere in the dead of night, and I don't like receiving severed heads in the mail. Call me crazy."

"Are you suggesting that *we* sent you a severed head?" asked the man in the center. "I have no idea what you are talking about. It's absurd."

"It may be absurd to think that the collective group of you did this, but it's not so crazy to think that one of you did."

"Humor us, Whitworth. Why would someone send you such a thing? And why do you assume it was one of us?"

"Very well. First, the why. Someone was trying to send me a message. Just as we were seemingly on the cusp of destroying Desmond Duquesne once and for all, I receive this package that changes practically everything I know about the Gleave-Duquesne scenario. Nothing like waiting until the last minute, huh? I shouldn't be surprised. You fellows have a history of doing that, don't you?"

The silhouette on the far right tilted its head slightly. "If I may ask, how did this surprise delivery change the situation with Duquesne?"

Whitworth flashed a crafty smile. "I think I'll keep that information to myself for now, thank you. I'm sure you under-stand why someone might keep secrets."

"Stay silent about your discovery if you'd like, Whitworth," resumed the one in the center, "but at least tell us what makes you think that one of us sent the package."

"I was able to read the head. I was able to trace it back two centuries, more even. However, when I tried to read the cardboard box in which it shipped, I could not. I may be old and a little bit crazy, but I'm no slouch. Not yet. Someone was protecting their identity with some pretty powerful magic. So I thought to myself, what group of people do I know that makes a regular habit of doing that?"

The five shapes stood silently for a moment before the center one spoke again. "Your reasoning is sound, except for one thing—something that you should know better than anyone. We do not change the course of events."

"That's right," said Whitworth. "You just sit back and watch, don't you? How noble. That is, until one of you grows a conscience and realizes how truly terrible it is for people with such power to do nothing. That's what I'm willing to bet happened here."

"If that is indeed the case, then the individual who sent this package to you will be dealt with appropriately."

"Because that's what happens to people who grow consciences. They get 'dealt with.'"

"Ms. Whitworth," said the man in the middle, his tone growing steadily more impatient, "these are the rules by which we function. You made it abundantly clear when you broke these rules that you disagreed with our principles, but having been removed, you get no say in them now. We do not interfere in the natural order of events. You know this, and you are abusing your privileges by even coming here tonight."

"Your principles are foolish and they cost lives."

"Your opinion is noted, as it has been noted in the past." Having heard one dismissive comment too many, Whitworth mustered a polite nod and turned to leave. She stopped after a few steps when she heard one voice say, "Still, we will investigate this issue internally. If one of our members is found to have acted out of bounds, we will handle the matter accordingly."

"Brilliant," Whitworth muttered as she gave a cursory wave to the shadowy figures. She walked back down the dank passageway and pulled on a wet, frayed cord, which would in turn ring a bell to alert Harry that she needed to be picked up. Today had been a long day, and tomorrow was going to be tricky. Her brain was tired. It was time to sleep.

TWENTY-SEVEN

Fallout

EACH MORNING, at precisely nine o'clock, Desmond Duquesne had his breakfast delivered to him. This morning, he regretted sitting at the dining table when he uncovered his platter to reveal a sliced grapefruit. Duquesne looked pleadingly at Ridgley upon seeing the bright pink citrus and mumbled, "Please tell me that you're joking."

"My apologies, sir," said Ridgley with a hint of empathy. "But I'm afraid not."

This exchange was not lost on Joanna Duquesne, who was thoroughly enjoying her light meal. "Come on, you two. You know that I've been wanting to make some changes in the menu options around here. I thought that this would be a good start."

"It's not that bad, Dad," said Daphne, who sat to her father's right.

"You're some help," Desmond joked. "I thought you were always supposed to be on my side!"

"She is," said Joanna. "She wants you to live longer. The grapefruit will help."

"Oh, well in that case," Duquesne said with a smile. He broke through the juicy pulp. "And here I thought I had to rely on ritual sacrifice for that." At this, Ridgley backed away uncomfortably and left the room, while Desmond's wife and daughter stared blankly at him from across the table. "Kidding, everyone!" he laughed. "Only kidding!"

"Well," said Joanna, wiping the corners of her mouth with her napkin, "aren't you hilarious."

Desmond forced a smile as he slowly chewed his fruit, but this disappeared when his son barged into the room carrying a tablet. "She did it again, Dad," he said, clearly aggravated. "That...woman...did it again!" He handed the tablet to his father, who fumbled with the touchscreen.

"Alex, you know that I have no idea how to use these things. What am I looking at?"

Exasperated, Alex took a few swipes at the screen and held it up for his father. Duquesne saw Eleanor Hornbeck's blog, *Horning In*, and smack in the center of the page, a headline that read "Desmond Du-Flame." He did not have to read beyond to know that it was in reference to the blaze that had erupted during the ribbon-cutting for the oceanfront park. Noticing the change in her husband's demeanor, Joanna asked, "What is it, dear?" He turned the device to show her the headline. "Oh."

"I'm really sorry that that happened during your big moment, Dad," said Daphne. "I couldn't believe it. What are the chances that a fire would break out right there, of all places?"

Desmond appreciated the sentiment but waved it off. "It's alright, Daphne. We're just lucky that no one was hurt." His eyes scanned the screen for a moment, and he nodded after receiving confirmation. "It says here that a few folks were treated for smoke inhalation, but that otherwise, everyone escaped the building just fine. Tragedy averted."

Alex was not as calm and insisted, "You've got to meet with Hornbeck again, dad. She's just trying to bury us because she's jealous."

"That may be," said Joanna. "But the woman does have every right to cover this story. After all, it was in every local paper as well. Still, I suppose she didn't have to lead with your father's name..."

"Desmond Du-Flame," her husband repeated, bewildered. "I mean, it's not even a pun. It's really not all that clever."

"Whatever," said Alex. "All I know is that if that woman comes anywhere near my party next week, I'll say something to her myself."

"You will do no such thing, Alexander," Duquesne admonished. "I will make sure that Emil keeps her away from the festivities, but if you ever see this woman, you are to be nothing but courteous and respectful. Remember what I said about stepping out of bounds. Now, will you be joining us for breakfast?"

"I'm going to the gym," he said curtly, and removed himself from the room.

Daphne rolled her eyes and smirked at her father. "Boy, you guys sure are lucky you had me, huh?"

Desmond took a sip of tea to mitigate the horrid taste of grapefruit and answered, "Too bad you didn't come first," with a wink.

Father and daughter laughed, while Joanna tried to suppress her amusement. "You are terrible, Des. Both of you are!" She finished up her own tea and said, "New topic. Daphne, have you decided which friends you'd like to invite to Alex's party?"

"So here's the thing, mom," Daphne sighed. "I don't have that many friends, and the ones that I do have can't stand Alex. Can't I get another perk instead? Like, can't I save you guys some money and just not attend? Get the house to myself for the night?"

"Now, now, Daphne," said her father. "You may not always get along, and Alex can be hard to deal with, but he is your brother. You're going to be there for his birthday."

"Though I suppose," Joanna offered, "if you want to stay home, Mrs. Ridgley would be happy to keep you company."

"I'll go," Daphne responded quickly, recalling the backrubs that Mrs. Ridgley used to demand when babysitting her as a child. "But I don't know about guests. I'll keep you posted."

"I'm glad to hear you'll be attending, though I'm sure that Mrs. Ridgley will be disappointed," said Desmond. "I heard her going on the other day about a herniated disc."

Daphne shot an alarmed look at Joanna. "Mom, make him stop."

Joanna laughed. "It's okay, Daphne. I'll give him a grape-fruit for every time he mentions that from now on."

"I thought I knew what evil was," Desmond said, feigning terror, much to his daughter's delight. "But you, Joanna—" He stopped midsentence and looked with anticipation at Ridgley as the servant reentered the dining room.

"Forgive the intrusion, sir, but Emil Havelock is here to see you. Shall I give him a time when you will be available?"

Duquesne frowned slightly and said to his wife, "I'd like to get this over with, Joanna. Would you two mind giving me a moment with Mr. Havelock?"

"He's all yours," said Daphne, her disdain for the visitor evident in her tone.

"Thank you, dear," he said softly to his wife as she followed the departing Daphne. Havelock passed Joanna on his way into the room but was met with only a half-smile as she left.

Desmond waited to see Ridgley slide the wooden panel closed and ensured that he heard the click of the lock before he clutched Alex's tablet and waved it at Havelock. "Have you seen this?" he asked, throwing it at his head of security. Havelock barely caught it and shook his head at the sight of the headline. "That," Desmond said, "is unacceptable."

"I know, sir," said Havelock in a rare moment of humility. "This was my fault. I should have been more prepared."

"Well, at the very least, I think it's evident that this Trammell kid is fireproof. Can you try something simpler next time? A bullet, perhaps?"

"I was trying to make it look like an accident, Mr. Duquesne. I was going for more subtlety."

"More subtlety," Duquesne said derisively. "Take another look at that story—at the picture of black smoke billowing out of an apartment complex—and tell me again how subtle your approach was."

Feeling his temperature rise, Havelock argued, "The head-hunters that *you* hired assured us the kid was dead. You're lucky I found out in time. Trammell was ready to put a hole in your head."

"Mr. Havelock," said Duquesne, rising from his chair and pointing to the remnants of his breakfast. "If you ever presume to tell me how 'lucky' I am again, your skull will be resting on this platter and I will take great delight in scooping out the pulpy mass that you call a brain, scraping the rim to ensure that every last ounce of tissue is removed from your thick head."

Havelock could practically feel the silver spoon that Duquesne held scraping against the inside of his skull and did his best not to shiver at the thought. Duquesne stalked toward Havelock with a crazed look in his gray eyes until the scene was interrupted by Ridgley, who said, "Mr. Duquesne, you have a phone call."

Duquesne turned his wrathful gaze to Ridgley and answered, "This is not the best time, Mr. Ridgley."

"I understand that, sir," said the servant. "But it's Frances Whitworth."

"Well, well," Duquesne said, his demeanor lightening. He handed the silver spoon to Emil Havelock. "Don't go anywhere. This should be interesting."

TWENTY-EIGHT

"You Are My Sunshine"

WILLIAM AWOKE at 10 a.m. to the sound of rain pounding on the window, feeling as though he had slept for days. While rested, he noticed as soon as he rolled onto his back just how very sore he was from head to toe. At first, he attributed this to sleeping motionlessly through the night, but upon standing, the shooting pain from his leg reminded him of all that he had been through in the days leading up to this welcome night of peaceful, dreamless sleep. He limped into the bathroom and only then realized he had fallen asleep wearing the clothes Gwen had gotten him the night before. Figuring that no one had seen him in them, he shrugged and decided to just keep them on for now. His body hurt too much to entertain the idea of changing again.

Will decided to head downstairs immediately to apologize to his aunt for falling asleep so abruptly. He grabbed the crutch that had seemed so superfluous yesterday and now was glad Dr. Creswell had provided it, considering the aches and pains that had set in overnight.

As he hopped down the stairs, trying to keep as much

weight as possible off his injured leg, delicious aromas wafted toward him, making his mouth water and inspiring him to fly more quickly down the last set of steps despite his body's resistance. Turning the corner into the dining room, he had the surreal feeling that he was having another vivid dream. On the table in front of him were all manner of breakfast items: eggs, bacon, sausage, French toast, and some of the most vibrant fruit that he had ever seen. However, despite this welcome sight, it was *who* sat around the table that made him second-guess the reality of the moment. Veronica Frost sat, as expected, at the head of the table, flanked on one side by Gwen Henley and on the other by Andy Lunsford.

Veronica and Gwen only smiled as Will hobbled over to his friend, beaming with excitement. "What the hell are you doing here?" he asked, and then, looking at his aunt, said, "Sorry. But...but what is he doing here?"

"At the moment," said Veronica with an amused smile, "he's regaling us with stories of your exploits, like when you filled your teacher's desk drawer with Jell-O..."

"Jelly," said Andy, his mouth full of French toast. "We couldn't make the Jell-O set. She took it remarkably well."

"I trust I won't find anything around here filled with jelly at any point?" she said with a raised eyebrow.

Will's face reddened slightly. "No, ma'am. I think those days are long behind me."

"It was last month," said Andy.

Will smacked him on the back of the head and said, "How did you even know where to find me? I'm so confused."

"That Whitworth lady," Andy answered. "She's cool. I like her. In fact, she even kind of gave me a job."

"I need to sit down for this."

"We'll get to all of that in good time," said Veronica. "But you must be famished, William. I wasn't sure what you liked, but Gwen and I threw this together this morning. I hope it's alright."

"It's better than alright," he said, excitedly fixing himself a plate heavy with every edible item he could get his hands on. "Are you a chef?"

"I dabble," said Veronica. "My husband was a chef and we were business partners. We own—or now *I* own—a restaurant called FrostBites."

"Get it?" Andy asked. "Because her name—"

"I get it," Will responded. "Thanks."

Veronica continued. "I'm sole owner of the business now, and Gwen acts as my personal assistant both here and at the restaurant. I don't know what I'd do without her."

"How are you feeling today?" Gwen asked Will. "Hopefully you'll be able to string some logical sentences together now that you've gotten some sleep?"

While she chuckled, Will sheepishly replied, "Yeah, I think I'll be better now. Sorry about that."

"No worries," she said. "And the clothes?"

"Great," he answered. "I can't thank you enough. You guys have been so good to me. This is the first time that I've actually felt safe and comfortable in days."

Veronica poured a cup of tea and handed it to him across the table. "Considering what you've been through, William, that's all we can ask."

"Well, thank you," he repeated.

"Oh, stop thanking us and eat," said Gwen as she stood and cleared her plate. "I need to head out to the restaurant for a bit, but I'll be back this afternoon. Do you need anything else?"

"I think we're fine for now, Gwen. Thank you and be careful."

This last comment caught Will's attention, and once Gwen had left, he asked, "Careful about what?"

Veronica hesitated for a moment. "The weather, dear. It's nasty outside."

"Oh," said Will. "So does Gwen live here also?"

"No, no," said Veronica. "She has her own apartment downtown. However, I could see why you might ask that. You'll see her around here quite a lot. She's basically my right hand. She used to work as a waitress at FrostBites, but she was far too bright and efficient to be stuck in that position. I made her manager, and then I hired her as my personal assistant. When her modeling career takes off, and I'm sure that it will, I'm going to experience quite a loss."

"Does she model now?" Andy asked.

"Here and there," she said. "She's been featured in several print advertisements, but the work is too sporadic for her to be able to support herself. It doesn't help that I'm holding her back."

"Why are you holding her back?"

"Oh, I'm not doing it on purpose, Andy. I would never do that. It's just that she's so devoted to me, and believe me, being my personal assistant is time-consuming. I'm sure that she's turned down opportunities out of loyalty to me and my business. It makes me feel terrible, but for so long she's been all that I've had." She lifted her eyes from her teacup at this point and looked lovingly at Will. "Until now, that is."

Will felt a bit on the spot but smiled back politely. "So it's just you here?"

Veronica nodded. "Technically, yes. But you'll see that people come and go all the time. For instance, as you were nodding off last night, I learned that you met Mr. Wisp." Will had nearly forgotten about the strange man in the kitchen. "You'll find he's something of a character."

"Seemed that way," said Will. "Is he...how do I say this? Does he have any special talents?"

"Oh, he has many," Veronica said with a mischievous grin.

"But I suppose you're asking whether he's like you? Whether he has the demonic strain as well?" Will nodded. "Yes, he does. He can read minds."

"Get out!" said Andy. "For real?"

"For real," Veronica replied. "Although I've asked him to refrain from doing so in this household. I guess I'll have to ask less politely next time. I apologize for that, William."

"It's okay," he said, though it was most definitely not. All he could do was try to think back to the embarrassing thoughts that Wisp may have extracted from his head. He suddenly empathized with the hotel clerk who had been influenced by Simon and felt, in a way, violated.

"So what can you do?" asked Andy, visibly excited by this brave new world of superpowers.

"Me?" Veronica responded. "I'm afraid I'm not in that club. I'm just as average a person as you are, Andy. You see, historically, only the men in our family have ever had any hint of the strain."

"Why?" Andy persisted.

"I really couldn't tell you," said Veronica, anxious to move onto another topic. "So William, when Gwen returns, she may have some news that concerns you. We can talk then. In the meantime, you two have some catching up to do. Feel free to watch television, explore the house, whatever you want. Just please don't leave, okay? This is the only place where we are sure that you're safe."

"Alright," said Will, somewhat disappointed that she did not seem in the frame of mind to talk further. He wanted to know more about her but decided not to push. There would be time enough later.

"Thanks for the food, Mrs. Frost," said Andy.

"It was my pleasure. Don't worry about cleaning up," she said, noticing that the boys had begun to stack their dishes. "I'll get that later, after I lie down. I have a slight headache."

Will noticed that she seemed drained of energy, so he let her go with a smile and a nod. "This is crazy," said Andy once she had left the room. "You need to catch me up on—"

"Shhh!" Will interrupted, holding a finger to his lips. He listened for a moment and heard his aunt humming an eerily familiar tune as she ascended the stairs. He shot up from the table and ran after her as quickly as his bum leg would allow. "Aunt Veronica?" he called up the stairs. She turned and looked at him with curiosity. "What is that song you're humming?"

"'You Are My Sunshine,'" she said to his amazement. "Do you know it?"

"Apparently," he muttered.

Veronica forced a smile but could not hide the sadness in her eyes. "I used to sing it to you when you were a baby. It used to put you right out. I guess just having you here is reminding me of that." Will did not know how to respond, and so he stood staring blankly as his aunt disappeared from the second-floor landing and the townhouse's lights flickered and dimmed from the storm.

FRANCES WHITWORTH FOUGHT BACK a yawn while she sat in her car outside of FrostBites. The previous day had been more taxing than she had expected, and today's dreary weather was not helping to keep her awake. Still, she needed to be on her game, so she took another sip of coffee and peered into the rearview mirror. There, she saw the blurry headlights of a black Mercedes that had not been there a moment ago. Taking a deep breath, she grabbed her umbrella and walked calmly to the shelter of the awning hanging over the front door of the restaurant.

Taking her cue, Gwen Henley unlocked the door from within and joined Whitworth in watching a trio of men step out of the Mercedes. Desmond Duquesne and George Brisbane each had umbrellas, while Emil Havelock chose to walk bare-headed in a sleek black trench coat. Upon reaching the awning, Duquesne first addressed Gwen. "Good afternoon, my dear. You must be Miss Henley. You're quite beautiful."

Gwen would have normally blushed, but her nerves prevented her from doing so. "It's a pleasure," she said, displaying no actual pleasure.

"This is Professor Brisbane, and this is Mr. Havelock. If you don't mind, Mr. Havelock is going to have a look around the restaurant—just in case." While Havelock stepped inside the restaurant with Gwen, Duquesne turned his attention to Whitworth. "So," he said. "It's been a long time." He held out his hand for Whitworth to take, but the latter did not reciprocate.

"Not quite long enough," said Whitworth.

The two stood quietly for a few moments, Duquesne grinning wryly and Whitworth playing with the Velcro strap on her umbrella, until George Brisbane broke the awkward silence with, "This weather is unfortunate."

"Yes," said Whitworth.

"Mmmm," agreed Duquesne.

Another stint of silence passed before Duquesne said, "Have you eaten here?"

"I have," said Whitworth. "Once or twice. You?"

"No," Duquesne responded. "I've heard good things. Management doesn't care for me."

"I went to Olive Garden last week," said Brisbane. The two old acquaintances met Brisbane's contribution with puzzled looks. "Breadsticks…" he said, as though offering a one-word explanation.

Luckily, Havelock reappeared at this point and ushered the three inside, where Duquesne felt able to speak more freely. "I apologize for the hoopla," he said. "But you must understand that I needed to make sure William Trammell wasn't sitting in the kitchen with a sniper rifle like he was sitting in that poor woman's apartment yesterday."

"I assure you," said Whitworth, taking a seat at a table indicated by Gwen, "with the exception of Miss Henley, I am very much on my own here. No tricks, as promised." She glanced at Brisbane and Havelock. "Which is more than I can say for you. What's wrong, Desmond? Don't you trust me?"

"Oh, I believe that you're a woman of your word," Duquesne replied. "I just don't trust Valentine, Brandt, or anyone else with whom you associate. In fact, I was surprised to see that Brandt was back in action. I thought he was retired."

"As it turns out, he hates you just enough to be drawn out of retirement."

Duquesne grinned. "Don't kid yourself, Frances. He hates both of us. You know what my theory is? He's jealous. He's always felt inferior to us, and that upsets him."

"And who are we that he should feel inferior?"

Duquesne sneered. "Come on, Frances. Don't feign humility. We each have more power in our little fingers than a thug like Brandt could ever hope to attain."

"Hope springs eternal," Whitworth mused. "After all, you weren't exactly born with power. What separates you from Brandt?"

Duquesne reeled from the perceived insult, but answered, "Ambition. Intelligence. Class."

Whitworth smiled knowingly. "Right...class," she said with a snort. "You can surround yourself with the priciest cars, the most beautiful homes, and the best help money can buy, but in my book, you're a sniveling coward who has only ever taken the easy way out. You're a child playing dress-up. You steal your power in cheap and underhanded ways, all because you can't accept how the world works. All because you're afraid to die."

Duquesne clenched his jaw and tapped the fingers of his right hand on the table. "I can't force you to like me, Frances, but why not just let me be? After all, I respect the mission of your organization, and I don't get in the way, do I? You do good work, important work. As do I. Why must you be so obsessed with my death? It borders on psychotic."

"Here's the thing," said Whitworth, leaning in with her hands folded on the table. "I'll say it slowly so that there can be no confusion: you are a murderer."

"Granted. But I'm also a philanthropist, a humanitarian even. I despise taking lives, but sometimes that's just what needs to happen for the greater good. History tells us so."

"So is it history's fault that James Lawrence is dead?" Whitworth asked.

"Who?" said Duquesne, knitting his brow.

Whitworth shook her head at the gall of Duquesne. It was common knowledge among their circle that Duquesne had bought the city authorities long ago, thus ensuring that any investigation of Lawrence's disappearance would go nowhere. Rather than continue her line of questioning, Whitworth addressed Gwen. "Miss Henley, could I bother you for a drink? Whiskey would be divine. With just a splash of water."

"Make that two, my dear," said Duquesne, "and I'll gladly treat my old friend here to the best you've got. And make mine neat." She nodded, and Duquesne leered as she reached for a bottle of amber liquid reserved for the establishment's most discerning guests. Once the glasses had been brought to the table, he thanked her with a wink and said, "Now, Frances, let's get to business. You said on the phone that you have an offer for me. I'll admit that I'm intrigued, especially now that you've sweet-talked me so much."

"I'm offering you the chance to do the right thing," Whitworth began.

Duquesne looked askance at the proposal. "Well, I'm not quite sure that would work out. It's been made abundantly clear from our conversation alone that you and I do not typically agree on what the right thing is."

"Hear me out," said Whitworth. "

I NEED you to give up on whatever ritual you are planning and leave William Kendrick alone."

Emil Havelock gave a derisive snort from the far corner of the room, but an unfazed Whitworth simply took a sip of her whiskey and awaited her opponent's response. When it came, it followed a long pause and a quizzical expression. "That's your proposal? Frances, you could have asked me this over the phone, and my answer would have been 'no,' just like it is now. I find it difficult to believe that your grand plan was to sit me down and ask me nicely to, for lack of a better phrase, 'knock it off.' I have the chance to gain immeasurable power, and I'm far too close to that brass ring to give up now."

"Desmond, what if I offered you the chance to attain a different kind of immortality?"

"Are you planning to dedicate a statue to me? Perhaps a painting? Thank you, but I've already got those as well."

Whitworth swirled her whiskey gently as she considered how to continue. "Listen, Desmond," he said. "Things have changed."

"Since when?"

"Since yesterday." This, Whitworth noticed, seemed to have finally caught Duquesne's attention. "Yesterday I learned that this prophecy, the one that says that William must be the one to kill you, was created primarily to drive a wedge between the Duquesne and Gleave families."

Duquesne's eyes lit up. "So it's not true?" he asked.

"Oh, it's still true," said Whitworth. At this, Duquesne's previous excitement dissipated. "However, long before this prophecy existed, another one was hidden—one that says only the combined efforts of Gleave and Duquesne will be able to fight back the coming darkness."

"What darkness?" Duquesne asked.

"From what I understand," Whitworth responded, "the Absence."

Duquesne stared at his fingertips as he tapped them together gently. Eventually, he took a tremendous swig of his whiskey and said to Gwen, "Miss Henley, if you could make it a double this time, I'd be forever grateful."

Havelock cleared his throat. "Would someone mind explaining what exactly this 'Absence' is? You know, for those of us who can't pull rabbits from hats?"

"The Absence is what it sounds like, Emil," Duquesne responded. "It's nothing. It's the purest of voids. It's what came before everything. It predates humanity. It predates the universe. It predates the Big Bang."

"Are you familiar with the biblical phrase 'In the beginning...'?" Whitworth added.

"Of course," said Havelock.

"Before that."

"And there are people—fanatics—who long for its return. They see it as a cleanse, a purge, or some such nonsense," Duquesne continued before returning his attention to Whitworth. "But how do I know that you are telling the truth?"

"You're a power-hungry lunatic who should have been dead over a century ago," Whitworth replied. "Can you think of any good reasons why I'd want to keep you alive? 'Preventing the end of the world' is pretty much the only item on that list."

"Fair enough," said Duquesne. "But why wasn't I aware of this prophecy?"

"I didn't know either," said Whitworth. "It was a well-kept secret."

Duquesne ignored Whitworth and instead focused his attention on George Brisbane, who was seated at the bar. His voice rising with anxiety, Duquesne asked again, "Why did I not know about this prophecy?"

Brisbane approached, grabbed a chair and hastily sat down between the two nemeses. "In all my research," he said, "I've never seen anything about it. How did you hear about it?"

"I received word of it from an anonymous party."

Brisbane eyed Whitworth incredulously, but Duquesne chortled. "Don't you see, George? 'An anonymous party.' It's those damn faceless friends of Frances' again, sticking their nonexistent noses in my business at the most inopportune time."

"Perhaps," said Whitworth. "Regardless of who sent me the news, the prophecy exists, so I recommend that you stop viewing young Mr. Kendrick as an adversary and begin looking at him as a possible ally."

"Well," Duquesne said, once more leaning back in his seat. "This *does* change things. Any other interesting information you'd like to pass on?"

"No other information," said Whitworth, taking another sip. "Only advice."

Duquesne's cocked his head. "Feeling bold, eh?"

WE KNOW each other very well, Desmond. I know that there are two things that matter more to you than anything else: avoiding the inevitability of death and preserving your family's legacy. So let's play this out. Tomorrow, you launch an all-out assault on the Collective. You kill me, you kill Brandt, and most importantly, you kill William Trammell. The path is clear for you to perform whatever ritual you're planning and add another few decades onto your life. Congratulations. But guess what? When the Absence comes knocking, you'll have no place to run. You will go to your death knowing that had you let William live, the two of you could have saved the world. You could have cemented your legacy as a hero. Don't be short-sighted."

Thunder cracked outside the restaurant and the rain hammered down harder than before, but the room fell silent as Duquesne digested the scenario that Whitworth had just laid out. "Well, I'll be damned," he finally said in a hushed tone.

A sense of relief washed over Whitworth as she saw what she sensed as understanding in Duquesne's eyes. Maybe catastrophe could be averted after all. "Do you agree to abandon your ritual and leave the boy alone?" she asked.

"This is my life's work," said Duquesne. "It's what I've scraped and clawed for since youth."

"Even immortality will be rendered pointless should the world end."

Duquesne pensively rubbed his chin a few times before responding. "How do you want to play this?"

"You agree to give up on the ritual. Beyond that, I ask that you meet the boy. Introduce him to your family. It's vital that this cold war between the Gleaves and Duquesnes ends."

"And you'll give the boy instructions not to try anything against me?"

Whitworth nodded. "As long as you give up on your schemes, I'll tell William to do you no harm. Believe me—he is not looking for a fight."

"That sounds amenable, but how do you know that you can trust me?" asked Duquesne with a devilish grin. "I may just be telling you what you want to hear."

"Make no mistake: if you give us no choice, we will put you down. Remember: the prophecy said that the darkness would be stopped by Gleave and Duquesne, and you're not the only Duquesne."

"Well played," said Desmond.

"Excuse me," said George Brisbane. "I'm not sure whether this has been considered, but just being in close proximity to the boy is dangerous for Mr. Duquesne. We know that he can kill him with a touch. Who's to say that he couldn't do the same to other members of the Duquesne family, perhaps even unintentionally? One handshake and Daphne or Alexander could be doomed."

"A solid point, Dr. Brisbane," said Duquesne. "How do I know, Frances, that I'm not unwittingly putting a hit out on my own children?"

Whitworth considered this for a few seconds before asking, "Would your daughter submit to a blood test? Our labs could determine the risk."

"We'll see," said Duquesne. He took a pause. "You don't think that Alexander should be tested as well?"

Whitworth realized her misstep. "Well, I mean, Daphne is William's age, right? I just assumed…"

"Frances, Frances, Frances," Duquesne said with mock incredulity. "If I didn't know any better, I'd think you were trying to play Cupid. Hedging your bets in case you feel the need to dispose of me?"

"Desmond…"

"Don't try to play me, old friend. I know you too well. You play the long game. I'll play along because I think I believe you about the Absence. And if William Trammell hits it off with Daphne, so be it." The relatively friendly tone of Duquesne's voice disappeared as he continued, "But if I catch wind that you're trying to manipulate my daughter, either through Simon or any other means, I will burn your entire organization to the ground."

"Threats are not necessary, Desmond," Whitworth said. "I would never think of manipulating your daughter."

"Of course you wouldn't," Duquesne grinned. "So where do we go from here?"

"I'd like to set up a meeting with you and Will tomorrow."

"He's welcome to come to New Covington. You, however,

are not. My condition is no Collective presence on my property. That doesn't end well."

"I figured as much," said Whitworth.

"Shall I expect the boy to come alone?"

"I'm not quite *that* trusting. Miss Henley has graciously offered to bring him tomorrow. A classmate of his will be tagging along as well. I'm trusting that what's left of your integrity will ensure their safety."

"They will all be welcome," said Duquesne, finishing his second drink and picking up his umbrella. "For now, though, I must be going. I have two parties to plan. I thank you for your candor, Frances. I've always respected that about you." After signaling for Havelock and Brisbane to make their way out of the restaurant, he took Gwen's hand, kissed it, and said, "And I look forward to seeing you again tomorrow, Miss Henley."

When the three men had left, Gwen slathered sanitizing lotion on her hands and said to Whitworth, "Did that seem too easy to you, or do I just not know what I'm talking about?"

"Gwen, from what your employer tells me, you always know what you are talking about, and in this case, I agree with you entirely. I was hoping to feel better after arranging this truce with Duquesne."

"And now?" she asked.

"I think I feel worse."

ONCE RIDGLEY PULLED AWAY from the restaurant, Havelock broke his silence. "With all due respect," he said to his employer, "after all this time, you can't possibly be considering abandoning your plans because of what that old crackpot said."

"I am considering it," said Duquesne. "But you're right. It would be foolish of me, after this one brief meeting, to throw away decades of preparation. I'll entertain the boy tomorrow.

We'll see how that goes. In the meantime, our plan moves forward, but with much greater discretion. Whitworth and the Collective are sure to be keeping an even closer eye on our movements."

"So we don't kill the kid?"

"No. Let's shelve that for now. If I play my cards right, this new turn of events could work in my favor." He chuckled to himself. "Frances Whitworth just handed me the key to creating the most powerful dynasty this world has ever seen. This may be too good to resist."

FROM THE MOMENT that his aunt excused herself, Will spent hours catching Andy up on what had transpired since the last time they had seen each other. Through it all, Andy sat with his mouth gaping, awed that his longtime friend was now, in his eyes, a kind of superhero. "Dude," Andy said when Will's story had reached its end, "You're literally a killing machine."

Will looked less than thrilled at this description but could only agree. "Seems that way," he said, "though it still feels weird that I'm supposed to kill a guy that I've never met based on what a group of strangers tell me."

"Yeah, but you've gotta avenge your family. I mean, this Duquesne guy killed them!"

"It's not that easy," said Will. "I feel bad saying this, but I don't even remember the Trammells. The more I think about it, the less it feels like revenge. At least, it doesn't feel like *my* revenge. It feels more like I'm taking out Duquesne for the sake of Brandt and the rest of them." He was a bit let down that Andy failed to offer any helpful suggestions, but then, how could anyone relate to what he was going through? "So," he continued, "how are you even here? Your parents just let you come to Boston on your own?"

Andy shrugged. "Sure. You know my parents—they're too

busy to bother catching me in a lie. I said I was looking at colleges with you and your parents, so remind me to pick up some brochures before I go home."

Will laughed. "Will do. What about this job that Whitworth gave you? You going to tell me what that's all about?"

"Ah! Perfect timing!" said Whitworth, entering the living room with Gwen. "We'll get to Andy's job in a second, but where is your aunt, William?"

"She went to lie down," he said. "She said she had a headache." Gwen and Whitworth exchanged knowing glances and then each took a seat. "Is everything alright?" Will asked.

"Absolutely," said Whitworth.

Gwen crossed her long legs and leaned in to address Will. "Will, while Mrs. Frost isn't here, there's something I feel I should tell you."

"Oh God," Will moaned. "What now?"

"Nothing bad," Gwen reassured him. "It's just—well—you may have noticed, but your aunt has had an uphill battle with depression. It set in years ago, just after the deaths of her son and husband."

"Understandably," Whitworth added.

Gwen continued, "What she did today is not unusual. She'll often find herself overwhelmed and will sequester herself in her room for a while. Don't think anything of it, okay?"

"Of course," said Will. "Is there anything I can do?"

"You're doing it," Gwen said. "Believe me, from the moment she received Ms. Whitworth's first phone call about your being alive, she actually showed an infusion of energy. I really think that your being here will make a world of difference."

"In many ways," said Whitworth. "Which brings us back to your reason for being here in the first place."

"Desmond Duquesne," Will offered.

"Exactly. Now, William, I have good news and bad news on

that front. The good news is that Miss Henley and I just came from a meeting with Duquesne himself, where we were able to reach a kind of truce."

"Meaning that I'm not expected to kill him?"

"Not at present, no. In return, Mr. Duquesne has vowed not to harm you either."

"So what's the bad news?"

"The bad news," Whitworth said, "is that you are expected for a visit at Duquesne's house tomorrow."

"What?" Will yelled. "Why the hell would that happen?"

"I arranged it, William. Hear me out. Nothing bad is going to happen to you, but it has become vitally important that you learn to coexist with Desmond Duquesne. The fate of the world could depend on it."

"I can't believe this," Will said. He turned to Andy and asked, "Do you believe what she's saying?"

"I kind of already knew about it," he admitted while avoiding eye contact with his friend.

Will shot Andy an incredulous glance, which then landed on Whitworth. "Andy's job is to be your companion. He and Miss Henley will be accompanying you to New Covington tomorrow."

Will shook his head in disbelief. "And what am I supposed to do when I get there, just hang out with the guy? 'Oh hi. Thanks for trying to have me killed. Want to play Scrabble?'"

"I hardly think you'll be there long enough for a game of Scrabble," said a befuddled Whitworth.

"I'll be there with you, Will. Trust me. To everyone but Desmond, we'll be there for a real estate deal. Andy and I won't let anything happen to you," Gwen promised.

"I appreciate that," Will said with sincerity. "But Ms. Whitworth, how much are Gwen and Andy going to be able to help if Duquesne tries to kill me?"

"He won't," said Whitworth. "I know you're there, Director

Valentine knows you're there, your aunt knows that you're there, and you'll be with two friends. He would be a fool to try anything that might harm you. Desmond Duquesne may be a lot of things, but he is certainly not a fool. Besides, I've taken a few precautions to ensure your safety."

"Like what?"

"I can't tell you now, but let's just say that there are more eyes on you than you know."

IN A VACANT TOWNHOUSE across the street, Eddie Garza watched through the rain-soaked window as Whitworth scurried to her car from Veronica Frost's doorstep. "You're going to get this boy killed," he murmured. "Crazy old loon."

TWENTY-NINE

The Meeting

HAVING BEEN BRIEFED on the restaurant business by his aunt and Gwen the previous night, Will assumed that he would retain enough information to be able to carry a conversation with Desmond Duquesne. But as they pulled up to the gates of New Covington, he found that he could only recall phrases such as 'New American' and 'point of distinction,' but had no earthly idea what said phrases meant. Instead, all he could think of when stepping out of the car was the grandeur of Duquesne's estate. The house was like something out of *Gatsby* with its stone columns and elaborate archways.

"I feel underdressed," Andy said when he saw Ridgley coming down the steps to greet them.

The older man overheard and said, "Nonsense, Mr. Lunsford. Don't let the facade fool you. Mr. Duquesne has a taste for classic architecture, but he prefers his guests to be as comfortable as possible."

"Oh. Thanks, Mr…"

"Ridgley," he answered, motioning for them to follow him up the stairs. As he led them into the expansive foyer, he explained, "My wife and I have worked for Mr. Duquesne for many, many years. We tend to the house and assist in any way we can. If you need anything while you are here, please feel free to let us know. Ah! Here's my wife now."

"I'm coming, I'm coming," said Mrs. Ridgley, evidently arriving from the kitchen, as she hastily wiped cookie crumbs from the corners of her mouth with the back of her hand.

"Mrs. Ridgley," said Mr. Ridgley, "this is Mr. Andrew Lunsford, Miss Gwen Henley, and this young man—this is Mr. William Trammell himself." He said Will's name proudly, as though introducing a dignitary, but Mrs. Ridgley, Will noticed, was unimpressed.

Looking him up and down, she did not offer a greeting, but rather said, "Him?"

Embarrassed, Mr. Ridgley attempted some damage control, saying, "Excuse my wife. She's on pain pills. She has a problem with...what was it now, dear?"

"My wrists," she said. "I think I'm getting carpal tunnel, what with all the potatoes I've been peeling and such."

"That must be a lot of potatoes," said Andy, whose comment was met with a scowl.

"It is," she snapped. "Mr. and Mrs. Duquesne have guests over quite frequently, and Mr. Duquesne always insists on a home-cooked meal. It's quite a bit of hard work," she said, massaging her wrist splint. "We can't all have fancy jobs with fancy clothes," she added, scowling at Gwen, who looked like a deer in headlights. "Or be skinny."

"Um...sorry?" was all that Gwen could think to mutter.

"Me too," Andy added, though he wasn't sure what for.

Not me, thought Will, who had immediately developed a strong dislike for the female Ridgley. He motioned with his crutch and said, "I guess we're in a similar boat. Stinks, right? I hope you feel better soon."

"Me too," she said, ignoring his injury. "Anyways, I guess I should go tell Mr. and Mrs. Duquesne that you're here."

"No need," said a voice from the landing atop the curving marble stairs. Will looked up and immediately recognized the face of Desmond Duquesne. The older gentleman was dressed in a dapper black suit with a royal purple tie and leaned slightly on a cane topped with a brass sphere. Will's blood ran cold as he slowly descended to the first floor, the tip of the cane tapping lightly on each marble step, his eyes locked on Will's the entire time. *Step, step, tap.*

Having reached the bottom of the stairs, Duquesne walked silently over to Will and stood eye-to-eye with him. Andy, Gwen, and the Ridgleys held their breath as the only sound to be heard was that of the brass tip of the cane coming to rest on the floor in front of Duquesne with a metallic knock. For the first time, Will felt how powerful he truly was as he noted that Duquesne stood at a safe distance. With one quick movement, he could lunge forward, grab Duquesne, and end it all right there and then. Part of him wanted to; part of him just wanted to see what would happen if he did, in fact, go after the old man. Duquesne stood staring icily with his gray eyes, similarly considering striking the boy down where he stood. "So," he said, still fixated on Will's face, "this is William Trammell."

Gwen Henley felt as though she were standing on pins and needles. *Come on, Will. Don't do anything stupid*, she thought.

"Mr. Duquesne," Will said. "I would offer my hand, but I doubt you'd want to shake it."

As Duquesne's stoic expression gradually twisted into a smile, the room let out a collective sigh of relief. "No, I suppose that wouldn't be prudent, would it? But I see no problem in shaking your friends' hands," he said, turning his attention to Andy. "You must be Mr. Lunsford," he said, shaking Andy's clammy, tremulous hand. "And of course, Miss Henley. What a pleasure to see you twice in as many days." She smiled politely and tried to hide her contempt as he once more kissed her hand. "Before we get down to the real estate business," he said, "I was wondering if there is a way for me and Mr. Trammell to speak privately for a few moments."

Andy and Gwen exchanged quick, worried glances, as they had each received instruction not to leave Will alone at any point of the visit. Noting their concern, Duquesne continued, "I assure you, I have more to fear from Mr. Trammell than he does from me. What do you say, Will?" he asked, bypassing the boy's less-than-enthusiastic support system.

Will was not sure how, but he could sense from Duquesne's tone that no harm was intended, and he saw this as an opportunity to fill in some of the blanks regarding his past. If anyone knew the truth about why he was what he was, it was Desmond Duquesne. "I'm okay with it," Will said with a small quiver in his voice.

"Admirable courage," Duquesne said. "You'll see your friends again in a matter of moments. I promise. Come this way. We can talk in my office." Will followed Duquesne into the main hall of New Covington and stood impressed by what he saw. The floors were brightly polished, light streamed in through innumerable windows, and the main hall itself stood three stories tall with wrought iron guardrails visible on each floor, no doubt to prevent guests from tumbling down into the vastness of the open space. Reaching into the center of this space was another marble staircase, much wider and more imposing than the one from which Duquesne had descended only moments earlier. Duquesne, who had remained silent as they walked, now acknowledged Will's injury. "What happened to your leg?"

"You sent people to kill me," Will responded.

"Well what on earth did they use?"

"Zombie bear."

"Huh. I swear, it's like no one I hire has ever heard of a bullet," Duquesne mused. "Why don't we use the elevator?"

"You have an elevator?"

"It would have been cruel of me to mention one if I didn't." He led Will to a far corner of the room and opened a broad wooden door. Inside, there was an old-fashioned elevator complete with retractable gate that they rode silently to the second floor of the mansion.

WILL SOON FOUND himself sitting in the same plush leather armchair that Eleanor Hornbeck had previously enjoyed, while Duquesne settled himself into the chair opposite. The older man spent what seemed like forever looking intently at Will, but eventually said, "Tell me, William: what do you know of me? I'd be very interested to know what you've heard."

"Well," said Will, not really sure in what direction to take his answer, "I've been told that you had my birth parents killed, and that you're practically immortal."

"This is true."

"Which?"

"Both," said Duquesne. "But before we get into a discussion of the magic business, I would like to look you in the eye and sincerely apologize for everything that the decisions of others, myself included, have put you through. It's not fair."

"No, it's not," said Will. "And I think it's messed up, but appropriate, that the only person to apologize so far is the one who caused all of this. My parents are dead because of you. You admit that. How am I supposed to forgive that? Why shouldn't I kill you right now?"

A slight twitch betrayed Duquesne's discomfort, but he quickly regained his composure and answered, "It would be too much for me to ask for your forgiveness, especially considering the fact that I ordered another hit on you earlier this week.

Perhaps that was rash. However, maybe I can at least get you to understand my perspective."

This guy's crazy, Will thought. But remembering that he was also very dangerous, Will decided it best to say nothing and play along.

"Let me show you something," said Duquesne, rising from his chair and unlocking a closet in the corner of the room behind his desk. The closet was stacked high with boxes, which were filled to bursting with what Will was surprised to see were awards. The old man dragged one particularly heavy-looking box out onto the maroon carpet, selected a silver plaque set on a block of cherry wood, and handed it to Will. The plaque was from the Feed a Friend Foundation and was etched with the phrase 'Humanitarian of the Year.' "Please don't think me ungrateful for keeping these awards tucked away, but I don't help people for the prestige. Besides, as you can see, my mask collection takes up most of my available wall space."

Will walked over to the closet and peered inside, noting that every award, plaque, or certificate in sight was from a different organization, but each reflected the same gratitude for Duquesne's generosity. "I don't understand," said Will. "How can you kill some people and save others?"

"It's about the greater good, William. You see, I enjoy helping people. I have been very fortunate and have made quite a bit of money, and it makes me feel good to give back. I need you to know that I deeply regret any loss of life that results from my actions, but can you imagine how many lives I have saved? Look at these awards. Each one symbolizes dozens of families who have benefited from my longevity and affluence. Why do I want to live so long, William? Because as long as I am breathing, I am able to better the lives of others. People like John Brandt and Frances Whitworth simply don't understand that. They'd rather punish me for my few crimes than allow me to continue my many missions."

"The person that the park was being dedicated to…that wasn't your father, was it? It was you."

"Correct," said Duquesne. "Many so-called 'normal' folks suspect that people like you and I exist, but for the most part, the world is not ready to find out about us yet. My extended lifetime has made it necessary to think creatively, and so I have essentially become my own son, grandson, et cetera. You may notice," he said, handing Will a sepia-tinted photo of himself that he retrieved from his desk drawer, "that I look slightly different now than I have in the past. Every few decades, when the time seems right, I take myself on a trip around the world. I disappear for a number of years and, during that time, have some minor cosmetic surgeries done. When I reappear, I do so as my own descendant. It gets tedious, but it is worth the annoyance."

"So you basically fake your own death?"

"Not often, but yes, that's the gist of it. Pretty tricky, huh?" Duquesne's eyes lit up as he briefly reveled in his own ingenuity.

"What about your family?" Will asked. "What happens to them when you decide to do this?"

Duquesne considered briefly before responding. "Honestly, it's never come up before. I've been married in the past, but for one reason or another, these marriages have never lasted. Also," he said in a more somber tone, "my current wife, Joanna, is the only one with whom I've ever been able to have children.

"William," he continued, "whether either of us like it, our fates have been intertwined by forces beyond our control. In that way, we are in the same boat. These forces want us to be at each other's throats, to be mortal enemies. I don't know about you, but I don't care much for being controlled. I say that we attempt to coexist. After all, we're apparently destined to save the world. Let's both be heroes, shall we?"

Will had experienced a flurry of emotions since entering Duquesne's home, but the one that had dissipated was fear. He looked at the delusional grin on the old man's face and realized that Duquesne truly believed in the prophecy that Whitworth had discovered, and that the opportunity to be known as a savior might just trump his desire to kill Will. He still wasn't entirely sure what to think about this character, but Will was at least relatively certain that, for now, he had nothing to fear from the owner of New Covington. "I'm new to all of this magic and prophecy stuff," said Will, "but I've seen enough in the past few days to believe that it exists. I don't want the world to end any more than you do. We're not buddies. I don't forgive you for what you did to my parents, but I won't kill you."

"There's a generous chap," Duquesne said with a smile that Will judged as either amused or condescending—possibly both. "And as a gesture of good will, I'd like to give you something." Desmond walked to a porcelain umbrella stand next to his fireplace and selected an ebony cane topped with a silver lion's head. He handed it gingerly to Will, making sure not to accidentally brush his hands against his rival's.

Will turned the cane over a few times, examining its fine detail and beauty. "It's really great," he said, "but I'm not sure that it's my style. Thank you anyway, though."

"I insist that you take it. Consider it a piece of your inheritance. You see, this was one of your great-great-grandfather's favorite items. He carried it everywhere. When he died, I just had to have it, so I offered his widow a hefty price for it. I always admired its beauty, and it actually inspired my collection. Since that time, I've purchased hundreds more, so while I'll always have a sentimental attachment to this one, I've got plenty of others. Besides, it's so much classier than that crutch."

Will couldn't help but agree with this but tried not to smile at the observation. He instead nodded stoically and said, "I appreciate the gesture. Thank you."

"Now let's show it off," Duquesne said. "I'm sure your friends are wondering whether either of us is still alive." He picked up a phone on his desk and said, "Ridgley, please bring our other guests up."

Within moments, Andy appeared in the doorway of the office, followed by Gwen, who immediately noted Will's new cane, and, comparing it to Duquesne's, said, "Well isn't this cute. A matching set."

Will suddenly felt ashamed for taking the gift from Desmond, but their host simply chuckled and said, "Not quite. His is much better quality. Now, shall we discuss business?"

Duquesne settled in behind his desk and opened a large binder full of real estate listings. "I wasn't sure exactly what Mrs. Frost is looking for, but I think that I was able to find a wide range of options. Take a look, and if you have any questions, please do not hesitate to ask."

Gwen and Will sat opposite Duquesne, and when Gwen took the binder from the real estate mogul, Will did his best to feign interest in the properties that she flipped through. Andy, in the meantime, made no effort to be interested, but rather examined the dozens of masks lining the walls of the office. Every now and then, Duquesne would call out, "That's from the Congo" or "That's a one-of-a-kind carved mask from Zimbabwe," to which Andy would typically respond with either "sweet" or "spooky."

"Yes," said Duquesne, "I suppose some of them do seem a bit spooky at times. My wife Joanna hated them for a long time, but she later found them to be great inspirations for her paintings. You should see them sometime."

Gwen closed the binder and interrupted Duquesne's musings. "Some of these look like they'd fit our needs. What's our next step?"

"Well, if William is agreeable, perhaps I could take you to see a few of the places over the next several days?"

He looked at Will expectantly until he answered, "Okay. As long as I'm here, I'd like to see Boston anyway."

Duquesne clapped his hands together, stood, and said, "Then we'll make a plan. Let me see you folks out now. I'm sure you're anxious to report about the progress we've made today."

"BEFORE I SHOW you to your car," said Duquesne as they stepped out of the elevator into the main hall, "I'd love for you to meet my wife and daughter. Do you have a minute to spare?"

Will looked at Gwen, who gave an approving nod, and said, "Sure." For a while, he had forgotten about Duquesne's beautiful daughter, but he was now grateful that the old man had thought to introduce them. Maybe what he expected to be the day from hell really wouldn't turn out that badly after all. He shot a glance to Andy, who winked all-too-conspicuously, having been told all about his crush during Will's briefing the day before.

"Just remember," Andy mouthed as they walked, "no touching."

Will shushed Andy and signaled for him to listen. As they walked toward the opposite end of the main hall, they heard the faint tones of a piano preceding the sound of a smooth, sweet voice singing, "I'm flying high, but I've got a feeling I'm falling…Falling for nobody else but you…" Will immediately associated this sweet voice with the face of Daphne Duquesne, knowing that it must belong to the stunning girl whom he had seen with her father at the dedication ceremony.

"Is that your daughter?" Andy asked, similarly impressed.

"It is, Mr. Lunsford. She's good, isn't she?" Duquesne held a finger to his lips as he slowly pushed open the door to the room in which Daphne was rehearsing. Daphne's back was to them, but facing them, seated at the piano, was a woman Will recognized as Desmond's wife Joanna. She would ever-so-slightly nod as her daughter hit the required notes, and to Will, every word seemed perfectly sung. The entirety of the song had almost passed by the time Joanna acknowledged their presence with a quick smile, which Daphne did her best to ignore, but could not. Her curiosity got the better of her during the last line of the song.

"Falling for nobody else but...Dad!" She had turned around mid-line, expecting to see her father, or maybe one of the Ridgleys, but instead saw a collection of strangers and shrunk in humiliation. "Really, Dad?" she exclaimed. "Oh my God, I'm so embarrassed."

"Don't be," said Will, almost instinctively. "You were great."

Her face grew an even deeper red, but she flashed a smile of appreciation.

"You're going to have to get used to an audience if you want to sing at the masquerade, Daphne," her mother said. "You'll be singing in front of hundreds of people." She turned her attention to her guests and introduced herself. "I'm Desmond's wife, Joanna," she said. "You must be William."

"Nice to meet you," said Will. He accepted her outstretched hand, but a sudden chill ran through his arm and his heart skipped a beat as he realized that he had already forgotten the 'no touching' rule.

Joanna observed his reaction and drew him closer to her to whisper, "It's alright, William. I'm not a Duquesne by blood."

William exhaled a sigh of relief as he realized two things. First, he had forgotten what Brandt had told him about blood being the key to everything. Beyond that, he had assumed that Duquesne acted in secret, that his nefarious deeds were well hidden from his family members. But Mrs. Duquesne had given the indication that the family might be well aware, not only of its patriarch's history, but also of Will's capability to kill Desmond. He wondered whether this was Daphne's reasoning for staying at a safe distance near the piano.

"And this is our daughter Daphne," Mrs. Duquesne said, her voice returning to a normal volume.

"Hi," she said shyly.

"She's usually more of a chatterbox," Desmond said. "But I suppose we gave her a fright by sneaking up on her like this while she was practicing."

"I wasn't scared, Dad," she insisted, giving him the 'stop embarrassing me' face.

"Of course not, dear," he said apologetically. "You know, you should talk to Will here. He's new to Boston. You've never been here before, have you Will?"

"You probably would have known if I had," Will responded.

Daphne tried to suppress a grin, but the corner of her mouth curved just enough to show Will that she enjoyed the light jab at her father. "Touché," said Desmond. "My point was going to be that perhaps you could show Will and his friend Andy around at some point. I think that you and William might find you have a lot in common."

Taking the not-so-subtle hints that she was being set up, Daphne's smile disappeared and she asked her father, "Like what?"

"Well...for instance—"

"Dad!" This shout from a man who had entered the room broke Desmond's concentration and visibly angered him. "I need your golf clubs," said the newcomer, brushing past Will, Andy, and Gwen without so much as an acknowledgement.

"Alexander!" Desmond pursed his lips and glared until the younger man gave him his full attention. "This is how you walk into a room when we have guests? Your rudeness knows no bounds."

Alexander, whom Will recalled as Desmond's elder child, granted Will and his companions a cursory "hello" and then returned to his initial request. "I need your clubs."

"For what? You have your own."

"Yours are better. Besides, I was going to let Carson use mine." Alexander motioned toward the doorway, where two of his friends, one male and one female, stood trying to avoid the awkward conversation.

"How many listing agreements have you gotten this week?"

"Don't ask me that now," Alexander hissed, looking around the room. Desmond Duquesne had now successfully humiliated each of his children with ten minutes' time, but on the plus side, Will noticed, Daphne now seemed to be thoroughly enjoying herself.

"I'm willing to bet that you haven't gotten any," Duquesne responded. "I'll tell you what. Finalize three agreements today and I'll let you have my clubs tomorrow. It's supposed to be a beautiful day."

"But Kara can't go tomorrow," he said, pointing to the dark-haired girl who waited for him in the doorway. "It's bad enough we don't have a fourth. We absolutely need a third."

"Well, why not William and Andrew here? They're from South Carolina, home of some of the most beautiful golf courses in the world. I'm sure they play."

The scenario had been entertaining for Will up until this point. Now, feeling on the spot, he looked at Gwen for guidance, but she was caught as off-guard as he was. Alexander, meanwhile, looked the two of them over and appeared less than impressed with what he saw. Andy could hear Alexander's friend Carson murmuring to Kara, "Great. A fat kid and a cripple."

"I play golf," Andy said. "Count me in. That is, unless you'd rather play with yourselves."

Alexander scowled as his father said, "Excellent! See? Now you're a threesome. William?"

"I don't think I should," he said, tapping Roderick Gleave's cane gently against his injured leg. "Doctor's orders. In fact, Andy, don't you have a condition too?"

The oblivious Andy gave Will a puzzled glance and said, "No. Not that I know of."

"Okay…" said Will. "Guess I'll just provide moral support."

"I have an idea," said Desmond.

"You seem so full of them today," his wife muttered behind his back.

"Why don't you two boys go golfing with Alex and Carson tomorrow, and then after, Alex and Daphne can show you the town." The siblings were surprised by their father's suggestion, but whereas Alex agreed begrudgingly, Daphne seemed more receptive to the plan.

So the tee time was set, and Gwen, Andy, and Will all left New Covington rather silently. Gwen dreaded the inevitable briefing with Whitworth and Mrs. Frost, feeling that she had been entrusted with not getting Will in over his head and she had failed. Andy wondered how he was going to learn to golf by the next morning. Maybe YouTube? Will simply could not wrap his head around what had just transpired, and every time he tried, his thoughts were interrupted by the recollection of Daphne Duquesne's voice. "Falling for nobody else but you…"

NOT LONG AFTER the visitors had left, Desmond Duquesne welcomed Emil Havelock into his office. "So," the head of security asked, "how did it go with the Trammell kid?"

"Shockingly well," said Duquesne. "I actually found myself enjoying his company."

Havelock knit his brow. "You're not giving up on the ritual, are you?"

"Not at all. In fact, Mr. Ridgley will be picking up the last of the supplies within the next day or so. We're full speed ahead."

"And did you tell the boy who really killed his parents?"

"No, no," Duquesne answered. "It is far too soon for that. I've got to earn the boy's trust first. Besides, I learned long ago to keep an ace up my sleeve."

THIRTY

The Demon and the Gargoyle

WILL HAD BEEN INSTRUCTED by Whitworth to report back as soon as his meeting with Duquesne had ended, and now he stepped into the lobby of the Stonegate Hotel, gaping at his surroundings. He had never seen anything like the massive room in which he stood. The lobby had at one time been the panopticon where the prison's four massive wings converged. Now, it served as a luxury lounge and waiting area, adorned with modern art, plush furniture, and arched windows that stood over thirty feet tall, allowing intense sunbeams to dance from one elaborate chandelier to another.

A gruff old man rushed by Will, knocking his injured leg with an overstuffed suitcase and snapping him out of his trance. He did as Whitworth had told him and approached the front desk, where he caught the eye of a dapper manager who spoke with a deep Jamaican accent but portrayed none of the hospitality often associated with the island. "Can I help you?" the man asked, clearly not a fan of dealing with younger clientele.

"I'm here to see Frances Whitworth," Will said. "She's expecting me."

The manager, whose nameplate read "Anthony" rolled his eyes and answered, "I will contact her when I can, but hotel business comes first." He motioned toward a large group that had just arrived, ready to check in, from the train station across the street. "When I have finished with this group, I'll help you."

Not eager to wait around, Will decided to try another approach. He looked around, leaned in, and whispered, "I'm William Kendrick."

Anthony's eyes went wide as he looked Will up and down. "*The* William Kendrick?" he asked. "Oh my goodness gracious!" Will's pride was short-lived as Anthony deadpanned, "Don't care. Take a seat."

More than a bit chagrined, Will moped away and plopped onto an ornate velvet couch, where he waited for thirty minutes before he saw Whitworth come through a door near the front desk. She looked disapprovingly at Anthony, who shrugged and continued to type away at his computer, before approaching Will.

"I'm sorry about the wait," said the agent. "Anthony can be a bit of a—what's that?"

The cane had caught her eye, the silver lion's head casting bright points of reflection throughout the lobby. "Desmond Duquesne gave it to me," said Will. "It belonged to Roderick Gleave."

Whitworth's mouth curled as an idea formed. "Duquesne may have just given us a lucky break," she said. She beckoned for Will to follow and led him down the hall to an unmarked door. They passed through into what looked like a standard hotel room, and Will hesitantly followed Whitworth's lead as she asked him to stand in the room's shower. The agent stepped in as well, and, after a quick tug of the showerhead, the tub jerked slightly and began to lower into Collective headquarters.

"You could not be weirder if you tried," Will mused as the tub settled in an alcove off the main atrium with the mosaic ceiling.

"You'd be surprised," Whitworth responded. As they traveled to the senior agent's office, Whitworth expanded on the thought that had crossed her mind in the hotel lobby. "As you've probably surmised by now, I am among those, like you, who have certain abilities. One of my particular skills is psychometry, which involves a kind of object memory. You see, each object takes up physical space, and when that object is moved, it leaves an energy signature. If you're lucky or well trained, like I am, you can see that signature and witness the history of an object. For instance, when I first arrived at your parents' house several days ago, I found your baseball mitt. I was able to follow its movements, which is how I knew that Brandt had paid you a visit after you returned from practice on the day he stole you away."

"So you can essentially go back in time?" Will asked as they entered Whitworth's office.

"In a sense, but the object needs to act as a tether. I could see where you carried the mitt, but not beyond that, and I couldn't interact with anything. I can only observe." She took Gleave's cane from Will, slowly twirled it a few times, and said, "I recently came into possession of a disembodied head. Don't ask me how. I don't know. But using my ability, I was able to track the head back to a particularly interesting meeting with Roderick Gleave. Now, with this cane, I may be able to not only show you this meeting but fill in some blanks regarding what truly happened between Gleave and Duquesne all those years ago."

"So I can see these memories too?"

"We'll find out." With the ebony cane in one hand and Will's wrist in the other, Whitworth instructed, "Close your eyes and stay as still as possible." Will did as he was told, bracing himself for what he expected would be similar to a science fiction movie. He envisioned himself zooming through a luminescent celestial wormhole, with Whitworth barely able to keep her grip as they plummeted into the past. Instead, he felt nothing before Whitworth whispered, "Alright. Open your eyes, William."

Will was disappointed by the lack of flair that their journey into the past had presented, but his disillusionment faded when he opened his eyes. He and Whitworth stood in a long dark room that appeared slightly askew—the boards of the floor warped into an undulating pattern and the walls narrowed unnaturally as they led to their focal point—the cane—which leaned against a stack of books at the far end of the room. Here, Will recognized his ancestor, Lord Roderick Gleave, hunched like a horrible gargoyle over his desk, furiously scribbling notes unintelligible to most human eyes.

To say that Lord Roderick had the look of a gargoyle would be neither a slight nor a misrepresentation. Flanked on both sides by towering bookshelves running the length of each wall, he tore through massive tomes that were only dwarfed by his own imposing form. What little moonlight could break through the midnight mist shone in through the window behind him, but any illumination that would have landed on his desk was blocked by his wide shoulders. The only light by which he read came from the low-burning candles, one on either side of the desktop, which shook and flickered precariously as he tossed books violently to the side. Will could not tell whether it was the candlelight or the strain caused by the lack thereof that made his downcast eyes seem a crimson red.

A gentle creak drew Will's attention to the other end of the room, where a familiar figure peeked its head through the open door. "Mr. Ridgley." The Gargoyle acknowledged him without lifting his full head of slate gray hair.

"Sir," Ridgley answered with a slight bow as he slipped through the door and gingerly shut it behind him.

Will did a double take as the servant walked in. His quick, efficient gait reminded Will of a tin soldier, as his starched clothes restricted his movements. "Wait a minute," Will whispered. "Is Ridgley immortal also?"

Whitworth answered, but with marked frustration. "No, William. The Ridgleys have been around for many generations as well. And, I imagine, they will always be around. They have a habit of surviving. The man we're watching now is one of several generations to have served the Duquesne family."

"Like cockroaches," Will mused.

"I suppose," Whitworth shrugged. With this motion, Will's view of the scene began to fade back to Whitworth's present-day office. "Now please, William, be still and pay attention. Let me concentrate. To follow an item this far back in time takes an extraordinary amount of effort." Will nodded and allowed Whitworth her concentration, which in turn brought Gleave's study back into focus.

As Ridgley inched closer to the desk, Lord Roderick's stony hand, which seemed to have given up on the concept of blood circulation long ago, continued to jot notes. "It seems rather late for you to be up and about, Mr. Ridgley," he said, finally raising his eyes to gaze at his visitor. "And looking so...unsettled."

It was now that Will was able to get a clear look at Gleave's features. His eyes did indeed have an unnatural tint of red to them, while the face that housed them possessed no color at all. Lord Roderick wore the complexion of a granite statue eroded from vast exposure to the elements. Although Will couldn't imagine him having been an outdoors type, he owned the deep fissures and rough skin of a farmer—without the healthy bronze glow.

"So?" Gleave asked. "Is there a reason for this interruption?"

"Yes, sir," said Ridgley, his voice steady. "I have just returned from Covington."

"Ah." Lord Roderick placed his pen in the fold of his book, making sure not to drip ink onto any of the strange symbols therein. "And what news from Sir Desmond?"

"Only this, sir," said Ridgley, his hand outstretched to offer his master the sealed letter.

His initial annoyance overcome by genuine curiosity, Lord Roderick took the letter in his cold craggy hand and peered at the crimson seal. The wax bore an image of the classical mask of tragedy, and almost in imitation, Gleave's lips curved downward. Mr. Ridgley watched with interest as his master unceremoniously cracked the seal with a flick of his thumb, unfolded the document, and read, his chapped lips moving ever so slightly.

By the close of the letter, Lord Roderick's eyes had become like two smoldering embers set in the horrific, twisted face of a stone idol. "Mr. Ridgley," he hissed through his teeth, "When did you receive this letter?"

"Just moments ago, sir," the servant answered. "I did as you instructed and brought the final piece of translation to Sir Desmond. He, in turn, handed me the letter."

Lord Roderick did not seem to care about this explanation after all, as while Ridgley was offering it, his master had thrown the letter on the floor and risen from his chair. He grabbed his cane and strode past Ridgley without another word, promptly leaving his study and heading for the foyer. Will and Whitworth followed effortlessly, essentially gliding just above the surface of the warped floor, as though pulled along by the faint blue energy trail that the lion-headed cane left behind. Following Gleave out to the street, Will looked back once more at Mr.

Ridgley and thought he could detect a furtive sneer as he calmly closed the door behind his master.

LORD RODERICK GLEAVE seemed a monstrous golem stomping and sloshing through the puddles in the broken cobblestones. Having given himself no time to do so before leaving his residence, he forced a top hat over his disheveled gray hair. This hat, along with his flowing cloak, effectively doubled his size, and the disreputable folks who lingered in the streets at this time of night found themselves thrown about by the barreling train that was Roderick Gleave. In fact, the only creature that made Lord Roderick pause was a peculiar, dark-haired woman who stood grinning at him near the end of an exceptionally dank and inhospitable alleyway. Infuriated by her obvious amusement at his situation, Lord Roderick took the woman's throat in his powerful grasp.

"And what, madam, do you find so amusing?" he asked, the threat of punishment more than implied.

The woman's icy features remained placid as she muttered, "It doesn't matter."

Gleave's eyebrows narrowed in a moment of vague recognition, and he released the woman, causing her to collapse with a splash into the grimy puddle below. "What do you know, hag?" he demanded.

Gathering her bearings enough to bring herself to one knee, the woman grinned once more, displaying a sharp snaggletooth. "I only know that you're running short on time, Lord Roderick Gleave. Why waste it on an old woman?" Will found it odd that she described herself as old. Yes, she showed some signs of aging around the corners of her eyes and mouth, but she couldn't have been out of her late thirties. Regardless, Gleave appeared to agree with her. He had no time to waste on this witch's nonsense. She cackled as Lord Roderick stomped off toward the end of the alley.

AS HE NEARED Duquesne's home, Will could tell that Lord Roderick was continuing to mull over the contents of the letter Ridgley had handed to him. Still, the time for thinking ended when he kicked open the wrought iron gate separating Covington from the rest of London. Perhaps forewarned that this might happen, two of Desmond Duquesne's servants came rushing from the door to greet him. "Lord Gleave," the first said in a quivering voice, "what a pleasant surprise!"

The man held out his hand in a gesture of feigned kindness, and Lord Roderick grabbed it with enough force to elicit a howl and mangle each of the servant's fingers. "Where is your master, Myres?" he growled.

"I...he...he's in his li-library," Myres whimpered.

His compatriot admonished him, shouting, "Thomas! Sir Desmond will have our heads for this!"

"No he won't," Lord Roderick quipped as he threw Myres into Duquesne's well-pruned rose bushes. The great Gargoyle took the second man's face in his hand and grinned. "He won't get the chance." Starting at the place where Lord Roderick's fingertips met his cheeks, the man's face began to take on a grayish hue, and he barely had time to scream before the head he had just been so worried about losing turned completely to stone. This was followed by his neck, chest, arms, and so on, until Lord Roderick stood grasping a life-size lawn ornament. When he let go, the statued servant toppled onto the grass with a wet thud. Taking no time to admire his handiwork, Gleave clomped up the granite stairs and entered the manor uncere-moniously through the door the servants had left ajar.

Wisps of fog followed Lord Roderick into the darkened marble foyer, weaving through and around his legs like serpents. All was quiet as he headed to the stairway. With Lord Roderick making his way up the stairs, Will noted the masks hanging on every wall, and recognized some from his trip to New Covington. They passed a mask meant to represent the demonic *oni* of Japanese folklore, complete with bulging black eyes, sharp vampiric fangs and a pair of delicately shaped horns. Beyond this was a Gabonese mask, this one twice the size of the *oni* due to its elongated face, but with tiny almond-shaped eyes. While not as overtly sinister as the Japanese mask, the lack of expression on this tribal totem was no less disconcerting. Finally, Lord Roderick came to a Burmese mask, the features of which were exaggerated into a grotesque, though colorful, visage with two rows of razor-sharp teeth formed into a kind of Glasgow grin below two large, hollow eyes. As Gleave reached the landing at the top of the stairs, Will turned to get a better view of the dozens of masks lining the walls of the foyer and felt an unshakable sense of discomfort. He remembered his history teacher telling him that many masks were created in an effort to ward off evil. *So much for that*, he thought.

It was after Gleave had taken a few steps toward the library that Will began to hear sounds coming from the far end of the hall. The noises were muffled at first, but as he neared the heavy doors behind which Gleave would surely find his old friend Desmond, they grew louder. The shattering of glass and the crashing of furniture did not seem to faze Gleave, but the unnatural, primeval scream that pierced his eardrums gave even the great Gargoyle cause to freeze in his substantial tracks.

As Lord Roderick stood listening to what sounded like the high-pitched din of an animal being slaughtered, Mr. Myres approached from behind, gingerly holding his crushed hand to his chest. "Lord Gleave," he said. "Please. Don't do anything that you'll regret. You of all people know how dangerous it is to interrupt these rituals."

Without turning to face the man whom he had crippled,

Gleave nodded his head in an uncharacteristically sullen, defeated manner. "You're right, Myres," Gleave conceded. Reaching under his cloak, he withdrew a pistol from his pocket. "But I think I'll stick around to test the effectiveness of your master's ritual." He looked at Myres' hand with a twinge of sympathy. They had both lost something tonight. "Go take care of yourself, Myres. If Sir Desmond is half the conjuror you think he is, he won't need your assistance." Gleave allowed himself a gruff chuckle. "Not that you could stop me anyway. Now go." He waved the gun carelessly in Myres' direction as the man bowed his head slightly, slowly backed away, and disappeared down the stairs.

No sooner had Myres taken his leave than the sounds from the library ceased. Checking to see that the pistol was indeed loaded, Gleave wasted no time in striding over to the door and forcing it open. The room was in a state of disarray. Books were strewn throughout the room, with hundreds of loose pages scattered on the floor, which itself bore deep scratches as though assaulted by a pack of hyenas. The once beautifully upholstered chairs oozed snow-white stuffing from open wounds. As Gleave barged through the upturned furniture, Will saw a familiar figure standing at the far end of the room.

Outlined by the flames in the brick fireplace, Sir Desmond Duquesne was the picture of composure, as usual. His straw-berry-blonde hair established his relative youth, though he did have some pronounced streaks of white poking through on the sides on his head. He stood, slim and rigid, adjusting his cuffs, as though he had not just completed a dark magic ritual, but rather had finished a simple game of backgammon. Dark eyes narrowed over his sharp aquiline nose as he saw Lord Roder-ick's shape approaching. "You're too late, my friend." Gleave's eyes followed Duquesne's down to the floor, where there lay a mummified corpse that resembled a human being, though smaller and with jagged bones protruding from its head, shoulders, and forearms. It reminded Will of the figures etched in stone beneath the Stonegate Hotel, and he knew at once that Duquesne had killed something not quite human.

"Years," said Gleave, his shaking hands betraying his gravelly voice. "Decades of my life devoted to tracking these texts down. Researching. Translating. Decades!"

Duquesne raised his hands as if to calm his old acquaintance. "Now, Roderick, can you blame me?"

"Yes, I can blame you! You stole my life's work! And you betrayed me!" Will watched with repulsion as purple veins bulged out of the Gargoyle's ashen forehead. "You were to wait for me, Duquesne. We were to do this together."

"You were going to betray me. I simply beat you to the punch."

"You really did it, didn't you?" Gleave's tone had softened slightly.

Duquesne nodded. "I summoned the demon and drained it, with minimal fuss."

"Do you feel…different?"

"No," said Duquesne. "There was some initial discomfort, but no, I cannot say that I feel much different than I did before."

"Good," said Gleave. "Then maybe it didn't take." He quickly raised his arm and fired a bullet through Desmond Duquesne's chest. The bullet lodged itself in a cracked fireplace brick as Duquesne's body flew backwards, hitting the mantel and crumpling on the floor. The room grew deathly silent following the blast from the handgun, and the scattered pieces of paper muffled Gleave's footsteps as he neared Duquesne's fallen frame. He looked at the wound in Duquesne's back—a bloody, jagged-edged hole discernible through the torn cloth of his shirt and jacket. He smiled, taking some satisfaction in the fact that his translation had, apparently, been incorrect. His moment of triumph did not last long, as Mr. Myres, who had rushed back upstairs at the sound of the pistol report, ran into the room, stumbling over the upturned armchair.

"What happened here?" he asked, looking first with disgust around the library, and then gasping at the sight of his fallen employer.

"Sir Desmond is dead," Gleave said, briefly turning to Myres. "See for yourself. All that work for nothing."

Gleave glanced back at the body and glared through the darkness, focusing again on the wound. That is, he would have, but the wound was gone. He turned Sir Desmond onto his back to check the spot where the bullet had entered, but as he placed his hand on his old friend's chest, he felt his own wrist grabbed with tremendous force. Duquesne's eyes shot open as he said, "It took."

Startled, Lord Roderick pulled away from Duquesne's grip and staggered back toward the library door, nearly knocking over the equally shaken Myres in the process. "You...you..." Gleave stammered.

"Can't be killed," Duquesne offered. "Apparently. And all thanks to you." The astounded Gleave had no response. Instead, he motioned to Myres to lift the torn chair into its proper position and simply sat down, a defeated creature whose once burning eyes were now little more than dying cinders. After a few quiet moments, the bloody but apparently healthy Sir Desmond put his hands behind his back and cleared his throat. "I hate to be insensitive, Roderick, but do you plan on sitting—"

"What now?" Gleave mused. "What's to become of me? You've ruined me."

"Oh, it's not that bad," said Duquesne. "You've still got your wealth, your health—"

The fire now returned to Gleave's eyes. "Don't you dare patronize me, you son of a bitch." He stood, resolved to see an end to Duquesne's pomposity. "I'll find a way," he said, his right hand crackling as it turned into a stone fist. With one sickening blow, he broke Duquesne's jaw, knowing full well that it would heal almost instantly, but sending a message nonetheless. Duquesne wiped the blood from his mouth as he watched Gleave stomp back toward the hall of taunting masks, ready for whatever his rival would throw at him.

Will was eager to follow his great-great-grandfather, but Whitworth, who had remained perfectly still during this entire scene, said, "I'd like to fast-forward to a particular night years after this, William. Close your eyes. This could make you dizzy." Will did as he was told, and Whitworth watched as the story she knew all too well flew by at breakneck speed. Over the next few years, Lord Roderick Gleave could think of nothing but revenge, and so declared war on the House of Duquesne. Despite what he had witnessed, something in Gleave refused to believe his counterpart had actually achieved immortality that night. His stubbornness nearly led to his downfall, as he poured immeasurable funds into the destruction of Desmond Duquesne. His assassins ranged from a group of London thugs to an Indian mystic to an American sharpshooter, but none were able to accomplish what he had not. Duquesne went on living, and Gleave's assassins were either never seen again or were delivered in gift baskets to Gleave's door. Mr. Ridgley, sensing the futility in his master's efforts, soon tendered his resignation, and, as a further insult to Lord Roderick, went almost immediately into the service of Desmond Duquesne. With Ridgley gone, the Gleave household began to crumble. His wife Elizabeth did the best she could to keep things in order, but the lack of good help—caused by Lord Roderick's growing reputation as a hot-tempered brute—left her exhausted and often ill. More importantly—to her husband, at least—was the fact that with Ridgley gone, his study remained in a constant state of disarray, making his continued research that much more onerous. But he refused to stop, and pored over his books and documents every night, often until the sun broke through the window behind his desk. The sun didn't do him any favors, though, as anyone who looked upon him in the light could tell that the old Gargoyle was starting to crack. Unshaven, with eyes like deep purple caverns, Lord Roderick began to look as though he had been awake for weeks on end. In point of fact, he often had been.

When Will was instructed to open his eyes, he saw that time had passed, and that he and Whitworth were standing back where they had started, in Gleave's study. Five years to the day after Duquesne had first betrayed him, Lord Gleave once more sat hunched over his desk, scribbling curious symbols on scattered pieces of paper. He paused when the large grandfather clock began announcing the midnight hour, compelled to lay down his pen and peer out the window, down to Mason Street. This night wasn't like that other one, years earlier. Tonight was clear and crisp, with a soft breeze circulating leaves beneath the lampposts. This appeared to calm the Gargoyle, until he saw an individual whom he had long forgotten emerge from the shadows and glance briefly up at him. "So the witch returns," Gleave said to himself. With that, he rose from his chair, grabbed his cloak and hat as he had five years ago, and made his way out to the street. Will and Whitworth again followed, and they were barely able to catch a glimpse of Gleave's quarry disappearing around a corner not a hundred feet from where he stood.

At first, Lord Roderick raced to catch up to the woman so that he would not lose her in the labyrinthine streets, but it soon became apparent that she was fully aware of being followed— so much so that when she finally reached her destination, she was sure to look back and catch his eye before ducking inside. Gleave did not hesitate in throwing open the door that the woman had closed, but not locked, behind her.

Lord Roderick needed to stoop as he stepped into the dark

dank hovel, and he immediately withdrew a handkerchief to cover his nose and mouth—a precaution to spare himself from the overwhelming stench of sulfur and opium. The space seemed to consist of only one room, though a number of raggedy sheets hanging around the perimeter suggested that there may have been more kept out of sight. This did not matter to Gleave, who had found what he came for. The woman was sitting sedately with two other hags, all three staring curiously at their guest. "So," said Gleave, taking particular note of the sister who only had one eye. "It's you."

"He knows us," said one of the sisters, sipping her tea and showing no surprise.

The one-eyed sister nodded. "Of course he does."

"Of course I do," Gleave repeated. "Your reputations precede you. Yaga," he said, naming the woman who had led him to their den. "Annis," he named her cyclopean sister. "And Mora. Three of the most powerful sorceresses in recorded history. Why are you here in London? And what do you want with me?"

"We know of your difficulties with Desmond Duquesne," said Annis. "And you know as well as we do that you'll never defeat him."

He looked to the hag named Mora—the one he had heard could see the future—for confirmation of this statement, and she offered it with a solemn nod. "Then why bring me here? To gloat? I suppose Duquesne put you up to this?"

"Far from it," said Mora, refilling her teacup. "We are no more allies of Desmond Duquesne than you are. He's an affront to our kind, and he's changed the natural order of things."

"Luckily," said Yaga, "we may have a way to put things right."

Now they had truly grabbed Gleave's attention, and without hesitation, he demanded, "Tell me how."

"Our powers are limited," said Annis, "and as you know, two of us are simply observers. I can see the present, while Mora can see the future. Yaga, though, has a stronger will than either of us, and can alter future events."

"She can write prophecy," Mora explained.

Gleave fidgeted in a subconscious display of excitement, but Yaga held up her withered hand to signal for him to remain calm. "It is important to know that I cannot give you the immediate satisfaction that you desire. Desmond Duquesne is right in that there is no living person capable of destroying him. I can do nothing to change that."

Gleave's excitement abandoned him as quickly as it had arrived. Deflated, he angrily asked, "Then why am I here? What good are you? I want Duquesne dead. Now."

"Be patient," said Mora, "and listen to our offer."

Yaga continued, "You may not be able to destroy your enemy, but I can see to it that your first male heir can. The heir to Roderick Gleave will have power to avenge you and to put an end to Duquesne once and for all. This is what I can do for you."

The idea of Duquesne dying at another's hand, and the realization that this death would be so far off, was not what Gleave had been hoping for. Still, he could take satisfaction in knowing that although Duquesne had gotten away with his betrayal for the time being, his rival's days would now be numbered. One question remained—the question that so often made or broke offers like this: "And what do you want in return?"

Annis' face contorted into a crooked smile. "Consider this one on the house."

"AND SO THE BLOOD FEUD BEGAN," Whitworth whispered while striving to maintain her concentration. "Now might be another good time to fast forward. We both know that Gleave had no male heir until you, so there's really no sense in watching his efforts to make one, if you know what I mean."

Thoroughly repulsed, Will nodded in agreement and watched the scene fade out on Gleave and the three sisters, and come back into focus on Gleave and one sister: Yaga. This Gleave was a man further changed by time. He slumped in a great crimson armchair, looking more ashen than ever, the bags beneath his bloodshot eyes having grown heavier. The Gleave that the old woman approached in his empty chamber was defeated.

The Gargoyle smirked between a series of brutal and painful coughs when he saw the old woman. "So, the great Baba Yaga graces me with her presence."

"You've grown old, Lord Roderick" said the woman, who had barely aged a day since their meeting in the opium den.

"I have," Gleave admitted. "Too old to control my power," he said, raising his left arm to show that his immobile hand had turned fully to stone. "And too old to produce an heir."

"I certainly hope you did not summon me here to blame me for that. I upheld my end of our bargain. It is not my fault that you could not do the same."

Gleave coughed again and spat blood at Yaga's feet. "You really think I'm stupid, don't you, you old bitch?" Yaga chose not to respond and remained unmoved. "Your sister can see the future. She would have known that I would only have a series of shameful, wasteful female offspring. So what was the point? Why even bother coming to me with this bargain? I deserve to know what your game was."

Yaga took a step closer, her dirty, bare foot landing in the bloody pool that Gleave's phlegm had left on the floor. "You consider yourself a king, Roderick Gleave, but my game is the oldest one there is, and you barely rank as a pawn in it. It was prophesied that when the end times come, only the united families of Gleave and Duquesne would be able to stop the Absence. My sisters and I could not have that. Now, thanks to our bargain, even if Duquesne does live forever, there will never be peace between your two families, and nothing to stop the eventual darkness. The slate will be wiped clean, and the world will be as it should. Tabula rasa."

"You're all insane," Gleave hissed.

"No," Yaga responded. "To fight against the inevitable as you and Duquesne are doing…that is insane."

Gleave coughed again. "Perhaps," he said quietly. Will could tell that it was becoming more painful for Gleave to speak. "But there is one thing that you didn't count on, despite all of your knowledge and power." Yaga looked at him askance as his choking continued. Gleave tried to get the words out, but his condition would not allow more than a few gasping breaths. He signaled with his one good hand for Yaga to come closer, and she did.

"What is it that you think I've overlooked, Lord Roderick?" she asked skeptically.

"The fact," he said, grabbing her arm, "that you won't live to see your plans take shape. Now you know how it feels." Yaga tried to wriggle out of his grip, but even in his infirm state, Gleave was too strong. He grimaced as the stone spread over his body and transferred to hers, crackling as it turned flesh, blood, and bone to granite. Lord Roderick Gleave finally wore a satisfied expression before the stone ultimately overtook his body. There he sat, his power having grown beyond his control, his transformation into a true gargoyle at last complete. In his cold hand he still held the arm of the great Baba Yaga, whose body had been turned half to stone before Gleave had expired.

"And there she would remain," Whitworth said, taking herself and Will out of the memory space, "until her head was removed and sent to me in a cardboard box."

Will was reeling from what he had just seen. The trip into

the past had certainly been enlightening, but he was at the same time disconcerted by the scope of what he was involved in. "Ms. Whitworth, what do I need to know about this Absence thing?"

Whitworth toyed with the ring hanging from her neck and answered, "It's an old wives' tale about how the world will end, William. It probably won't even happen during your lifetime. The important thing is that the rift between the Gleave and Duquesne families is mended by the time it does happen. If you can do that, everything will be fine." She patted Will on the back and led him from the office. "Everything will be fine," she repeated. "I'm sure of it."

THIRTY-ONE

FrostBites

WILL FELT as though he was with a celebrity when he walked into FrostBites with his Aunt Veronica. Employees in the bustling restaurant seemed to stop in their tracks when they spotted the owner coming in for an unexpected visit. Then, all at once, everyone began to move more quickly, as though making up for lost time. Servers straightened up, busboys became table-clearing blurs, and two of the three bartenders abruptly stopped chatting with their customers and started restocking glasses. The one bartender who remained unfazed was a good-looking late twenty-something who poured two glasses of cabernet and handed them across the bar to Veronica and Gwen.

"Always great to see you, Mrs. Frost," he said with a blindingly white smile. He glanced at Wisp, who had invited himself along, but gave no such greeting.

"You too, Jackson," she responded, accepting the drink. "Jackson, this is my nephew Will and his friend, Andy. Boys, this is our head bartender, and Gwen's boyfriend, Jackson Palmer."

"Hey guys," said Jackson. "What'll ya have?"

"Just a Coke," Will answered.

"Whiskey neat," said Andy. Upon a glare from Aunt Veronica and a nudge from Gwen, he amended his order. "I meant to say iced tea. I'll have a regular iced tea."

"And you?" Jackson asked Mr. Wisp without a tinge of affability.

"Let's go with a Rob Roy," he said with an unnecessary wink. "Classic."

"Well, well," slurred a drunken overweight man with a shock of white hair and a matching walrus-like mustache. "She graces us with her presence!" Obviously trying to get Veronica's attention, the man nearly fell off his stool to lean over the bar and catch her eye. He caught it, but he would have been better off catching pneumonia.

"Dean Calendar," she explained to Will. "He's a restaurant critic who never met a drink or a hostess that he didn't like." When Jackson returned with their drinks, she addressed her employee. "Mr. Calendar is finished for the night."

Jackson nodded, and Will watched attentively as his aunt scanned the restaurant with an unblinking gaze, quietly registering every other bit of activity that occurred in the bustling scene. She led the party to a vacant table in the middle of the expansive dining room, followed closely by Gwen, to whom she muttered, "Jackson is doing a fantastic job, as usual. Please be sure to tell him." Gwen nodded and flashed a proud smile. "Now, who is that server back there?" Veronica asked, motioning toward a young girl currently taking another table's order.

"That's Karen. She's new this month."

"She slacks. Please let her go tomorrow."

Gwen was taken aback. "How do you...?" She let her question trail off upon receiving a cautionary glance from Veronica. "Yes ma'am," she complied. "I'll get it done."

With this bit of unpleasantness over with, the group took their seats and eagerly ordered several of the menu's most enticing dishes. Since the table included Veronica Frost, these dishes arrived more quickly than either of the boys could have expected—not that anybody was complaining. Veronica, Gwen, and Wisp listened politely as Andy told the story of how he and Will had met in first grade and faked enthusiasm when Andy provided another litany of pranks that he and Will had played on their teachers, though Andy's idea of an edgy gag was replacing the number two pencils with number ones before a test.

Finally, sensing the boredom that Andy couldn't, Will intervened and asked his aunt, "So how did you meet Mr. Wisp?"

"Well," said Wisp, seizing the opportunity to out-talk Andy, "it was back when your uncle, God rest his soul, was still alive. You see, I used to be a consultant. Do you know what they do?" The boys both shook their heads. "They point out the obvious and tell people what they want to hear. As you can imagine, when you can read minds, there's just no easier money out there."

"Did you *ever* have scruples?" Veronica asked.

"Not sure. But if you sauté them and add them to this menu, I'll surely try them," he smiled. "So we were at the Christmas party of some big muckety-muck…I forget who… and I spied your uncle from across the room. Of course, he had this gorgeous woman on his arm, so who wouldn't have noticed him?"

"It helped," Veronica interrupted, "that my husband had just purchased this very restaurant and was looking to make a name for himself."

"Quite right. And who better to help him do so than old Wisp?" her friend said with another unnecessary wink. "Naturally I approached Mr. Frost and started working my magic, but little did I know that I was about to meet one of the only people who has ever been able to see through my charm." With this, he pointed to Veronica. "She wasn't falling for my shtick, which of course upset me, but also intrigued me. She put me in my place, and at the same time, won my unwavering devotion."

"Did you end up doing business together?" Will asked.

"Not at that time," Veronica answered. "But in the years since my husband died, Mr. Wisp has proven to be invaluable. Just as long as he stays out of here," she said, lightly tapping her temple.

"I wouldn't dream of it, my dear," said Wisp. "Now, William, I hear you had an interesting experience with my old buddy Whitworth today."

"Yeah, your great-great-grandfather was kind of a dick, huh?" Andy asked.

"Apparently," said Will. "I originally thought Duquesne was the villain in this, but now I see that Gleave was probably just as bad in his day."

"It's important to remember, though," said Veronica, "that regardless of how cruel Roderick Gleave was, this does not make Desmond Duquesne any less dangerous."

Will would have conceded that she was correct, but their conversation was interrupted by shouting from one of the nearby tables. Will's party looked to see a man of around thirty yelling furiously at his female dining companion. Tall, muscular, and displaying a large tribal tattoo on the back of his neck, he cut an intimidating figure as he stood to tower over her. He had clearly been drinking and was now wielding his steak knife like a baton, swinging it carelessly as he berated the poor, embarrassed woman.

"She cheated," Wisp offered nonchalantly, and took a sip of his Rob Roy.

"You read his mind?" Andy asked.

Wisp shook his head. "Don't have to be a mind reader to figure that out, my friend. I've seen it all before."

Behind the bar, Jackson was readying himself to address the disruption, but Veronica signaled for him to stay put. Despite Gwen's objections, Veronica walked over to the table herself and began talking to the man. When he did not calm down, her face grew sterner and she leaned in to whisper something in his ear. What this was, Will did not know, but it must have been an invitation to settle the dispute outside, since he followed Veronica through the front door. "Ronny's got a way with people," Wisp mused. "Neck-tattoo chose the wrong restaurant to pitch a fit in."

"Do you think she's alright?" asked Will. "Should I go out there?"

"Your aunt puts out fires," Wisp responded. "She's better than anyone I know when it comes to that. You just wait. She'll be back in no time, problem solved."

Sure enough, by the time Wisp had finished his sentence, Veronica was back. She approached the man's humiliated date, sat with her for a moment, held her hand compassionately, and seemed to console her. The woman left embarrassed, but grateful, and Veronica returned to her group.

"Job well done, Ronny." Wisp raised his glass in her honor, but she did not appear appreciative of the gesture.

"Well," she said, "job done, at any rate. And you folks wonder why I don't come out much." She managed a slight chuckle, but then said, "I think I may call it a night."

"Oh, come on, Ronny! The night is young and I'm sure the boys would love to stay!"

Gwen offered a suggestion. "If you're alright with them staying, I'm sure that Jackson could keep an eye out and make sure they don't get into any trouble." She glanced at the boys as she said this, as if she fully expected trouble to ensue.

"We won't do anything stupid," Will said.

"Promise," said Andy.

"Cross our hearts," Wisp drawled.

Mrs. Frost reached into her purse and handed a wad of bills to Will. "Here's money for a cab. Be home by eleven." She glanced at Wisp and then at the boys. "If I smell a hint of alcohol on your breath, I'll make that bear that attacked you look like Winnie the Pooh. Understood?"

"Understood," said all three men.

With that, the two women left the boys in FrostBites, and Wisp immediately moved them to the bar, where he took a seat next to Dean Calendar.

"How's the coffee treating you, buddy?" Wisp asked Calendar with a hard slap on the back.

Calendar, who looked like he was half asleep and was obviously seeing double, looked right past Wisp and answered, "Like I was saying. I am the most important fucking restaurant critic in Boston. Maybe…maybe even in the, um, the country. I will drink what I want!"

"Good for you!" Wisp mocked. He spun on around on his stool and said, "Tell me, William, what else can you do besides have prophetic dreams?"

"Nothing," he said flatly. "Apparently everyone else has some sort of cool ability, like how you can read minds or Simon can make people do what he says."

"A piece of advice for you, my friend. There are plenty of other ways to make people do what you say apart from infiltrating their minds like your pal Simon does."

"What do you mean?"

"Power," Wisp said. "If you have enough of it, regardless of what form it takes, you can make people do whatever you want. The problem is that you fail to realize just how much power you truly have."

"I told you," Will insisted. "I don't have any. Brandt said that my only real power was the ability to take out Duquesne."

"John Brandt *would* say that. You know he's afraid of you, right?"

This was news to Will. "What? Why?"

"He's afraid of all of us. He thinks that we've got too much power, that it's unnatural. But I ask you, how can it be unnatural to use the skills that we were born with? It's in our blood—yours especially!"

"Do you seriously think I can turn people to stone like Roderick Gleave could?"

Wisp shrugged. "If you wanted to, I suppose, but that seems like a waste of talent to me. Try for something more useful, more versatile. Try this." He removed a quarter from his pocket. "I'm going to flip this coin. Try to stop it in midair."

"Are you for real?" asked Andy.

"Hush, Andrew." Wisp returned his gaze to Will and repeated, "Try to stop it. Concentrate really hard. Ready?"

Will shrugged, said "Okay," and concentrated on stopping the coin in the air. It plunked down onto the bar. "Well that was fun," Will said dryly.

"You'll never get it on your first try," Wisp said. "However, once you do…oooh boy. Once you push yourself past that threshold, there's no going back. It'll be a piece of cake for you. Let's try again."

For the next half hour, Wisp flipped his coin and Will tried to stop it, but to no avail. In the meantime, Andy attempted to excuse himself to use the men's room but was stopped by Jackson. "Hold it in," said Jackson.

"Why? Is something wrong with the bathroom?"

"No." Jackson leaned in and whispered, "Just don't leave your friend alone with this guy."

Andy now had his misgivings confirmed. He watched as the smooth-talking Wisp attempted to tutor his friend and realized that he felt more uncomfortable now than he had hours earlier in the halls of New Covington. Before long, he decided to do something about this, so he approached Will and said, "I think I'm going to head out. Big day of golf tomorrow."

Will nodded in agreement and said to Wisp, "Sorry to disappoint."

"No disappointment here, my friend," he answered. "It was worth a shot, right? Sometimes it takes an emotional catalyst the first time it happens. We'll find it before long."

As Will and Andy headed for the door, Wisp slapped a hundred dollars down on the bar, put his mouth up to the still inebriated Dean Calendar's ear and said, "Bet you won't tell the kid what you really think of Ronny Frost."

Calendar sprung to life again, looked to the door, and yelled, "Hey kid! Say goodnight to your bitch of an aunt for me!"

A wide-eyed Andy looked back, and Will paused momentarily, but decided not to give that lush the satisfaction of a response. As Will angrily balled up his hands, Calendar's scalding coffee tipped into his lap, and an elated Wisp said to himself, "There you go, boy. Emotional response." When Andy and Will had gone, Wisp threw his arm around the wavering Calendar and said, "Come on, you old bastard. Let's go get you another drink."

WILL and Andy paced the sidewalk in front of FrostBites, dodging the odors being blown their way by the restaurant's smoking patrons and looking up and down the street for any sign of a cab. "That Wisp guy gives me the creeps," Andy said with a slight shudder. "And Jackson seems to agree."

Will shrugged. "I'm not sure what to think about him, but he is friends with my aunt, so I feel like I should give him the benefit of the doubt. I'd like to think she's smart enough not to get involved with anyone shady."

"I'm sure she's very smart, but anyone could—"

"Here's a cab," Will interrupted as he hailed the yellow car. The cab decelerated and hugged the curb, but out of nowhere, a black Mercedes pulled in ahead of it. The tinted window lowered and the boys saw Mr. Ridgley seated behind the wheel.

"Are you two gentlemen heading to Mrs. Frost's? If so, I happen to be going your way."

A brief but silent argument consisting of several head shakes, nods, and darting eyes ended with Will making the first move and sliding into the back seat of the car. Andy followed reluctantly but was quick to question Ridgley about his coincidental appearance. "I've been out running errands, Mr. Lunsford," he answered, motioning toward a collection of bags on the passenger seat. "But in all honesty, I was heading to Mrs. Frost's place as my final chore for the evening."

"And why were you going there?" Will asked.

"To give you this." As Ridgley sat idle at a red light, he leaned over and removed an envelope from the glove compartment. He handed it back to Will and said, "Please be careful with that, Mr. Trammell. The vials are fragile." Noting the boys' looks of confusion, he explained, "Vials of blood, courtesy of Mr. Duquesne. Ms. Whitworth requested to run some tests. Sir Desmond was not eager to do so, but upon meeting you, he changed his mind. Please tell Ms. Whitworth to accept the samples as a gesture of good faith."

Will held the envelope more gingerly once he had heard what it contained. "Um, well, thank you. I'm sure that Ms. Whitworth has a good reason for asking, and that she'll appreciate the gesture."

"I'm sure," said Ridgley.

While his friend was speaking to their driver, an object on the floor of the car caught Andy's eye and, seeing that neither of his companions were paying attention, he moved quickly to scoop it up. He had trouble seeing it in the dark, but in the fleeting beam of each streetlight that they passed, he turned it over in his hands, until he came to recognize it as a stamp. It was a simple stamp, a small wooden block, but the design on the rubber underside was a complex and confusing series of squiggles that Andy could not identify. Normally, he may not have thought anything of this, but since he was currently being driven around town by the manservant of an infamous occultist, he thought it best to pocket the stamp so that he could present it to Whitworth. Surely she could make something of it.

"Well," said Ridgley as he pulled the car in front of Veronica's brownstone, "I'm glad that I was able to be of service. My regards to your aunt."

Thanking Ridgley, the boys made their way up the steps, with Will taking the lead. Andy stayed back, though, gazed across the street, and was relieved to see that Eddie Garza had followed them home from the restaurant. He gave a curt wave, to which a tired-looking Eddie cracked a smile and waved back.

THIRTY-TWO

A Day of Duquesnes

"I THINK you're doing it wrong," Will said to Andy as they waited for Alexander Duquesne and his friend Carson to arrive at the golf course.

"What do you mean?" Andy had been taking practice swings, but Will was convinced that several passersby mistook his motions for convulsions.

"You need more control. You look like you're fighting off a moth with a newspaper."

Andy stared at his friend and shook his head. "Why would a moth have a newspaper?"

Will sighed. "Look," he said, swinging his cane as though it were a club. "You have to do it smoothly and follow through. You don't stop the club once it hits the ball."

"Ooooooh... See, when Ms. Whitworth lent me some clubs, I was kind of hoping they'd be enchanted or something."

"Why the hell did you tell the Duquesnes that you play golf?"

"Alex's friend was making fun of us. He called me fat and you a cripple."

"Well that's not cool," Will said. "I probably don't even really need this cane anymore. I was just relying on it to get me out of having to golf."

"You, sir, are an ass."

"Speaking of, here come your opponents."

Alex and Carson pulled up in their golf cart and immediately started laughing at Andy's vintage golf bag. "My God," said Alex. "Did you steal them from the set of *Caddyshack*?"

"I…enjoy that movie" was the best comeback that Andy could muster, to which Carson replied,

"And I enjoy winning, so we may as well get on with it."

"Where's your cart?" Alex asked.

Will and Andy looked at each other. "I knew we forgot something," said Will.

Alex guffawed. "That leg's going to be hurting today, Billy."

As Alex and Carson drove off toward the first hole, Andy looked quizzically at Will. "I kinda feel like he should be nicer to the guy who can kill him with a touch." Will nodded and they began walking. "Are we sure his father is the bad guy? Maybe there was a mix up. Everyone probably really wants you to kill Alex."

"'Everyone' being you?"

"Yup."

WILL DIDN'T LIKE reality shows. It wasn't so much that he found them offensive or stupid. No, the problem was that he had a difficult time watching other people make fools of themselves. While flipping through channels, he would often come upon reality talent shows with tone-deaf people attempting to become the next big thing. Inevitably, he would watch until the third or fourth bar of the song, and then either change the channel or mute the volume. This was the same reason why he did not frequent karaoke nights. It was also the same reason why he found it difficult to watch Andy attempt to play golf.

"That was my practice swing," said Andy, having struck himself in the shin with his own club. "I just need to walk my practice swing off and then I'll be ready."

"We told you on the last hole," said an already-exasperated Alex. "There are no practice swings. It is what it is."

"And no kicking the ball into the hole. That's costing you strokes, you know," Carson advised. "Though I'm thankful we got off the last hole before sunset."

"Ha ha," Andy retorted. "What hole is this anyway?"

"Three."

Andy groaned and took a swig of water. In the meantime, Carson addressed Will. "So if you guys are from South Carolina, why are you up here?"

Alex smirked. "Yeah, Will, why *are* you here?"

This all but confirmed to Will that Duquesne's entire family knew what was going on, but he was not going to give Alex the satisfaction of putting him in an awkward spot. "I came to visit my aunt. I haven't seen her in a long time."

"His aunt is Veronica Frost," Alex said to Carson.

"The one who owns FrostBites? I heard she went crazy a while back, that she never leaves her house."

"She leaves," said Will, restraining his anger. "Just not often."

"Why not?"

Will shrugged. "Guess she'd rather not run into people like you."

"Watch yourself, Billy," said Alex. "My father could buy and sell your aunt and her shitty restaurant."

"Alright, fellas," Andy interjected. "Let's all be friends here. Just wait til you see this swing."

"Shouldn't you be wearing a helmet?" Carson joked.

Andy tried to ignore the remarks, but at this point he was

sweating bullets. His hands shook as he took his stance, and he kept repeating to himself, "Please don't suck...please don't suck..." Will was thinking the same thing. He wanted more than anything for Andy to do well. Putting these two in their place would make this whole excursion worthwhile.

Andy took a wild swing that nearly resulted in him knocking himself over, but at least the ball left the tee this time. Alex and Carson laughed derisively at Andy's contortions, but Will kept his eye on the ball. His gaze remained fixed as it headed down the fairway. It was going much further than anyone's shots had gone all morning, and no one could believe what they were seeing.

"Guess I don't know my own strength." Andy had a spring in his step as he walked toward where his ball had landed. Alex and Carson followed behind, each stunned into silence by this sudden display of strength and skill. When he approached the hole, Andy was dismayed not to see his ball anywhere. He looked around a bit, and when nothing appeared, he decided to take a leap of faith and look in the hole itself. There, to his astonishment, was the ball. Trying to show humility, he told his competitors, "Um, looks like a hole in one, guys. Sorry..."

"Bullshit," said Carson. "There's no way."

Carson and Alex ran over to the hole to see that he was correct and then proceeded to mutter streams of obscenities between one another. "How'd you do that?" asked Alex.

"I don't know," said Andy. "Practice?"

Carson and Alex's grumbling continued onto the next hole, and the next, and the next. By the time they had reached the halfway mark, Andy had successfully made five holes in one while the others, their egos deflated, had fallen farther and farther behind. At this point, Carson picked up his phone and could be overheard saying, "Hello? Yes, this is he. A meeting *now*? But I'm on the golf course. No, no. That's alright. I'll be there." He hung up. "Sorry fellas, but I've got to get out of here. My friend has an internet start-up that I'm going to be a part of, and he wants to meet with me ASAP. Alex, you ready?"

"Yeah, that's cool," said Alex. "Looks like we'll need to finish this another time. Too bad, too, since I tend to hit my stride on the back nine."

"SO ALEXANDER JUST QUIT?" Whitworth leaned back in her chair and wore a bemused grin as Andy and Will recounted the story of their golf excursion from the other side of her desk.

"Yeah," said Will. "But what's even better is that Andy basically left him no other choice. I've never seen anyone play like that. It was pretty much the biggest comeback ever. It was unbelievable."

"It was, wasn't it?" Andy eyed Will suspiciously, but otherwise held his tongue.

"Well, hopefully Andrew's victory on the golf course is an indicator of future successes," said Whitworth. "Now, you're still going out with Alexander and Daphne tonight?" Will nodded, but Whitworth's cheeriness faded. "Are you sure about this, William? Please don't do anything that will make you too uncomfortable."

"Oh, I don't think that being around Daphne is going to make him uncomfortable."

Will blushed and punched Andy in the arm. "Jackass."

"She is a beautiful young lady, isn't she?"

"She's…yeah…I mean…"

Whitworth smiled warmly. "Believe me," she said. "I know what you're feeling. I just need to ask you to remember that we currently have no idea what could happen should you so much as touch Daphne."

"What about the blood that Ridgley gave us?" Andy asked.

"I've sent it to the lab. Dr. Feng is currently trying to verify that the two vials are, in fact, samples of Desmond and

Daphne's blood. William, on your way out today, I'd appreciate if you could stop by the lab to give another small sample of yours. From there, we should be able to draw a conclusion fairly quickly."

"Can I go do that now?" Will asked anxiously. "I need to get ready."

Whitworth gave him a somber go-ahead, and in a flash, Will was gone. Left alone, Andy read Whitworth's face and asked, "You're really worried about him, aren't you?"

"I am. William's already been through more than most people your age could handle, and he's holding up remarkably well. I'm concerned that involving him with the Duquesnes was a mistake. This burgeoning relationship with them is only going to confuse him further."

"If it's any consolation," offered Andy, "I trust that you're trying to help him, and I think he does too. Oh! And I have this," he said, reaching into his pocket for the stamp. "I thought it might help."

He handed the small block of wood and rubber to Whitworth, who pushed her glasses onto the bridge of her nose and peered at it curiously. "Where did you get this, Andrew?"

"The floor of Ridgley's car—er, Duquesne's car. You know what I mean."

"Interesting… Do you happen to know what this is?"

"No idea."

"It's called a sigil. It's akin to a crest or a seal. This one in particular is the sigil of Beleth, an ancient and extremely powerful demon."

"So you've seen this before."

"I have," Whitworth said, removing a folder from the top drawer of her desk. "In fact, I've seen it quite recently." She handed Andy a photo of a stone column with Beleth's symbol, as well as five others, carved into it.

"Where was this taken?"

"In a chamber beneath New Covington. Beleth is one of the demons that Desmond Duquesne was planning to summon, apparently. I have to tell you, though, I'm stumped as to why he'd go to the trouble of making a rubber stamp with a sigil on it."

"He doesn't seem to be playing with a full deck," said Andy.

"No, but he's definitely playing at something. Here," she said, handing the stamp back to Andy. "What I could read from the stamp was entirely innocuous. Ridgley picked a batch of them up from a stationary store downtown. This one, at least, never made it to Duquesne. Take it back to New Covington when you go. Drop it in an inconspicuous place, but don't let anyone know that you had it. It's best if Duquesne believes that it never went missing."

"So what does this mean?"

"For now, all it means is that Desmond Duquesne lied to me. If he still has Ridgley running errands that involve demonic sigils, odds are he's still planning to go through with his ritual. I'm relying on you, Andrew, to be our eyes on the inside, especially now that William has gotten a bit...distracted."

WHEN WILL and Andy arrived at New Covington later that day, they were greeted by Mrs. Ridgley, who they were surprised to see was now in a wheelchair. "Oh my God, Mrs. Ridgley," said Will, mustering as much compassion as he could. "What happened now?"

"Well," she answered, spinning around and leading them to the main hall, "my sciatica has been acting up again. On days like this, it's difficult just to get out of bed. I only wish that I could rely on something simple like the cane you carry around, but you have youth on your side, and your ailments aren't quite as severe, are they?"

Will thought back to the way he had had to clamber through a kitchen to avoid being devoured by a bear three times his size. "I suppose you're right, Mrs. Ridgley. You've got it worse. I hope that you feel better."

"At this rate, she'll answer the door in a body bag tomorrow," Andy murmured.

Will suppressed a chuckle as Mrs. Ridgley shot a piercing glare in Andy's direction. "Miss Duquesne is upstairs in her room," the injured woman sighed. "I suppose you'd like me to go announce your arrival?"

Unsure of how to respond to this, Will and Andy exchanged glances, and each started to muttered, "Okay..." when Joanna Duquesne interrupted. "It's alright, Mrs. Ridgley," she said with a knowing smile directed at the boys. "Why don't you go rest? I know you've had a...um... rough day."

Mrs. Ridgley consented with a thankful nod and wheeled herself from the room. "Wow," said Andy. "I have to ask you: how do you put up with that woman?" He pointed in the direction of Mrs. Ridgley, who had found one of her wheels caught on the corner of an area rug.

Mrs. Duquesne shrugged. "Mr. and Mrs. Ridgley predate my time in this house. My husband insists that we keep them around. Although, between you and me, I find it embarrassing to have anything resembling servants in this day and age." They followed her into a large parlor, empty but for a number of canvas paintings hanging on and leaning against the wall. They were masterfully done, in Will's opinion, and in each one, he recognized one of Desmond Duquesne's prized masks. Each painting represented the appropriate era and location in which they would have traditionally been used.

"You did all of these?" Will asked.

Joanna assayed her own work and answered, "I did. Desmond's masks always bothered me, but I find that giving them context helps me to appreciate their history and craftsmanship." She added, "I know that you'd literally be watching paint dry, but you're welcome to keep me company while my daughter is getting ready."

Will nodded and began to slowly travel around the room, understanding what Joanna meant by being able to find the beauty behind many of the masks. Before long, though, Andy tugged at his sleeve and gestured for Will to observe the canvas that Joanna was currently working on. When he did, his blood ran cold. In a painting that she had nearly completed, Joanna portrayed a figure dressed in a long black cloak, wearing an avian mask and presiding over what looked to be a bonfire. In an instant, Will found the creature from his dream brought to life by the strokes of Joanna's brush.

"Is that one of Mr. Duquesne's masks too?" asked Andy.

"It is," Joanna responded. "One of his favorites, though I can't for the life of me see why. I find it horrible."

"It is a particularly gruesome piece of work, isn't it?" said a gravelly voice. Will turned to see a man that he recognized from Brandt's files—a stout, balding man with thick tortoise-shell glasses.

"Dr. Brisbane," Joanna said politely. "I had no idea you were here."

"I have an appointment to see your husband," he said. "But when I heard that Mr. Trammell was here, I had to come meet him." He held out his thick hand and formally introduced himself. Despite his bookish appearance, Will noted the power in his grip and the calluses on his fingers, surely from years of work at archeological sites.

"What can you tell me about that mask, Dr. Brisbane?" Will asked.

Brisbane stepped closer to the painting, seemingly trans-fixed by the chilling visage. "This is the mask of a plague doctor. During the time when the Black Plague was rampant in Europe, plague doctors would don these uniforms, if you will, and set out to deal with the dead. Note this elongated, beak-like structure. Any idea why they chose this shape?"

"Because they acted like vultures, flocking to dead bodies?" Andy offered.

"An apt connection," said Brisbane, "but not quite. This beak was functional, not ornamental. Think about it. Their job was to traverse the streets in search of disease-riddled and decaying bodies. Imagine the smell." Will, Andy, and Joanna exchanged disgusted looks. "Indeed. These men, quite understandably, would often pack their masks with herbs and fragrances to keep the stale stench of death away. Even the vilest work can be made more palatable through a simple trick of the senses."

Giving his audience a moment to digest this, Brisbane continued, pointing to the long black rod that the plague doctor held in his right hand. "Now, as for this instrument here, it was often nothing more than an ordinary staff or cane, used for sifting through the bodies, giving them pokes every now and then to determine whether they were alive or dead. You can understand, given the degree of contagion, why the doctors would not have wanted to get in there with their hands."

Will shivered as he thought back to his recurring dream, the one where the plague doctor poked at the charred bodies of the Trammell family. "And the fire?" Will asked, though he was sure that he knew the answer.

"Well, those are the bodies, of course," Brisbane said matter-of-factly. "Am I right, Mrs. Duquesne?" She nodded, and the professor returned his gaze to the painting. "It's interesting," he said. "The plague doctor may have been the closest humanity has gotten to seeing the Grim Reaper himself. After all, when an unfortunate individual saw this figure heading in his direction, he surely must have known that the end was near."

"Yes," said Joanna, with a tone implying that Brisbane had

outstayed his welcome. "On that happy note, why don't I go find my husband for you?"

The group traveled back into the main hall, where they were practically run down by Alexander's friend Kara, looking more than a bit disheveled. "Kara," said the unpleasantly surprised Joanna. "Are you looking for Alex?"

"Alex?" Kara said, trying to regain her bearings. "Um...yes. Is he around?"

"I'm afraid not," Joanna answered flatly. "I believe he's still with Carson." She paused to collect herself before asking, "Do you happen to know where my husband is? Dr. Brisbane is here to see him."

Kara's eyes shifted as though she were strapped to a polygraph. "I *think* I just saw him near his office," she said. "But I'm really not sure."

"Of course you're not," Joanna said. "Mrs. Ridgley will show you out, Kara."

Taking her cue, the girl hastened toward the entrance hall, while Brisbane, appearing uncomfortable, gave a quick bow of the head and excused himself to find Desmond. Sensing tension, Joanna turned to the boys and divulged, "I don't like that girl."

"Who does, really?" Daphne mused, bouncing nimbly down the long marble staircase. She looked as much a visitor to the grandiose manor as they did, wearing a casual outfit consisting of jeans, a T-shirt, and a light, olive-hued jacket.

"Hey. Your brother isn't coming out with us?" Will asked hopefully.

Daphne looked intently at Will, raised a curious eyebrow, and addressed Andy. "I hear you completely humiliated my brother and his friend." Andy reddened a bit and began to apologize until Daphne stopped him. "No, don't apologize. That's awesome."

"Really?"

"Yeah. Those two walk around like they're God's gift. I kind of love that he's refusing to come with us."

"Because Andy beat him on the golf course?" Will said, trying to disguise his delight with the situation.

"Totally. He's busy sulking. It's fine, though, because he'd just hold us back."

"Okay," said Will, positively beaming despite his best efforts. "So what are we doing?"

"I have ideas," Daphne answered. "But I hope you like fish."

AFTER SAYING their goodbyes to Mrs. Duquesne, the trio were dropped off in the center of the city by Mr. Ridgley and made their way to Boston's famed Faneuil Hall. "Are we due in court or something?" Will asked as they approached the entrance to the imposing brick building.

Daphne laughed. "It looks like that, doesn't it? But it's actually a pretty cool marketplace." They entered the building and found themselves among a bustling throng of tourists checking out various crafts and souvenirs. The smell of roasted nuts smothered with cinnamon wafted through the air and Boston Red Sox memorabilia surrounded them on all sides. "Established in 1742 as a public meeting place by local merchant Peter Faneuil, blah, blah, blah…" Daphne said. "Bottom line: this place has some of the best, most authentic clam chowder that you'll find anywhere in Boston—or in the world, for that matter."

"I've never had clam chowder," Will admitted, almost ashamed. "I'm not sure that I like it."

"You do. Trust me," Daphne replied just before she ordered three cups at a small kiosk. She flashed a black credit card at the boys and added, "By the way, today is on my father. I guess he knows that people who have been kidnapped sometimes don't happen to have full wallets."

Will's eyes went wide. Having been under the assumption that she knew little about his recent adventures, he was shocked to hear her mention his abduction at the hands of Brandt. "You know about that?"

"I know more than you think," she said with a mischievous curl of her lips.

Upon receiving their chowder, the threesome grabbed a high-top table nearby, and Andy dug ravenously into his soup. Will, on the other hand, had been stunned into silence by Daphne, who obviously knew that his cover story about helping his aunt with a real estate deal was a sham. "So," said Daphne, picking up on his discomfort, "I'll just come out and ask it. Are you planning to kill my father?"

Andy choked on a clam and sputtered, "Awkward..."

It took Will a moment to respond, but when he did, he knew enough not to answer the question directly. "Daphne, are you aware of my family's history with your father?"

"What I know is that some prophecy somewhere says that if you so much as touch him, he'll die, and that you're the only person in the world capable of doing that."

"I'm surprised you know that much," said Will. "What do you guys do? Sit around the dinner table discussing the latest prophecies?"

"Not exactly, but my father keeps us in the loop. I know that he's not exactly normal, that he's over two hundred years old, and that he has a lot of enemies. That isn't the kind of stuff someone should keep from his family."

"Are you aware that he had my family killed?"

"Okay, kids," Andy interjected. "Aren't there better things that we could talk about? Maybe anything aside from past murders, attempted murders, or potential murders?"

"It's alright, Andy," Daphne answered. "This was bound to come up eventually. Yes, Will, I have heard that, but do you have definitive proof that my father's enemies aren't just trying to use you? They don't like the idea of him living forever, and I'll admit that it's out of the ordinary, but you've seen some of the great things that my father's done. He's not perfect by any means, but overall, he's a good man who cares deeply about other people. And he likes you a lot. He's already told me that several times."

"Really?"

"Really."

"Hey guys, you know what I like?" Andy asked, desperate to change the topic of conversation. "This chowder. It's pretty great."

Daphne laughed. "Okay, Andy. You're right. Let's have fun. I know just the place."

FOR THE NEXT hour or so, Daphne led Will and Andy around Boston, pointing out historic sites, acclaimed restaurants, and local hotspots. During this time, Will filled her in on the journey he had taken over the past week or so. By the time they reached the harbor, not far from where he had first seen Daphne and her family from a sixth-floor window, the sense of unease from Faneuil Hall had lifted, and Will began to feel as though he had known her for years. Her warmth and lightheartedness was a marked difference from the doom and gloom that had surrounded him lately, and it was intoxicating. For the first time in days, he was able to banish thoughts of Brandt, Duquesne, and the Collective. He was with friends, and things felt—oddly enough—right.

The late afternoon sun reflected off the blue-tinted windows of a tall, uniquely-designed building that Daphne excitedly conducted the boys toward. "Come on," she said.

"This is one of the best aquariums in the world. We need to be able to see everything before they close."

Will and Andy followed her into the sprawling aquarium and joined her at a rail overlooking the first exhibit, a penguin refuge. She leaned on the brass rail and looked down at the birds with an expression of childlike glee, glancing back at Will periodically to see whether he had caught one of their antics. He approached the rail, placing his hand dangerously close to hers, until Andy squeezed between them. Her trance broken, Daphne excused herself to use the ladies' room but implored her companions not to go on without her.

She followed the signs for the restrooms but seemed to be walking in a daze. She had not expected today to go this well. Really, she had not expected the day to go well at all. When she had first heard her father's would-be assassin was coming to Boston, she had imagined someone with the look of a hard-ened criminal. Instead, she found herself attracted to this clean-cut, charming everyman. But what was she to do? How was she to play this? Distracted by these thoughts, she paid no attention to the man who stood in the shadows near the hallway that led to the restrooms. Folding up his map of the aquarium, Simon followed Daphne down the dimly-lit passage.

"WHAT EXACTLY DO you think you're doing?" Andy asked in an almost parental tone.

"I didn't do anything wrong," Will said. "What's your problem?"

"Will, I get that you're falling for her and I can't fault you for that, but your hand was like an inch away from hers, and for all we know, the minute you touch her she'll...I don't know...explode or something."

"I doubt she'll explode."

"Whatever. It doesn't matter how it happens, all I know is

that there's a good chance this curse of yours—or whatever you want to call it—means you can't touch her…at least not until Ms. Whitworth gets the results of the blood test."

"I'm not going to do anything to hurt her," Will reassured his friend. "I would never allow myself to do that. I'm in control."

"I hope so, Will. I know you've been through a lot, and God knows you've been able to handle it better than most would, but if you accidentally kill this girl…I don't know, man. That's not something you're going to be able to bring yourself back from."

"I appreciate your concern," Will said, patting his friend on the shoulder. "But I'll be careful. I swear."

"Good," Andy responded, a bit relieved. He held his stomach and said, "Especially good, actually, because the clam chowder is fighting back, and I think I may be dying." He looked over his shoulder to see Daphne returning. "I'm going to head off to the bathroom myself. I'll take my time, if you know what I mean, as long as you promise that you'll both still be alive when I get back."

"Promise. Now go," he said to his friend, who was rapidly turning as green as the water in the penguin exhibit. "Hope everything comes out alright."

Andy scrunched his nose. "You're disgusting." With that, he hustled off to the restrooms, giving Daphne a pained smile as he passed.

"The chowder?" she asked upon returning.

Will nodded. "If I know Andy, he may be a while. We'd better move on without him." Daphne consented and before long, they had arrived at the centerpiece of the aquarium: a large cylindrical tank that spanned the height of the building. It was filled with an incredible menagerie, ranging from rays and nurse sharks at the bottom to barracuda and lionfish closer to the top. The creatures swam in circles as the human visitors traveled a spiraling ramp along the perimeter of the tank, making it difficult to tell which was following the other. "This is incredible," said Will. "Who knew that all of these different fish could coexist in one tank?"

"And not only fish," Daphne responded. "Look at this guy." She pointed to a sea turtle whose size rivaled any other creature in the tank, gliding placidly along behind a school of small indigo fish. "He reminds me of George Brisbane," she mused.

Will chuckled. "Are he and your father good friends?"

Daphne shrugged. "I honestly can't say that my father has many friends. They're mostly acquaintances, or more like employees. People like Brisbane only care about money."

"And people like your father?"

"They care about the greater good."

For a moment, Will's veneration for Daphne turned to sympathy. She really had herself convinced that her father could do no wrong. He wondered what she knew about Desmond's past dealings, wondered if she would feel the same way if she had seen the altercation between her father and Roderick Gleave. "And who's this?" Will asked at the sight of a toothy, menacing reef shark.

"Oh, that's an easy one," she said. "Emil Havelock."

Will nodded grimly. "He's the man who killed my family. I'm sure of it."

Daphne looked at Will in the blue glow of the immense tank. "I would believe that in a heartbeat. I just can't believe that my father would give an order that terrible." She wanted to take his hand, but after a brief hesitation, gently placed hers on his shoulder. Startled, he moved away quickly and looked at her as though expecting her to burst into flames. "It's alright," she said. "My father explained the rules to me. I can't touch you. That doesn't mean I can't touch your T-shirt." She smiled warmly, stood beside him again and slowly ran her fingertips up and down the small of his back. "See? No one's dying." Her relaxing touch caused him to instinctually close his eyes. The sensation of her hand on his back had quickly become the best part of his day. "I'm sorry about your family, Will. If I could bring them back, I would."

"I know," said Will, sensing her sincerity. "But none of that is your fault, obviously. Besides, if we're being honest, I don't even feel as though I ever met my real parents. I have no memory of them. That's what makes this so difficult. I'm furious that my life has been tampered with so much, but I'd probably be much more gung-ho about avenging my parents' deaths if I felt more of an emotional connection."

"Like the connection I feel with my parents?" Daphne asked. She did not receive an answer, but then, she had not expected one. Instead, she continued, "I have nearly twenty years' worth of memories with my father, Will. Birthdays, graduations, holidays, even arguments. Of all the people that you've spoken to recently, you're looking at the one who knows Desmond Duquesne the best, and I'm telling you that he's not capable of the evil he's been accused of."

"I don't know what to believe anymore."

"Believe what you want, Will, but just answer my question. Are you planning to kill my father?"

She positioned herself between Will and the glowing indigo fish tank as she asked her question, her dark intense eyes fixated on his. For a moment, he felt weak in the knees, almost as though he were back in school and preparing to present in front of the entire class. Being put on the spot like this created an anxiety that manifested throughout his entire body. He knew that the only way to stop it would be to speak. "No," he answered. "I won't take your father from you. I promise that I won't."

"Promise you won't what?" asked the returning Andy.

"Make me look at the jellyfish," Daphne lied. She shuddered and explained, "They always gave me the creeps."

"So does that mean we're finished here?"

"Not quite," said Daphne, leading the way down a narrow corridor. "There's one more tank I always have to look at when I come." After only a few paces, she stopped in front of a tank no larger than the one at Andy's parents' house, and the boys exchanged mocking glances. "What?" she asked.

Will took a closer look at the creatures in the tank and said, "Really? This is what you were so excited about?" He chuckled. "They're just seahorses!"

"I know," she said, indignant at her companions' pronounced lack of enthusiasm. "But they've always been my favorite. I always asked for one when I was younger, but my parents told me that they were too fragile...that I wouldn't know how to take care of them." She chose a lone seahorse drifting along near the bottom of the tank and traced her shape on the glass. "She's just so graceful and beautiful." In an instant, Will went from scoffing at Daphne's childhood wish to empathizing with it.

AFTER THE AQUARIUM, the trio headed to a local pub for dinner, during which Daphne asked numerous questions about their school lives. Unlike Veronica and Wisp, she did not need to politely feign interest in Andy's stories, and she punctuated his 'drawer full of jelly' story by saying, "Oh my God, that's great! I am so jealous of you guys!"

"Why would you be jealous?" Will asked. "It's just normal stuff."

"Exactly," Daphne responded. "You don't understand how much normal stuff I've missed out on. I was homeschooled, which was fine, but you guys have so many more friends than I do, and so many more experiences. I love my father, but he completely sheltered me, and now he wants me to go into the family business, so I guess it won't end any time soon."

"Well, what would you want to do if not real estate?"

Daphne looked sheepishly at her two new friends and muttered, "Maybe a vet?"

"I could totally see that," said Andy.

"Me too," said Will, "but only if you've learned by now how to take care of seahorses."

She chuckled and continued to speak to Will and Andy as though she had known them for her entire life, the awkwardness of the early afternoon dissipated by Will's vow to not take action against her father.

Their discussion continued into the night until Andy's exaggerated yawns finally had their intended effect and Daphne called for Mr. Ridgley to pick them up. He did so promptly and the three filed cozily into the backseat. Andy insisted upon sitting between Will and Daphne, acting as a buffer to prevent any inadvertent contact. Disappointed at first, Daphne was at least relieved when Andy nodded off within the first few minutes of their drive. Will stifled a laugh as Andy's head came to rest heavily on her shoulder.

When Will spoke, he did so silently to avoid waking his friend. "I had a great time today," he said. "Thanks for showing me around town. It was nice to get away from all these crazy people."

"I know the feeling," Daphne confided. "What are you doing tomorrow night?"

"Probably either getting shot at or set on fire. You?"

Daphne snickered. "It's my brother's birthday. My parents are throwing him a little party at a restaurant near our place. It won't be nearly as big as my father's masquerade next week, but it should still be nice. Do you want to come?"

Will's excitement at the invitation was abated only by the identity of the guest of honor. "I'm not so sure your brother is going to love the fact that I'm there."

"I'm not so sure that matters," Daphne responded. "I was

told that I could invite some people, and I choose you and Andy. If Alex doesn't like it, that's too damn bad."

Will appreciated her candor and readily agreed to attend. "I have to ask, though," he said. "Are you inviting me because you want me there, or are you inviting me because you still don't trust that I'm not going to go after your father?"

"Maybe a little bit of both," Daphne answered with a mischievous glint in her eyes. "But I suggest you don't look a gift horse in the mouth."

She was toying with him. He knew it, but he liked it. "Noted," he said with a nod as Ridgley pulled to a stop in front of Veronica Frost's residence. Although hesitant to break the gaze that he shared with Daphne, Will knew that he had to go, and so roused Andy with a nudge.

The two young men stepped out onto the sidewalk before Ridgley could come around to open their door, and Will immediately felt torn. Having arrived home, he realized how very tired he was, but while his body longed for bed, his heart longed to be back in the car with Daphne, preferably without the Andy buffer. At the very least, he wanted to kiss or even hug her goodnight, but he knew that he couldn't. There was some consolation, though, in feeling that she wanted the same thing.

When Ridgley closed the car door, Will made his way up the short flight of stairs and fumbled briefly with the set of keys his aunt had provided him. Andy followed his friend groggily and leaned on the wrought iron railing for support. Daphne, in the meantime, had slid across the leather seat to the door from which Will had just exited.

"I don't want to speak out of turn, Miss Duquesne," said Ridgley, "but is it wise to get involved with this boy?"

"Nope," she muttered. "It's absolutely not." Still, she placed her finger on the tinted glass and traced the silhouette that he cast against his aunt's front door.

THIRTY-THREE

Mr. Wisp Spins a Web

THE EXPOSED bulb hanging in the stairwell leading up to Eleanor Hornbeck's third-floor apartment gasped for life as she trudged up the stairs, fighting with two handfuls of plastic grocery bags. She stopped just below it, heaved a sigh, and slammed the wall with her elbow. The light stopped flickering and shone brightly. She continued on her way, though with the next step, the defiant bulb started its buzzing and flickering again. Upon reaching the landing she fumbled for her keys and, after several minutes, found the proper one for her dead-bolt. When she turned the key, however, she realized that the door was not, in fact, bolted. Having lowered her bags to the floor as silently as possible, she slowly turned the tarnished brass knob and peered cautiously into the apartment.

"Jesus," she said upon spotting the man standing at the far end of her leaving room. "How the hell did you get in here?"

He had been standing with his back to the door, gazing through the cloudy pane of a window into the small courtyard below, but now Mr. Wisp turned and said cheerily, "Can't a man visit his sister?"

339

"Stepsister. And I thought you were a burglar. You're lucky I didn't call the police and have you shot." She dragged her plastic bags through the door and slammed it shut.

"Well, thank God for small favors," Wisp replied.

"Don't count your chickens," she said. "I'm still considering it. What do you want?"

"Such hostility, Eleanor," he said in a soothing tone. He took the bags from her hands and carried them into the kitchen. "You know you're my pride and joy…et cetera."

Eleanor rolled her eyes and followed him into the kitchen. His good deed done, he took a seat at her antique wooden table, leaned back, and removed his yo-yo from the pocket of his blazer.

"Again I'll ask: what do you want?"

"Fine, fine," he said. "I saw your smear job on young Alexander Duquesne the other day, so I came to speak to you, as it seems that our interests are converging."

"And what interests would those be?" Eleanor asked.

"You, sister dear, are intent upon debasing the Duquesne family and have been digging your claws in like a raptor as of late."

Eleanor simulated outrage as best she could. "I don't know what you're talking about. Why would I go after the Duquesnes?"

Wisp shrugged. "Jealousy? Potential blackmail? The fact that he's one of the wealthiest moguls in the world, and finding a big enough story could put you and your little dirt sheet on the map? Tell me when I'm getting warm…"

"It's my job to keep track of what the rich and famous are up to," she snapped. "The real question is, why the hell are you suddenly so interested in them?"

"Who? The Duquesnes?" Wisp asked, affronted. "I assure you, I'm not. My interest lies with a certain young man who— one way or another—is about to change the Duquesnes' lives."

His fingers were now the anchors of a beautifully symmetrical web of string, the red yo-yo swinging pendulously in the center.

Eleanor leaned back against the kitchen counter, clearly intrigued, but still suspicious. "Who?"

Wisp's grin widened as he purred, "William Trammell."

"William Trammell?" Eleanor searched her memory for the name and eventually found it with a tilt of her head. "He's the one you said could off Desmond Duquesne."

"Correct. But get this, sister dear. William Trammell has a thing for Desmond's charming daughter Daphne. Ain't that something?" His stepsister grinned slightly while he continued, "And this boy's got *power*. I can sense it. He's going to be the next big thing. He'll be worth our time and effort."

"And how do you know that?"

"Because I've taken him under my wing."

"God help him," she said under her breath.

"I see that you've received an invitation to Duquesne's masquerade ball." He pointed toward the refrigerator, upon which hung the black and white invitation.

"I was invited," she said, stooping to pour cat food into three bowls in the corner of the kitchen. "But I haven't decided whether I'll be attending. It's a charity fundraiser, so it would cost me a fortune to go."

"Your altruism truly knows no bounds," said her stepbrother. "I, on the other hand, would be more than willing to make a generous donation—should you agree to bring me as your plus one."

"Will Trammell be at the masquerade?"

"If I were a betting man," said Wisp with a smile, "I'd put money on it. Now, I know that you loathe the Duquesnes and would rather not spend time at a charity gala, but the way I see it, you could end up with an exclusive headline if you stay on top of things."

Now Eleanor's gears were turning. "The headline: 'Star-crossed Lovers Unite Duquesne and Frost Families.'"

Wisp nodded with indifference. "Possibly."

"Or maybe 'Duquesne Killed by Daughter's Beau.'"

"Or more interesting still," said Wisp, "would be if William ends up killing poor little Daphne. Now wouldn't that set off a powder keg?"

Eleanor's eyes lit up. "And I can be in the front row."

Wisp nodded slowly. "Things are going to get interesting, my dear. Why not make the most of it?"

"And to what do I owe this uncharacteristic display of generosity?"

Eleanor's stepbrother stood and approached, grabbing her face and smooshing her cheeks together. "I just wuv my wittle sister so vewy much." He released his grip and chuckled as she dourly tried to rub his red fingerprints from her face. "Just kidding. You know I enjoy a good show, and you just happen to be the one with the ticket."

He headed back out to the hallway but stopped halfway through the door. "I almost forgot. Meet me at the club before Duquesne's party. We can take a car service."

Eleanor shot daggers in his direction but did not bother to leave the kitchen. "And what if I already have a date?"

"Oh, Eleanor, you must never lose that sense of humor. I'll see you in a few days." Wisp chortled as he shut the door and left his stepsister alone to consider his proposal.

THIRTY-FOUR

Bad Blood

THE NEXT DAY, Will showered, dressed, and threw open the curtains to see that it was a beautiful morning in Boston. He hopped down the stairs and found his aunt sitting in her office with Gwen, reviewing the restaurant's books and revising an ad for a new waitress. The bemused Veronica peered over her reading glasses when he entered the room. "Well, good morning," she said. "You seem to have a spring in your step today. Is the leg feeling better?"

He hadn't given it much thought, but now that she had put him on the spot, he realized that this was the first morning he did not reach for either a crutch or Gleave's cane. "Actually, yeah," he answered. "Much better."

"Glad to hear it. And yesterday? How did it go with Daphne and Alexander?"

"It went great," he said, noting too late that he should have contained his enthusiasm a bit more. He knew his aunt was not entirely comfortable with throwing her nephew into the snake pit of New Covington more often than need be. "Alexander actually didn't go because Andy beat him so badly on the golf course, so that was pretty funny."

Veronica raised an eyebrow. "So it was just the two of you and Daphne?"

"Yeah, but I think it worked out better that way."

"Mmm…" was the only response he received. Still, at least Gwen made him feel better with a look that said, 'Don't mind her.'

"So…" Will hesitated, but he knew he needed to break news of tonight's plans sooner rather than later. "Andy and I were invited to Alexander's birthday party later today, and I said that we could go. I just wanted to let you know."

"Who invited you?" Gwen asked. "Desmond?"

"No. Daphne."

"William," said his aunt, taking off her glasses and closing the thick binder on the desk in front of her. "Are you sure that this is a good idea? I mean, until we hear from the Collective regarding that blood sample, there's a very real chance that you're putting that girl's life in danger every time you are around her."

"I understand that, but I can be careful. I was careful yesterday."

Veronica sighed. "Do you care for the girl, William?"

The discomfited Will looked to Gwen for support but got none. "What do you mean?"

"I think you know what I mean. I'm trying to be delicate to spare you some embarrassment, but are you developing feelings for Daphne Duquesne?"

"Yes," he admitted. "I am. Does that matter?"

"It absolutely matters," said Veronica. "As these feelings develop, it is going to get more and more difficult to avoid a situation that leaves you with blood on your hands. I can't even bear the thought of what it would do to you if you even inadvertently let anything happen to that young lady."

344

He knew she was right, but the draw to see Daphne again was too powerful. He was going to the party tonight, whether she liked it or not. "I'll be careful," he reiterated. "Now I'm going to make some breakfast. Does anyone need anything?"

The two women both quietly and politely said no, and Will left the office with much less enthusiasm than when he had entered it. "I feel bad for him," said Gwen.

"You know I do too, but it is an incredibly tricky situation. The boy's been through enough. Could you imagine if he accidentally killed this girl? I can't stand by and let that happen."

SHE PICKED up her phone and dialed. Seeing Gwen's quizzical expression, she held her hand over the receiver and explained, "Maybe he needs to hear this reinforced by someone who isn't his meddling old aunt. Let's see if Frances Whitworth has any concrete information for us yet."

WITHIN THE HOUR, a Collective contingent comprising of Whitworth, Donovan, Valentine, Brandt, and Feng had arrived at Veronica Frost's doorstep, and Will and Andy had been summoned to join them in the living room. When Will entered the room, he felt as though he was entering an intervention. Not only did everyone appear exceedingly grim, but several members of the group, including Gwen and Valentine in particular, seemed unable to look him in the eyes. "Hey everybody," Will said as he took a seat. "Is something wrong?"

"Will," said Valentine, trying his best to achieve some semblance of eye contact. "We do have a bit of news that you're not going to want to hear. You see, well—"

"Director," Whitworth gently interjected. "If you don't mind, I'll handle it." Relieved, Valentine stepped back and perched himself on Veronica's window seat. "You see,

William," said Whitworth, "the test results came back from the lab, and it has been confirmed that you pose just as much a risk to Daphne or Alexander as you do to Desmond."

Will filled with emotion upon hearing this but did his best to maintain his composure. "I can't believe this. It makes no sense."

"It makes perfect sense," Drayton Feng hissed. "I ran the tests myself. Twice. Each time that your blood was exposed to one of the Duquesnes', a reaction occurred that would doubtless be fatal. Dr. Creswell observed the tests as well, if that for some reason strengthens the findings in your view."

Will glared at the disfigured researcher. "You know, doc, I can see why you're not working in a real hospital somewhere. Your bedside manner is really lacking. No wonder they lock you underground."

Brandt laughed in appreciation of Will's newfound backbone, but the rest of the room was far less supportive. "William, please don't speak to people like that," his aunt requested. "I know that you are upset, but it is not Dr. Feng's fault."

"She's right, Will," Valentine added. "When the results came to me, the first thing I requested was that they run another set of tests. None of us wanted this to be true. It just is."

"And there's nothing that can be done about it?" Will asked.

"The only thing we can do right now," said Whitworth, "is make sure that you bring no harm to Daphne. She's an innocent victim of circumstance."

"So am I."

Whitworth lowered her head and her tone. "I know. But a prophecy is a prophecy, and Baba Yaga's magic is as strong as any I've known. That doesn't mean that we won't keep trying to find solutions, but it does mean that—for now at least—it is imperative that you do not lay a finger on Daphne Duquesne."

The high of the previous night came crashing down. Will

wanted nothing more to do with this conversation. "I get the point. Is that all?"

Valentine cleared his throat. "Um, not quite. Dr. Feng?"

Feng looked to still be reeling from the berating he had suffered, and clearly had as little interest in continuing the meeting as Will did. Still, he did as he was told. "Aside from the aforementioned tests, I've been working on an additional project regarding your blood sample." He reached into his pocket and removed a vial filled with clear liquid. "I was able to isolate some of the acute irregularities that make your blood unique, and I have incorporated them into this. Essentially, it is poison, though it will only really have an effect on someone in the Duquesne family bloodline. It is tasteless, odorless, and may be our best means of assassinating Desmond Duquesne."

"So if we put it in Duquesne's wine, for example, it's essentially like he's drinking Will's blood?" Andy asked.

"Yes, and once ingested, the desired effect should take place almost immediately."

"Cool."

Donovan spoke next. "Will, your aunt told us that you were invited to Alexander Duquesne's birthday celebration. We think that this would be the perfect place for you to slip Desmond the poison. He'll have his guard down, and he seems to trust you now."

"Do you people hear yourselves?" asked Will, addressing the entire room. "The perfect place to kill a man is at his son's birthday party? My God."

"I'll admit that we're getting desperate, William," said Whitworth. "But if we don't stop him soon—"

"You're not just desperate," Will snapped. "You're hypocrites. You just finished telling me that one of our main priorities is to make sure that no harm is done to Daphne. Don't you think that killing her father in cold blood constitutes harm being done? Not all pain is physical, you know."

At this, Brandt stepped in. "You self-righteous little prick. You're eighteen, and you're going to lecture the people in this room about emotional pain? We've been through more than you know. Your aunt lost her family, Whitworth lost her fiancée, Feng damn near almost lost his face, and I—" He was trembling as he waved his weathered finger in Will's face, but Veronica threw herself between the two of them.

"That is enough! This is my home, and everyone will be respectful of it! I understand what you are trying to accomplish, but watch your tone, John Brandt, or get out!"

Brandt recoiled like a scolded pit bull, adjusted his demeanor, and responded, "I just want an answer from him, Veronica. Will, are you going to do it or not? Are you going to the party, and will you agree to kill Desmond Duquesne?"

"I'm going to the party," said Will. "I will not be killing Desmond Duquesne. Meeting adjourned." With that, he walked out, leaving the crestfallen group silenced by the strength of his resolve.

"We're not going to convince him to do this before the party," said Valentine. "He's adamant."

"Damn it!" Brandt shouted, ignoring Veronica's reproachful glance.

"Calm down, John," said Whitworth. "There may be another way."

"Him?" Donovan asked, pointing to Andy.

Whitworth nodded. "What do you say, Andy? You're the only other person in this room who's been invited to tonight's party. Want to be a hero?"

THIRTY-FIVE

Damage

It took some convincing before Veronica, who hadn't driven in the years following the accident that took the lives of her son and husband, agreed to call a car service to take Will and Andy to Alexander Duquesne's birthday celebration. Before long, she answered the door to a man Will had never seen before, but with whom Andy was quite familiar.

"Mrs. Frost?" said Eddie Garza. "I believe you called for a ride?"

"I did. It's for my nephew and his friend, actually."

As they walked toward the door, Will noticed that Andy looked as pale as the times Will would forget to buckle his seatbelt on the way to school. "You okay, man? You don't look too good."

"Fine," said Andy. "Must be something I ate." He approached Eddie and held out his hand. "Hello, sir. It is a pleasure to meet you. My name is Andy Lunsford."

"Um, okay," said Eddie, who had far more undercover experience than Andy. "How's it going?"

"Good, sir, good," he said with an overstated wink. "Shall we go?"

Will and Veronica exchanged glances before she gave him a hug and whispered, "Be safe."

"Will do," he promised, and they were off.

THEY ARRIVED AT AGOSTINO'S—A beautiful Italian restaurant—fashionably late, as Andy described it. After all, he explained, they really would not know anyone but the Duquesnes themselves, so there was no point in arriving early. The two agreed that they fully expected an evening of standing by themselves in the corner, watching wealthy people make fools of themselves, and they were pretty much fine with this. What they did not expect was that they would arrive to a more intimate affair of only about thirty people, and that their seats would be reserved at the head table between Daphne and Joanna Duquesne. "Guys!" Daphne shouted upon seeing them and waved them to their seats. The warmth from the night before returned, albeit briefly, as Will checked his impulse to give her a friendly hug hello. He hated that instead of being able to have an enjoyable time, Whitworth's words from earlier echoed through his head. Still, he tried his best to make this preoccupation as subtle as possible while Daphne named everyone in the room and explained their connection to the family. This went on for several minutes before the boys were startled by a hand on each of their shoulders. "You boys going to be ready for the quiz later?" Desmond Duquesne laughed.

Will looked nervously at the hand that Desmond had placed precariously close to his neck. There was a heightened confidence about Desmond tonight. He knew that Will had no intention of working against him. "I'm glad that you could make it," Desmond continued. "I'm heading to the bar. Can I get anyone anything to drink? Andrew, you look like you could use something."

Andy felt the weight of the vial sitting like a lodestone in his blazer. "Um, no. I'm good with water, thanks." He indicated the bottle of sparkling water on the table and Desmond left for the bar, followed by his bodyguard Emil Havelock.

Desmond addressed Havelock as they stood at the bar. "I've been assured that William has no intention of taking action against me tonight. However, his friend, Andrew, is going to try to poison me. I don't imagine he's too slick, but just in case, keep a watchful eye on him."

Havelock agreed. "You want me to have a talk with him?"

"No, no. Let's not go causing a scene. We'll see how it plays out."

"IS EVERYTHING ALRIGHT, ANDY?" Joanna Duquesne asked.

"Sure," he lied. "Everything's fine." He was nervous enough with his assignment, but when he considered how this woman had shown him and Will nothing but kindness, the weight of Feng's poison grew heavier and heavier. He reached into his pocket and felt the vial that held the key to stopping all this madness, but he also came across something else which, until now, he had forgotten he had brought with him. Sitting next to Desmond's wife, now seemed like the perfect time to discuss the small wooden stamp he had forgotten to leave at New Covington the day before. Removing Beleth's sigil, he looked around cautiously before showing Mrs. Duquesne. "I meant to give this back to Mr. Ridgley," he said. "I found it a few days ago and thought that it might be important. Any idea what it is?"

To his surprise, Mrs. Duquesne looked as though she had seen a ghost. She quickly snatched it from Andy's hand and examined it closely while cupping it in her hands to ensure that no one else could see. "Oh," she said, suddenly attempting to act casual. "It's just a stamp that we're using for the masquerade party."

"I don't follow," Andy admitted.

"It was Desmond's idea. There are going to be over two hundred guests of all different ages. He thought it might be wise to stamp the hands of anyone twenty-one and up so the bartenders know they can serve them."

"Ah," said Andy. "That makes sense. But, um, what is that symbol?"

Joanna pretended to examine it closely, screwed up her lips, and said, "I have no clue, but I'm sure Desmond has a reason for whatever it is. He always has a reason," she muttered. "Thank you for returning it, Andy. The last thing we'd want is to get in trouble for serving someone underage." She placed the stamp in her purse and shut it up tight.

IN THE MEANTIME, Daphne and Will were reminiscing about their day at the aquarium when Daphne noticed a distinct change in how much attention Will seemed to be paying to what she was saying. "Will, what's wrong? You're acting very different from how you did yesterday."

She sat, legs crossed elegantly in a simple black cocktail dress, her hair flowing in delicate waves over her sun-kissed shoulders. He had not yet seen her dressed for such an occasion, and all he wanted to do was feel her hand in his as he swept her onto the dance floor. Instead, he felt impelled to be honest with her and risk putting a damper on her good mood. "I got some bad news today," he said. "At least, from my perspective it's bad. You know those blood samples that your father gave to have analyzed?"

She did not react visibly but said, "Let me guess. It's official. If you touch me, you kill me."

Will nodded somberly. "I can't believe it."

"Then don't," she said, to his surprise. "Don't lose hope. If things are meant to be, they will be, and no amount of magic can change that. They'll figure something out. In the meantime, let's have fun, okay?"

"Are you sure? You're not afraid?"

"You don't want to hurt me, do you?"

"Of course not!"

"Then I know you won't," she smiled. "Come on, let's dance." She lured him with a beckoning finger, and the two of them joined the rest of the younger crowd on the dance floor. The only two that held back were Alexander and his friend Carson, who, spotting Will for the first time, shot drunken daggers of disdain in his direction.

"I can't believe your sister invited that kid," Carson sneered. "He's a punk. What does she see in him?"

"Agreed," said Alexander. "She could do better."

"She could do me."

Alex turned his glare toward his friend. "Watch it."

DAPHNE AND WILL DANCED until dinner was served, at which point they returned to the table to rejoin her family, save for Alexander, who had insisted upon sitting with his friends when he heard that Will and Andy were his sister's chosen guests. "You look like you could use a cold shower," Andy whispered to Will upon his return.

"I know," said Will, tugging at his starched collar. "I'm sweating. That dance floor is hot."

"Yeah. Because that's what I meant," said Andy with an eye roll.

Dinner went well and was filled with lively conversation that caught the Duquesnes up on the events of the previous day, including Andy's aversion to clam chowder and Daphne's identifying a turtle that resembled George Brisbane. Almost immediately upon finishing her meal, Daphne begged Will to return to the dance floor—a request that he declined for the time being, as he had started to feel an ache in his wounded leg. Instead, Andy was lucky enough to be dragged away to join Daphne and several of Alexander's female friends.

Before long, Will found himself alone at the table with Joanna Duquesne, who scooted over two seats to sidle up next to him. She watched him watch Daphne before leaning in and saying, "I don't envy you, William."

This broke his gaze. "What do you mean, Mrs. Duquesne?"

"Please, call me Joanna. I don't envy the position that you are in. It's clear that you care for my daughter very much, but at the same time, the whole purpose of you being in Boston is to kill my husband."

"I'm not going to, though."

Joanna took a deep breath. "I'm not going to be one of those people who tell you what you should or should not do. I can tell you, though, that I can relate in more ways than you know. Some look at my husband and see a humanitarian and philanthropist. And that is all true." She directed Will's gaze toward her husband, who stood shooting the breeze with several of Alexander's friends, enthralling them with what appeared to be quite an exciting story. "Others," Joanna continued, "see a monster. Someone who would sacrifice anything to achieve his goals, someone who will use others like pieces on a chessboard." Joanna's eyes began to moisten as Alexander's friends all left the faraway conversation, except for Kara, who hung flirtatiously on Desmond's arm. He leaned in to whisper something in her ear and she blushed. Will noticed the opposite reaction in Joanna's cheeks. "And that may all be true as well."

"Mrs. Duquesne, are you saying that you're in favor of me killing your husband?"

"I'm saying that the best way to protect yourself is to learn to realize when you are being played, and by whom. As for you and my husband, do what you feel is right, not what anyone else tells you is right." Will nodded in appreciation of her forthrightness. "For the record," she added with a lighter tone, "I think that you and Daphne would make an adorable couple." She leaned on his shoulder as she excused herself from the table with a kind, but pensive, smile.

Will considered what Joanna had said and noticed that Desmond and Kara were nowhere to be found. He felt sorry for Mrs. Duquesne, but reasoned that Desmond's character flaws were not enough to warrant cold-blooded murder. With this settled for now, he turned his attention back to Daphne, who seemed to have entirely worn down a practically-panting Andy. He weighed whether to return to the dance floor to relieve his friend, but before he could decide, the two removed themselves and Daphne excused herself to go freshen up in the powder room.

"I'm going to get a drink," said Andy, and despite not being invited, Will got up to join him at the bar. "What are you doing?" Andy asked as they walked.

"Going to the bar with you."

"Why?"

Catching a strange vibe from his friend, Will leaned on the bar and asked, "Is there a problem?"

"I'm just…no," Andy stammered. He ordered a Coke and a whiskey while Will looked on with curiosity.

"Thirsty?"

"I thought I'd get something for Mr. Duquesne," said Andy. "Just to be nice. His is the whiskey."

Will observed his friend nervously tapping his fingers on the polished wooden bar top before darting his hand into Andy's coat pocket and removing the vial of Feng's poison. "I knew it," Will said. "You were really going to do it, weren't you?"

"Will, come on," Andy pleaded. "Give that back. Let's just get this over with."

"You were just dancing with Daphne. She has been nothing but friendly to you, and you're about to kill her father right now?"

"Don't look at it like that, Will. If we don't do something, he may keep hurting people." He tried unsuccessfully to snatch the vial back. "Come on."

"So you've bought into the company line, huh?"

"The sooner this guy's gone, the sooner we can go home, Will."

"You can go home whenever you want, Andy." With that, he opened the vial and poured it into the sink behind the bar. Andy fell silent as he watched his hopes of saving the day trickle down the drain. "Frankly, none of this concerns you."

When Andy finally spoke again, it was in a muted tone. "I know you're confused, Will. I was just trying to help. I feel like you're going to regret not doing something."

"I just did something," said Will. "And I don't regret it."

Andy nodded. "Okay. I'm just going to get out of here. I don't belong with this group of people, but maybe you do." Will watched as Andy walked to the stairs leading down to the restrooms, but he refused to chase after him. He slammed his fist on the bar and gulped the whiskey that had been ordered for Desmond while Emil Havelock looked on with satisfaction.

ANDY TRIED to collect himself as he walked down the long flight of stairs leading to the restaurant's lowermost level, which housed offices, restrooms, and a powder room. He regretted having come to Boston. Once he got outside, he would ask either Eddie Garza or Ms. Whitworth to book him a ticket home. He was in over his head, as was Will, but at least Andy was in a position to leave.

To make matters worse, when he was halfway down the stairs, he heard a voice coming from the basement, an obnoxious drunken voice that he recognized from the golf course. Great. Carson. This was not what he needed right now. Then he heard another familiar voice. It was Daphne and she sounded distressed. Realizing that the noises were, in fact, coming from directly beneath the staircase, he raced down the last few steps, turned the corner, and saw Daphne being assaulted by Carson. His fingers were pressed viciously into both of her arms as he pinned her against the wall. She was kicking frantically, so much so that she had already lost one shoe, but to no avail. In his drunken state, he seemed immune to her desperate attempts at self-defense. "Please…" she whimpered. "Let go!"

Ignoring her tearful plaints, Carson mumbled something incoherently as he sloppily kissed her neck.

"Hey!" Andy yelled without hesitation. "Get the hell off of her!"

At the very least, this turned Carson's attention from Daphne, but when he saw that he was being addressed by Andy, he responded with a vicious sneer. "Get lost, fat boy."

Having had enough, Andy lunged at Carson, wrapping his forearm around his neck and screaming for Daphne to run away. She tried, but Carson, realizing that he could not let her run back up into the crowded hall, found enough energy to throw Andy violently to the floor. He grabbed Daphne's arm as she tried to run and dragged her back to the darkness of the stairwell. "Come on, Daphne," he slurred. "You know you've always wanted this. Let me show you how much better I am than that asshole upstairs."

He got as far as unbuckling his belt when another hand grabbed him by the shoulder and spun him around. Carson found himself face to face with Will, who said, "I'm not upstairs," and punched him as hard as he could in the jaw.

Carson went reeling back and Daphne tried to run, but she tripped and stayed slumped on the floor at Will's feet, sobbing. He wanted to help her up. He wanted to grab her and hold her and tell her that everything would be alright, but he knew that he couldn't. Seeing red, he waited for Carson to get back to his feet. He would punish him.

Daphne's drunken assailant spat blood and ran at Will, and that's when it happened. Andy watched as Carson was lifted off his feet and sent careening through the air, his body crashing through a wooden end table, smashing both it and the ornate vase that had been resting on top of it to bits. By the time Emil Havelock arrived at the foot of the stairs, Carson lay knocked out among splinters of wood and shards of porcelain. Alex and his mother soon followed, while Desmond stumbled out of one of the catering offices, followed by Kara, who tried desperately to fix her tousled hair. Joanna knelt and held her daughter in the way that Will could not while watching her husband trying to tuck his shirt back into his rumpled pants.

"What the hell did you do?" cried Alexander, directing his anger at Will and Andy. "This never would have happened if you two hadn't come. I want you out now!" He looked to Havelock for support. "I want them out now!"

Havelock, who was not accustomed to taking orders from his employer's whiny kid, deferred to Desmond, who nodded in agreement. "Party's over. Emil, please show these two gentlemen out before tempers continue to rise."

"YOU TWO WANT to tell me what happened back there?" Havelock asked as he led Will and Andy out into the glare of the setting sun.

"Carson was trying to rape Daphne," Andy answered. "I tried to stop him but couldn't. Will tried to stop him and could."

"So what happened? He tripped and fell through the table?"

"I threw him through the table," Will answered flatly.

Havelock eyed Will up and down. "I'm supposed to believe that?"

"I couldn't care less what you believe," Will retorted.

"Watch your mouth, kid," Havelock fired back. "I'm just trying to find out what really happened. I don't recall ever doing anything to you that you should be acting all pissy toward me."

"No?" said Will with newfound courage. "Then I guess you don't remember killing my parents."

Havelock couldn't help but grin. "No, I don't. Have you been under the impression that I was the one who killed your parents this whole time?" Will didn't answer but grew irate when the usually mirthless Havelock chuckled. "Let me clue you in to two facts, kid. One: I've killed a lot of people for a lot of different reasons. Two: you don't scare me. That said, if I had killed your parents, I'd have no problem admitting to it, believe me."

Will and Havelock remained engaged in a stare-down until interrupted by Eddie Garza. "Everything alright here?"

"You their ride?"

"I am."

"Your boys here got into a bit of a scuffle with one of the other party guests." Eddie noted a growing lump on Andy's head and Will's rapidly bruising fist. "You should see the other guy," Havelock quipped.

THIRTY-SIX

Breaking Points

WILL and Andy rode home in silence, neither one knowing quite how to address the other after the evening's dramatic turn of events. While Will's memory replayed the image of Carson flying through the air, Andy's thoughts leaned more toward concern over how the Collective would react to the fact that he had not gotten the job done, that he had not killed Desmond Duquesne. Eddie also worried about what reaction that news would bring and pitied the boy who had only wanted to help his friend but was now a quivering mess of anxiety.

When they were close to home, Andy finally broke the silence. "I'm going to the hotel to report to the Collective. Maybe I'll just stay there. Can you tell your aunt that for me?"

Andy had been hoping that Will would say, 'I'll join you,' but instead, all he got was, "Yeah. I'll tell her."

Soon enough, Eddie drove off toward the Stonegate with Andy, and Will was left alone on his aunt's doorstep. Upon entering the house, he found Veronica lying on the couch with an icepack on her head. "Are you okay?" he asked with concern.

She smiled weakly. "I'm fine, William. Just a mild headache. I get them every so often. How about you? How was the party?" She sat up and almost immediately noticed the bruising on his right hand. "Oh, Will. What now? Here. Take this." He sat next to her on the couch and she wrapped the icepack gently around his knuckles. "Did you get into a fight?"

"I did, but for the right reasons. Honest."

"I suppose I need to believe you," she teased. "I'm sorry it didn't go well. I really am. Is there anything I can do for you?"

"Actually," he said, "I'd like to speak with Mr. Wisp."

"THIS IS UN-FUCKING-BELIEVABLE," Brandt growled after Andy had given his report of what occurred at the party. "Not only is the kid not playing ball, but now he's actively sabotaging our efforts. Duquesne must be loving this!"

"John, we need to remain calm," said Whitworth.

"I don't know, Fran," said Valentine. "While I'd normally be on your side, in this case, I think Brandt's response is entirely appropriate. We're very clearly running out of options."

"Let's put our heads together," Donovan suggested. "I'm sure we can think of a way. Can we just get more of William's blood? Make a new batch of poison?"

"Maybe," said Whitworth. "If William is willing…"

"If he's willing," Brandt sneered. "Bullshit. I'm through with this team-player crap. I gave you all a chance. You almost had me convinced that if I worked with you, we'd get this done, but even all these years later, it's obvious that the same level of incompetence runs rampant around here."

Valentine pleaded as Brandt stood up. "Please, Brandt. This isn't the time to go running off. We'll need all hands on deck soon. Duquesne wants our group to splinter. If you leave, you'll be playing right into his hands."

"If I stay, I'll be playing into yours. Frankly, I don't know which is worse. I'm out of here. I'll get it done myself."

"Let him go," said Donovan. "He's toxic."

With Brandt gone, Valentine moved to reconvene in the morning, hoping Brandt would have come to his senses by then. Alone with Whitworth, Andy now felt comfortable enough to speak up. "Ms. Whitworth, I don't know if this will help, but I did find out two things at the party."

"And what were they?" Whitworth asked, somewhat distracted.

Andy cleared his throat and sat up straight in the conference room chair. "Well, Ms. Whitworth, I'm going to have to play hardball. If you want my info, I'll be needing a room for the night, preferably here at this fine establishment."

Whitworth smiled. "You want to stay in the Brig?"

"Oh, um, no. I meant that establishment," he said, pointing up. "The hotel."

"You drive a hard bargain, Andrew," Whitworth said. "But done. I'll even have Anthony throw in a continental breakfast. Now what do you know?"

Swollen with pride from his negotiating skills, Andy spoke. "Well, first, I found out that the sigil stamps are going to be used to identify people of legal drinking age at Duquesne's masquerade ball."

Whitworth rubbed her chin. "Now that's interesting. What else?"

"I also found out exactly what my buddy Will is capable of as far as magic goes."

MR. WISP TENTED his hands and tapped his fingertips together rhythmically as Will related the story of what happened between him and Carson. His eyes lit up when Will reached the part about the shove that knocked Carson clear

363

through a solid wood table. "My, that must have been some-thing," he said with a hint of admiration.

"I guess it was," said a slightly less enthused Will. "I was wondering, is this what you were talking to me about in the bar the other day?"

"Could be," Wisp answered. "Tell me, how were you feeling when this Carson character was coming toward you?"

"I wanted him to. I wanted to hurt him for what he tried to do to Daphne."

"Yes, yes, but what were you *feeling*?"

"I don't know," said Will, not really grasping the nature of the question. "Anger?"

"Mmm...I don't think so." Wisp shook his head. "What you were feeling went beyond anger. You were feeling rage. So much rage, in fact, that I believe it manifested in the form of telekinesis." Will's face wore a blank expression. "Moving things with your mind, essentially."

"Oh."

"It seems we may have found your latent ability. See? I told you prophetic dreams could not possibly be your only skill. This skill is much more...promising."

"But how do I control it? I mean, I could have killed that guy tonight."

"Well, it's all about finding a way to focus your energy and making sure you're only putting out the required amount at any given time. It's like being a marathon runner. If you give every-thing you have the moment you leave the starting line, you'll expend yourself and never reach the end. The same tenet holds true for those of us with these special gifts." Wisp walked over to Veronica's desk and grabbed a ballpoint pen. "Let's try this. Pretend this pen is your only means of defense against a thug like Carson. And let's say that, hmmm, this," he said, drawing a rudimentary figure on a thick notepad, "is Carson himself." He handed the pen to Will, took several steps back, and held the pad at arm's length. "Now William, use your weapon. Show stick-figure Carson what you can do!"

Will looked at the pen, took aim at the pad, and threw the pen as though it were a dart. It bounced off the pad after leaving a small mark and an even smaller indentation. Wisp's smile disappeared. "I don't quite think you get what I'm saying, Will," he said, handing the pen back to him and once again taking a few steps back. "Use your emotion. Think back on earlier tonight. Think of poor Daphne. Think of the terror in her eyes as that fiend clawed at her, trying oh-so-desperately to remove her clothes and prove that his manhood could compare to yours. Think of your friend, what's-his-name, lying helpless on the floor, obviously no match for someone of superior strength and prowess." As Wisp pushed further, he noticed a faraway look in Will's eyes, and saw that the pen was rising on its own. "There you go. Think of your Daphne, lying at home in bed right now, tears seeping through her tightly shut eyelids. This night will haunt her for the rest of her life. Think of what could've happened if—" Like a javelin, the pen cut through the air and pierced the heart of the effigy on the page. It tore clean through the pad and stuck in the wall behind Mr. Wisp. The older man removed the pen, admired the depth of the hole in the wall, and whispered, "Fantastic, William."

Will was not sure how to feel about this newfound skill, but at the very least, he was shocked by his own ability. "Do I always need to be angry for that to happen?"

"Well, I'd guess that any emotional impetus might work just as well. Remember, the emotion is the catalyst that you needed to show you that you're capable of this at all. Now that you know what you can do, you'll be able to practice, to hone your skill. If you're anything like me, and I like to think that you are," he said with a wink, "you'll soon be able use your skill whenever and wherever you want."

"So it gets easier?"

"In a way. With some practice, you'll be able to throw pens around left and right by the end of this week. However, that does not mean you'll be throwing cars. You were able to launch Carson, but that was during an extremely emotional situation. Moving objects larger than yourself would wear you out in no time. You've got to pace yourself."

"So the more practice I get, the larger the objects I can move?"

"Probably. It also depends upon the sorcerer's personal strength. I know of a girl who has the same ability as you. She's a master telekinetic. Her precision is unmatched. Still, she's never been able to use her power to lift anything heavier than a stapler."

"That sucks."

"Let's just say she makes it work."

JOANNA DUQUESNE STAYED up with her daughter until nearly three in the morning, when Daphne finally fell asleep, half from exhaustion and half from the sleeping aids they had found in Mrs. Ridgley's private stockpile of medications. Brushing Daphne's hair gently away from her face, she gave her daughter a soft kiss on the forehead before heading downstairs to confront her husband.

She found him in his study, surrounded by his masks, which were exceptionally unsettling at such ungodly hours of the night. Past midnight, they always seemed to take on lives of their own. Desmond sat fiddling with the wiring on the back of one particularly heinous mask made of carved wood. "This fell off the wall," he explained without looking up. "I used cheap wire the first time around with this one. Won't make that mistake again."

"Good," said Joanna. "It's nice to know that there are some mistakes you're not willing to make twice."

Sensing this was not going to be a pleasant conversation, he set the mask down on his desk and gave his full attention to his wife. "Is there something wrong, dear?"

"Des, our daughter was almost raped tonight. How can you ask if there's something wrong?"

"Joanna, you know me better than that. You know I was asking if there's something wrong *besides* what happened to Daphne tonight. How is she, by the way?"

"Finally asleep. Hopefully, it will last through the night. You know, if it weren't for William Trammell and his friend, things could have been much, much worse."

"I agree. Who knew?" he mused.

"I knew," said Joanna. "I think they're a good match. They seem to care a lot about each other already. It's such a shame this ridiculous restriction is imposed on them."

"Believe me, Joanna. I'm of the same mind as you, and trust me when I say that after I settle my own affairs, my next order of business will be to find a way to circumvent that pesky prophecy and get those two together."

"Desmond, you're still going through with your plans, aren't you? After you told everyone from me to Frances Whitworth that you wouldn't?"

Duquesne looked at his wife for a long time before finally answering. "Joanna, it's for the best if you don't know some things."

"I already know, Desmond. It's one thing to hide your other indiscretions from me, but you told me that you were not going to go through with your sacrifice. You promised me you would be satisfied with what you've got. And then I find this." She threw the sigil of Beleth onto his desk with a look of disgust.

"Where did you find this?"

"It doesn't matter. You still plan on committing mass murder, and I will not be a part of it."

"You already are, Joanna," Duquesne said with an eerie

calmness. "I told you what I was a long time ago, and you accepted it."

She closed her eyes and tried to remain calm. "We didn't have children then. Besides, I was convinced you were doing all of this for selfless reasons. I'm not convinced of that anymore. Things have changed."

"They have not. I still plan to dedicate my life to helping others. It just so happens that I will have more power and time to do so. And you'll be right there alongside me!"

"Until I die," she said, breaking down in tears. "Then what? You replace me with a girl half your age. What am I saying? You replace me with a girl one-tenth your age! And you see nothing wrong with this?"

"Joanna, I love you," he said, returning to his mask. "But I've spent too much time planning this final step for you to start going off-script. Know your role and stick to it."

She held her tongue, knowing it was useless to argue with her husband once his course of action was determined, and left. With his wife gone, Duquesne immediately called for Havelock, who arrived shortly thereafter. "I apologize. You wanted to speak to me earlier, Emil, and I was indisposed, but clearly Alexander's celebration did not go quite as planned."

"It's alright, sir. How is your daughter?"

"Resting well, thank you."

"And what about Carson? Would you like me to put the screws to him?"

"I appreciate the offer, Emil, but there is no need. He's already on the guest list for the masquerade, and while she surely won't want him there, I'm very much looking forward to having him front and center."

Emil grinned. "On another note, sir, I thought you might find it worth mentioning that William Trammell saved your life tonight."

Duquesne raised an eyebrow. "Do tell. The poison?"

"Dumped it right down the drain."

"Well, isn't that something. I was already wondering what I could do for William to express my gratitude for saving my daughter, and now I find out that he went out of his way to save me as well. You know what, Emil? Let's get him here tomorrow. I think that it's about time he learned what truly happened to his parents."

"Are you sure, sir?"

"I've atoned to the boy, Mr. Havelock. I have nothing to hide. But I think it's important for him to know that we did not pull the trigger, so to speak." He hung the tribal mask back in its place on the wall and took a moment to straighten it. "I've gained his trust. The Collective, it seems, has not. Let's drive the final nail into their coffin."

THIRTY-SEVEN

Truth and Consequences

THE NEXT MORNING, Ridgley showed up unannounced on Veronica Frost's doorstep and claimed that Desmond Duquesne insisted upon personally thanking Will for saving his daughter from the drunken Carson. Mr. Duquesne, Ridgley said, was in the car and would gladly come in to express his gratitude to Will, but Veronica objected. "Did he lose even more of his mind overnight, Mr. Ridgley?" she asked. "You know what my answer is. Desmond Duquesne will never step foot in this house."

"Understood, Mrs. Frost. It was my job to ask."

Will, who was standing within earshot, chimed in with, "I'll meet with him. I'd like to ask how Daphne's doing, and to apologize for ruining the party."

"I assure you, Mr. Trammell," said Ridgley, "everyone is entirely of the opinion that Carson ruined the party—not you."

"Good to know. I'd still like to meet with him," said Will, looking with pleading eyes at his aunt.

She frowned but knew that Will would find a way to contact

the Duquesnes regarding Daphne anyway. "Not here," she reiterated.

"What about the Common?" Ridgley suggested.

BOSTON COMMON WAS a short walk from Veronica's place, which made it the ideal location on such a gorgeous day. It felt good to get out in the fresh air again, and even though Will was convinced he was being followed by the Collective, he had almost grown accustomed to the feeling and did his best to put it out of his mind.

Within ten minutes, he found Desmond Duquesne sitting on a bench in front of the Park Street Church. For some reason, in this setting and in this light, he realized how truly old Desmond was. His many surgeries, regardless of how expert they were, became twice as obvious as they were in the soft lighting of New Covington. "I want more than ever to shake your hand, Will, but I suppose that wouldn't be wise."

Will smiled. "I suppose not."

"You know, each day I'm starting to see why those original prophecies have our two families coming together to do great things. You're a remarkable young man, and the apple has fallen very, very far from Roderick Gleave's branch of your family tree."

"Thank you," said Will, genuinely appreciating the compliment now that he knew more about the kind of person Gleave had been. "How is Daphne?"

"Doing better this morning, thanks in no small part to you. If you and Andy hadn't been in the right place at the right time, I shudder to think how much worse she could be right now."

"I did what anyone would have done."

"No, you didn't, Will. You went above and beyond, which is why I'm going to attempt to repay you."

"I can't take money, sir," Will said, shifting awkwardly.

Duquesne laughed. "You misunderstand. I heard you had a conversation—or should I say a confrontation—with Emil Havelock after leaving the party last night." Will nodded but thought it best to remain silent. "I've been hesitant to bring the deaths of your parents and your sister up again, Will, for obvious reasons. We've been able to coexist and you've been getting along famously with Daphne. However, because I've taken to you, I have started to feel terrible about how much you've been misled. Will, do you want to know what happened to your birth parents?"

"I do," he answered earnestly.

"It's true that in my regretful attempt at self-preservation, I ordered your parents' deaths. You've got the wrong idea about Emil Havelock, though."

"I know," said Will. "I could tell that he was telling the truth yesterday."

Duquesne nodded. "He was. Tell me, who told you that Havelock killed your parents?"

"Well, I don't know if he ever outright *told* me, but Brandt led me to believe that it was Havelock."

"And how much do you know about Mr. Brandt?" Will didn't answer. He knew what was coming and he felt sick. "He's not a very open fellow, is he? Did you ever see the burns all over his back? Your family did die in a fire, didn't they?" Will wanted to stand up but couldn't. His legs felt like jelly. "Mr. Brandt is a very angry man, but I often wonder—is it anger at me for ordering the hit, or is it guilt for having carried it out? I'd ask the same thing about Mr. Simon."

Will could barely speak, but managed, "Simon? He was in on it too?"

"Oh, Simon is even more culpable, William, though he at least seems to regret it. Still, he didn't quite tell you the truth either, did he?"

373

"Who else knows about this?"

"Well, that's difficult to say. Obviously I know, as do Brandt and Simon. I'm really not sure who else, but they *are* former Collective members, so I wouldn't put it past the one person who seems to know everything…"

"Whitworth."

"I'm truly sorry to burden you with all of this, William. But I couldn't see you having your strings pulled any longer, not after what you did for my daughter. I've made mistakes. I've done horrible things. But ultimately, I want you to remember the one person who has owned up to his mistakes and been honest with you."

"I have to go," said Will.

He started to walk away when Duquesne tapped his arm with his cane. "Be careful, William," he said. "You are dealing with dangerous people who have worked very hard to hide their secrets."

Will resumed his walk, which gradually turned into a run. He fought through the pain in his leg as he ducked and weaved through the crowds of Cambridge Street on his way to the Stonegate Hotel.

PEG ALMOST FELL off her chair when she was startled by the banging on the door of Whitworth's office. "Calm yourself," she muttered as she approached the door. Whitworth had gotten the heads up from Anthony at the front desk that Will was on his way and was anxiously looking forward to seeing if he had had a change of heart concerning his stance on whether to join the cause against Desmond Duquesne. Before Peg could even close the door behind Will, she could tell that the young man had not.

"Will," said Whitworth, "I'm very glad you came by. I think

I've figured out when and how Duquesne is planning to perform his ritual."

"Great," said Will, seething. "I don't care. We need to talk."

"Peg, would you mind giving us a few minutes?" the agent asked. While clearly put out by the idea, she reluctantly obeyed, taking a magazine from her desk and heading out to the hallway. "What's on your mind, William?"

"Have you always known what happened to my family? Have you always known who was responsible?"

"You've been told that Desmond Duquesne was responsible. That's the truth."

"Stop playing word games. I know he gave the order. He admitted to that. Do you know who he gave the order to?"

Whitworth braced herself for Will's rage and said, "You mean Simon and Brandt."

Will went wide-eyed. "You've really known about this the whole time! I trusted you! You of all people seemed to be straight with me, and now I find out you were keeping me in the dark the entire time? Do the others know? Do Donovan and Valentine? Feng and Creswell? Hell, does Peg know?"

"We are all aware of the scenario, William. I'm sorry that you feel misled. Perhaps I should have been more straightforward with you."

"Why?" Will ranted. "Why didn't you tell me?"

"Because it would have complicated things. Like it or not, you are the only one who can stop Duquesne. When I found out Brandt had hidden the truth from you, I couldn't fault him much for that. The reasoning was that as long as you felt Desmond Duquesne was solely responsible for your parents' deaths, you'd want revenge and you'd focus your energy on him."

"But there's one of the flaws in your reasoning. How can I want revenge for the deaths of people that I have absolutely no memory of?"

"You want revenge on Brandt and Simon right now, I imagine. Is that not for your parents' deaths?"

"In part, maybe," Will admitted. "But I also don't appreciate being manipulated, lied to, used and otherwise jerked around. Where are those two, anyway?"

Whitworth sighed. "We don't know. Brandt was here last night, but he left upon hearing about what happened at Alexander's party. I fear he may come after you soon."

"Good. Let him come. It's time he and I had a conversation."

"Will, I understand you are upset, but will you spare an old woman just a few minutes of your time?" Whitworth motioned for Will to take the seat in front of her desk, and after a brief hesitation, he did. She removed the chain from around her neck and handed it to Will. "For ten years, no one has touched that chain but me. Do you see what is on it?"

"It's a ring."

"It's a woman's ring—my fiancée's, in fact," Whitworth clarified. "She inherited it from her grandmother and wore it practically every day of her life." Will had not previously noticed, but Whitworth wore a similar ring of her own on her left hand. "Years ago, I was engaged to the most incredible woman I've ever had the pleasure to meet. Her name was Sarah. Sarah and I were so happy for so many years, and I felt nothing and no one could ever come between us. Well, as it happened, I was wrong."

Despite his anger, Will couldn't help but feel sorry as Whitworth very obviously fought back tears. "Sarah was an artist. A truly talented one. I was too wrapped up in my work, though, to give her the support she needed. One day, I came home to discover that Sarah had disappeared with someone who promised to make her wildest dreams come true, but he was a con man who took advantage of her and soon abandoned her. Well, of course she came back to me after things went south, and I was all too happy to refuse to take her back. You see, despite what I currently feel for her, my rage was still fresh back then. I refused to forgive her for the way she had hurt me. She went away with her tail between her legs. I had taught her a lesson."

"Did you ever see her again?" Will asked.

Whitworth shook her head somberly. "She overdosed on sleeping pills a few days later. It was accidental. I know it was. She was too strong a woman to let me break her completely. But I had broken her enough. So now I live with that, and I live with that ring that you're holding in your hand. Every night, before I go to sleep, I trace the history of that ring back to better times. I relive our first date, our first kiss, the night I proposed …good times that I'm fortunate enough to be able to recapture. Times when she was so in love with me." Whitworth closed her eyes and smiled at the thought of Sarah. "I thought I lost my love because someone else stole her away. In truth, I lost the love of my life because my hatred and bitterness blinded me to what was important."

"I'm very sorry for your loss, Ms. Whitworth. I really am. But with all due respect, John Brandt is not the love of my life."

Whitworth managed a faint smile. "I'd be worried if he was. Regardless of whom you direct your hatred toward, William, it is bound to come back to you twofold. Please just consider that before you go looking for Simon and Brandt."

Will had been successfully calmed, but something was still bothering him. "If you all knew that those two killed my family, why aren't they in the Brig with Steampunk and the rest?"

"The truth is a complicated thing, Will. I'm guessing you're still uninterested in helping us take down Duquesne?"

"No," said Will. "Ironically, he seems to be the most trust-worthy one around here."

"I think I can change your mind, but I won't press you until after you visit room 1602 of the hotel. You can't afford to lose your best friend at this point, can you?"

Will conceded that Whitworth was right about this. Regardless of who knew what about the events that led to the death of his family, Andy had absolutely no involvement in it. In fact, he had striven to be nothing but helpful throughout this whole ordeal. So, while Will assumed that this was doubtless a ploy to try to win him back to their side, he did feel compelled to smooth things over with his friend.

WILL KNOCKED on the door of 1602 but received no answer. Maybe he had gone out for a bite? Or maybe, Will thought, Andy was heading to Veronica's house to similarly try to smooth things over. He decided to knock one more time and was answered by Andy's tremulous voice asking, "Who is it?"

"It's me, buddy. Open up." Curious as to what was taking so long, Will held his ear to the door in time to hear a familiar voice say, "Andy, please open the door." Will gave some thought to running away, but he strengthened his resolve and waited for Andy's inevitable appearance. When Andy did open up, his complexion was a sickly shade of green and he mouthed, "Run."

"Can't do that, pal," Will said, entering the room to find Simon, as expected, standing behind Andy. "See, I'm just dying to have a chat with these guys. Where's Brandt?"

Will felt a sudden thwack on the back of his head just before everything went dark.

THIRTY-EIGHT

Game Over

VERONICA FROST LOOKED ANXIOUSLY at the clock in the hall as she paced back and forth, waiting for her nephew to return from his meeting with Desmond Duquesne. It was now well past dark, and she had heard nothing from either Will or Desmond. The house was quieter than it had been since Will's arrival and the silence made her increasingly nervous.

"I'm sure the boy's fine," said Wisp from the comfort of the living room, where he poured himself another scotch. "Come join me for a drink, Ronny. I'll bet the glass will only be half empty by the time he walks through the door."

Veronica declined with a dismissive wave of her hand. "Something's wrong. I can feel it. William would not just run off like this and leave me wondering."

"Maybe he met up with Daphne?" suggested Gwen, who nervously watched her employer pace from her perch in the middle of the staircase.

"That wouldn't make me feel much better, frankly," said Veronica.

Having resolved to take action, she hastened into her office while Wisp called from across the hall, "Now what could you be up to?"

"Calling Ridgley," she responded, picking up the phone.

"You have Ridgley's number?" Gwen asked.

"Of course," she responded. "And if he knows what's good for him, he'll tell me where William is."

PEG HAD LEFT for the day and Whitworth's office was still, save for the ring which she turned over in his hands. She lay on the leather sofa on which Will had first sat upon arriving at the Collective and pleaded for some divine intervention. "Sarah," she said, "I know that I'm always asking for favors and I know that I don't deserve it, but I need your help. I finally know what Duquesne is planning, and it's as bad as we feared. Inspire me, my love. How am I going to stop this without the boy?" At that moment, her phone nearly vibrated off her desk. "I don't suppose that's you," she mused to her fiancée as she got up to check.

She answered the phone just before the call went to voice-mail. It was not Sarah. "Hello, Detective. Is everything well?"

"I was about to ask you the same thing, Ms. Whitworth," Eddie Garza responded. "I take it you won Will back to the cause?"

Whitworth suddenly had a terrible feeling about this call. "Unfortunately no, Mr. Garza. What makes you ask?"

"Well, I tailed Will this morning, and seeing as he's been in the hotel since before noon, I figured you were having a war meeting or something."

"William never left the hotel, Mr. Garza?"

"No, ma'am."

Whitworth grabbed a gun out of her desk and bolted from her office. "Meet me in the hotel lobby, Detective. We may have a problem."

. . .

WHEN WILL AWOKE, he was nauseous but he did not know why. The stench of fish and the rhythmic clinking of rigging lines against masts suggested that he may be on a boat. Still, he had never been known to get seasick. No, this queasiness was caused by something else, something he could not quite put his finger on.

He opened his eyes slowly to see that he was not on a boat but in a warehouse, and he was accompanied by the three people he had expected. Gagged and tied to a nearby chair was Andy, who did not seem to be injured, but who looked as bad as Will felt. Simon was seated at a cheap card table, while Brandt stooped over a low filing cabinet, tinkering with a number of small metallic objects. He placed the objects gently in a black satchel and turned to face Will when Simon casually announced, "He's awake."

"Hello, Will," said Brandt. "Just like old times, huh?" Will tried to get up, but found that he was bound to his chair just like Andy. The room spun from his sudden movement and it became apparent that even if he had stood up, he would have promptly fallen over. "Standing up isn't really an option right now. I imagine you're feeling slightly dizzy."

Will felt a throbbing in the back of his head and remembered what had gotten him into this situation, to begin with. "You know," he said weakly, "you didn't have to knock me out again. Ironically enough, I was about to go looking for you."

Simon was visibly intrigued, but Brandt refused to engage in guessing games. Instead he explained, "See, that's where you're wrong, Will. I did have to knock you out. Otherwise, I doubt that you would have willingly given blood."

"You...you took my blood?"

"That's why you're feeling so weak right now. Unfortunately, I had to take quite a bit, just to be sure I had enough.

It's too bad it had to come to this, but you forced my hand. After all that I told you, you still chose the wrong side, which means that if you won't kill Duquesne, I have to." Brandt took a syringe from his black case and held it up to the light of an exposed bulb. "Do you know what this is?"

The substance in the syringe looked black at first, but when the light struck it, glimmers of crimson were evident. "My blood," he answered.

"Well, yes," said Brandt. "But more specifically—your blood in what would otherwise be a tranquilizer dart. Not bad for a dumb thug, huh? One shot of this, and your girlfriend's father finally turns to dust. Of course, I had to fill quite a few darts. I don't expect Duquesne to allow an easy shot."

"So glad I could help. Guess we could have skipped the whole abduction. I mean, the first abduction," Will said with disdain. "Why is he here?" he asked, motioning with his head in Andy's direction.

"We needed him to get to you," said Simon. "Nothing more. He hasn't been harmed."

"You didn't need to harm him because you've gotten into his head."

Simon looked ashamed but conceded that Will was correct. "I told him to let you into the hotel room. I told him to come with us when we left for…here. We couldn't leave loose ends."

Will looked at Andy's sweating face. He felt terrible for what he had gotten his friend into. Now he had to get him out of it. "Look, you got what you wanted. Just let us go."

Brandt snorted. "Right, so you can run back to Whitworth, or even worse, to your buddy Duquesne? I don't think so. You'll be staying right here until Desmond Duquesne is dead."

"I'll stay," said Will. "But why can't Andy go? Please. He doesn't have anything to do with this. I know that you've got some decency in you. I've seen it. Let him go."

Simon looked back at Brandt. "The boy was blindfolded

the entire time. He has no way to lead anyone back to us, Brandt."

"Wipe his memory," said Brandt, "and I'll let him go."

Simon shook his head. "I won't do that. Just take him out of here and drop him wherever. Will is right. He's served his purpose."

Brandt stared at Simon for a long moment before giving an annoyed huff and saying, "I have to get some more supplies anyway. I'll take the kid with me, but I swear to God—you keep Will in this warehouse. He doesn't step foot outside until Duquesne is dead."

"Agreed," said Simon.

Will breathed a sigh of relief as Brandt led Andy up the stairs and left him alone with the man to whom he really wanted to speak.

ANTHONY USED his master keycard to allow Whitworth, Donovan, and Garza into room 1602. The room was in pristine condition, as if no one had stayed there in days. "Did your staff get to the room already?" Donovan asked.

"No," Anthony insisted while double-checking on his phone. "According to my records, no one has been in here for turndown service since last night."

His police instincts kicking in, Garza scoured the room. "No sign of forced entry from either the door or the windows. Everything seems to be in place."

Whitworth remained silent, but Donovan suggested, "I'm thinking Simon 'convinced' the kid to let him in. I mean, that seems like the most likely scenario, right?" He watched as Whitworth traversed the room, looking for an object to read. "Are you going to do your thing?" Donovan pressed, handing her the television remote control. "See what happened."

Whitworth took the remote but shook her head. "This

won't work. I follow object memory, meaning the object needs to be at least somewhat in motion. Otherwise, it's static, and thus leaves no energy signature. Unless Simon, Andy, or Will left something behind, I don't have much to work with here. Simon's too smart to have let that happen."

"Maybe the two boys just went out for a while. They *are* teenagers, after all," Anthony suggested. "I wouldn't be surprised if—"

Whitworth interrupted Anthony with the 'one minute' gesture and answered her vibrating cell phone. "Yes, Veronica," she said. "No, I don't… We're working on it as we speak… Don't panic… We'll find him. I'm sure there's nothing to worry about… Alright. We'll be in touch."

Whitworth's face had gone white by the time she hung up. "No one knows where the boys are, including the Duquesne household," she said. "Which lends to the abduction theory. We don't have time to waste. We need to find them. Mr. Donovan, please get every available man out looking. Detective, you stick with me. I know some of Brandt's old haunts."

"If you're not going to be with me, I'm going to need Hex," Donovan said.

"Good idea. Take her. Call in any lead."

"Excuse me," Anthony interjected, "but should I be calling the police?"

"We'll do it faster," said Donovan.

"Agreed," said Whitworth. "Let's brief the Director and hit the road."

MR. RIDGLEY HAD BARELY HAD time to inform his employer about the panicked phone call from Veronica Frost before Duquesne received a call of his own. Ridgley, Brisbane, and Havelock exchanged concerned glances as Desmond grew increasingly anxious during the call. "What do you mean

384

Simon has the boy?" they heard him say. "Damn it. Let me think." He held the phone away from his ear and addressed his cronies. "The Collective knows what I'm planning, stamps and all, and now Simon has William Trammell. Tell me what I need to hear."

"Sounds like the kid has to go," Havelock said without hesitation.

Brisbane cleared his throat uncomfortably. "If you want your plans to go uninterrupted, I, um, agree."

"Mr. Ridgley?" Duquesne asked.

"It pains me to say it, sir, but you may have no choice."

Desmond sighed. "That's what I thought." Raising the phone back to his ear, he gave the order. "We're too close, and there's no telling what Simon's already instructed him to do. I'm not happy about this, but when you find the boy, kill him."

AGENT DONOVAN FOLLOWED Hex as she glided effort-lessly above the streets of Boston, leading to the harbor. He parked his car a stone's throw from the aquarium and leaned down to pet the exhausted cat. "Good job, Hex. I knew you'd still have Will's scent. You deserve a treat." He held out a hand full of crunchy cat treats and smiled as Hex ate them ravenously. When she was finished, he watched her slump to the ground and close her eyes. Looking around grimly, he grabbed the cat by the nape of her neck and walked her over to a nearby dumpster. Dropping her in amongst the putrid trash bags, he clapped the filth from his hands and walked back to his car, remarking, "Sorry, puss. I'm more of a dog person."

He moved the car to a crowded lot facing the water, and it wasn't long before he was able to spy Brandt leading a worse-for-wear Andy Lunsford out of a weathered warehouse on the far end of the pier. He watched as Brandt loaded Andy into a rented car and took off. This was proving to be even easier than he thought.

ANDY COULD NOT BELIEVE what was happening. Earlier today, he had been visited in his hotel room by Simon, whom he had thought was still working with the Collective. The next thing he knew, he was leading his friend directly into a trap. Now he was being driven around Boston by a psycho who reeked of whiskey and tobacco. He had to think. He hadn't recognized any streets or landmarks thus far, so there was no way that he'd be able to lead Valentine's crew back to Will unless he came up with something creative. His hands were not bound, so he began to feel around the car. Nothing.

Brandt watched Andy in his peripheral vision, almost amused that the boy considered himself slick. "If you're looking for a weapon," Brandt said, "you're not going to find anything."

Andy had to think fast. "I'm looking for your cigarettes."

Brandt couldn't help but chuckle. "You smoke?"

"Sometimes. When I'm stressed, which would be now. Besides, it's the least you could do."

"You know what?" said Brandt. "I guess you've earned that. Like Will said, I'm not completely heartless." He removed the pack from his pocket and handed it over to Andy. "Take one as a parting gift." Andy placed a cigarette in his mouth as he felt the car pull to a stop. "Enjoy your smoke," said Brandt. "And God help you if you try anything funny. Don't make me regret letting you go." With that, he signaled for Andy to remove himself from the vehicle. He did, and when Brandt peeled away, Andy found himself on a street he did not recognize.

Exhausted and sore, he walked for nearly an hour before his eyes lit up at a directional sign for Faneuil Hall. "That's where I had the chowder," he said to himself. He picked up the pace until, panting, he reached the open expanse of cobblestones leading to the historic brick building. From here, he remembered where he was. "Only a few blocks this way," he said, as though trying to convince himself that his memory was accurate. As he walked, he grew more and more confident that he was traveling in the right direction, and twenty minutes later, he stepped wearily into FrostBites.

"I WANT to ask you a question, Simon," Will said weakly. "And unlike you, I have no way of making you answer, so I just want you to think about how you would feel if you were in my situation. I know you're not a bad man. I'm just asking how you could do such a terrible thing."

Simon regarded Will's statement with curiosity, but admitted, "I'm afraid I don't quite follow your question, William."

"What happened to my family? I know that Duquesne ordered the hit, but you never indicated that you worked for him. Why did you do it?"

Simon lowered his head, averting his eyes from Will's. "I suppose you've been speaking to Duquesne about this?" Will didn't respond to what he knew was a rhetorical question. "I never *worked* for Desmond Duquesne. One thing you must know about him is that he holds a hell of a grudge. While Brandt and I worked with the Collective, we were thorns in his side. In fact, it was me, Brandt, and a colleague named Miranda Simms who were able to take away the source of Duquesne's power, the Heart of Murena. Without it, he is unable to perform the rituals he needs to increase his power and longevity. Naturally, he didn't take kindly to our interference and we earned places on his extensive enemies list.

"Now, when he found out about your existence, of course, he wanted to put an end to it. He could have used any of his own people but chose instead to kill two birds with one stone and destroy the Collective too. Miranda was already long gone, having disappeared with the Heart." He paused for a moment to gather his thoughts, and continued with, "He got hold of my family. My wife and two daughters. He threatened their lives, knowing that I would do anything for them. He had me use my powers of persuasion to tell Brandt to kill you and to have him kill himself in the process. Brandt had no idea what he was doing. It was all me. I pulled Brandt's strings because I felt I had no other choice. Duquesne did not indicate how you were all to be killed, so I chose the use of the firebomb. It was the best way that I saw to deflect blame from the Collective. Your father, Daniel Trammell, was already the target of an organized crime boss, Chilnos Villovich, whose enemies were known to suffer similar fates. I assumed the authorities would naturally turn to Villovich for the arrest, which they did."

"I thought that Brandt had left the Collective by that time?"

"Oh, he had," Simon answered. "But that didn't matter to Duquesne. By using me, Duquesne could still strike at the Collective. By using Brandt, Duquesne could settle his old grudge."

"So what happened?" Will asked. "How did I survive?"

"Not due to any heroism on my part," Simon said regretfully. "Duquesne requested that I persuade Brandt to kill you, which I did. My powers are significant, but there are others out there who have far greater abilities than I do. Have you heard of the Nowhere Men?"

Will shook his head.

"The Nowhere Men are an elite group of magic users. Their powers have grown so great that they voluntarily take a vow not to use them to affect the lives of others. They see everything, but they are to react to nothing. That's how things are supposed to go in theory, anyway. On the night when you were to die, Brandt had already planted the bomb in the basement of your family's house. He stayed there silently, as I instructed him to do. The bomb was set to go off at twelve. However, one of the only people with the ability to override my commands showed up at the house before that could happen."

"A Nowhere Man?"

"Yes. Whoever this person was had caught wind of what was happening and knew that it was imperative that you stay alive. He snapped Brandt out of his trance and sent him racing upstairs to get you out of the house. Without my guidance, he didn't know how to disarm the bomb. Instead, he grabbed you and ran. The two of you barely made it out alive. The flames caught Brandt as he carried you from the house. He shielded you, but he was burned quite severely over a large portion of his body. Though injured, he was able to escape the scene with you."

"So, in a way, he saved me?"

"That would be the glass-half-full way of looking at it, yes. As soon as news of the fire hit the media and the report claimed no survivors, I told Duquesne that my job was done. He agreed and lifted the threat on my family. They were safe, but I soon received a call from a young doctor, Robert Kendrick, who was treating Brandt's burns. Brandt had asked for me. As you can imagine, he was less than thrilled that I had betrayed his trust, and that I had—in his words—violated his mind."

"That's why he doesn't trust anyone with powers."

"It's certainly one of the major reasons. While he was furious at my actions, the one thing we both agreed upon was ending Duquesne. We knew you were the key and that you needed to be protected at all costs. Dr. Kendrick overheard our conversation. He was going to be moving down to South Carolina within the next month, and he and his wife were hoping to start a family there. He offered to—for all intents and purposes—adopt you, as long as we could fudge the necessary paperwork. With my powers, that was easy enough. Finally, the decision was made to wipe your memory and send you with the doctor."

This last part made the hair on Will's neck stand on end. "You wiped my memory? That's why I have no recollection of the Trammells at all?"

"I'm sorry, Will." Simon looked genuinely haunted by this decision. "We did it to protect you. I've refused to do it ever again, though. I could barely live with myself once I had sent you off with no memory."

"Barely," said Will. "But you did live with yourself. You found a way. You had your own family back and that was all that mattered, right?"

"Will, my wife packed up my daughters and left immediately after that. This business all became too much for her to handle, and frankly, I don't blame her."

"I'm sorry," Will said.

"As am I."

"So who was the Nowhere Man that saved my life?"

"I have no idea," Simon responded. "But whoever it was is almost certainly not in the club anymore. For better or worse, that individual changed things in a major way. There is no way that he was welcomed back."

"What about the Collective? Once people found out that you and Brandt were responsible for the deaths of innocent people, why wasn't the Collective held accountable?"

"Like I said, the public was led to assume that Villovich had planted the bomb. It was my way of trying to save face for the Collective. The evidence, though mainly circumstantial, was enough. Of course, people in higher places discovered the truth, but Senator Valentine was able to save the organization from being dissolved. Still, I resigned, funds were pulled, and their skeleton crew has not grown since the fallout of the Trammell incident. Several in Washington still believe that the group is needed, but support is dwindling."

Will was starting to feel like a fool. "Duquesne really has played everyone, hasn't he?"

"He has," said Simon, glad that Will finally seemed to be catching on. "Including you. It seems like you don't even remember that he sent Candace and the others after you back in Memorytown. As soon as you saw Daphne, I knew we had a chance to get you close enough to kill Desmond, but who knew you'd fall for him as well?"

"Desmond Duquesne admitted to his mistakes, unlike you two. Why wouldn't I be just as angry with you? I don't even remember my family, thanks to you. Besides, you and Brandt have this righteous indignation about being used, but what have you been doing to me?"

"I'm sorry that you feel used. I truly am. But getting rid of Duquesne is about more than just revenge. It's about saving lives. The only way for him to get what he wants is to kill people, Will. Are you willing to let that happen because you're under the impression that, deep down, he's a nice guy?"

Will found himself unable to directly answer the question. "I just can't see myself doing to Daphne what you did to me."

"I understand that you care for her, but sometimes the difficult decisions have to be made. If you're not ready to make them, if you'd rather spend your time wandering around aquariums, then we grown-ups will have to make the decisions for you. I almost wish that Whitworth had never heard about that second prophecy. There would have been no need to push you and Daphne together."

"What do you mean 'push us together'? That was…" Will's heart sunk as a terrible thought popped into his head. "How did you know about the aquarium?" Simon, caught in his own web, declined to answer. "You were there, weren't you?" As Will finished this question, he spied movement over Simon's shoulder. Someone was tiptoeing down a flight of metal stairs, someone who was not Brandt. When the figure descended further, Will recognized it as Agent Donovan, who held a finger up to his lips. Will did his best not to let on, as he actually did not want Donovan to interrupt. He needed answers. "Did you speak to her at the aquarium?"

"I did," said Simon.

"Oh my God. What did you tell her to do?"

"I suggested that she invite you to her brother's party. At the time, we thought it would get you close enough to kill her father."

"What about her feelings for me? Did you do that? Did you make her have feelings for me?" Will was about ready to jump out of his skin. "Answer me!"

"Will, listen to me," Simon began, when he caught a glimpse of Donovan in the reflection of a broken window on the far side of the room. He spun around to meet Donovan's gaze. "Donovan, I need you to—"

Will's eyes went wide as Donovan shot two bullets through Simon's skull. "No more Simon says," he sneered as the body slumped to the floor.

"What did you do?" Will yelled. "He wasn't going to hurt me! You didn't have to do that!"

"Well," said Donovan, "I kind of did. Those were my orders."

"From Valentine?"

"From Duquesne." Will sat speechless as Donovan gazed around the cavernous space. "I can't help but notice that you look a tad on the anemic side, Will. Ah!" he said, discovering Brandt's cache of tranquilizer darts, "That explains it." He cautiously held one of the darts and flashed a cruel smile. "How clever. I will really need to commend Brandt on his ingenuity when he returns. When *is* he returning?"

"I don't know. I have no idea where he went."

"That I believe. You haven't been that quick on the uptake over the past few weeks, have you?" Donovan spun a chair around and sat with his gun pointed at Will. "I guess you finally found out that Brandt and Simon killed your family. So now you realize what I've known for years: that John Brandt is a piece of shit. Well, don't worry. When he gets back, I'll make sure he gets flushed."

Will looked frantically around the room for something to use as a weapon against Donovan, and he noticed that among the darts filled with his blood, there were still several that appeared to be filled with some clear liquid—potentially tranquilizers. He remembered what Mr. Wisp had taught him and tried to focus his energy on the dart, but nothing happened. He kept trying, imagining the dart flying through the air and lodging itself in Donovan's neck. But his head hurt and his blood loss had left him in such a weakened state that he was unsure whether, if untied, he could have even walked to the dart.

After a long few seconds, Donovan caught on and looked over his shoulder at the dart, which Will had been able to rock back and forth. "Nice try," said the agent. "Whitworth told me about your little show at Alexander's party. I've got to be honest, I was worried you'd be in fighting form when I found you, but I have to hand it to Brandt—his brilliant idea to take your blood makes it pretty unlikely that you'll be performing any magic tricks today. I know how it works. You don't have the energy for it. So just calm yourself."

Will resigned himself to the fact that Donovan was right. He didn't have the strength. He could only hope that Brandt would be able to overpower Donovan, which he thought easily possible until Donovan himself approached the darts. "You just gave me an idea, kid," he said, picking up the dart gun. He raced to load a tranquilizer into the weapon when he heard heavy footsteps on the landing above. "Don't you say a word," he rasped.

As Will watched Brandt come down the stairs, he thought,

Why not say a word? He's going to kill me anyway. So, before Brandt reached the bottom of the staircase, Will screamed, "Look out!"

But it was too late. Donovan shot a dart into Brandt's back and watched as Brandt gradually lost consciousness, first falling to one knee and then collapsing next to Simon's lifeless body.

THIRTY-NINE

Your Greatest Failure

WILL WATCHED as Donovan strapped the unconscious Brandt to a chair next to his, noting that he tied the ropes around Brandt's wrists with an especially tight knot. Simon and Brandt had not bound his own hands so harshly, but Will noted there was still very little give as he squirmed in his seat. When he had finished with Brandt, Donovan evaluated Will's restraints, pacing in a circle to eyeball both the bound ankles and the hands that had been tied against the back of Will's folding chair. Satisfied, he unholstered his gun, leaned against a table in front of his captives and fixed his eyes on Brandt, whose head was slumped into his chest.

Will knew he would never be able to untie his knots without Donovan noticing and even if he could, the turncoat would shoot him before he could get to his feet. He looked around the room and assessed his surroundings. His back was to a large window that looked out over the rough waters of the harbor. The warehouse itself was a long, expansive space, so he imagined that they were positioned at the end of one of the longer docks. The ceiling was crisscrossed with rusted steel beams and red metal shipping containers of various sizes were meticulously stacked in multiple rows on either side of the room. A plan was forming, but it was a stupid one and it would rely upon his ability to stall Donovan.

"Why are you doing this, Donovan? Why betray the Collective?"

"Shut up," the agent answered without so much as blinking.

Okay, Will thought, *this stalling thing works better in the movies.* "You're the reason Candace and the others were able to find us in Pennsylvania, aren't you? You clued Duquesne in as soon as Whitworth discovered where we were."

Donovan turned his gaze from Brandt and gave Will a disingenuous grin. "Can't get much past you, huh?"

"And that first time we came to the harbor—on the day of the dedication ceremony—you didn't even shoot at Havelock, did you? You let him get away."

"Unfortunately, yes. Do you know how easy it would have been to just let you three burn? But with Whitworth on her way, there was no way I would have gotten away with it. So here we are. No Candace, no Havelock. Just the two of you tied up with someone who is actually capable of getting the job done."

"Yet here you stand, not getting the job done. What are you waiting for?" Will hoped this strategy wouldn't backfire. As Donovan indulged in a stilted chuckle, Will concentrated on his training. He was still weak, but he felt the ropes around his ankles gradually loosen. One down.

"If you must know, I'm waiting for Brandt to wake up. You see, it's important to me that you die first. He's going to watch his last chance at redemption go up in smoke."

"You really hate him that much. Why?"

"Why?" asked an incredulous Donovan. "Your family is dead, and you're tied to a chair because of him, and you're asking me why? If anyone could relate, Will, I would have assumed it would be you. Brandt—simply put—is an asshole. He blames everyone else for his shortcomings. Who did he blame for your parents' deaths? Duquesne? Simon? Did he tell you about why he left the Collective in the first place, about what happened in Prague? Who did he blame for that? Whitworth? Valentine? *Me?*"

Will had clearly touched a nerve, and Donovan was unraveling in a way he had not expected from the usually reserved agent. He thought of Whitworth's advice from earlier. *This is what you become*, he thought. *This is what you become when you can't let go.* "I don't know anything about that," Will said. "But I do know that you've both helped a lot of people. Why throw all that away?"

"Don't," said Donovan with a smirk. "Don't try to make this into a therapy session like Frances would. I've been waiting for this for too long."

"Then shut up and get it done," muttered Brandt, his heavy head lifting just enough to glare at his former colleague.

Will used this brief distraction to concentrate on the ropes that tied his hands, loosening them but grabbing them before they hit the floor.

"Alright," said Donovan. "Now that everyone is paying attention, perhaps we can finish this."

"I'VE GOT TO SAY," Whitworth mused while Eddie Garza followed her direction and sped toward the docks, "it was quite ingenious of Andrew to ask Brandt for one of these." She twirled the cigarette between her fingers. "This should lead us right to William."

"I really hope so," said Garza, trying to remain calm. "Any word from your partner yet?"

"No." Garza saw that Whitworth wore a frown, but there

was something more to her expression than mere concern. "What is it?" he pressed.

Whitworth sighed. "I don't know," she said. "I just get the feeling that I made a mistake in sending Donovan after Brandt. I'm worried that—turn here! Dock 19!"

Garza did as he was told, tires screeching as he brought the car to a stop facing a series of cranes and shipping containers. Beyond these, a warehouse loomed large on the end of the dock. "The cigarette's trail leads here?"

"What? Oh. Probably. I just saw Donovan's car." Whitworth removed herself from the vehicle and hustled toward Donovan's sedan. "No sign of him," she said.

SHE LOOKED out toward the warehouse with foreboding until a feint mewing sound interrupted her thought process. "Hex?" She followed the sound to the dumpster where the cat had been disposed and lifted the glassy-eyed creature out by the nape. "Who did this to you, my love? Show us the way."

Hex shook off the last vestige of Donovan's poison and ran toward the warehouse.

"LOOK AT HIM, BRANDT," Donovan demanded, grabbing Brandt's head as though palming a basketball and twisting it to face Will. "This may not be your greatest failure, but it will be your last."

At that moment, the sound of screeching tires traveled over the water and through the broken panes in the warehouse's industrial windows. "Shit."

Donovan left his captives to climb on a table and glance through a raised window on the side of the building, allowing Will an opportunity to whisper, "Can you swim?"

"Not well," Brandt responded weakly. "And not bound."

"Don't worry about that," said Will. He stared at the bindings on Brandt's wrist as they came loose. "I don't know how much strength I have, but you're going to have to trust me."

Brandt nodded and looked up at the returning Donovan. "They found you, didn't they?"

"Enough," said Donovan, panicked. He aimed his gun at Will's forehead. "Time to—"

With a burst of energy, Donovan flew backwards, his gun firing into the ceiling and echoing through the building. Will and Brandt were likewise thrown backwards, shattering the windows behind them and plummeting into the cold waters of the Atlantic. Will's plan had worked, nearly. He had loosened his own bonds enough that the chair to which he had been tied remained in the warehouse, and he was able to use all four limbs to keep himself afloat in the choppy water. Brandt, however, was not so lucky. Will had run out of time before loosening the ropes around Brandt's ankles, and the half-sedated man now struggled feebly to stay above water using only his arms, which were still feeling the effects of the tranquilizer.

Will tried in vain to use his powers to lift Brandt and himself out of the water, but he'd used what little energy he had to escape the warehouse. With no magic left, he needed to swim for his life. He grabbed the floundering Brandt under his good arm and tried to swim to shore, but the current was working against them, and it didn't take long to realize they were getting nowhere. He watched helplessly as Brandt choked up water through his black beard, matted to his face by seawater, and despite his efforts, soon found himself in the same position. Wave after wave crashed against his face as he made one last effort to reach the harbor. He gasped as he swallowed mouthfuls of the dark briny water, until the gasping finally stopped and Brandt slipped from his grasp.

· · ·

EDDIE GARZA KICKED in a metal door on the far end of the warehouse, snapping its rusted hinges. He entered quickly but cautiously, gun drawn. "Will? Will, we're here to help! Are you in here?"

An unarmed Whitworth followed closely behind. "It appears we're alone here, Detective."

"Almost," said Garza, approaching a body Hex had found lying prone near the bottom of a flight of stairs. "Friend of yours?"

Whitworth stepped carefully to avoid the pool of blood and somberly answered, "Yes, actually. I'm so sorry, old friend." The agent closed Simon's eyes and bowed her head in reverence for a moment. "I should have known. Why didn't I know?"

"Know what?"

"Donovan did this," she said with grim resignation.

"Your partner? Where is he?"

Whitworth pointed to another door across the expansive warehouse floor. "Probably back in his car by now. It's alright. There will be time for that later. Let's find William."

Garza nodded and walked toward an overturned chair near a shattered window. Leaning to pick up a length of rope, he noted, "It looks like someone was tied up here. Do you think Donovan took Will with him?"

"No," Whitworth responded, picking a piece of cloth from the broken window pane. "I believe that—Detective! In the water!"

Eddie raced to the window and peered some twenty feet down into the choppy waters of the Atlantic. There, he saw two bodies floating limply with the tide. "Will!" Without hesitation, Garza dove into the harbor, his muscles tightening as they were submerged in the surprisingly cold water. He swam toward the body he recognized as Will and struggled to get his arm around the young man, the waves working against him and threatening to send him crashing against the barnacle-covered pier.

"Well, that won't do," Whitworth said to the mewing Hex. "Let's try this." The agent held her hands in front of her, palms facing the harbor, and concentrated her attention on the three men in the water. "The itsy-bitsy spider climbed up the..." Before she could conclude the melody, a series of waterspouts shot forth from the harbor, lifting Eddie, Will, and Brandt high above the crashing waves. Eddie stared in amazement as he and his unconscious companions were lowered gently onto a floating dock nearby, but as soon as they had alit, he knelt on the creaking, splintered wood and began administering CPR to Will.

Whitworth raced down to the dock as quickly as her sore knees would allow and was relieved to see that Will was coughing up water by the time he'd arrived. "I didn't know you could do that," said Garza.

"Yeah," Will rasped. "It seems like today has been a learning experience for all of us."

"Sure has." Garza waited for Brandt to finish spitting out seawater and gasping for breath before punching him in the face.

FORTY

The Return of the Doctor

WHEN WILL FINALLY OPENED his eyes, he was greeted by a silhouette outlined by bright sunlight streaming through his bedroom window. As the shape drew closer, he was able to distinguish Daphne's warm smile. "How long have you been here?" he asked as he moved his stiff joints to sit up against the headboard.

"Long enough," she said. "We were all worried about you."

"How long have I been out? It feels like days."

"It has been days," Daphne answered. "You missed my father's party. It was so much fun." She shied away and peered out into the sunlight. "I was sorry that I didn't get to dance with you."

Will blushed. "Me too. So everything went alright?"

"Everything went according to plan," she said with a chipper tone. "Now come downstairs. Everyone's here. They want to see you. Can you get up?"

"Yeah..." he groaned, feeling like the Tin Woodsman when he struggled to bend his legs. She handed him Gleave's ebony cane and together they made their way downstairs. Halfway

403

down the stairs, Will got the familiar sense that something was not right. Daphne had said that everyone was there, but the silence was deafening. He could not even hear their own footsteps as they traveled toward the dining room. "Are you sure that everything's okay?" he asked, but Daphne ignored the question and disappeared through the dining room door.

When he entered the room, she was gone, but there were more than enough people there to take her place. Somehow, his aunt's dining space had expanded to the size of a banquet hall, and there was a large, beautifully decorated table running down the center of the room. Veronica Frost sat at the head of the table, flanked by what must have been upwards of thirty strangers on each side. They sat motionless and expressionless, their faces hidden by ornate masks. Finally, a small noise pierced the silence and Will looked to the corner of the room to see a cloaked figure fiddling with an old phonograph. The record spun for a moment before the familiar opening chords of 'You are my Sunshine' began to play. As Will had feared, when the figure faced him, it was once again wearing the mask of the plague doctor.

"You missed the first party, William," said the muffled voice of the Plague Doctor. "So I invited everyone back. They were so eager to meet you."

In one synchronized movement, the guests seated around the table turned their heads to look at Will, and one by one they began to remove their masks. The first was an overweight man whose puffy lips were a sickly shade of gray and whose eyes were glazed over with a putrid, viscous sheen. The woman next to him removed her peacock mask to reveal fresh, deep gashes across her face. She too had blank dead eyes. Another man was missing half his face. It looked as though it had been torn off by an animal and gave him the ghoulish appearance of having a perpetual smile. The others followed suit, each grislier than the last, until they reached

Veronica, who sat mask-less and stoic at the end of the table. "Help me," she mouthed as the Plague Doctor approached her.

Will ran with all his speed toward the Doctor, but the undead party guests scratched and clawed at him, trying to hold him back from reaching his goal. "Stop it!" he screamed. "I need to help her!"

The Plague Doctor drew a blade from his cane and stood poised to plunge it through the back of Veronica's chair. "Perhaps you should have thought of that earlier," the shadowy figure said. He shoved the blade forward, but Will closed his eyes, unable to bring himself to watch the horrific scene. When he opened them, the room was back to normal and was empty again, save for Daphne.

"Where did they all go?" Will asked frantically.

"There's been no one here but you and me, Will," Daphne responded. "Just the two of us," she continued, leaning in closer, her face only inches from his. "Just like you want it."

He felt a sense of euphoria as her soft lips pressed gently against his. After a few seconds, she pulled away and smiled. "That was—" She stopped with a jolt and put her fingers up to her lips. She suddenly looked frightened, and Will could only watch in horror as she began to deteriorate before his eyes. "Will…" she pleaded, but nothing could be done. In an instant, she had grown emaciated and had taken on the pale blue hue of death. Will did not allow her corpse to slump to the floor, but instead scooped her into his arms and held her tight, tearfully repeating, "I'm sorry, I'm sorry" over and over.

"WILL! Will! Calm down! It's okay!"

Will opened his eyes to see that rather than clutching the dead body of Daphne Duquesne, he was, in fact, clutching the very alive body of Gwen Henley. Immediately upon realizing this, he let go and fell backward onto his pillow, mortified. "I-I didn't realize that was you."

"I figured," Gwen grinned. "Glad to have you back," she said, patting his hand. "Let me get the others." Only when Gwen had left the room did Will realize he had broken into a sweat from his latest dream. He wiped his brow with his forearm and followed up with a quick pinch to his arm, since according to all the films he had seen, that was pretty much the only way to know whether or not he was still dreaming. The pain from the pinch had barely subsided when Gwen reentered the room, followed by Veronica and Andy.

"Oh, thank God," said his aunt, leaning in to gingerly wrap her arms around him. "You had us all so worried."

"How long have I been out?" Will asked.

"For a while. You lost quite a bit of blood and then you nearly drowned. Luckily we found an amazing doctor who makes house calls. He's been looking after you the whole time." Upon saying this, Veronica beckoned for someone standing in the hallway to come in.

Will's eyes widened as Robert Kendrick entered the room. "Dad?"

"Frances Whitworth called me just before you got into trouble in that warehouse. I took the first flight I could. How are you feeling?"

Will leaned forward and hugged his father in response. It seemed like it had been years since he had seen his adoptive parents and having Robert in the room with him provided immediate comfort.

"From what Andy's told me, you've been through a lot since I last saw you." Will simply nodded, and as he did so, he noticed the melancholy expression on Robert's face. Addressing Veronica, Robert said, "Would you mind giving me a moment with my, um, with Will?"

Veronica politely assented and ushered Gwen and Andy

back downstairs into the den. With the others gone, Robert closed the door and pulled a chair up next to Will's bed. "I'm sorry, son," he said with his head hung low and his eyes focused on a speck of dust on the carpet. "Emily's been beside herself since you've been gone, and I honestly haven't been much better. I know that nothing I say can make up for what you've been through, but I just needed you to know how much I regret putting you in harm's way."

Will sat silently for a moment before responding. "For over a decade, you treated me like your own son. You were always there for me and although I didn't know it, you were always protecting me. As far as I'm concerned, I've been placed in harm's way by nearly everyone I know at this point. You and Mom were pawns, just like I am. There was nothing else that you could have done."

Robert raised his head and looked his son in the eyes. "Will, I appreciate that you understand the strange situation that we found ourselves in. However," he said, growing sterner, "I've got to say that I'm very disappointed in you right now." Will could not believe his ears. After all that he had been through, now he was going to receive a lecture? "As your father, I refuse to let you sit here and call yourself a pawn. Your mother and I taught you better than that. Andy's filled me in on the story so far, and it certainly looks like you've ended up injured in this bed because you're under the impression that it's acceptable to have other people pull your strings. We both know that's bullshit." Will had never heard his father swear before, and in this context, it was almost inspiring. "I need you to promise me one thing. When you get out of this bed, you're going to be your own man. You've got a hefty responsibility that's been pushed upon you; there's no doubt about that. But how you address this responsibility is up to you and you alone—not me, your aunt, Brandt, Whitworth, or anyone else. Will, you are going to leave this room in the driver's seat—no more just going along for the ride. Do you understand me?"

"Yes, sir," Will said with a new sense of empowerment.

"And understand one more thing," said Robert. "No matter what decisions you make, I'm sure you'll make me and your mother proud."

WILL STAYED in bed for the remainder of the day, gradually feeling his energy return as he entertained a steady rotation of visitors. Shortly after Robert had left the room, Andy came in to fill Will in on the details surrounding his escape from captivity and his trek through the streets of Boston in search of help. He also explained who Eddie Garza was and how—if it had not been for him—Will may not have made it out of the warehouse at all.

He heard a similar story when Jackson and Gwen visited later, but he was more intrigued by the small envelope Gwen had smuggled past his aunt. "Here," Gwen said quietly, slipping the note into his hand. "Ridgley delivered this today. It's a note from Daphne. Your aunt would not approve of me passing this along to you. In fact, she doesn't know it was delivered at all, so please be sure to keep it under wraps."

Will nodded, took the note, and read it. It was short, but sweet: "Guess we're both having pretty bad weeks, huh? I heard about what happened, and I'm so sorry. I was glad to hear that you're okay. Hopefully you'll be better in time for the party!"

"So I didn't miss Duquesne's party after all?" Will asked.

"No," said Gwen. "It's tomorrow night. Why?" She raised her eyebrows and shook her head vehemently. "Oh no you don't, Will. You're not really considering going, are you? Look at where all your involvement with that family has gotten you!"

Will pursed his lips. "Let's just say I'm thinking about it.

Now, I need to ask you a huge favor, but you've got to keep it a secret. Also, it may require borrowing some money."

"I'm sure your aunt will give you all the money you need," said Jackson.

"Not for this."

WILL SAT ALONE with his thoughts after Gwen and Jackson left, rereading Daphne's note and considering what step to take next regarding the Duquesne situation. He was not alone for long before he heard a gentle knock and saw Veronica slowly open the door. "Do you mind one more visitor?" she asked.

"Not at all," he responded.

She came in and sat in the chair that had been formerly occupied by Robert. "I don't suppose I could convince you to eat something? There are plenty of leftovers from dinner…"

"It's okay," said Will. "I don't have much of an appetite yet but pencil me in for breakfast."

"Will do. Dr. Kendrick has been entertaining us with tales of your childhood."

"Anything embarrassing?"

"Just about all of it," she said with a smile. "You got lucky, William. He seems like a great man, and he really cares for you."

"Yeah, it's great to see him again. I guess I didn't realize how much I missed my family." He caught his error as soon as the words had left his mouth and stumbled to recover. "I mean, aside from you. I'm sorry. I didn't mean to imply…"

"It's alright, William. I get it. It takes a lot of getting used to." She paused and rested her hand on his arm. "Listen, William, I came in here to tell you that I just had a long discussion with Dr. Kendrick, and he filled me in on the advice he gave you earlier. I not only want to second that advice, but I want to apologize for being one of those people who have been pulling you in all different directions."

"But I never felt that way about you," said Will. "Actually, you're one of the only people aside from Andy and my father who I still feel I can trust."

"Well, thank you. That's certainly a relief to hear. And despite my personal feelings toward Desmond Duquesne, I promise to support whatever road you choose to take."

Will saw that it had taken a lot for her to express this sentiment and said, "Desmond Duquesne killed your husband and son, didn't he?"

"He did. I mean, there wasn't any evidence, but when a man who has no enemies in the world has his brakes cut, there can only be so many suspects."

"But it wasn't about your husband. It was about your son, Matthew. I don't know why I never realized this until now, but he was the first male descendent of Roderick Gleave. I was born later. Duquesne succeeded in killing your son, but he failed when it came to killing me."

"That's exactly it," his aunt said. "So now you know why you remind me of Matthew in more ways than one."

Will took her hand and said, "I won't let anything happen to you. Ever."

Veronica looked puzzled. "What do you mean? What would happen?"

"I don't know," Will said. "I just had another dream and you were in it."

"With Duquesne?"

"I think so. And there were others."

"Who? People that you know?"

"No. Duquesne was throwing a party, but all of the guests were dead. There were a lot of them. I'd say maybe…"

"Seventy-two?" suggested a voice from the hall. Will was

not surprised to see Frances Whitworth enter the room, but his aunt was taken aback.

"Who let you in here?" she demanded. "I told you that William needed to recover. This is not the time to be discussing Collective business."

"My apologies," said Whitworth, walking sheepishly toward the bedside with her hands folded in front of her. "But while I wish William the speediest of recoveries, this may be the *only* time left to discuss Collective business."

Will was not thrilled about the intrusion, but could not help but ask, "Where did you get the number seventy-two? Seems oddly specific."

"For too long now, Desmond has possessed an ancient book called the *Lesser Key of Solomon*. It contains the instructions for unleashing a horde of demons whose powers Desmond would kill to possess. In order for Desmond's plan to come to fruition, a substantial number of sacrifices will need to be made. One for each demon he plans to summon from the sigils that the *Key* provides."

"Seventy-two."

"You got it. We're lucky if the casualties end there, though. What he's planning is incredibly reckless and I doubt even he fully comprehends what he's about to unleash. As your dream indicates, he intends to go through with this during his masquerade tomorrow night. He'll have plenty of potential sacrifices and they'll be sitting ducks. We need you, William. You are our surest bet to stop him. I'm asking one last time: will you please help?"

Will looked into Whitworth's eyes and wanted to believe her, but his recent experience made him think the better of it. "I trusted Donovan," he said. "That landed me here."

The elder agent bowed her head in shame. "I trusted him too, William. He fooled us all, and I'm very sorry for what happened to you."

"Have you caught him yet?" Veronica asked.

"Not yet," replied Whitworth. "I'm sure he's staying close to Duquesne now. But we'll get him. We will."

"And Brandt?" Will inquired.

"Brandt," said Whitworth, "is in our custody. He's acted in a reckless manner and placed your life in danger. He'll be dealt with accordingly, but he's no longer a factor." Whitworth stopped here and looked at Will expectantly. "So?" she eventually continued. "Can we depend on you?"

Duquesne had once more ordered his death, and now his most recent dream had indicated that no one was safe from his reach. But Will's thoughts remained fixed upon what Robert had told him earlier. He was in more control now than when he had held the gun on Brandt in the Pennsylvania woods. "I'll let you know," he said. Noting a slight grin on Veronica's face, he settled back into bed.

"Fair enough," Whitworth said. "We still have the blood samples that Brandt took from you. Hopefully, that will be enough, should you decide not to help. Just remember that this is our only chance to stop him. Once he performs this ceremony, all bets are off." She closed with that and, with a nod to Veronica, drifted out of the room.

BRANDT STARED at the blank wall of his cell, giving no indication that he had caught Valentine's entrance with his peripheral vision. "What in the hell were you thinking, Brandt?" When he received no answer, the Director continued, "You could have easily gotten that boy killed."

"Really?" Brandt retorted. "I took some blood from the kid. As I recall, it was *your* man who murdered Simon. By the way, how many years ago did I warn you about him?"

Valentine sighed. "Fine. You were right. Feel better now?"

"It would make me feel better to take out Duquesne, and

412

hopefully Donovan, and then never see this place again. But you're not about to let that happen, are you? What do you plan to do with me? Are you going to stick me in the Brig with Steampunk and the rest of your freak show?"

"You'll be sitting tight here for a while…at least until Duquesne is dealt with. I don't need you screwing things up further."

The Director cringed as Brandt subsequently exploded with laughter. "Me? Are you insane? Again, if it weren't for that sniveling shit Donovan, I'd be on my way to kill Duquesne now. Did you at least rescue the tranqs?"

"We did. Dr. Feng is diluting them into more darts now. It was a clever idea, Brandt."

"It was," Brandt concurred. "And as its originator, I should be pulling the trigger."

"Not happening."

"No, you do it your way. Because that always works." Brandt shook his head. "Tell me, Director, when you go home at night, what do your wife and kids think of the blood on your hands?"

Finally losing his cool, Valentine removed his jacket as he walked toward his captive. "Tonight, the blood will be pretty easy to explain, you miserable bastard."

Brandt did not flinch as he neared, but merely pointed to an agent who had shown up at the door of the cell. "Director?" said the agent before Valentine had reached Brandt, "You've got a call."

"It can wait," Valentine snapped.

"Sir, it's the Senator."

Brandt flashed a mocking grin. "Uh oh," he taunted. "Someone's in trouble."

Valentine stormed into his office, slamming the door behind him and throwing his jacket over a nearby chair. He sat, took a deep breath, put on a fake smile, and placed his caller on speaker. "Hello, Dad," he said. "How are things?"

"Don't bullshit me, Nathaniel. What the hell is happening up there? Why is Duquesne still alive?"

Trying hard to maintain his composure, Valentine answered, "We've been running into some roadblocks, but we're making progress."

"You have the boy?"

"We have what we need to get the job done."

"And yet," said the polished voice, "it's not done."

"Duquesne is planning the ritual for tomorrow. We still have some time. Not much, admittedly, but enough. We plan to head to New Covington and—"

"I don't recall asking for a play-by-play, Nathaniel, nor am I interested in hearing one. I'm solely interested in receiving word that the son of a bitch is finally dust. To that end, I suggest you call in the other agencies. Perhaps you don't have the manpower to get the job done."

"No." The Director wiped the sweat from his brow. "We're enough of a laughingstock already. We can do this. Let us do this."

There was a period of silence on the other end before the Senator continued, "Have it your way, Nathaniel. Just know this. If you screw this up, I will be unable to come to the Collective's defense again, and frankly, I may not want to. Your objective is clear: kill Desmond Duquesne. Use any means necessary. Collateral damage can be cleaned up."

"Well, we've been trying to avoid that as much as possible."

"Perhaps that's where you are going wrong. Do not tread lightly. Hit Duquesne hard. Use all your resources. Leave his house in ashes if you must, but get it done. Covering up for a mess will be a whole hell of a lot easier than dealing with Duquesne post-ritual. Am I understood?"

"Yes, sir," Valentine responded faintly.

. . .

AFTER MULLING his options within the privacy of his office, Valentine returned to Brandt's cell carrying a large black canvas bag. "Did Daddy lay down the law?" Brandt asked.

"Shut up," Valentine said, dropping the bag at his tormentor's feet.

Curious, Brandt cautiously unzipped the bag and removed one of the tranquilizer darts that he had filled in the warehouse. The blood was a bit more transparent from Feng's dilution process, but it would still do the trick. "What am I supposed to do with this?"

"I've had a change of heart," said Valentine. "Consider yourself drafted."

FORTY-ONE

The Calm

WITH JOANNA DECLARING herself in no mood to breakfast with her husband, Desmond Duquesne was able to steal away with the croissant that Ridgley had set out for him and walk down to the lake adjacent to the rear lawn of New Covington. He sat on the lone bench, and, realizing that he had no appetite, tossed bits of the pastry into the water, each delicate flake creating barely a ripple on the dark, glass-like surface.

Desmond could not have asked for a more beautiful day to precede his big moment. The sun shone brightly, burning off the last vestiges of the morning mist, and the only sound to be heard was the brushing of reeds against each other as they swayed in the gentle breeze. He closed his eyes and smiled as the scent of lakeside hydrangeas wafted toward him. He would not remain forever young, but he could at least remain forever alive.

"Where's your grapefruit?" he heard Daphne say. He opened his eyes to see his daughter sitting next to him. She looked tired, but she was every bit as strong as he had taught her to be. "Is it already at the bottom of the lake?"

He chuckled and motioned to put his arm around her, stopping himself mid-stretch. "I'm sorry, Daphne. After what happened…"

"It's okay," she said, allowing his arm to rest across her shoulders and snuggling close to his side. "I'm okay. Will saved me."

Desmond nodded pensively. "He certainly did. He's a good man."

Father and daughter sat for several minutes, the silence only broken by the dancing reeds and a gaggle of squawking geese passing overhead. "I used to be afraid of that, you know," Daphne eventually said.

"Afraid of what?" Desmond asked, looking out onto the lake, trying to discern what her eyes were focused on.

"The mist," she explained, nodding toward the vaporous columns that rose from the still water. "I used to think it was ghosts."

Desmond grinned and gave Daphne a playful pat on the shoulder. "I did not know that," he said. "But don't worry. I have it on good authority that ghosts do not exist."

"Good," she said with a smile. Still gazing at the mist, she continued, "What about an afterlife? Do you believe that we go somewhere after we die?"

"Oh yes," said Desmond, similarly staring at the apparitions dancing on the lake. "I do indeed."

Daphne sat up at this point and looked at father. "Can I ask you something?"

"Anything. Always."

"Is that why you want to live forever? Are you afraid of what comes after this?"

Desmond retained his composure, but he was taken slightly aback by the question. It was not the question itself that surprised him, rather that it came from the mouth of his daughter, who he never thought interested in the philosophical or metaphysical. "Daphne," he said, placing his hand on her knee, "look at this scene, this morning. Could anything be more perfect? After two hundred years, I've never grown tired of waking up to mornings like this, and I can honestly say that I never will. If there is something that you love to do, you should do it as much and as wholeheartedly as you can. I love to live— so I plan to do so for as long as I can."

"And what you're doing tonight is going to make that happen?"

"It certainly is. One quick ritual, and I'll be able to live for many, many more generations."

"Can you promise me one thing?"

"Of course."

"Promise me that you're not going to hurt anyone."

Desmond took a deep breath and looked his daughter in the eyes. "I promise you, Daphne: everything will be fine." Daphne nodded slowly and stood up, but Desmond could sense that something was still bothering her. "Are you alright, Daphne?"

"I'm fine," Daphne replied with a shrug. "And I'm happy for you. I guess I just feel bad that your 'perfect mornings' are eventually going to get very lonely." She managed a sad smile and walked back to the house, leaving her father with the ghosts in the mist.

PEG STARED at Frances Whitworth as she sat pensively at her desk, clutching Sarah's ring. She brought it up to her lips and seemed to mutter something, but Peg could not make out what it was. She had rarely seen her boss like this, but when it happened, she knew that it was best to stay on the sidelines. Still, Whitworth had been in this state for nearly an hour, and to Peg's knowledge, just across town, a lunatic was planning a mass ritual sacrifice. Having seen enough, she finally marched over to the desk, leaned both hands on it and said, "Snap out of it, Fran."

Whitworth looked wide-eyed at her secretary. "Peg, what am I supposed to do?"

"We still have the darts with Will's blood in them," she suggested.

"Right. And now that Duquesne knows about them, they'll be all but useless."

"Well then have Feng mix up another batch of that poison."

Whitworth shook her head. "We're out of time, Peg."

"I beg to differ," said a voice from behind Peg. Whitworth looked around her to see a worse-for-wear Will Trammell leaning against the doorframe.

"William…" she whispered, shocked at his sudden appearance.

"The way I figure, time is on our side," said Will.

"What do you mean?"

"Why don't we talk as a team?" Will suggested, motioning with his head in the direction of the conference room.

Whitworth smiled from ear to ear, and with a renewed energy, she shot up from her chair. "Peg, gather the others. Everyone. Now."

"You got it," she answered, and with a spring in her step, headed for the phone. "You want my shotgun?"

Whitworth chuckled. "You hold onto that. I've got my secret weapon right here." The agent put her arm around Will's shoulder and led him into the hall as Peg barked into the phone, "All hands on deck for what looks like a rare opportunity to kick some ass. Bring the cat."

DESMOND DUQUESNE GAZED into the smooth, blood-red stone that Havelock had taken from the departed Miranda

Simms. Tonight was the night, and although Donovan had botched his last assignment, Duquesne was feeling confident that the ritual would go off without a hitch. "Just one more step," he mused. "Once the ritual itself is complete, all of our hard work will come to fruition."

His words echoed through the chamber, bouncing off the etched columns that surrounded him. George Brisbane, the only other person currently occupying the space, nodded and placed a black cushion on the altar in the center of the room. "It is sure to be spectacular," he said. Taking the stone from Duquesne, he gently rested it on the pillow. "Have you decided how you'd like to approach this?"

"I certainly have, Professor. As my guests arrive tonight, any guest over the age of twenty-one will receive a stamp on his or her hand. The stamps are all unique, and each represents one of the seventy-two demons mentioned in the *Lesser Key*." Duquesne tapped the worn cover of the hefty tome that lay next to the Heart of Murena on the altar. "After I make an initial appearance at the party, I will head down here and wait for my stamped guests to join me."

"That much I assumed," said Brisbane. "But why would they come down here? Will all seventy-two be brought at once?"

"No, no," said Duquesne. "They will be ushered down in small groups by our own pied piper, Mr. Ridgley, under the pretense of being invited to imbibe a sample from my extensive wine cellar. Once they get down here, you, my friend, will work your magic and summon the appropriate demons. The demons will feast on their sacrifices and regain their full strength."

"At which point you will use the Heart of Murena to absorb that strength, and by the end of the evening, essentially gain the strength and vitality of all seventy-two."

"Exactly," said Duquesne.

"But what happens," Brisbane persisted, "when your guests

begin to notice that their numbers are dwindling? That their friends and family are not coming back to the party?"

Clearly beginning to tire of his colleague's questions, Duquesne sighed, "It will be fine, George. Trust me. If people begin to catch on, then they will be next. Otherwise, that's why we have Mr. Havelock and his men. They will keep order. The process will go smoothly."

Brisbane nodded grimly. "So what will you do when this is all over? What becomes of Desmond Duquesne tomorrow?"

Duquesne grinned. "At this time tomorrow, George, I'll be the most powerful man in the world. And despite what any prophecies say, I'd be willing to bet that even an army of William Trammells couldn't stop me. Tomorrow I begin a new world order—one of peace and prosperity—led by the only man capable of making it a reality." A mischievous glint appeared in Duquesne's eyes as he mused, "Of course, I might not be able to resist taking a trip to the Stonegate Hotel to gloat."

"And what about me?"

"I'm a man of my word, Dr. Brisbane. After you perform this ritual tonight, your life will never be the same. You'll have wealth beyond your wildest dreams."

Brisbane's mouth twisted into a covetous smile. "Enjoy your party, Mr. Duquesne. I need to continue the preparations."

"Good man," said Desmond. "I'm going to send a few of my men down here, just in case Valentine and Whitworth get any ideas." He stopped halfway up the ramp leading to the ballroom and asked, "Would you like something from the bar? I have a feeling that I overbought."

FORTY-TWO

The Storm

CHARLIE MCMILLON, one of Desmond Duquesne's security personnel, sat in a makeshift security booth at the main gate of New Covington, ready to stamp the hands of anyone on the guest list who was over twenty-one years of age. He guessed that the idea of hand stamps made sense from a legal stand-point, but he could not for the life of him figure out what the funky shapes were supposed to be, or why each guest needed an entirely different stamp. Still, he was getting paid good money, so as the guests passed through, he stamped their hands and promptly tossed each used stamp into the trashcan at his feet. He needed to be sure to remember to check the guests against the photos hanging in the booth labeled 'Do Not Admit.' He had unfortunately forgotten to do so when the line of guests had stretched into the street, but now that the party was underway and latecomers were trickling in, he would be more vigilant.

The sun was just setting when a pair of individuals approached the gate wearing two of the more elaborate masks he had seen that evening. The masks were embellished with

423

everything from jewels to feathers and seemed to make use of every color in the rainbow. With masks twice the size of their heads, the pair looked like a two-person Mardi Gras parade.

As they approached the booth, Charlie readied two stamps and said, "Good evening, folks. Before I let you in, would you mind removing your masks and checking in?"

"No, I would not mind," said the female figure, hefting her mask gracelessly off her face. "This thing is ridiculous, and I can't believe I'm out in public with it. You couldn't have just gotten a cheap plastic thing?"

"I wish I could have," said her male counterpart, removing his own mask to reveal a sly grin and a distinguished head of silver hair, "but unfortunately she was busy tonight." The man winked at Charlie, who didn't get the joke, and said, "Eleanor Hornbeck and guest."

Charlie found Hornbeck's name on the list, crossed it off, and picked up one of the stamps. "Could I have your hand, Ms. Hornbeck? This is just so that you're able to enjoy the bar tonight."

Eleanor held out her hand, but her brother gently lowered her arm before she could be stamped. "Oh, that won't be necessary, my friend," Wisp said in his smooth, slight southern drawl. "She's in recovery."

Hornbeck's face contorted into a sneer as she asked, "Recovery from what?"

Giving Charlie a knowing look, Wisp explained, "She just crawled out of the bottle a few weeks ago. This will be her first sober night out in public. We tried on Tuesday, but I found her drinking tequila with the busboy behind the dumpster at The Cheesecake Factory. Sad…"

Eleanor swatted at him with her oversized mask, knocking off jewels and sending up a flurry of feathers. "You son of a bitch," she screeched. "I'm going to take that mask and shove it up your—"

"It's going to be a long night," Wisp said to Charlie as he led his sister up the driveway. "You stay well, my friend. Wish me luck!" Once out of earshot, Wisp leaned into his belligerent stepsister and whispered, "Trust me. You'll thank me once the show begins."

Back in the booth, Charlie muttered, "Better him than me," and checked the guest list. With very few names left to check off, he assumed that the most boring part of his night was about to begin. But before he settled back to download a few time-killing games, he heard a faint, pleading voice. "Can you help me?"

Peering through the window of the booth, he had to lower his gaze to see a young, very tired-looking girl holding a porcelain doll and pleading, "I lost my mommy. Can you help me?"

Charlie left his post and approached the girl, stooping down to meet her at eye level. "Is your mommy at the party?" he asked.

She shook her head adamantly. "She was over there," she said, pointing across the street to a dark, wooded area.

"Are you sure?" Charlie wanted to help the girl but wasn't too eager to stray that far from the front gate. If Havelock caught him away from his post, he'd have his head.

"Uh huh," said the girl. "Our dog ran away, and she ran after it and I lost her."

Charlie resigned himself to the fact that he'd have to at least take a cursory look for the mother. "We'll look quickly, and if we can't find her, I'll call the police for you."

The girl took his hand as he led her across the street, and to Charlie's relief, almost as soon as they reached the spot near the woods the girl had pointed to, he saw a beautiful young woman running down the road to meet them. "Rose?" she cried. "Oh, thank God!"

"This is your daughter, miss?" asked Charlie.

"It is," said Gwen, hugging Rose.

"What about your dog? Did you find him as well?"

"No," Gwen answered. "I did find this, though." Charlie watched curiously as she reached into her purse and held out her hand. Seeing a small hill of what looked like baby powder resting in her palm, he did not have time to react before she blew it in his face. He futilely tried to wave away the cloud of dust, but once inhaled, it was a matter of seconds before he hit the ground.

Once Charlie McMillon was out, Will, Andy, Garza, and Whitworth emerged from the woods. "Well done, Miss Henley," said Whitworth. "Couldn't have done it better myself."

"Your fairy dust worked like a charm."

Whitworth chuckled. "Fairy dust. Like fairies exist…"

Trying to remain on task, Garza offered, "Let's not waste any time. Gwen and Rose, your job here is done."

Rose yawned. "That's good. Lilibeth's tired."

"I'm betting you are too?" Gwen asked.

"Not really," she said. "Ice cream?"

THE FOUR INTERLOPERS snuck into the security booth McMillon had abandoned to find fewer than ten unused sigil stamps resting in an open lockbox. Tossing them into the trashcan, Will said, "Well, we're late, but at least we can prevent Duquesne from getting all seventy-two sacrifices."

"Every little bit helps, I guess," said Andy before getting distracted by the 'Do Not Admit' photos hanging on the wall. "Hey! That's us!"

Will took a closer look to see his face posted alongside the faces of Andy, Gwen, Veronica, and a slew of Collective agents. "What an exclusive party," Will mused. "Good thing we brought masks. You *did* bring masks, right?"

"Of course," said Andy, feigning offense. "What do you

take me for?" He opened the bag that had been slung over his shoulder and removed a full rubber clown mask, complete with bright green hair. A collective sigh filled the booth. "It's a bit on the nose, isn't it?" Garza quipped.

"Andy, you know that there's a difference between a masquerade party and a Halloween party, right?" Will asked.

The abashed Andy donned the mask anyway and said, "It's not easy finding masks in June. Maybe next time you should find the masks and I'll save the world."

"I don't know," said Whitworth, pondering the clown mask. "It's comical, if a bit unsettling."

"Thank you!" Andy said with a clap of vindication. "Now here's yours." He handed Will a black domino mask. "See? It's not as attention-grabbing as mine."

"It also doesn't cover much of my face," said Will.

"I'm sure it will be fine, William," said Whitworth. "Duquesne truly does not expect you to show tonight. Just keep a low profile and you should be able to glide beneath his radar. With any luck, we'll stop the ritual and no one at the party will even know that anything's wrong. Now go."

Andy gave a salute to Whitworth. "We'll do our best to blend in, ma'am," he said through the clown mask.

"We're all going to die tonight, aren't we?" Garza asked Whitworth while watching through binoculars as the boys entered the mansion.

"Oh, I doubt that," the older woman answered. "I'd guess that nearly half of us will live through the night."

Turning to glare at Whitworth, Garza noticed the comedy mask that McMillon was to have worn later in the night as part of Duquesne's security detail. He handed it to Whitworth without saying a word and proceeded to point his binoculars once again in the direction of the entrance to New Covington. There, he saw another of Duquesne's troops stationed at the door with a similar comedy mask. "Maybe more than half," said Garza. "I know how we're getting into the party."

"YOU HEARD DETECTIVE GARZA," Valentine said into his phone. "Security is wearing the classical mask of comedy. Let's take them down quickly and quietly so that we can get to the big fish." He hung up and looked at Brandt in the rearview mirror. "Get one of those damn masks as soon as you can. Do not take it off. We don't need anyone distracted by the fact that I've let you in on this."

Brandt nodded and Valentine continued, "You, me, and Jenny will be heading into the sacrificial chamber through an entrance located in a tool shed out back. Whitworth and the rest will be making their way through the party and entering the chamber through the entrance that Agent Lawrence found in the ballroom. Hopefully we can keep this contained to the underground area. Our primary goal is to destroy the Heart, the *Key*, or both. If Duquesne happens to wind up with a dart in his neck, all the better. We're looking for no civilian casualties and no showboating, got it?"

"Well, look at you acting like a leader. Good for you," Brandt taunted as he left the vehicle.

Valentine and Jenny followed suit, with the Director addressing his agent, "I trust you'll be discreet about Brandt's inclusion here?"

"Yes, sir," Jenny answered.

Valentine nodded and approached Brandt, standing toe-to-toe with him. "One more thing, Brandt. When this is over, I never want to see your face again."

Brandt grinned. "I'll give you my word on that one."

. . .

"I FEEL UNDERDRESSED," Andy told Will from beneath his rubber clown mask. "Especially compared to you." He tapped Gleave's cane that Will had brought along. "Looking all distinguished with your fancy cane."

Will ignored him. His attention was already elsewhere. A familiar voice was serenading the crowd with 'That Old Black Magic,' and Andy watched Will maneuver his way through the partygoers as though in a trance until his eyes locked with Daphne's. She stood on stage in front of the band, elegant in a sleek black dress. Will's heart beat faster as the corner of her mouth curled up and she aimed her lyrics in his direction. "...'cause you're the lover I have waited for, the mate that fate had me created for..."

"Will, I know she's hot and everything, but we really need to find her father," Andy said under his breath.

"Right," Will said half-heartedly. "I know."

"...under that old black magic called love..." The song had ended, and the crowd gave their host's daughter an enthusiastic ovation.

"Come on, Will," Andy urged.

They watched as Joanna joined her blushing daughter on the stage and jokingly, but lovingly, insisted that Daphne take a bow before letting the hired band take over. Will looked around the room cautiously before removing his mask.

"You should really leave that on," Andy warned.

"There are enough people here for me to get lost in the crowd," Will said. "I'm more worried for them. They shouldn't be here."

"Who? Daphne and Mrs. Duquesne? They live here."

"I know, Andy, but what if things get ugly? We need to make sure they're safe. Give me just a minute to talk to Daphne."

Andy frowned, but he knew that there was no talking his

friend out of this. "I'm going to get some food, act like I belong," he said through the rubber mask. "Please be fast."

Will nodded and made his way to the side of the stage, where Daphne had been cornered by a gaggle of gaudily dressed middle-aged women who poked and prodded at her hair and shoes. She appeared more than relieved when Will approached and she was able to excuse herself. "There he is," she said. "My hero."

Now it was Will's turn to blush, especially as they were still within earshot of the chattering women who were now looking him up and down. "You were amazing up there," Will said. "And I, um, I got you something."

Daphne gave a quizzical smile. "What's the occasion?" she asked as pulled a small box wrapped to perfection in purple paper out of his pocket. "Really, I can't..." But despite her feigned protestations, she could not resist unwrapping the gift. She opened the box to find a necklace with a small jade pendant carved into a familiar shape. "A seahorse!" she grinned.

"Now you own one," Will said, relieved that she seemed pleased.

"Put it on me!" she requested, holding the open chain in front of him.

"I...I shouldn't. You know that."

"I trust you," she said softly. He took the chain and she turned around, lifting her hair to expose the smooth, sun-kissed skin of her back. Will's hands trembled as he struggled with the latch, but he eventually secured the chain and let it fall onto the back of her neck. "See?" she said, turning back to face him and adjusting the charm so that it rested squarely above her chest. "It looks beautiful, and no one died."

"Can't ask for more than that," Will joked nervously.

"You know, if our lives were normal, this would have earned you a kiss," Daphne said, straining for levity. Will wanted to grab her, to pull her close and finally taste her perfect pink lips, but all he could manage was a melancholy smile and an understanding nod. "I'm glad that you came tonight, Will."

"Me too."

"But something's wrong, isn't it?" she asked, noting that his gaze had begun shifting around the room.

"Can we go someplace more private? We need to talk about your father."

THE BALLROOM WAS STEADILY FILLING up with guests, and Alexander was in his element. The crème de la crème of New England was in attendance, including several of his friends' wealthy and influential families. He flitted from one to another like a drunken moth before he at last reached Carson, recognizable only due to his neck brace. "You've got some balls showing up here," said Alexander. "If my parents or sister see you, they'll freak out."

"Thank God it's a masquerade, then," Carson laughed, tapping the ornate jester's mask on his face. "Besides, you know I would never do anything to your sister, right? I hope that you defended me after that."

"I tried," said Alex, "but for some reason, that kid has them all wrapped around his finger."

"That punk," said Carson, melodramatically rubbing his brace. "If he were here, I'd kick his ass for sucker punching me like he did."

"Is that so?" said Kara, her drunken voice emanating from behind a cat mask. "Prove it."

"I wish I could," said Carson.

"You can," Kara pressed. "Isn't that him right over there?" She pointed to Will, who was following Daphne out of the ballroom.

431

Alexander cursed and excused himself. Scanning the room, his eyes settled on a rotund individual removing a clown mask to wipe sweat from his face. He immediately recognized Andy, grabbed him by the collar, and pushed past a security guard to duck into the secret panel at the far end of the ballroom. He dragged the protesting Andy awkwardly down the ramp, which he had only ever traversed once or twice in the past, until he reached the bottom and found George Brisbane reading nervously from a book, while his father paced impatiently in a long black cloak. "What are you doing down here?" his father asked. "You're supposed to be entertaining."

"I know," Alexander said, panting. "But something's wrong."

Emil Havelock stepped forward from a dark recess of the chamber. "Who is this?"

Alex removed the clown mask to reveal Andy's terrified, perspiring face. "I…I was invited by Daphne," he stammered.

"Where is your friend, Mr. Lunsford?" Duquesne demanded.

"He's with Daphne," said Alex. "They just left the ballroom. I don't know where they went."

"He's a resilient little bugger, I'll give him that. Mr. Havelock, please incapacitate him in the quickest way possible. Mr. Donovan, we may as well get the process underway. Bring me some guests."

"I thought that was Ridgley's job," said Donovan.

"We're moving up our timeline. Just get the process started," Duquesne demanded with a growing impatience. Havelock and Donovan nodded and hurried off, while Duquesne addressed Brisbane. "Dr. Brisbane, are we ready?"

Brisbane was sweating nervously, but knew he had little choice but to be ready. "Everything is set. Once the sacrifices are brought down, I can start opening the seals."

"Excellent. We'll need to expedite the process. So much for

pageantry." He almost sent his son back to the party, but even amid the musty air of the cavern, his nose wrinkled as he detected the distinct odor of whiskey. "Is that alcohol on your breath, Alex?"

"I-I just had one or two, Dad. I know you told me not to drink, but…"

"It's not about the drinking, Alex. It's about the—" He grabbed his son's hand and saw the demonic stamp on it. "It's about the sigil, damn it." He let go of his son's hand and twisted the silver head of his walking stick. "I hope it was worth it, Alex. Hold out your hand." Alex, terrified, did not know what to do. "Hold it out!" Duquesne shouted. Alex held his stamped, trembling hand out in front of him as his father pulled a long, narrow blade from its sheath. When Alex realized what was happening, he screamed, but it was too late. With one stroke, Desmond lopped off his son's hand at the wrist, sending it plopping onto the cool stone floor. As the tears streamed down Alex's face, Duquesne sneered, "Don't make me regret saving your life."

Duquesne summoned the two masked security guards who remained in the chamber and said, "Gentlemen, please help my son out the back way. Get him to a hospital. In the meantime, radio for some of your colleagues to come down here and take your place."

"And what about me?" Andy said.

"You, Mr. Lunsford, have become my trump card," Duquesne responded. "If your friend makes his way down here, he'll have to choose between stopping me or saving you. Forgive me for making you the damsel in distress, but I really cannot risk you mucking this up." He concealed the blade in his walking stick once more and approached the altar in the center of the room. He gently stroked his own reflection in the blood-red stone. "Dr. Brisbane," he said, "please begin."

. . .

"SO WHAT'S UP?" Daphne asked when she and Will had successfully removed themselves from earshot.

Will, stunned by her nonchalant attitude toward the evening's true purpose, could not help but ask, "Do you know what's really going on here tonight? Do you know what your father is doing?"

She rolled her eyes, disappointed that the conversation had once more returned to this. "I know, Will. He's doing that ritual thing, but it should be relatively quick, and it's not hurting anybody."

Will's jaw practically hit the floor. "Oh my God," he said. "You really have no idea, do you? No wonder you've been so okay with this. He told you that it was harmless, didn't he? Of course he did."

"Will, what are you saying?"

"I'm saying that not only did your father try to have me killed yesterday, but as we speak, he's getting ready to sacrifice most of the people at this party. Doesn't sound so harmless anymore, does it?"

She shook her head. "No. I can't believe that. It can't be true. He wouldn't do that."

"I'm afraid he would," said Emil Havelock, pressing the barrel of a gun into Will's back. "And your boyfriend is here to stop it. I can't let that happen. If you two would be good enough to walk with me..." He led them up the wide marble staircase and into Duquesne's study. "The ritual shouldn't take long. Afterwards, I'll let Desmond decide what to do with you two. In the meantime, I'll be right outside this door. And remember, no touching!" He leered at Daphne as he pulled the door shut and locked it from the outside.

Daphne went pale. "This can't be happening," she said as she lowered herself into an armchair. "It can't. He promised me. He promised me that he wasn't going to hurt anyone. I don't know what to do. What do we do?"

Will looked around the room but saw only Duquesne's collections of books, masks, and walking sticks, none of which would be much help. "I don't know," he replied. "I guess we hope that the Collective does its job."

"If they do, my father's a dead man."

EARLIER IN THE EVENING, Mrs. Ridgley had parked her wheelchair in the corner of the kitchen, and she'd been barking out orders to the waitstaff ever since. Her husband, on the other hand, silently worked to ensure that each tray of hors d'oeuvres was impeccable. Now, as he wiped clean an empty silver platter, he caught a glimpse of a patchwork figure in the reflection. The figure spoke in a deep, muffled voice, but after a few repetitions, the butler was able to make out enough of the message. He handed a tray full of hors d'oeuvres to his wife and said, "It's time for you to take a turn, dear. Go hand these out, will you?"

"And how am I supposed to do that?" she asked, demonstrating that she would barely be able to navigate her wheelchair with one arm.

He took the tray of food and placed it on her lap. "Figure it out," he said, and rushed off.

LURED by the promise of a rare wine sampling from Duquesne's cellar, four guests followed Donovan through the barely-lit tunnel and into the chamber where their host awaited them. He now wore his full masquerade regalia, his prized plague doctor mask complementing the long black cloak. He stood at the altar holding his cane in one hand and the crimson stone in the other. Over his shoulder, his guests could see George Brisbane mouthing incomprehensible words from a book that looked beyond ancient.

"What is this?" asked one of the guests, gazing with fear and awe at the eighteen columns lining the cavernous space.

"It's something I'm eager for you to be a part of," Duquesne said from behind the avian mask. "And it's something you should feel honored to be a part of. Dr. Brisbane, release the first of our *true* guests!"

Brisbane spoke under his breath, his lips moving faster than even he thought possible. From his position in the shadows at the far entrance of the cavern, Brandt could not tell what the professor was saying, but he knew that things were going to end badly if they did not step in now. He looked to Valentine for approval, but Valentine hesitated, whispering, "Once a ritual begins, it should not be interrupted. It's too unpredictable."

"So what do we do?" Brandt growled.

Valentine was shaking. "I don't know."

AS WHITWORTH, Garza, and the rest of the Collective contingent made their way down the tunnel, they felt the walls shake around them. "We're too late," said Whitworth. "The ritual has already started."

"What now?" Garza asked.

"At the very least, we get the guests out." She motioned for silence as they came up behind Donovan and the panic-stricken party guests. But before she could do anything she noticed that Andy was slumped, wrists and ankles bound, against one of the pillars.

Andy's face blanched as the four sigils on a nearby pillar began to glow and eventually crack. From the top sigil, he saw a clawed hand come forward, then another, until an eight-foot-tall creature, lanky and spotted with patches of mottled fur, leapt forward, screeching. From another sigil came a much smaller creature, this one snake-like, but with four legs on each side of its body.

"This is insane," said Brandt, having seen enough. "We need to stop this." Before Valentine could prevent it, Brandt readied his tranquilizer gun, took off his mask and shouted, "Hey Duquesne! I'll see you in hell!"

Duquesne whipped around to see who the intruder was. "Brandt. You should really—" Brandt fired his first dart before Duquesne could finish his sentence, sending it rocketing toward his target's heart. In a lightning-fast move, Duquesne swung his walking stick and batted the projectile away. After it clinked uselessly onto the ground, he continued, "As I was saying, you really should know better than to interfere with magic, Brandt. George, keep reading. Gentlemen," he said, addressing his security force, "kill that man." He pointed to Brandt with the tip of his cane, but no one budged.

"What are you doing?" cried Donovan, drawing his own weapon. "The man said Brandt goes." The disgraced agent's bravado subsided when he looked around to see each of the comedy masks removed to reveal the faces of his former Collective colleagues.

Duquesne was similarly thrown off when he recognized the faces of Valentine and Whitworth, but he soon recovered, noting the creatures that continued to emerge from their sigils and holding the red stone high above his head. "It doesn't matter!" he shouted. "You're too late! These demons will get their sacrifices, and by the end of the night, I will be a god!"

"Over my dead body," said Brandt, removing a concussion grenade and tossing it into the center of the room. The grenade went off with a blinding flash, sending Duquesne and Brisbane flying in opposite directions.

MR. RIDGLEY HASTENED UP the stairs as quickly as his starched suit would allow and found Havelock keeping guard outside Duquesne's office. "Emil," he panted, "there's trouble downstairs."

"At the party?"

"No," said Ridgley, "*downstairs*. Mr. Duquesne needs you immediately. I'll stay here."

While Havelock was sure that, if given the chance, William Kendrick could overpower Ridgley, he knew that it was more important to attend to his employer. He nodded and ran off, leaving the butler to fish through his pocket for the appropriate key.

"Mr. Ridgley?" Daphne, armed with a fireplace poker, was shocked to see him open the door.

He nodded and said, "Miss Duquesne, I suggest that you remain here. Mr. Kendrick, follow me."

"So when did you decide to turn on Duquesne?" Will asked as they raced through the halls of Covington.

"I've known he was out of control for quite a while now, Mr. Kendrick, but my hands have been tied. He would have had my head if he knew I couldn't be trusted. That's why I had to do things surreptitiously, like dropping the stamp Mr. Lunsford found in the car."

"You meant for us to find it?"

Ridgley nodded. "I knew you and Whitworth would decipher Duquesne's plan, but I was hoping you would take action a bit sooner than this. Come now; we need to get you to the chamber before all hell breaks loose."

"...ALRIGHT? ANDY? ARE YOU ALRIGHT?" Andy opened his eyes to see that Eddie Garza was hurriedly untying his bindings, and as his hearing gradually returned, he was able to acknowledge Garza's concern.

"Yeah, I'm okay," he answered, checking to see if his ears were bleeding. He stood slowly, noting that everyone in the chamber was doing the same. The concussion grenade had done its job and then some, the reverberations in the chamber neutralizing man and demon alike. The small snake-like creature had scampered off, but the tall, hairy beast was stirring below its own sigil.

"You idiot!" Duquesne screamed, breaking the silence. "What have you done? Where is the Heart?" He had dropped the stone in the blast and was now frantically searching around the altar on his hands and knees.

"Desmond, stop yelling," said Whitworth. "We have bigger problems." Andy and Garza approached the fallen George Brisbane, who lay wide-eyed on his back, muttering what sounded like gibberish.

"What happened?" asked Valentine as he approached the altar.

"It looks like Dr. Brisbane is broken," Andy answered. "What is he saying?"

Garza gazed upon the blithering professor with concern. "Something's wrong."

Whitworth nodded slowly and looked around as light began to shine from each of the remaining seventy-two sigils. The columns around them shook and cracked and Desmond Duquesne rose to his feet, his lips quavering. "And that's why you don't interfere with a ritual."

FORTY-THREE

Pandemonium

MR. WISP WAS BORED. He leaned against the bar, having sweet talked the young bartender into serving him despite being stamp-less. His sister pointed to yet another high society snob, and he obligingly offered, "She's having an affair with the man in the tacky green tie. He's a plastic surgeon. Actually, he's more interesting. He's been with half the women in this room."

"Oh?" said Eleanor, greedily typing the info into her phone and snapping as many candid pictures as she could. "Who?"

Wisp sighed and rolled his eyes. "I don't know. Look for women with big fake—hold on."

"Huh?"

"Did you just see that?" he asked, pointing to the area of the room where the band played. "It looked like something just ran under the stage. I could have sworn it was a lizard, but it had too many legs."

Eleanor took his drink and finished it herself. "You're drunk."

Not far from the bar, Kara was waving down a waiter with a tray of shrimp. "Care for a bite?" he asked politely.

She flashed a glassy-eyed smile. "Don't mind if I do." She bit into the snack just before the floor beneath her erupted and screams filled the ballroom. Like a great white preying upon a seal, an enormous eel-like demon burst through the floor, tossing Kara into the air and swallowing her with a sickening snap. It gave a reptilian roar and hovered over the heads of the panicked guests, searching for more victims.

Eleanor leapt to the other side of the bar in the most graceless manner possible, while Mr. Wisp poured himself another scotch. "Now this is more like it," he said with a grin.

WILL HAD ONLY MADE it halfway down the marble staircase when he saw the demon devour Kara. From there, he had a bird's eye view of the ensuing chaos, as partygoers ran for any exit they could find and a horde of demons began to filter out of the hole that had been created in the center of the ballroom. Horrific creatures of all shapes and sizes flew, leapt, crawled, and slithered in the midst of the guests who, in their drunken states, had little chance of getting away.

Ridgley went pale, wished Will luck, and ran away down the remainder of the stairs, disappearing into the throng. He found his wife still in the kitchen, asking the terrified waitstaff what all the commotion was about, but receiving no answer. "Time to go," Ridgley said to his wife, swinging the kitchen door open just long enough to show a glimpse of the carnage.

"Jesus!" she cried, ripping the brace from her leg and springing up from her wheelchair. She shoved her husband out of the way and ran to the pantry next door, where their bags were already packed.

Will, in the meantime, spied a familiar shape amid the bedlam and called loudly for Hex to come his way. The cat dropped the dead eight-legged demon from her mouth and dashed to Will who, after convincing himself that the rules were out the window, said, "I'm not sure if you even understand English, Hex, but if you do, go to Daphne. Stay with her until this is over." The cat blinked twice and was off like a shot.

DAPHNE PACED in her father's office, frightened by the screams that now emanated from the main hall. She hated feeling this powerless and had nearly resolved to jump from the second-story window into the shrubs below when she heard a faint scratching at the office door. She hesitated, not knowing what kind of unearthly creature her father might have unleashed. But when she heard a plaintive meow, she cracked the door open to see Hex, who appeared harmless enough. Scooping the cat into her arms, she moved to shut the door but found a foot stuck in the opening.

"Thank God," said an out-of-breath Carson. "Let me in."

"Go to hell, Carson."

He looked down the hall and so did Daphne, each spying the creature crawling over the railing to the landing. It was an infant, bald and cherubic, with blank eyes, jagged teeth, and a third arm growing from its forehead. The bottom half of the creature was that of a tarantula, eight-legged and hairy. It giggled as it approached. "Oh God," said Carson, suppressing the urge to vomit. "Let me in you stupid little—"

With a sudden and ferocious swipe, Hex tore at Carson's face, sending him reeling back and allowing Daphne to shut the door just before the spider creature reached them. She locked herself in and ran to the far corner of the room with Hex as she heard Carson scream and saw streaks of blood seep into the room from beneath the door.

IN THE SACRIFICIAL CHAMBER, the battle raged on as Valentine, Jensen, and the rest of the Collective unloaded their weapons into the demonic horde. "These are demons, right?" Garza asked Whitworth as they ended up back to back. "Are my bullets even doing anything?"

"They should eventually do the trick, so long as the particular demon that you're shooting at has not regained its full strength…that is, as long as it has not taken a sacrifice."

"And how will I know?" Garza persisted, hobbling a demon that resembled a thin, barren tree.

"You'll know," Whitworth responded.

"Most of the demons are heading out to the main house through that hole in the ceiling. Let's head up and try to make sure that civilian casualties are minimized," said Valentine, reloading.

Whitworth reached into her pocket, removed what looked like a bag of seeds, and handed them to Garza. "In case you get overwhelmed."

"Magic beans?" he joked. "Do I eat them?"

"Oh God, no," said Whitworth. "I'm sure you'll figure it out." The elder agent rushed with startling speed back up the darkened passage, toward the ballroom.

Andy, who had stuck close to Garza during the fight, watched Duquesne ignore all that was going on around him as he continued to search for his Heart of Murena. "What do we do with him?" Andy shouted to Valentine.

"Leave him," the Director said as he followed Whitworth into the passage. "Without his toys, he's nothing."

"Come on, Andy," said Garza. "We've got to move."

"Okay…" But as Andy turned to leave, he noticed an object on the floor under the altar. He ran to grab it, shoved it into the wooden box from the top of the altar, and hurried after Eddie, leaving Duquesne in the dark with the rest of his demons.

. . .

"OKAY, CAT," Daphne said to Hex. "I can't just stay here when I don't know what's happening to my family." She picked up the fireplace poker again and took a few practice swings. "I guess this will have to do," she shrugged. "Unless, of course, you've got any better ideas…"

Hex closed her eyes and stretched, and as she did so, her leathery wings grew out. When she opened her eyes again, they glowed a brilliant purple. If Daphne had not just witnessed a killer spider-baby, she probably would have been more impressed. As it stood now, she simply said, "I appreciate the effort, but I'm not sure that'll do it."

Cocking her head slightly and meowing, Hex stepped away from Daphne and closed her eyes once more. She again began to change, but this time in a more substantial way. Her muscles grew and her fur shed to reveal an entirely different, striped layer beneath. Her teeth and claws grew to the size of daggers, and her wings practically knocked Daphne over when they flapped open, spanning nearly the width of the room. Frightened at first, Daphne's anxiety was relieved when the new and improved Hex bowed her head obediently. "Yeah," said Daphne, gently petting her new companion, "that'll work."

"YOU KNEW that this was going to happen!" Eleanor Hornbeck screamed while she struggled to keep herself hidden behind the bar.

Her stepbrother stood surveying the damage and holding a bottle of Duquesne's finest scotch close to his chest, shielding it from danger as best he could. "Now why would you think that?" he asked, taking a sip from his glass. He peered up to see a massive demon affixed to the metal girders that had once held a panel of the domed glass ceiling. The creature writhed languidly, a mess of viscous tentacles originating from what appeared to be a huge, beaked barnacle. "Well that's troubling," he mused, finishing his drink. As he poured another, he found himself joined by two more individuals behind the bar.

"Are you two alright?" asked Eddie Garza, leaning down to check on Eleanor. She waved him away and returned to cowering, but Wisp nodded and generously offered a swig. Eddie ignored the gesture but realized he recognized the silver-haired man from the time he had spent monitoring Will's movements. "You're Veronica Frost's friend, right?"

"Her very best," said Wisp.

"Good. Andy," Garza said, turning to his companion, "stay with these folks. Stay hidden behind here. I'm going to help clear the room. Hopefully this will all be over soon."

Neither Andy nor Wisp appeared thrilled to be left with the other, but given the alternative, they each silently assented, and Garza was off. Sensing that the woman behind the bar had the right idea, Andy promptly ducked down alongside Hornbeck and left Wisp the only standing spectator. Wisp loosened his tie and cracked open the bottle of scotch but found himself held at gunpoint before he could take a drop. "How rude of me," he said to his assailant. "Would you like a glass? I can try to find one that's not broken."

The former Agent Donovan met his offer with a stony expression. "Keep your drink. I just want the boy."

Without hesitation, the relieved Wisp took his swig and said, "Mr. Lunsford, it's for you." He pulled Andy up by the collar and presented him to Donovan.

Aiming his handgun at Andy's face, Donovan said, "I saw you sneak that box out of the basement. I'll be taking the Heart now. Hand it over."

"I don't know what you're talking about," said Andy. "I don't have the Heart."

Eleanor, privy to the conversation from her hiding place, spotted the box that Andy had placed on the floor near her and snatched it. Rising quickly, she slammed the box on the bar and said, "Here! Just take the damn thing and leave us alone!" In a flash, she had once again disappeared behind the shelves of alcohol.

"Wow. Thanks a lot, everyone," said the disgusted Andy. However, seeing the greedy look on Donovan's face as he grabbed the box, Andy's disposition changed. "You know what? On second thought, you've earned this."

"Damn right I have," Donovan responded. The traitorous agent opened the box and stood staring in disgust. "What the hell is this?" Having expected to see a smooth crimson stone, Donovan was unpleasantly surprised when the box revealed a severed hand with a symbol stamped onto it. Before he could drop the hand, a powerful tentacle wrapped itself around Donovan and lifted him, screaming, into the snapping maw of the Lovecraftian demon on the ceiling.

Wisp slapped Andy on the back and poured him a small shot of the scotch. "See there? Teamwork!"

JOANNA DUQUESNE WATCHED as Agent Donovan was devoured by the tentacled beast and turned stoically away. Her husband had betrayed the family, he and his cronies had insisted upon shedding blood, and she had been complicit through her inaction. "Oh, Desmond," she whispered, though her husband was nowhere to be seen. She glided like a phantom through the fray, unable or unwilling to hear or see any more of the violence surrounding her. She only came to her senses when she was nearly knocked over by the Ridgleys, their suitcases stuffed to bursting with expensive souvenirs of their time at Covington.

"Mrs. Duquesne!" said Mrs. Ridgley, obviously not having expected to run into her employer. "I was just...we were just..."

"Leaving," said her husband, nudging his wife toward the door.

Joanna said nothing.

"Yes, well, good luck with all this," Mrs. Ridgley continued. "If I do need a reference——"

Their employer snatched a silver candlestick that had been tucked under Mrs. Ridgley's arm and continued to stare blankly at the couple, which seemed to instill more fear in them than the rampaging demons had done. Mrs. Ridgley stumbled over her baggage as she turned tail and ran from the house and Mr. Ridgley followed not far behind, though he was courteous enough to suggest, "Leaving is the wisest course of action, Mrs. Duquesne. You should do so as well."

Joanna turned back toward the ballroom and muttered, "I'm going to see my husband."

HAVING ACCEPTED ITS SACRIFICE, the tentacled creature dropped to the floor with a thunderous, sickening splat and made its way toward Andy and Wisp. "The pods!" Whitworth shouted to Garza who, taking his attention off the demon he was engaging, ran to Andy's side and looked skeptically at the black spheres which he poured from the small satchel into the palm of his hand. Shrugging at Andy, he dodged a swiping tentacle and ran toward the nucleus of the demon, the rock-hard core with the protruding, parrot-like beak, and tossed the spheres into the beast's gullet. Figuring that the best course of action at this point would be to run, Garza did just that, instinctively jumping over the bar upon hearing the first of several loud explosions rock the room. The walls splattered with black gunk, and a squirming green arm fell alongside Eleanor Hornbeck who, having had her fill of scares for the evening, finally fainted.

"That was crazy!" said Andy, covered in the tar-like substance. "Do you have any more of those things?"

Garza did not respond but looked beyond Andy at a large crack in the wall that ran like a lightning bolt up toward the domed ceiling. The explosion had killed the demon, but Garza now saw that he may have inadvertently killed the rest of them as well. Powerless to do anything but shoo Andy and Wisp away from the area, he struggled to wrap his arms around the limp Hornbeck. "Come on, lady," he pleaded in vain. "We've got to get——" But it was no use. A substantial portion of the ballroom ceiling was falling in, and he and Hornbeck would be crushed in an instant.

Eddie braced himself for the falling stone and glass, but it never hit. He opened his eyes to see Will Kendrick, arms outstretched, struggling to levitate the crumbing debris only inches above Garza's head. "I don't know how long I can hold this," he said, breaking into a sweat. "Go. Now."

Garza continued to drag Eleanor out of the way, but there was just too much weight for Will to hold. He thought he would have to drop it, have to watch his father's good friend disappear in the rubble, until help descended in the form of Hex. The creature swooped down and scooped Eleanor gently up, moving her to safety so that Garza could fend for himself and get out of the area just in time for the stone and glass to come crashing down.

"Hex, old friend!" Whitworth smiled despite a significant gash on the side of her face. "I had almost forgotten you were here!"

"That's Hex?" Will asked.

"It is, and I think she's got the right idea. It's time to take the kid gloves off." Whitworth dropped her gun to the floor, seemingly unaware that a large, mantis-shaped demon was creeping up behind her.

Will shouted as he saw the creature raise one of its bladed

forearms to strike at the old woman, but it was too late. The creature had swung its weapon, and Whitworth had no time to move out of the way.

She did, however, have time to make herself incorporeal, allowing the blade to slice through her shape without receiving any injury. "How did you do that?" asked Will, amazed.

"Practice," Whitworth winked. "Now go help people. I've got work to do." Whitworth cracked her knuckles and made a compressing motion with her hands. The mantis demon shrunk to the size of a mouse and was promptly devoured by Hex. The spider baby had since crawled back downstairs and was the next to attempt an assault on the elder agent. But Whitworth, with a wave of her hand, melted the marble on which its eight legs stood, submerging it halfway and solidifying it, assuring that the demon would not be bothering anyone else.

Spying the tall, hairy demon that had been among the first to escape from the sigils, Whitworth gathered the shards of glass that had fallen around the bar and whirled them into a deadly cyclone that shredded the beast mercilessly. Whitworth, who hadn't engaged in a battle in years, could not manage to suppress her grin as she took control of the situation.

AGENT JENSEN WAS WINDED, but he was holding his own against the demon horde he had followed up from the subterranean chamber. The sea of panicked guests was beginning to thin out as they either made their way frantically from the house or, in less fortunate situations, were slaughtered by the remaining demons. He stood back-to-back with Director Valentine, each firing his weapon at a steady clip, careful not to hit bystanders. He sensed that they were gaining the upper hand, but there was still one major problem.

"They're getting out," said the Director, pointing toward

the partially-collapsed ceiling and wall. "Our priority now needs to be containment."

"I agree, sir," said Jensen, "but that ain't going to be easy." He pulled the trigger of his gun solely to show his supervisor that he was out of ammunition. "These things take a hell of a lot to bring down."

After two more shots taken at a reptilian demon attacking a nearby socialite, Valentine realized that he too was out of bullets. "Damn," he said. "Grab anything you can, Jenny. We need weapons."

This command was met with a guttural laugh that made Valentine's blood run cold. Now unarmed, he and Jensen stared with dread as a figure took shape before them. As tall as two men, it stood in a burgundy cloak that flowed like waves of blood. Its face was a bare, weathered skull, almost human, save for sharp protrusions at the chin, cheeks, and scalp. The arms were similarly composed of bare bones, and where the hands should have been were the skulls of carnivorous, lupine creatures.

"Why waste your energy?" the shape hissed. "Accept your fate and consider yourself honored to be victims of Asmodeus." Jensen and Valentine watched helplessly as bony tendrils slinked out from beneath the demon's cloak, each culminating in the skull of a viper. Hydra-like, eight heads appeared and snaked their way toward the unarmed agents.

"Screw this," Jensen said, taking a swing at one of the skulls. He connected, but promptly recoiled, nursing the fist that had been lacerated by a razor-sharp fang. "Oh well," he said, resigned to his defeat. "It's been nice working with you, sir."

Both men winced as the snake heads sprung forward but were taken off-guard by a sudden bang and a shower of skull fragments. Daphne Duquesne had appeared on the scene, guns blazing. With a weapon in each hand, she took expert aim at each of the skulls, shattering them all in turn, and leaving a stunned Asmodeus reeling. His snakelike appendages reduced to nothing more than flailing skeletal whips, the demon raged and disappeared through the collapsed ceiling, cloak and bones alike scattering into the wind.

"If you guys need guns," Daphne said once the demon was gone, "you might want to check over that way. A few of my father's security guys bit the dust over there."

"Yes, well, thank you," said Valentine, dusting the bone fragments from his jacket. "But where in the hell did you learn to shoot like that?"

"I was homeschooled by Desmond Duquesne," Daphne winked, tossing a weapon to Valentine. "We didn't spend much time on arts and crafts."

With a raised eyebrow, Valentine nodded and said, "Fair enough. Now you stick with Agent Jensen." He looked past Daphne, toward the gaping crater in the middle of the ballroom. "I've got to run."

"I DON'T NEED HELP," Brandt said to Valentine upon the Director's arrival at his side.

"No? Because your problems seem to be multiplying."

Sure enough, Brandt shot a bat-like demon to the ground, which then proceeded to tear itself in half and rise back into the air as two smaller, but fully-formed, demons. "I could kill these bastards all day," said Brandt, blasting the two bats into four pieces. He and Valentine unloaded on the rapidly multiplying demons, going shot for shot with each other until the reanimated creatures seemed barely large enough to be dangerous. "I shot more than you," Brandt bragged as he sent a bullet whizzing past Valentine's head and into one of the few remaining bats.

Valentine took aim at Brandt and returned the favor,

shooting a bat only inches from Brandt's ear. "Let's call it even," he smirked.

Brandt gave an approving nod. "Just this once."

"Are you sure? You've still got some skills for an old man. We'll probably have some freelance work after—"

"Down!" Brandt threw the Director to the ground, taking a cluster of bullets into his own chest. Will watched from across the room as the force of the blast flung Brandt over the edge of the chasm that led to Duquesne's chamber below.

"Havelock," Valentine said, scrambling to his feet. "Do you see what's going on around us? Duquesne's plans are in tatters. What's the point in continuing to fight us?"

With both hands on his weapon and a smug grin, Havelock answered, "I guess I just like shooting people..." Before he could pull the trigger a second time, though, the gun was yanked from his hands and flipped in the air so that in a split second, Havelock found himself looking down the barrel.

"Can you handle this?" Will asked Valentine. The Director grabbed Havelock's weapon from midair and nodded to Will. "Good. I'm going to find Brandt."

FORTY-FOUR

Proving Ground

THE BALLROOM WAS IN CHAOS, and without a Duquesne or Ridgley in sight, Will had no way of knowing how to get down to the lower chamber where Brandt lay writhing. His head jerked as he looked around frantically for a stairway of some sort, but only saw an uninterrupted series of mirrored panels that lined the curved walls of the ballroom. He was growing dizzy from watching his own reflections in these mirrors, until his eyes alit on one where he didn't appear. Instead, the lanky form of the Patchwork Man from his dreams had manifested in this one mirror and, upon getting Will's attention, reached a digit up to point out a small lever. Without time to question the figure's motives, Will pressed the same lever that James Lawrence had pressed weeks earlier and was hit with the same cool draft.

With the panel propped open, he bolted down the dank corridor until he reached the lower chamber, where he almost slipped on the puddle of blood that Brandt was lying in. He knelt next to the rasping man and made a cursory assessment of his injuries. Brandt was much worse off than he had been in

Memorytown, but Will still gingerly attempted to at least stop the bleeding from Brandt's abdomen. Brandt painfully pushed his hand away. "Enough, William. Finish what we've started. I'm not getting out of here alive."

"None of you are," said a muffled voice. Will jerked his head around to see the plague doctor of his nightmares, Desmond Duquesne, standing behind him—a motionless harbinger of death amid the chaos surrounding them. From behind the beaked mask, he continued, "I gave you the opportunity to avoid all of this, William, but you and your friends chose to act in a selfish and foolhardy manner. Now you've not only spoiled my plans, but you've sentenced your companions to death. Tell me, have Mr. Brandt's lessons paid off?"

"I guess we're about to find out," Will responded as he gripped Gleave's ebony walking stick tightly. "I'll tell you this much: I should have listened to what he said about you. You had me fooled for a while there, but it's clear now that you're nothing but a coward."

Duquesne cocked his head. "A coward? Truly? Come. Let's see who backs down first." He swung at Will with his cane, but his younger opponent was able to leap back in time to avoid the silver tip. Now it was Will's turn, and he swiped at Duquesne from a number of angles, but likewise missed. "You're quick," Duquesne said. "But I seriously doubt that Brandt taught you much in the way of hand-to-hand combat. He's always been of the mind that guns win the day. Brute." He landed a blow against Will's right arm and followed up with a slash that took Will out at the knee. Howling in pain, Will fell backwards, but he maintained his grip on Gleave's cane.

"I don't need guns. I'm an Aberrationist."

Duquesne stood still and cocked his head. "A what?"

"An Aberrationist," Will said proudly, pulling himself erect with the cane.

"Are you calling yourself an abolitionist?"

"Jesus Christ," Brandt groaned from the floor. "Still not a thing."

"Regardless, William, the only word I'd use to describe you right now is 'outmatched.'"

Will knew this to be true, but he hoped that he would only have to keep Duquesne occupied until reinforcements arrived. He looked plaintively at the entranceway, hoping to see Whitworth, Valentine, anyone... "Looking for allies?" Duquesne mused. "I count one." He pointed with the tip of his cane to the bleeding and useless Brandt.

"Two," said a voice from the darkness. Will stared in shock and concern as Joanna Duquesne stepped out of the shadows, candlestick in her quavering hand. "Stop this," she said to her husband. "Stop this madness now."

"Sweetheart," Desmond hissed through the mask, "how can you be against me too? What will it take for you people to realize that what I was trying to do here was ultimately a positive thing? Yes, people would die, but I would make up for that ten-fold. I would have all the time in the world to—"

"Enough!" Joanna shouted. "You lying bastard. William's right. You are nothing but a coward. There's nothing philanthropic about this," she said, motioning to the corpses surrounding them. "No matter how you attempt to justify it, these are little more than the actions of a pathetic old man who fears the inevitable. You should have died a long time ago and we all know it. You're just too gutless to accept that."

She raised the candlestick to strike him, but he was too fast. Grabbing her arm before she could land a blow, he screeched, "Bitch!" and slapped Joanna to the ground. "You want me to die so badly? Show me how."

Something snapped in Will when he saw Desmond strike Joanna, and now, with the cloaked figure standing over her, he sprang into action. The look on Joanna's face betrayed that Will was fast approaching from behind. "This is for the Trammells!" Will swung his cane furiously at Desmond's head, and even though he turned to face his attacker quickly, Duquesne was unable to avoid the blow. The lion's head cracked against the Venetian mask, sending it falling to the ground and breaking into several pieces.

With Duquesne's face exposed, Will forgot all about the promise he had made to Daphne. He wanted to land a solid blow—one crack across the jaw, fist on face, that would end Desmond Duquesne for good. But Duquesne could sense what Will was thinking and similarly resolved to finish the conflict. "Enough child's play," he said. Within seconds, Will found himself facing an onslaught from Duquesne. The silver-tipped walking stick seemed to strike every part of his body, and he was soon backed against the stone altar, feeling as though he had been repeatedly lashed by a whip. "Kudos to Brandt," said Duquesne. "He tried. But whatever he taught you, it simply wasn't enough."

Brandt's eyes fluttered open when he heard his name, just in time to see Duquesne draw the long blade from inside his cane and thrust it through Will's gut. Will fell to the ground within arm's length of Brandt, still breathing, but shallowly. Joanna ran to Will's side but was unable to break his fall. She knelt next to him, holding his hand gently and cautioning him not to move. "I'll get help," she said. "I'll be back as soon as I can."

Will nodded weakly. Releasing his hand, she attempted to run off, but was grabbed by her husband. "You're not helping him," he said with a mad look in his eyes. "You're joining him."

Will wanted to help but had no idea how. He knew he had been seriously—perhaps mortally—wounded and would merely collapse if he attempted to stand. Not knowing where else to turn, he asked Brandt, "What do I do?"

"Duquesne's wrong," said Brandt with a bloody smile. "I did teach you enough. Remember, it's all about…"

"The blood," Will said, staring down at the blade protruding from his gut. He grinned weakly at Brandt. "This is gonna hurt."

Brandt nodded and grabbed Will's hand. Will closed his eyes and recalled hearing Wisp's smooth, southern drawl. *Once you push yourself past that threshold, there's no going back. It'll be a piece of cake for you.*

"Piece of cake," he repeated, trying to ignore the pain as he used his power to slowly withdraw the blade. He winced as he felt the last of it slide out and, opening his eyes, saw the weapon floating in front of him, dripping his own blood onto his lap.

"You've got this," said Brandt. He watched as the blade lifted higher and began spinning like the wheel of a gruesome carnival game.

"Hey Duquesne," Will muttered. "Guess what I can do."

Desmond Duquesne released his grip on his wife's neck and looked wide-eyed as the spinning blade careened through the air and plunged through his heart. He stood in disbelief for a moment before breaking out into a hysterical laugh. "Nice try, William," he said. "But you never learn! Weapons can't kill me."

"No," said Will, "but my blood can."

Duquesne stopped laughing. He peered down at the piece of steel jutting from his chest and touched the crimson liquid that coated the blade with his gloved hand. His grin disappeared as the realization of what had happened finally sunk in, and a burning sensation began to spread throughout his body. "Well, I'll be damned," he muttered.

Will, Brandt, and Joanna looked on in horror as Desmond Duquesne's age caught up to him. He decayed rapidly, turning from a ghastly shade of gray to a sickly shade of green, his hair and nails growing out, his eyes and organs dissolving, his jaw and limbs falling off, until only a pile of bone and rot remained in the place where he had stood, covered by the empty black cloak that slumped to the floor next to the broken ceramic mask.

Joanna knelt alongside her husband's remains, devoid of any expression that Will could read. Brandt, however, wore a discernible smile despite his worsening condition. "I never thought you'd pull it off, kid," he confessed. "I need to…" His voice trailed off as he tried to work through his wounds.

"It's alright," Will said. "Save your—"

"Shut up and let me finish," Brandt demanded. He struggled to turn his head and look Will in the eyes. "You'll never hear these words leave my lips again, but I'm sorry, William. I'm sorry about your family, and I'm sorry for what I put you through. Make sure that it ends here…" The grip that Brandt still had on Will's hand finally loosened, as did his grip on consciousness. Will watched the wounded veteran's eyes close and saw Joanna Duquesne run to get help just before everything faded to black.

Above the scene, at the edge of the crater that now led from the ballroom to the chamber, Mr. Wisp stood with his hands clasped behind his back, surveying the scene with his icy blue eyes. "Party's over," he said to no one in particular.

A SHORT TIME LATER, Andy jumped into the ambulance into which Will had been wheeled. "What now?" Eddie Garza asked as the ambulance drove off with the two boys.

Director Valentine responded, "Now we make sure that the property is clear of any lingering demons, we scour the premises for the Heart, and you, at least, call it a night."

Once the flashing red lights of the ambulance faded from sight, Garza noted the eerie calm that fell over the property surrounding New Covington and took in the sight of the once great house that now stood half in ruin. "Where are the police? There's no way they don't know about this."

"Oh, they know," said Valentine. "We told them we'd handle it. Believe me, it took very little convincing when the bigwigs were asked to look the other way on this one. Most of them have been on Duquesne's payroll for years and make a habit of ignoring any strange events at New Covington."

"This whole thing ran deeper than most people realized, huh?" said Garza. Valentine nodded. "So what about me?"

"Well, you handled yourself pretty damn well in there," said the Director. "And we lost a number of good men, plus Donovan. Would you give some thought to moving to Boston?"

"I'd consider it," he said. "And the guests who were here? Are you going to offer them jobs as well? How do you plan to keep this from spreading?"

"I believe that Agent Whitworth has that well in hand."

WHILE HER COLLEAGUES lingered around the devastated husk of Duquesne's ballroom, Whitworth sat with her back to them, listening to the quiet gurgle of the creek from the bench where Daphne and Desmond had conversed earlier that morning. She turned Sarah's ring over in her hand and addressed the man who stood behind her without bothering to turn around. "Did you have any difficulties?"

"Not many," said the faceless form. "Neither the guests nor the staff will remember what took place here. At the moment, they are making their way home, convinced that the party was tragically ruined by a gas leak and subsequent explosion. Only two were able to resist. Wisp and his companion."

Whitworth waved this off. "They should prove nothing more than a nuisance, but I'll keep an eye on them nonetheless."

"Have you been able to confiscate Duquesne's materials?"

"The *Key* is in our possession, though it is relatively inert now that the demons have been set free."

461

"And the Heart?"

"Nothing yet, but our men are looking for it now. They're sure to locate it, and when they do, I will personally see to it that it does not cause any further difficulty."

"Your vault."

"Exactly," Whitworth nodded. "My friend, I truly appreciate the favor that you've done for me tonight. I understand the risk that you've taken. I'm in your debt."

"Yes, you are," said the figure. "We'll talk."

FORTY-FIVE

Closure

SOMEHOW, Will knew that he was dreaming this time. He was aware that the cemetery through which he walked was once again a figment of his imagination, but still he feared the reemergence of the plague doctor. He walked across the open plain toward the mausoleum, but when he arrived at the stone arch, the wooden door slammed shut before he could enter. Relieved that he was not bound to relive the same nightmare forever, but confused as to what to do now, he spotted a small stone bench next to a motionless lake and took a seat. He watched the sun rise from behind the opposite bank, burning off the dreary darkness and revealing a mist rising from the surface of the water.

Peering at the mist, he was not surprised to see a dark, humanoid shape form—the same shape that had guided him in his earlier dreams, that had led him to the secret panel in Duquesne's ballroom. "Who are you?" he asked the Patchwork Man. The water rippled slightly, but the shape remained inert. "I never believed in ghosts, but you're one, aren't you? You've been helping me all along. Why?"

The figure gave no audible response but flew from the surface of the lake and disappeared behind a large tree in the near distance. This being a dream, Will's injured leg did not prevent him from chasing after the shape, and as he neared the tree, he heard the now-familiar hum of 'You Are My Sunshine.' On the other side of the sizable trunk, he found a young couple seated at a picnic table. He immediately recognized them as Daniel and Linda Trammell, but this time, Linda was holding a small bundle in her arms, rocking it gently back and forth, smiling as she hummed.

Daniel greeted his son. "Hello, William."

"Am…am I dead?"

His father let out a hearty laugh. "You'll be just fine. You're just getting some much-deserved rest. It's over, Will."

"Are you the Patchwork Man?"

"Your mother and I have been with you all along. You should know that."

Will took solace in what his father said, but his recent experiences had made him wary. "I appreciate that, but that's not exactly what I asked…"

Daniel Trammell smiled and arose from his bench. "We're very proud of you, Will," he said and wrapped his arms around his son. "But it's time to wake up now."

Will closed his eyes as he felt his father's strong, comforting embrace for the first time that he could remember. "But I don't want to wake up yet. I want to talk to you. I want to learn all about you and mom and my sister. Please…I don't want to wake up…"

"Well, I certainly don't blame you, Will," said a new voice. "I'd want to sleep for weeks if I were you."

Will opened his eyes to find his adopted father, Robert Kendrick, standing over his bed. "Check it out, Will," Robert continued. "You've actually been brought to a real hospital this time. Now that Duquesne is gone, you're free."

Will had always hated hospitals, but he felt as though he had been hit by a bus and so was immensely relieved to see that what his father said was true. He was also glad to look around the room and see only friendly faces: Robert, Eddie Garza, and his Aunt Veronica. "How long have you all been sitting here?"

"A while," said Veronica. "Though I have to admit to dozing off, Detective Garza remained ever vigilant. I think I owe you a dinner, Eddie."

"If you make pot roast, you're on," Eddie answered, resting his hand on Veronica's shoulder. "Anyway, I only did what your father would have done. He'd be proud of you, kid," Eddie said. "You'd make a hell of a cop."

"I should probably finish high school first," said Will, noting for the first time that he had missed his graduation while in Boston, and came to the terrible realization that he'd probably have to repeat his senior year.

"Your aunt and I have already discussed that, Will," Dr. Kendrick said. "We're going to ask Frances Whitworth if she can pull some strings."

"I don't want anyone brainwashed into letting me graduate," Will insisted.

"Nothing like that," Veronica assured him. "Frances can be very convincing and she knows all the right people. Besides, if you ask me, it's the least she can do to repay you for putting your own life on the line. A lot. Tell me, do you enjoy being knocked unconscious? Because I'm beginning to worry."

Will laughed with his aunt while Dr. Kendrick cleared his throat and said, "Will, you do have another visitor who has been anxious to see you."

"Robert," said Veronica with a worried expression, "are you certain he shouldn't rest?"

"I'm sure it will be fine, Veronica." Addressing Will, he said, "We'll show her in on our way out."

The three left, and Daphne Duquesne entered the room

shortly after. Will could tell that she had been crying, but she had also done the most she could to cover up the fact with a combination of makeup and forced composure. She sat in the chair next to his bed and instinctively reached out to take his hand but caught herself at the last minute, recalling her hand gracefully and offering a warm smile. "How are you?" she asked.

Will smiled back but did not immediately answer. It broke his heart to look into the face of the girl he had grown to care for, the girl whose father he had killed. He had never broken a promise in his life until the one he had made to her, the most important one he had ever made. "I'm fine," he lied. "I can hardly feel a thing. Apparently, the blade missed any major organs."

"I'm willing to bet that was intentional," said Daphne. "My father really liked you. I don't think he wanted you dead. He was just too obsessed to let anyone get in his way. If he had wanted to kill you, he would have."

"Yeah," Will responded, recalling the many hits that her father had put out on him and not quite knowing what to say. "Listen, Daphne," he began, his face flushing as his heart rate monitor gradually began to beep faster, "I'm so sorry. I just had to stop him. I never meant to—"

"Will, stop it," Daphne demanded. "My mother told me what happened. You have nothing to be sorry for."

"What do you mean? What did your mother tell you?"

"She told me that my father stabbed you to get you out of the way, and that Brandt took the blade right out of your stomach—with no regard for your well-being—and killed my father with it. In the end, my father and Brandt killed each other, and you were just caught in the crossfire."

Will lay dumbfounded in his hospital bed as his heart rate returned to normal. "So Brandt is dead?"

Daphne nodded. "He used his last ounce of strength to kill my father. Then he succumbed to his own injuries."

Tell her. Will thought. *You have to tell her the truth now.* "Daphne," he said, wanting desperately to take her hand, "I'm so sorry for your loss. If there's anything I can do..."

She smiled warmly and rested her hand on the side of his bed. "I'm just glad you're alright."

"So am I," said Andy, peeking his head through the door. "Sorry to interrupt."

"Not a problem," Daphne responded. "I should go check on my brother anyway." She shot a smirk in Andy's direction. "And if you ask me whether I'm going to 'give him a hand,' I'll tell Hex to scratch your eyes out."

"Well that would just be cruel," said Andy. "And funny. But cruel. Mainly cruel. Tell him I said hi."

Daphne chuckled. "Not gonna do that, but can you tell Will something for me?"

"Me?" asked Will, confused.

Daphne gave him a knowing smile and said to Andy, "Tell him this." She planted a kiss on Andy's cheek, gave Will a quick wink, and closed the door behind her as she stepped into the hallway.

Andy, flustered and blushing, said, "Um, I'm not going to..."

Will shook his head, "Yeah, no. I got the message."

"So things between you two are..."

"Difficult," Will admitted. "I mean, it's really not ideal to fall for a girl that you can't touch."

"Hey," Andy said, sitting in the chair alongside Will's bed. "Now you know how it feels to be me. There must be a prophecy keeping Sam Foster and I apart too." Will practically fell out of his bed to punch Andy, and the two laughed through their pain.

. . .

THE NEXT MORNING, Veronica arrived to take Will home. While being steered through the corridors in a hospital-mandated wheelchair, he turned to his aunt and said, "Not that I'm disappointed, but I kind of assumed that Gwen would be coming to get me. I'm really glad to see you out and doing...better."

"I've got a long road ahead, I'm sure," said Veronica. "But it's a huge relief to know you're safe and I don't have to worry about Desmond Duquesne threatening my family anymore. Who knows? Maybe I'll work on getting a life now. I may even take Mr. Wisp up on his invitation to go out for a drink this weekend."

"Whoa! Slow down, party animal," Will joked, earning a light slap to the back of the head. He breathed in the fresh air as his aunt wheeled him through the sliding doors of the hospital exit. He hadn't felt this free since that last baseball practice weeks ago, before he had met Brandt or learned anything about Desmond Duquesne. "You seem much better as well," Veronica suggested.

"Like a new man. It feels strange to know that no one is trying to shoot me, blow me up, or set me on fire."

"Well, it's the little things in life, I guess," she quipped. "By the way, I spoke to Dr. Kendrick—I'm sorry, your father—this morning. We were discussing all the great colleges in the area..."

Will looked back at his aunt with wide eyes. "I-I just got out of the hospital, and—"

"And like you said, no one is trying to kill you! So it seems like the perfect opportunity to check out a few schools." She chuckled. "Come on. You'll have fun. Your mother and father are both going to come up next week for a college visit or two before they take you home."

"Sounds awesome," Will conceded. "But maybe this weekend I can just do nothing but eat pancakes?"

"Oh my goodness," said Frances Whitworth, leaning against a wall as the wheelchair turned a corner in the hospital parking lot. "May I join? I could drink maple syrup like water. I'm ashamed to admit that. Peg thinks that it will give me diabetes, but I've lived a good life, I mean..." Eddie Garza, leaning out the passenger side window of Whitworth's car, cleared his throat to get the older woman back on track. "Sorry! Sorry! Where was I? Pancakes...pancakes...demons! That was it. William, you're looking like the picture of...some degree of health, and we'd like to ask for your help."

"But I don't work for the Collective, Ms. Whitworth, and frankly—no offense—I don't plan to."

"Well, here's the thing," Whitworth persisted. "By my count, there are still at least a few dozen demons running loose as a result of Duquesne's ritual, and because of this, in an unprecedented move, the Collective has been given a budget to hire several more agents." She paused, noting Will's disinterested expression. "I've also been given permission to bring on a freelancer or two. No commitment. You help me stop the things that go bump in the night—if you want to, when you want to. I hear that college books are expensive, and it sure beats waiting tables."

Will glanced at Garza, who shrugged as if to say, 'Why not?'

"If I help," Will negotiated, "I want you to work on finding a way for me and Daphne to be together."

Whitworth nodded. "Deal. In fact, Drayton and Angela are already hard at work, and I plan to consult every resource I have."

Satisfied, Will bit. "So what's the scoop?"

"We've gotten word that there's a particularly nasty demon named Phenex causing all sorts of problems in the woods out near Concord. Feel like taking a ride?"

Will looked at his aunt, whose concerned frown gradually

turned into a sly grin. "I'd appreciate it if you'd be back by midnight."

"And not a minute past," said Whitworth, clapping her hands together excitedly. "Or I'll turn myself into a pumpkin." She opened the trunk of her black sedan and removed Gleave's ebony cane. "The woods are no place for a wheelchair, William. Think you can manage?"

Will caught the cane, kissed his aunt on the cheek, and hurried to the car. "And for God's sake, let someone else get knocked out this time!" Veronica called after him.

"Let's make magic, kid," said Garza as Will shut the door and they made their way toward Concord.

About the Author

Born and raised in New Jersey, Ray O'Meara developed a fondness for the written word at an early age, when his mother would read him Golden Books. (*The Little Red Hen* and *The Happy Man and His Dump Truck* remain his favorites.) It was in high school, though, when he realized the true importance of literature, and that the classics that had always seemed escapes from reality were just as instructional as his childhood favorites. He learned to love Dickens by reading *David Copperfield*, and saw that Dickens reflected life as it is: sad, joyous, frantic, and filled with too many oddball characters, many of whom have purposes in our lives that are not always revealed right away.

After attending Monmouth University in Long Branch, New Jersey, for his bachelor's degree and Seton Hall University for his master's, Ray remained in the academic field, tutoring writing and teaching composition, research, and literature courses at Monmouth as well as at a local community college, Brookdale. During his time at these schools, he participated in conferences including several hosted by the Northeast Modern Language Association, presenting on pop culture icons like Batman and Walter White, often drawing parallels between these characters and those of classic literature. This melding of two worlds can hopefully be seen in Ray's own writing, as it certainly helped to shape it.

Currently, Ray is preparing for his wedding to his fiance Kristen, whom he has been with for just over two years. They live at the Jersey Shore and enjoy traveling, attending concerts, hosting Christmas parties, and cooking together. Most of all, they enjoy experiencing whatever bits of culture—pop, high, or otherwise come their way, from Broadway shows to beer festivals. And of course, they rarely turn down a happy hour. After all, there's no better time or place to find characters.

Did You Enjoy The Aberrationists?

You can help by leaving your review on either GoodReads or the digital storefront of your choosing.

Thank you!

The Parliament House

THE PARLIAMENT HOUSE
WWW.PARLIAMENTHOUSEPRESS.COM

Want more from our amazing authors? Visit our website for trailers, exclusive blogs, additional content and more!

Become a Parliament Person and access secret bonus content…

JOIN US

Made in the USA
Middletown, DE
23 October 2020